THE UNFREAKINGBELIEVABLE ANTHOLOGY

Betsey Kulakowski, Jenny Simard LaBranche, *and*
JB Caine

Dedication

This anthology is dedicated to our listeners. To those who press play late at night, on long drives, and in the quiet spaces where stories take root. These stories are for you.

Thank you from Betsey, Jenny, and Jen
The UNFREAKINGBELIEVABLE Podcast
www.ufbpodcast.com

Contents

Lying In State

PARANORMAL COMEDY BY JENNY SIMARD LABRANCHE

Part 1: "I Wasn't Ready for This Shit"

Nick woke up dead.

At least, that's what everyone else seemed to assume. He hadn't exactly received a memo. One minute, he'd been making terrible coffee in his apartment, and the next, he was hovering above a varnished casket in a room that smelled like floral sadness and despair. Not his favorite smell, by the way. He wrinkled his nonexistent nose. Roses, lilies, and the faint trace of old carpet cleaner. Lovely.

And the lighting. Whoever had decided that funeral homes needed fluorescent lights deserved a smack upside the head from beyond the grave. The glow was harsh, cruel, and made his skin, well, what was left of it, look like a corpse. Which, apparently, he now was. Thank you, Captain Obvious.

Nick took a slow spin in the air above the casket. Yep. That was him. Lying there, all stiff and meticulously arranged in a suit two sizes too tight. He definitely hadn't chosen it. Some well-meaning relative with questionable taste must have decided navy blue looked "so dignified." Dignified? He looked like a mannequin that had been vacuum-sealed for shipping.

The mortician, a nervous man named Edgar, fumbled with his gloves and muttered something about "final touches." *Final touches.* Ha. If only the poor man knew. Nick leaned over and whispered, "You do realize I can hear you, right?" Edgar jumped so violently his glasses slid down his nose, and he swore. Not the kind of swearing Nick admired, but points for enthusiasm.

Behind him, the funeral staff shuffled about like extras in a poorly-rehearsed play. Sharon, the one responsible for flowers, tripped over a baseboard, and her tray of half-dead chrysanthemums tipped over, scattering petals across the carpet. The cat of irony would have pounced on the moment if there had been one. Nick made a mental note to haunt her later.

"This is fine," he muttered to himself. Not under his breath technically, since he didn't have breath, but somewhere between audibility and spectral resonance. Nobody responded. "Really? Fantastic. Exactly what I wanted. Fluorescent humiliation, slightly crushed flowers, and my friends crying in the corner like toddlers who lost their goldfish."

He floated lower to get a better look at his own body. It was ... weird. Really weird. Sure, it was technically him, but in a way that made him think, *Wow, the human body is horrifying.* Pale, waxy, frozen in a pose that suggested mild serenity but actually screamed *help me, please ... someone—anyone!* He winced at the stiff hands laid over his chest. They'd tried to make him appear peaceful. He looked as peaceful as a traffic accident looks serene: not at all.

And then there was the hair. Or rather, the lack of his signature disaster hair. Apparently, the mortician had thought "polished" was a good look. The reflection in the polished casket lid mocked him—smooth, shiny, antiseptically perfect. His usual bedhead, the rebellious tufts that gave him that *I-just-rolled-out-of-bed-and-somehow-still-look-good* vibe, gone. Forever.

And the smell of formaldehyde. God, he hated it. Not just the sharp, chemical sting, but the memories it dragged up: hospitals, death, that one time he'd tried to dissect a frog in high school and cried for an hour. That smell was back, haunting him in olfactory form.

He floated up to a corner of the room. Relatives milled about, crying, hugging, whispering in hushed tones perfect for a movie scene. He tried a ghostly wave of annoyance. Nothing happened. Of course not. Ghosts, apparently, were terrible at influencing the living unless they went full *Poltergeist*.

The first eulogy came from Aunt Cindy. Nick was not a fan of Aunt Cindy. She had a way of making every mundane story about him sound like he'd crossed the Atlantic to rescue orphans from a burning village.

"Nick was always so kind," she said, voice trembling. "He always thought of others before himself."

"Oh, please," Nick groaned. "Always kind? The last time I thought of others was when I borrowed money from Joe and forgot to pay him back for a year."

He drifted closer, glaring at the mourners. A few tears dropped near the edge of his casket, probably for dramatic effect.

Edgar kept glancing around nervously, as if he *felt* Nick's presence. At least someone in the room had a shred of awareness. Nick almost felt camaraderie. Almost.

Then came the flowers. Sharon, back from her earlier fumble, placed a bouquet near his head. Nick floated down to inspect. Roses. Lilies. Some purple thing he couldn't identify. Very tasteful, as far as "you're dead now" décor went. He whispered to the bouquet, "Nice job. Really. A funeral essential."

Across the room, his coworkers huddled together, faking pained expressions. He could practically see the thought bubbles above their heads: *We really liked him!*

"Oh, spare me," Nick muttered. "You stole my pens and blamed it on the office cat."

His patience or whatever ghosts had instead of it was wearing thin. Then came the final straw. Reverend Higgins, a nervous man with a squeaky voice, began a monologue about life, death, and the "moral lessons" of Nick's so-called career.

"Nick taught us the value of patience," he said solemnly.

"Patience?" Nick shouted, hovering above him. "Patience is what you need when your Wi-Fi dies, Reverend! Life is chaos. *I* was chaos!"

No one so much as blinked. Typical.

He drifted back above his casket, crossing his arms—or trying to, given the lack of corporeal form—and surveyed the room. Everything was in place. People were crying. Flowers were arranged. His body looked absurdly serene.

And him? He was stuck in between floating, watching everyone lie about him, embellish his life, romanticize him, and ignore the parts that made him who he really was.

And that was how Nick realized death was going to be a lot more annoying than life.

Part 2 : "The Parade of Liars"

If Nick had known death would involve this much socializing, he might've worn a name tag that said *"Still Not Dead Inside."*

He hovered near the open casket, watching as the first mourners shuffled in. The air smelled like lilies and reheated coffee, a scent that could make even Heaven seem depressing. The soft organ music droned on, and the funeral director, a man who looked like he ironed his hair, greeted guests with the same tragic smile he probably used when upselling coffins.

"Ah, the late Mr. Callahan was dearly loved," the man said to a weepy woman at the door.

Was I? Nick thought. *Pretty sure Brenda here once reported me to HR for eating her yogurt.*

Brenda dabbed her eyes with a tissue that looked suspiciously clean for someone "so devastated."

"Oh, he was such a good man," she whispered to another coworker. "Always so ... professional."

Nick floated closer, peering at her like a gossiping poltergeist. "Professional? I once told you the copier was haunted just so you'd stop hovering near my cubicle," he muttered. "And it worked, didn't it?"

The other coworker, a guy named Doug who had all the charisma of wet cardboard, nodded solemnly. "Yeah. He was a mentor to me. Always said, 'Hard work beats luck.'"

Nick froze. "The hell I did. I said, 'Luck beats Doug.' You're misquoting me at my own funeral!"

Doug sniffled dramatically, probably hoping someone noticed his single tear. "He was like the big brother I never had."

"Oh, please. You're the reason I started working from home."

Nick drifted away before he accidentally ghost-slapped someone. The funeral home's viewing area was now filling up, co-workers, neighbors, distant cousins, and that one guy who always showed up to funerals just for free food.

In the next room, a small group clustered around the coffee urn, balancing Styrofoam cups and sympathy sandwiches. Nick recognized his ex-girlfriend Stacy instantly. She was the kind of woman who could turn a breakup into a public art installation. He could already tell from her posture, chin up, eyes glistening, that she was preparing to perform.

"He never stopped loving me," she said softly, as if auditioning for a tragic movie."Oh, come on," Nick groaned. "We broke up five years ago because you 'needed space,' specifically the space between me and your yoga instructor."

One of Stacy's friends patted her arm. "You were his muse, I can tell."

"Exactly," Stacy said, her voice quivering. "He told me once that I was his reason for living."

Nick threw his hands up. "My reason for living was pizza and bad TV! You were my reason for therapy!"

Nearby, his cousin Tim was explaining how close they'd been growing up."We were like brothers," Tim said. "I'll never forget how he taught me to be brave."

Nick squinted. "I *taught* you how to hotwire Grandpa's lawnmower, you little liar."

Tim wiped away an imaginary tear. "He said once, 'Fear is temporary, regret is forever.'"

Nick blinked. "No. No, I did *not* say that. I said, 'Regret is temporary, fear is forever, especially if you're being chased by a goose!'"

The lies kept coming. Every corner of the room buzzed with false memories and exaggerated tributes. A neighbor claimed Nick once saved her cat from a tree, he distinctly remembered throwing a broom at it because it attacked him. A high school classmate said Nick was "the funny one who lit up every room", which was true, but only because he once accidentally set a curtain on fire at prom. And his old boss, Mr. Palmer, was currently holding court near the casket, speaking like a man at a TED Talk about leadership.

"Nick was a visionary," Palmer declared. "He taught me the value of integrity."

"Integrity?" Nick snapped. "You used to steal my pens!"

Palmer leaned dramatically against the podium. "He once told me, 'A man's worth isn't measured by what he earns, but by what he gives.'"

"Oh, for shit's sake, Palmer, I said that about *parking spaces!*" Nick floated through him in frustration, making the man shiver. "Yeah, that's right, enjoy that ghost draft, liar!"

It didn't stop there. People who barely knew him were crying harder than his own family. Nick's sister, Claire, stood in the front row, holding a tissue box and muttering to her teenage son to sit still; she was just exhausted. He could tell. But then she leaned over to her husband and whispered, "He never did find love. Poor Nick."

Nick frowned. "Excuse me? I had love! It just came with Wi-Fi and takeout!"

He floated to the back of the room, trying to calm down, but the sound of Stacy's voice carried across the crowd again. "I know he's still with us. I can *feel* his spirit here."

"Yeah," Nick grumbled. "Because I'm glaring at you."

Then she turned toward his casket and said tearfully, "If you're here, give us a sign!"

Nick crossed his arms. "A sign? How about this, stop lying!"

Suddenly, the lights flickered. The room gasped. Stacy let out a small shriek.

"Oh great," Nick muttered. "Now they think I'm *haunting* them because I *care*."

Someone whispered, "He's here!" and the panic spread like bad cologne. The funeral director scrambled to calm everyone down, and the organist hit a wrong note so sharp it sounded like a scream.

Nick hovered above it all, watching the chaos he'd accidentally caused. "I'm not haunting you! I'm just trying to correct the record!"

He floated toward the coffee table, glaring down at a trio of mourners swapping tales like they were at a pub.

"Yeah, I remember Nick," said one. "Didn't he once wrestle a bear?"

"That was a *dog*," Nick said. "A poodle. And it bit me!"

"Oh right," the man continued. "And he was in a band in college."

Nick groaned. "I played tambourine once at a keg party."

They clinked their cups together. "A true legend."

That was it. "No!" Nick shouted. "I am not a legend! I'm a guy who couldn't keep a houseplant alive!"

But the more he yelled, the less it mattered. Their stories kept coming, reshaping his life like a cheap made-for-TV biopic. Each one made him feel smaller, blurrier. It was like they were overwriting him.

He floated toward the casket, staring down at his own still face. "That's not me," he said quietly. "That's the version of me they made up."

The organ started playing again, off-key, hauntingly bad. Someone whispered about how peaceful he looked. "He's finally at rest."

Nick rolled his eyes. "I'm not resting. I'm raging!"

Yet, even as he said it, he felt the weight of exhaustion creeping in. The laughter, the lies, the falseness of it all, it was draining him. Maybe that's how ghosts fade, he thought. Not from unfinished business, but from being misremembered.

As the last few guests filtered out, Stacy paused at the casket one final time. "Goodbye, my love," she whispered. "You were too good for this world."

Nick sighed. "I was *barely* good enough for this one, sweetheart."

She left the room, dabbing her eyes, and for the first time, the room was quiet. Just him, his empty body, and the faint hum of fluorescent lights.

He looked around at the flowers, the photographs, the sympathy cards that all had the wrong idea of who he was.

Then he chuckled softly. "Maybe it doesn't matter what they say. They're the ones who have to live with the lie, not me."

He drifted toward the door, muttering, "Besides, they'll find out the truth when I start haunting their bathrooms."

Part 3: "The Eulogy from Hell"

Nick had survived, or rather, *outlived*, the parade of liars, but nothing could've prepared him for the eulogy.

He'd retreated to the corner of the viewing room, sulking like a toddler in timeout, when the funeral director clapped his hands and called for everyone's attention. "If we could all take our seats, Reverend MacLeish will now say a few words about our dearly departed Nicholas Callahan."

Nick squinted. *Reverend who?* He didn't even remember being religious, much less acquainted with a reverend.

The man who stepped up to the lectern looked like he'd been carved from a single piece of polished driftwood. His white hair gleamed under the soft lights. His voice was syrupy, the kind of voice that made people nod gravely even when he said nothing.

"Friends," the reverend began, hands clasped as if auditioning for a toothpaste commercial, "we gather here today to celebrate the life of a man who touched so many hearts."

Nick crossed his ghostly arms. "Yeah, usually with annoyance."

The reverend smiled benevolently at the crowd. "Nick was, above all else, a man of kindness. A man of generosity."

Nick barked out a laugh. "I once charged my brother interest on a loan of *five dollars!*"

Reverend MacLeish continued, "He never spoke ill of others. His spirit was gentle, his heart pure."

"WHAT?!" Nick shot up into the air like a helium balloon. "I called my boss a human hemorrhoid *to his face!*"

He floated down toward the reverend, peering over his shoulder at the notecards. The handwriting was looping, graceful, and utterly fake. "Where did you even get this crap?" he demanded. "Google 'generic funeral speech'?"

The reverend droned on. "He loved deeply, laughed often, and lived with purpose."

"I loved pizza, laughed at cat videos, and lived paycheck to paycheck," Nick snapped. "Let's not rewrite history here."

As the reverend shifted to talking about Nick's "philanthropy," something in Nick snapped. He zoomed toward the podium, furious. "Philanthropy? I once donated blood because I thought I'd get a free T-shirt!"

He hovered so close that the reverend's toupee rippled in the chill. A woman in the front row shivered. "Did anyone else feel that? Like ... a cold draft?"

"Yeah," Nick said. "That's honesty blowing through for the first time today."

He looked around at the crowd, people dabbing their eyes, nodding along like this eulogy was gospel truth, and the unfairness hit him like a truck. This stranger was painting him as some kind of saint. A sanitized version. The version that never lost his temper, never said something stupid, never died with a half-eaten burrito on the passenger seat.

Nick clenched his fists and shouted, "I'm not who you think I am!"

And that's when the lights flickered.

The crowd gasped. The organ groaned to a stop like it had been personally insulted. The reverend paused mid-sentence, blinking up at the ceiling.

Nick froze. "Wait ... did I just—?"

He focused, really focused, on the nearest lightbulb. It trembled. He grinned. "Ohhh, I can *work* with this."

The bulb popped with a loud *crack*, showering the podium in sparks.

The audience screamed.

Reverend MacLeish ducked. "The spirit is among us!" he shouted.

"Damn right, I am!" Nick yelled, giddy now. "Welcome to your haunted story hour!"

He zoomed toward the back of the room, flicking lights one by one like a vengeful electrician. Mourners shrieked. A child started crying. Someone fainted into the cookie table.

"Oh, this is *so much better* than social media," Nick said gleefully.

He spotted his ex, Stacy, clutching her pearls. "Nick, is that you?" she whimpered.

"Yes, it's me," he said, swirling around her coffee cup until it tipped over and splashed her blouse. "Consider that karmic dry cleaning."

"Merciful heavens!" she shrieked. "He's angry!"

"Oh, I'm *beyond* angry," Nick said. "I'm post-mortem petty!"

A man in the second row crossed himself and muttered a prayer. The reverend, sweating bullets now, raised his voice to be heard over the chaos. "The spirit is restless! He must be yearning for peace!"

"Peace?" Nick barked a laugh. "I'm yearning for accuracy!"

The coffin rattled.

Every head in the room snapped toward it.

Nick hadn't meant to, but apparently, when he got emotional, things *moved.*

"Oh boy," he muttered, watching the lid tremble like a popcorn bag in a microwave.

Someone screamed. A woman in floral print fainted. Another guest grabbed her purse and bolted for the door.

"Okay, maybe I went a little far," Nick admitted.

The lid of the coffin closed an inch.

The room *erupted.*

Screams. Stumbling. Coffee everywhere. The reverend dropped his Bible and ran for the exit of the room like his shoes were on fire.

Nick tried to shout over the chaos. "Wait! I'm not trying to haunt you, I just want to clarify a few things!"

But no one listened. They stampeded out of the room, leaving behind trampled programs and half-eaten finger sandwiches.

The silence afterward was almost comical.

Nick hovered above the mess, staring at the chaos he'd created. "Okay," he said slowly. "Maybe that got away from me."

The lights buzzed, flickering weakly. He glanced up at them. "So that's what power feels like, huh? Not bad."

He drifted toward the podium, where the reverend's notes were still scattered. He leaned over it, and squinted at it.

"'Nick Callahan was a man who always sought the good in others.' Yeah, sure. I sought the good parking spot, not the good in *people*."

He floated back to his casket in the other room, looking down at himself again. The suit still didn't fit right. His hair was weirdly parted. And now the lid was crooked from when he'd accidentally rattled it.

"Well," he said, "at least they'll have a fun story to tell. 'Remember when the corpse almost sat up?'" He chuckled, shaking his head. "Honestly, I'd haunt me, too."

The sound of hesitant footsteps echoed from the hallway. Nick turned. His sister, Claire, poked her head in, clutching her son's hand.

"Is everyone okay?" she whispered.

Nick sighed. "Define 'okay.'"

Her son tugged on her sleeve. "Mom, I think Uncle Nick's ghost is mad."

Claire looked around nervously. "Don't be silly. Ghosts aren't real."

Nick grinned. "Oh, you sweet summer child."

Then, feeling impulsive, he flicked the light above her head. It buzzed, then went out.

She gasped. "Okay," she said quickly, "maybe we should wait outside."

As they left, Nick laughed to himself. "You always did hate awkward family gatherings."

For the first time since he'd died, he didn't feel powerless. Sure, he was technically a ghost, but he could *interact* now. Influence things. Maybe he couldn't fix his reputation, but he could make sure people stopped pretending to know him.

He floated back toward the podium, thinking. The next person who tried to deliver a speech full of lies was going to get a real show.

But as he looked down at the chaos, the spilled drinks, the fainted mourners, the broken lights, something inside him softened. He hadn't meant to scare them. He'd just wanted the truth to matter. To not be erased by platitudes and polite fiction.

He looked back at his body and whispered, "I wasn't a saint. But I wasn't all bad either."

The last flickering bulb finally died out, leaving the room bathed in dim, peaceful light.

For a moment, it almost felt like he was glowing.

Part 4: "Grave Mistakes"

After the chaos he caused at his own funeral, Nick decided to take a breather in another room. Which was ridiculous, considering he didn't breathe anymore.

Still, floating out of the viewing room into the dim hallways of the funeral home felt like stepping into another world, or more accurately, another *afterworld*. The air shimmered faintly with something he hadn't noticed before, like the walls themselves hummed with restless energy.

He wasn't alone.

The first ghost he met was sitting cross-legged on top of the soda machine in the break room, humming "Sweet Caroline" to herself. Her clothes were vintage: bell-bottom jeans and a paisley blouse that practically screamed *disco fever*.

She looked up as Nick drifted in. "You new?"

"Yeah," Nick said, glancing around. "Just died this week. Rough crowd in there."

She grinned. "Funerals usually are. Everyone suddenly loves you when you can't talk back."

He chuckled. "You get it."

"Sure do." She hopped off the machine, hovering an inch above the floor. "Name's Darlene. Been here since '74. Nixon's still president, right?"

Nick blinked. "Oh, uh ... no. He's been gone for a while."

Her smile faltered. "Well, that explains why nobody gets my Watergate jokes."

Before Nick could reply, another ghost drifted through the wall, an elderly man in a powder-blue tuxedo, his expression sour as old milk.

"Polyester," he groaned by way of introduction. "They buried me in *polyester.* Can you believe that?"

Nick stared. "You're ... haunting this place because of your *outfit*?"

"Wouldn't you?" the man snapped. "It doesn't breathe, it clings, and every time I manifest, I *squeak.*"

Darlene rolled her eyes. "Ignore George. He's been squeaking about that for fifty years."

Nick floated closer. "So, what's the deal? You guys just ... hang out here?"

"Pretty much," Darlene said. "Some go toward the light. Some stay for snacks."

George crossed his arms. "Some stay because their loved ones made unforgivable fashion choices."

Nick snorted. "You people are ridiculous."

George narrowed his eyes. "Oh, and you're *so much better?* What's your unfinished business, Mr. Fancy Suit? Someone said your eulogy wrong?"

Nick opened his mouth to retort, then stopped. "Yes, actually."

Darlene grinned. "Oh, he's one of *those.*"

"One of what?" Nick said defensively.

"The righteous ones," she said. "You know, the ones who can't move on because they think the living owe them a proper narrative. Newsflash, buddy, once you're dead, nobody cares what version they tell."

"That's not true!" Nick said. "They're spreading lies! They're acting like I was Mother Teresa when I was just— "

"Human?" George said. "Flawed? Self-centered, but not evil?"

Nick hesitated. "Well, yeah."

George shrugged. "Welcome to the club."

Darlene floated closer, her tone softer now. "You think it's about them, but it's not. It's about you not being ready to be forgotten. None of us were."

Nick didn't reply. The hum of the vending machines filled the silence. Somewhere down the hall, he could hear the muffled sound of laughter, the guests from his funeral, probably at the reception now, telling more stories.

He floated toward the sound, but Darlene grabbed his sleeve. "You don't wanna go back there. That part's over."

He shook her off. "Maybe for you. But I'm not done yet."

"None of us are," George muttered. "That's the problem."

Nick drifted through the wall into the next hallway and found more ghosts milling about. A woman in a veil was sobbing dramatically into a lace handkerchief, even though she had no tears. A man in military uniform polished invisible medals, muttering that no one remembered his middle name. Another ghost sat staring into space, repeating, "They spelled it wrong on my tombstone."

The funeral home was crawling with regret.

And for the first time since he'd died, Nick realized how pathetic they all looked, himself included.

Darlene's voice echoed faintly behind him. "You can haunt every liar in the world, honey, but they'll still forget your name eventually."

Nick stopped. He looked back toward the doorway. She was leaning against the wall, arms crossed, her form flickering slightly like a dying candle.

"You sound like you've given up," he said.

"I've just had time to think," she replied. "You've had, what, a few days? You'll get there."

He hovered there, torn between fury and exhaustion. The funeral home lights buzzed overhead, one of them sputtering weakly. He couldn't tell if it was from his presence or just bad wiring.

Maybe both.

George drifted past, muttering, "Just wait until they cremate you. Then we'll see what polyester smells like."

Nick sighed. "You're all insane."

Darlene smiled faintly. "Probably. That's what eternity does to you."

He floated toward the far window, peering out at the night. Snowflakes swirled in the glow of the streetlights. People were leaving the funeral, their laughter muffled through the glass. Life was already moving on.

His name was still on the sign outside: *In Loving Memory of Nicholas Callahan*. But tomorrow, it would be someone else's.

And the world would forget him.

For the first time, the anger felt smaller. Pettier. Like a balloon slowly losing air.

Maybe Darlene was right. Maybe this wasn't about lies, it was about his refusal to fade.

He looked back at her and said quietly, "What happens if you stop fighting it?"

She tilted her head. "You mean ... if you let go?"

"Yeah."

She smiled sadly. "Then you find out what's next."

Nick nodded slowly. "Right."

He turned toward the reception room again, where the laughter had turned into the faint hum of background music. He could almost see his reflection in the glass, translucent, fading at the edges.

"Grave mistakes, huh?" he muttered. "Guess we all made a few."

Darlene gave him a knowing smile. "Yours just made better headlines."

Nick laughed, soft and genuine for the first time. "Yeah. Figures."

He floated down the hallway, his voice fading behind him. "Fine. One more round with the living. Then maybe I'll see what comes after."

Part 5: "The Truth According to Nick"

Nick had gotten used to the murmur of lies by now, the hissing hum of gossip and half-remembered anecdotes that seemed to fuel his own funeral. The air was thick with perfume and bad breath and worse intentions. He had tuned most of it out, lingering by the snack table and flicking pretzel crumbs at an aunt who was still loudly insisting he'd "always loved cats." He hadn't. He'd hated them. The feeling had been mutual.

But when the crowd began to thin, the red faces retreating toward cars and casseroles, he noticed someone left behind.

A man stood by his casket. Alone.

"Sam?" Nick floated closer, squinting. "Is it, Jesus Christ, huh."

Sam Hennigan, his old best friend. The guy who'd been there for all of it: the beer-soaked college nights, the botched proposal, the road trip where Nick had puked out the window and blamed it on altitude sickness. The two hadn't talked in years. Some argument that started about politics, or money, or one of those things that seemed world-ending at the time.

Sam's hair was thinner, his gut thicker, but his eyes were the same, wide and too honest. He was staring at Nick's body like it might answer him if he just waited long enough.

Nick hovered behind him, torn between relief and irritation. "Well, look who finally decided to show up," he muttered. "You couldn't pick up the phone, but you could pick out a black tie."

Sam let out a shaky breath.

"Hey, man," he said quietly, voice trembling. "You look ... not great. But they did their best, I guess."

Nick rolled his eyes. "Oh, sure. Lead with a compliment."

Sam chuckled softly, though it sounded more like a sob. "I don't know if you can hear me, but ... I hope you can. Because I owe you a lot of apologies."

Nick froze.

Apologies? That was new.

Sam rubbed the back of his neck. "You were a pain in the ass, Nick. You always had to be right. Always had to win. Every argument, every damn debate, you'd drag it out till everyone else gave up."

Nick crossed his arms. "Still not hearing the apology part."

"But," Sam continued, "you were also ... loyal. When my mom got sick, you were there. You showed up when nobody else did. You sat in that hospital room for hours, eating pudding cups and making her laugh about old nurses you thought were vampires."

Nick blinked.

He remembered that. He'd almost forgotten.

"I don't know why we stopped talking," Sam said, voice cracking. "I mean, I do, but ... it's so stupid now. You were pissed because I didn't show up for your birthday, and then you said something about how I was turning into a corporate sellout. I hung up on you, and that was it. Ten years of friendship gone in one phone call."

Nick wanted to interrupt, to say he hadn't hung up first, to defend himself, to make a joke about Sam's old Bluetooth obsession. But instead, he found himself silent. Just ... listening.

Sam took a deep breath. "You weren't easy to love, man. But you mattered. You mattered to a lot of us, even when you thought you didn't."

Nick glanced at his own face in the coffin, the waxy imitation of himself. The mortician had combed his hair wrong. His tie was crooked. He looked like a guy who'd lost every argument he'd ever picked.

Sam sniffled and reached out, brushing dust from the coffin's edge. "You know, when we were kids, you told me you never wanted a funeral. You said, 'If I die first, just toss me in a lake and play AC/DC.'"

Nick smirked. "Still stands."

Sam smiled faintly. "Guess I blew that one."

For a long while, neither of them said anything. Sam stared at the body. Nick stared at Sam. And for the first time since waking up dead, Nick didn't feel angry. Or amused. Or detached.

He felt ... tired.

"You were my best friend," Sam whispered. "Even when I hated you."

Nick wanted to say it back, to admit he'd missed him, too, that he'd thought about calling, that every sarcastic voicemail draft he'd deleted had been a pathetic little olive branch. But the words didn't come. Not out loud, anyway.

Instead, he found himself drifting closer. His hand, or the ghostly version of it, hovered just above Sam's shoulder. And though it passed right through, for a moment, Nick could've sworn Sam shivered like he'd felt it.

"Yeah," Nick murmured, voice softening. "Me, too."

Sam cleared his throat and straightened. "Anyway. I should go before your cousins start another fight about the will. I just ... I needed to say that."

He lingered a second longer, eyes glassy, then turned and walked away.

Nick watched him go. And something inside him cracked, a small, almost imperceptible sound, like a dry twig snapping underfoot. The bitterness that had fueled him, even in death, started to feel stupid.

He floated back toward his casket. The room was empty now, save for the flowers and the faint hum of the lights.

He laughed quietly to himself. "You know, Sam, you're right. I was a pain in the ass." Then, after a pause: "But I was a good one."

For once, the joke didn't feel like armor. It felt like truth.

Nick sat cross-legged in the air, staring down at himself. Maybe he'd wasted too much time proving he was clever instead of just being kind. Maybe every fight, every grudge, every sarcastic jab was just noise to drown out something he didn't want to feel.

He reached for the edge of the coffin again. This time, when his fingers brushed it, the air around him shimmered faintly. Like static.

He smiled. "Guess that's progress." He leaned back, letting the hum wash over him.

"I get it now," he said softly. "Not about heaven or hell or any of that crap. Just ... what it means to stop talking for once." The overhead light flickered, not in anger, not in mischief. Just once. Like a nod.

Nick chuckled. "Alright, fine. You win, universe. I'll shut up for a bit."

And as the faintest hint of warmth crept into the cold edges of the room, Nick felt something loosen, a final thread unspooling.

For the first time in his life, he didn't have the last word.

And that was perfectly okay.

Part 6: "Fading the Hell Out"

By the time Nick drifted back into the main viewing room, the lights had gone dim, and the smell of wilting lilies had settled into something vaguely chemical. The crowd had thinned to the stragglers, the diehards of mourning. The ones who couldn't leave without being seen leaving.

Aunt Cindy was still there, of course, holding court by the casket like she'd been knighted in grief. "He always wanted to be a pilot," she said dramatically, hand clutching her chest.

Nick groaned. "I wanted to *go to Hawaii*, Cindy, not *fly the damn plane.*"

She continued, undeterred. "Such dreams he had."

"Yeah," Nick said. "Dreams like not having his aunt exaggerate for attention."

In the back corner, his coworker Dale was nursing a Styrofoam cup of coffee and talking to a group of bored relatives. "We were real close, me and Nick. He told me once that if anything ever happened, I should take care of his cat."

Nick floated closer. "I didn't even *have* a cat, Dale! You're allergic to air conditioning, what would you do with a cat?"

Dale sipped, nodded solemnly. "That was the kind of guy he was. Always thinking of others."

Nick threw his hands up. "I was thinking of how to get out of the lunch meeting, you liar."

Across the room, an old flame, Lydia, red hair perfectly curled, face carefully mournful, dabbed at her eyes. "He never stopped loving me," she said to a small, eager audience. "He told me once that I was the one who got away."

Nick barked a laugh. "The one who got away? Lydia, you left me for your gynecologist because he had a boat."

Her friend sighed. "You must miss him so much."

"Oh," Lydia said, with a practiced quiver in her voice, "every day since we broke up."

Nick crossed his arms, smirking. "You blocked me on everything, sweetheart."

He started pacing, floating in lazy circles as the human noise swelled around him again, stories, corrections, embellishments. Every one of them wrong in some way. Some minor, some spectacularly off-base.

But this time, something was different. He didn't feel the need to fix it.

He hovered over his own casket, looking down at the stiff version of himself, and laughed. It wasn't bitter or sharp anymore. Just tired, wry amusement.

"Alright," he said to no one. "You win, people. Tell whatever story you want. I'm done arguing."

He drifted toward the preacher, who was packing up his notes from the eulogy. The man muttered something about "what a beautiful soul."

Nick leaned over his shoulder. "I cheated on my taxes and yelled at a Girl Scout once. Beautiful soul, my ass." Then he caught himself grinning. "Eh. Maybe I was wrong."

He floated up, high above the room, taking in the scene from a wider angle: the folding chairs, the pale carpet, the fake ferns drooping under fluorescent light. It all looked small now. Insignificant.

"I wasted so much time on this crap," he said, almost to himself. "All these people, all these lies. And I thought if I just shouted loud enough, I could make them *see me.*" He sighed, chuckling softly. "Turns out, you fade either way."

Down below, Aunt Cindy gasped. "I think I felt his presence!"

Nick smirked. "You felt gas, Cindy."

The lights flickered once, briefly, like a laugh from somewhere above, or maybe below.

That got him going again. He started circling the room, his old energy flickering back in bursts. "Alright, fine! You want a legend? Make one! Tell them I rescued orphans! Say I cured gluten intolerance! Hell, say I invented brunch!"

Someone in the crowd looked up, startled, as a floral wreath toppled from its stand. Gasps filled the room.

Nick snorted. "Yeah, that's right, give them a *show.* Tell them Saint Nick saved humanity with nothing but sarcasm and a bad attitude!"

His voice echoed strangely now, as if coming from farther away.

He kept going, pacing in midair, gesturing dramatically like some drunken ghost of Hamlet. "You know what? Fine. Tell them I made peace with all my enemies. Tell them I was brave, noble, generous. Go ahead, make me a folk hero. I'm tired of correcting morons!"

His voice wavered. The edges of his hands blurred. His reflection in the window had already started to fade, like steam on glass.

He glanced down at himself one last time. The body was still there, mouth slightly open, the expression half-smirk, half-surprise.

He chuckled quietly. "And for the love of God," he muttered, "close my mouth. I look like I'm catching flies."

For a moment, he lingered, the air shimmering faintly where he hovered. The hum of lights buzzed in his ears.

Then he laughed again. A small, satisfied sound. "Not bad," he said softly. "Could've been worse."

And as the hum dimmed, so did he, fading out mid-smile, mid-thought, mid-sarcasm. The air rippled once and then stilled.

Down below, a draft stirred the flowers. Aunt Cindy gasped again. "Did you feel that? That was him. I know it."

Dale nodded solemnly. "Yeah. He's at peace now."

From somewhere unseen, a faint, fading whisper replied, "Peace? Don't push it." And then Nick was gone.

The lights steadied. The room went still.

The living resumed their chatter, spinning new stories, shaping his memory into whatever version of him fit best.

But somewhere, not above, not below, just *elsewhere,* Nick Callahan, lifelong cynic and reluctant ghost, finally stopped correcting the record.

He didn't need to anymore.

The conversation was over.

No Boys Allowed

PARANORMAL THRILLER BY BETSEY KULAKOWSKI

"The unanswered mystery is what stays with us the longest; and it's what we'll remember in the end." — Stephen King

Children go missing all the time. Some are taken by strangers; others are taken by a non-custodial parent or a family member. Sometimes it's to protect the child. Sometimes it's to punish the estranged spouse. In the US, a child goes missing every ninety seconds. Tragically, one in 10,000 is not recovered alive. Some are never found.

In the US, an estimated 460,000 children are reported missing each year, according to the FBI. Two-thirds of missing children are between the ages of fifteen and seventeen years old. More than half return home in the same week and the overall return rate is 99%.

Amber Beecham was one of those children: the lost. She disappeared in 1977. Her case was one of the more *unusual* missing person cases still on the books. It was a case OSBI Agent Jon Bowen couldn't let go of; refused to forget. As a cold-case investigator, it was his job, but this case—*this* case—was personal.

Jon had just turned ten years old the summer when it happened. While his sister, Madeline, went to summer camp, he was at a football camp in North Texas. Maddie and Amber had been friends since kindergarten. Jon knew Maddie, but just as well as any boy knew his little sister's best friend.

To him they were two silly little girls who giggled too loud and interfered with his own plans far too often.

The summer of 1977 was a summer of tragedy. It was Maddie and Amber's first time going to sleep-away camp and both girls had been excited. When Maddie came home, she was traumatized and silent. Amber didn't come home.

Maddie never talked about Amber or what had happened; not to her family, not to the police, not even to the psychologist who tried to help her through the ordeal. She didn't speak to anyone. She didn't speak; not for a long time.

The *Sunshyne Girls' Camp*—founded in 1968—was sponsored by the *Ladies' Cotillion of the Northern Star* and was one of the highest rated summer camps for girls in Southeastern Oklahoma. To attend, a girl had to be recommended by a member of *The Cotillion,* of which there were seventeen chapters spread across Oklahoma, Arkansas, and Texas.

Jon's Aunt Kathy, a flight attendant and graduate of *The Sunshyne Girls' Camp*, had vouched for the girls. The mission of the *Sunshyne Girls' Camp* was to provide girls with the skills to become independent world travelers. The organization had been created by Sunshyne Gaylord, a wealthy socialite who—in her later years—had been appointed as an Ambassador for UNICEF. Sunshyne traveled the world in this role and was surprised to find there weren't enough young women like her who fed their taste for adventure as she did.

Her father had been a wealthy businessman-turned-politician who made an unsuccessful bid for first the Senate, then the US Presidency. Long after her father died, Sunny continued to devote her life to the *Cotillion* and its mission with the hopes of empowering girls to embrace a spirit of wanderlust and a passion for discovery. She never married and hated seeing her sorority sisters graduate with an expensive and useful degree, just to accept a proposal from a wealthy young man. Too often, she watched their dreams die as they were bound to house and hearth; serving at the whims of their husbands who never allowed them to travel the world. It broke her heart to see the most excitement they had was hosting the garden club or baking cookies for the PTA bake-sale—at least, that's how Sunny saw it.

She was one of the first women's rights advocates to reject marriage and children, but it didn't keep her from becoming Aunt Sunny to hundreds—if not thousands—of girls over the years. Her camp gave young ladies the skills to navigate the world, beginning with wilderness survival abilities. Many of the camp's graduates went on to become independent world travelers in their own rights. The camp also taught them about the customs of other countries, how to navigate airports, public transit; they even taught self-defense classes.

On June 13, 1977, something happened at the *Sunshyne Girls' Camp*; something no one had been able to explain, not even those who'd seen the whole thing. Now, thirty-five years later, it had happened again. Three girls were missing. Not far from the camp, the bodies of two young men had been found. They were later identified as Kevin Buescher and Jeremy Anders. Neither had any affiliation with the camp, though both seemed to have some relation to a couple of the camp counselors. Kevin was dating one of the older girls, and Jeremy was his friend he had intended to introduce to one of the other counselors.

"Jon, I know this is going to be a tough case for you, and I hate to have to ask you to investigate it." OSBI Director Karen Armitage was a no-nonsense woman. He knew she had taken a moment to consider this assignment. She planned every move with great care. "But you know more about the 1977 case than anyone and this one has all the earmarks of a repeat event."

"Is there anything to suggest this might be a copy-cat killing?" Jon asked.

"It may be too soon to say," she said. "Local authorities are preserving the crime scene now. OHP has a chopper fueled and ready to go. How soon can you meet them at the airfield?"

Jon already had his duffle bag down out of the closet, knowing he might be down there for a couple of days. He didn't need much. He glanced at the clock by his bed. "I can be there in thirty minutes," he said.

"I'll relay that to OHP," she said. "Jon?"

"Yes, Karen?"

"You don't have to do this," she said.

"I do," he answered. "And you know it."

Years had passed since Maddie lost her best friend; since she'd gone missing herself. She never could tell the Agents what had happened, even after years of counseling. She continued to disavow any memory of what had happened, but then—there were the nightmares.

Stephen King once said, "*Nightmares exist outside of logic* ..." but Maddie's nightmares had been founded; considering what she'd seen, even if she couldn't remember it. The doctors said her mind was blocking it to protect her from reliving it again and again. Unfortunately, her psyche couldn't block it entirely, thus the dreams; nightmares continued.

Jon had nightmares of his own. He'd only seen the crime scene photos from the 1977 murders. Seeing the bodies of the dead men now was much more traumatizing. "Who's been past the crime scene tape?" He asked, his tablet and stylus at the ready.

"Two hikers found them," Sheriff Scott Taber said. "My deputies arrived approximately forty minutes after the call came in. They taped off the scene and let me know of the situation. I called OSBI straight away. Deputies have held off any entry awaiting your arrival."

Jon jotted down notes. "How many victims?"

"Two, we think," the sheriff said, waving over one of his deputies. "Agent Bowen, this is Kirk Holt. He's been with me since he got out of the academy. Kirk, please tell Agent Bowen what you found."

"Agent Bowen," the deputy began.

"Please, call me Jon," he said, holding up a hand. "We'll be here all night if we're worried about titles."

"Call me Kirk," the deputy nodded. "Jon, when Leo, my partner, and I arrived, we found what appears to be two bodies."

"Why do you say 'appears'?"

"Because we had to count the pieces to be sure," he said. "They have been dismembered. It appears to be two men in their early twenties. A group of campers from Broken Bow reported that two of their party had gone missing."

"How long ago?"

"Reported missing yesterday," the Sheriff said. "Three girls from the camp are also missing."

Jon felt his blood pooling in his feet and his face went numb. He didn't have time to be squeamish or sentimental. "No one's been past that crime scene tape since you arrived?"

"No, sir," Kirk said. "We have a crime scene unit and medical examiner from Durant *en route* as well."

"I figured they'd beat me here." Jon forced a smirk onto his face.

"You had a helicopter," the Sheriff said. "In case you haven't noticed, this is pretty rural. It takes time to get here."

Jon glanced up at the rugged climes around him. Most people thought Oklahoma was a flat, and barren grassland, but that wasn't the big picture. Geographically, Oklahoma was a transition zone in the western United States. Most of the landscape was unmistakably part of the Great Plains; home to wheat farms, wind farms and oil fields. But southeastern Oklahoma was a different story. A large portion of the Ouachita Mountains dominated the region. While southeastern Oklahoma was the most mountainous part of the state, it was also home to its lowest point. At 289 feet above sea level, the Little River in McCurtain County wasn't far from where they were standing. Deep pine and oak forests covered the region, making the rugged terrain even less accessible.

"Do we have an ETA?" Jon asked.

"Thirty minutes to an hour, the way I figure it," the sheriff said.

"Alright, we'll wait." Jon nodded, tucking his tablet back into his pack.

"Most of the first body is over here." The deputy led the medical examiner and crime scene unit supervisor up the hill and around a stand of pin oaks. The local law enforcement had done a great job setting up a generous boundary around the actual crime scene. They had ample space to work with; unlike crime scenes in a congested city. Jon followed, keeping well behind the local authorities.

Jon scanned the landscape looking for tracks ... traces of boot marks or anything that might identify the killer or killers. The pine and oak litter was dry, and combined with the rocky terrain, there was little chance of it being that simple.

Jon's normal systematic approach of a crime scene was to start at the body and work his way out to the yellow tape in the four cardinal directions before he scanned a grid pattern looking for evidence. He would look at the body position, gather information on the physical anthropology of the victim, look for clues to the cause of death, then begin the detailed work of collecting evidence that might lead to his killer.

But, the first thing Jon noticed here was how *pristine* the crime scene was. There was no blood; no bits of flesh scattered about the dismembered corpse. There were no weapons, no signs of a struggle, nothing to explain how the body got here, or how it ended up in its current state. Immediately he began to suspect this was a secondary crime scene, meaning the victim had been killed elsewhere and the body dumped here.

He stopped at the edge of the clearing to begin snapping a series of photographs, being sure to document the big picture, then zooming in to catch midlevel details before collecting a series of up-close photographs of the body—what was left of it. He watched one of the crime scene units doing the same and wished he had a camera like hers. His was just a Nikon he'd bought to take on a vacation four or five years ago. It wasn't big and fancy, but it got the job done. The date-time-stamp feature was essential, and it took high resolution pictures as good as the cameras used by the CSI teams.

The body—or more properly, pieces of body—was almost white; bloodless and pale. That was abnormal. The torso lay prone, with bits of ivory bone showing through the flesh. A few feet away, lay one of the arms. Jon snapped a series of pictures. He noted through the lens as he zoomed in that it was the left arm, even though it lay on the right side.

The right arm lay much farther away. He found it with the last three fingers curled down, the pointer finger and thumb both extended as if pointing toward something. He snapped some more pics and then looked to follow the direction the arm pointed to. There, the head sat on a rock. Jon looked away, not prepared for what he saw. But he steeled his courage and lifted the camera as if to shield himself as he studied the victim's face through the lens. It was most certainly a male; his dark beard bisected the ashen face. The lifeless eyes were open, black like a doll's eyes. They gazed empty toward the trees above but saw no sky, no hope for tomorrow.

"The second body is over here," Kirk said, carefully stepping around the scene toward a second clearing. Jon glanced back at the face, but turned away as he swallowed hard to keep his lunch down. He fell in behind the deputy and picked his way down a rocky embankment through a stand of pine and oak trees. "We suspect that was Danny Mulgrew," he explained, nodding back up the hill. "We think this is Coyle Norwalk."

Jon didn't need to ask how he knew. This man had been African American, with long dark dreads that lay fanned out behind his head, as if each one had been precisely placed. His head was still attached—more or less—to the torso. Three legs lay nearby; one belonging to the first victim, clearly. While the man had been black, the skin now was more of a pale blue gray.

Jon had to step away, turning his back on the scene, taking a deep breath to calm his stomach and settle his nerves. Then he realized he could take a deep breath without smelling the sweet tang of death that so often accompanied such a scene.

"You okay, Agent Bowen? Jon?" Kirk came up behind him. "You're not going to pass out, are you?" He put a hand on Jon's back. "I never expected an OSBI Agent to get squeamish."

"I'm okay," Jon said. "You notice anything unusual about these crime scenes?"

Jon moved where he could meet Kirk's eye. The younger man was a few inches shorter, but not by much. Kirk's lip curled up. "You mean any of this is usual?" The deputy's voice cracked.

"Take a deep breath," Jon said. Kirk did. "Smell anything?"

Kirk shook his head. "No, not really."

"My point exactly."

Jon sat at the hotel reviewing the pictures, knowing he wouldn't sleep after what he saw today. He compared the photographs to those taken by the CSI teams thirty-five years ago. The images were similar—just as unsettling. Jon realized there was more to this than what he'd read in the earlier case files from so long ago. He needed to know the truth about what happened, and the murder book—that's what cops called a case file—didn't tell the whole story.

In the 1977 case, three campers and two camp counselors had gone missing in the blink of an eye. Both of the adults had been found within days of the event. Neither could tell authorities what had happened. The young men's bodies had been found miles from the camp; mutilated—dismembered some time later.

Jon's college professor had been the State Medical examiner at the time. Maybe he'd be able to tell him more. Dr. Nathanial Peterson had long since retired and had taken up residence in a house on the banks of Lake Eufaula in south central Oklahoma, a few hours drive from the crime scene. He found the old man sitting on his back porch beneath a sign with a large mouth bass etched into the wood. It read, *life is better at the lake*. The old man brightened when Jon introduced himself.

"OSBI, huh?" Nate chuckled. "I always knew you'd do well. You were one of my best students."

"Doc, I have a case I need your help on," Jon said. "Remember the Sunshyne Girls' Camp case?"

The old man's smile fell, and his countenance darkened. "Hard to forget that one. One of those little girls was your sister, if memory serves me right."

"Yes," Jon said. "Madeline. Maddie."

"How's she doing now?"

"Still won't talk about it," Jon said. "Never has, as far as I know. Not to anyone. It's happened again. Two more young men were murdered. Girls are missing. I need your help to find them and bring them home."

"It's been so long," Nate rose and went into the house, leaving the door open behind him. Jon took it as an invitation and followed. Nate went into the kitchen and poured two cups of coffee, handing one to Jon. He sniffed it but recoiled behind the doctor's back. It was thick and skunky; and the Doc offered no cream or sugar.

"What do you want from me, Jon?"

"Tell me about the 1977 case," Jon said, taking the chair Nate motioned to at the kitchen table.

"As a forensic pathologist, it was my job to observe the condition of bodies and collect evidence that I could draw conclusions from," Dr. Nate Peterson explained as Jon sat back nursing the bad cup of coffee, holding his breath as he pretended to drink it. It was scalding hot, so actually drinking it was impossible, even if he'd wanted to.

"You know, them TV cop shows get it all wrong," he started, and Jon realized this would not be a short story. "We call it the five faces of death." Jon took a sip of the coffee and at once regretted it.

Nate might have been a great medical examiner, but he made lousy coffee. He'd spent the last years of his career teaching at Southeastern Oklahoma State University — SEOSU—that's when Jon met him. It showed. Every conversation was a lecture. "The major changes that occur to a dead body are *rigor mortis*—everybody's heard of that; but then there is *livor mortis*—or lividity—that's how the blood pools, then there's *algo mortis*—when the tissue begins to cool, then there's *palor mortis*—a change in skin color, and last, decomposition."

"So what were the conditions of the bodies of victims from the 1977 case?" Jon asked.

"Well, that's a good question, Agent Bowen," he said, tipping back his own cup, swallowing down the hot liquid; his Adams' apple bobbed up and down as he drank the scalding hot coffee. *Freak. It's almost 100 degrees outside and he's drinking this battery acid?* "Within a half-hour of death, gravity takes effect on the stagnant blood. After six to twelve hours, the victim's blood will pool and settle in the body. The parts of the body with less blood will turn white ... the pooling blood turns the body red and purple. The skin gets all blotchy, you know."

"I've seen a few dead bodies in my day, Doc."

"Even when a body exsanguinates, there will still be traces of lividity. We can use these signs to tell when a body has been moved after death."

"Had the bodies been moved?" He hadn't seen anything about that in the 35-year-old case files. But then, there wasn't much in that thirty-five-year-old case file; forensically speaking. He thought that odd considering Nate was one of the most preeminent forensic specialists in the state, if not the country.

"Typically, there are three things you need to figure out: the location of the body, the time elapsed since the heart stopped and the cause of death. Once you know that, only then can you figure out the manner of death."

That didn't answer Jon's question, but he wasn't telling Jon anything he didn't already know. He'd taken no less than three forensics classes since graduating from college; and several more while in college. Before becoming an OSBI Agent, Jon had done an internship at the State Medical Examiner's office. He'd schlepped body bags and scraped up gray matter on countless crime scenes before joining the Durant Police Department right out of college. That'd been ten years ago, and he'd seen all five manners of death: natural, accidental, suicide, homicide and undetermined. The average *Joe-on-the-Street* would be surprised at how rare the *undetermined* cause of death was; especially these days with all the tools at the fingertips of modern day law enforcement.

"Well, we know the location where they were found, at least," Jon muttered under his breath. "Doc, I've read through your case file. There's a lot you don't say."

"Oh, I said it," Nate grumbled, shaking his head. "Dang Federal Government scrubbed my files."

Jon did a double take, almost dropping his coffee cup. "What?"

"FBI, CIA, NSA, every federal agency known to law enforcement came in, scrubbed the files, issued gag orders and pulled a major bait-and-switch to keep it out of the media."

"Gag order?"

"I shouldn't tell you anything," he said, getting up with great effort. "But what the hell do I care? I'm almost ninety. What can they do to me? Lock me up at Big Mac?" He asked, referring to the State Penitentiary in McAlester. "Eh, better than ending up in that lousy nursing home my kids wanna send me to."

"I am not asking you to put yourself in jeopardy so I can find these missing girls, Doc. I'm a realist. It's been thirty-five years. The odds are good that Amber isn't coming home ... ever. But these new missing girls? Maybe I can help bring them home." Jon set the cup on the table and leaned in. "I'm doing this for Maddie, as well as the other girls who never came home."

"If you want answers ... you need to work your way up," Nate said.

"Up?"

"All the way up, Jon," Nate continued, leaning heavily on his chair. "A steely-eyed detective like you, might just be able to cut the red tape and get to the truth."

"What truth am I looking for?" Jon asked, tightening his brow.

"The truth about how a body can be completely exsanguinated, without a trace of blood left anywhere. How arms and legs can be removed from the corpse with no sign of scalpel cuts ... how two virile young men can be found weeks later with no sign of decomposition. How the five faces of death can be masked from law enforcement for thirty-five years—and how the government's been able to white-wash it to the point those missing girls' names have never been mentioned in a single newspaper or television report."

Jon knew at least one of those answers. Amber Beecham's family had requested the media not mention their missing daughter; insisted on it vehemently. Law enforcement had no problem complying and now Jon understood why—yet wondered even more.

"Remember your training, Jon," Nate said. "You remember my classes, don't you?"

"Of course," Jon said. "They were some of my favorites."

"Well, once you go back through the basic steps, then ... you need to think outside the box. You're not going to solve these cases through traditional old-fashioned police work."

"I'm not?"

"No. You won't." Nate turned and picked up the fishing pole sitting in the corner. "Now are we going to cut bait or are we going to fish?"

"I'm going to have to take a raincheck on this one, Doc. I've got some outside-the-box thinking to do."

"Roll on, *Savage Storm*," the old man chuckled, referring to the college's new mascot. "Roll on!"

Think outside the box? Hm. Okay. Jon went home and pulled out the box on the top shelf of his closet and set it on the foot of the bed. He took out one of the notebooks and thumbed through it. Not finding what he was looking for, he rummaged around until he found the right one. These were his notebooks he'd kept from his introductory Forensics courses back in college. Jon was a copious note-taker and he'd had the foresight to keep these notebooks all these years. He referred to them often.

Cold cases can be the most frustrating and difficult cases a detective will ever be assigned to, he'd written on the first page of this notebook. *A cold case unit is often an integral part of a well-formed police department, but not every law enforcement agency can devote the resources necessary; especially in areas with high crime rates. But cold case units can effectively reduce the crime rate by catching serial criminals, who often engage in other types of crimes, not just murder. It also leads to improved community relations which means citizens are often more willing to cooperate with police.*

Jon closed the notebook, knowing this was a rabbit trail that could take him off course. He'd already reviewed the OSBI files from thirty-five years ago, he'd scoured through them no less than once a year since it'd been assigned to him. He'd gone back to the basics with the case. "Time to think outside the box," he said, tossing the notebook back in its place, glancing at the novel laying on his bedside table. It gave him an idea; one he might regret. But if he was going to solve this case, he needed help. He knew just who to call.

Best-selling author Sabrina Bishop hadn't gotten to the top of the *New York Times* Best Seller list without knowing a thing or two about a criminal case. One in particular had been her bread and butter. She'd helped Jon Bowen catch a serial killer—more or less—even though he insisted he didn't believe in all that *mumbo-jumbo psychic stuff*. If he didn't *believe* in it, why did he come to her for help? Most law enforcement agencies wouldn't even consider it; those that did, considered consulting with a psychic as a *tool-of-last-resort*.

The file in front of her didn't have much information. Resting her hand on the aged manilla folder she could feel the black markers in the hands of Federal Agents redacting large sections of the information. Over the years entire pages had been removed and the file recreated to obliterate the history of changes—so no one would know. But Sabrina knew.

The first narrative of the facts was—by and large—still intact. What was missing were the witness statements, testimony of several persons of interest and most of the crime scene photographs.

Three girls had gone missing; one mysteriously returned to the camp office in the middle of a blinding rainstorm. The next night, little Madeline Bowen walked into the camp; ashen and drenched to the core. Her teeth chattered. She had looked at the scout leader and said simply. "They tried to take me."

"And now, three more girls are missing?" Sabrina looked up at Jon, trying to see past his eyes and read him; past his fear and concern, which were hidden just below his confident exterior.

"And two more young men are dead," he said. "I know this is nothing like *The Handyman* serial killer cases, but ... I thought you might be able to help."

"You know this case file has been ... altered, right?" she asked, stabbing a neatly manicured nail into the top of the stained folders.

"I do. I talked to my professor. He was the ME at the time," Jon said. "He told me the government had redacted most of the pertinent information."

"And your little sister was the sole witness?"

"Yes," Jon said. "At least ... that we know."

"What did she tell you?"

"She won't tell me anything," Jon confessed, explaining Maddie's condition.

Sabrina pursed her lips as she stared at him, letting the emotions on his face flood into her. His heart broke for his sister. He was afraid for those missing girls. He was disappointed in himself for not being able to put the pieces together. You didn't have to be psychic to know that. You just had to know Jon, and she did.

"She'll tell me."

His eyebrow lifted. "You think so?"

"I know so," she nodded. "Can you call her?"

"She'll know that it's a set up," Jon said.

"Tell her ..." Sabrina hesitated a moment. "Tell her we've started talking again, and you think it might be getting ... serious."

"You want to go there *again*?" Jon snapped.

"We tried, Jon." She fought to keep her expression neutral and her tone casual. "I'm sorry things didn't work out between us, but ... we *tried*."

"You're the one that broke off the engagement," he snapped. "In case you forgot."

"I have not."

"Are you saying you want to try again?"

"No, but your sister doesn't know that."

"Ooohhh." He dragged the word out. "So, that's how it's going to be?"

"You want answers?"

"I want the truth."

"Then call your sister and let me help you find it."

Maddie smiled when she opened the door. "Jon! Come in! Come in!" She stepped back and allowed Jon to lead Sabrina into her home. It was a cute little colonial in a historic neighborhood in Oklahoma City, not too far from the State Capitol. The area had seen a renaissance over the past few years. Still, it was a lot for a single woman to manage, Jon thought.

Maddie seemed to manage fine, though. The front lawn was verdant; neatly manicured. The flower garden had been done in the English style, with neatly groomed privet hedges and colorful flowers including lavender, echinacea, geraniums, foxgloves, hollyhocks, and daisies, as well as roses and peonies.

"Welcome. You must be Sabrina," Maddie said.

"I am." Sabrina stuck out her hand. "Sabrina Bishop."

"Best-selling author, Sabrina Bishop," Maddie beamed, shaking her hand vigorously. "I can't believe you're here. I can't believe you're dating my brother!"

"I'm wounded," Jon feigned insult. "Why is that such a surprise?"

"You're a dork, for one thing," Maddie goaded him. "Who wants lemonade? I just made some."

"I'd love some," Sabrina said, as Maddie led them into the kitchen. "You have a beautiful home."

"Thank you," Maddie beamed.

Jon had told her Maddie was an architect and knew it would be a compliment that would win her favors. "Did you design it yourself?"

"Oh, heavens, no." Maddie poured three glasses. "It was built in 1916 and was in horrible shape when I found it. I did design the renovated floor plan though." Maddie handed her the lemonade. Sabrina used the moment to her advantage. She let her hand connect with Maddie's when she wasn't expecting it. She reached out and found the memories she'd been suppressing and extracted what she was looking for.

Maddie flinched and her eyes rolled back in her head. Jon caught her and scooped her up in the same motion, while Sabrina saved the glass from falling from her hand. She watched as Jon carried Maddie to the sofa and lay her down. Sabrina lifted the glass to her lips with a trembling hand, draining the glass. Drawing memories like that was draining, and she felt woozy. The sugar in the lemonade would help and she got it down before she passed out herself. Jon came back and caught a hand under her arm, taking the glass from her unsteady hand. “You okay?”

“Yeah,” she managed. He sat her down in a chair and brought her a second glass of lemonade, knowing how her abilities could drain her. “Drink.” He held it to her lips. She reached up to help as she drank greedily.

“Thank you,” she said when her thirst was sated.

“Get what you need?”

“Yeah,” she nodded. “But ... you’re not going to like it.”

Sabrina explained everything in the car. “Your sister was abducted, but ... it wasn’t what you think.”

Jon signaled and pulled the car over to the shoulder. He put it in park. “What?”

“Have you considered that the abductor might not have been someone of this world?”

“What?” Jon’s expression dropped. “Are you kidding me? Aliens? What is this? ‘The X-Files?’”

“Maddie remembers going with her friends and the counselors to watch the meteor showers by the lake, not far from camp. Two boys came to join them. They lit a camp fire and made s’mores and told ghost stories until the meteor showers began.

One minute they saw a shooting star, the next ... a blinding light. She heard screaming and the next thing she knew she was in a room with these ... beings. Do you have a pen? Paper?”

Jon pulled a notebook from his jacket pocket, and a pen from his shirt pocket. Sabrina sketched an image, before turning it where Jon could see it. The being had a large head with an elongated skull. The eyes were large and dark, but menacing, too. Jon handed the picture back, shaking his head. “I’m not sure about this, Sabrina.”

"Look, do you know what's going on in the astronomical world right now?" Jon shrugged. Sabrina continued. "The Perseid meteor showers occur around this time of year, but this year, they're even more spectacular because the full moon doesn't come until late in the month."

"Meteor showers?" Jon scoffed.

"The same meteor showers your sister and her friends went to see," Sabrina said. "Look, in 1977, the Swift-Tuttle comet came dangerously close to the Earth. The meteor shower occurs when the Earth passes through the comet's tail, you know?"

"I didn't," Jon said.

"That same comet is almost as close now as it was in 1977. It won't be this close again until 2126." Sabrina held his gaze. "I think we need to go back to the Sunshyne Girls' camp."

"To what end?"

"To find the missing girls," she said. "So we can bring them home."

"For the record, I don't like this," Jon muttered. "I don't like this one bit."

"For the record, I'm not too happy about it myself," Sabrina intoned. She aimed the flashlight at the rugged path before them. Jon used his own light to scan the woods around them.

"This was your bright idea," Jon said, flinching and swinging the light across her when he heard a branch snap. She froze and he almost knocked her down. "Just a deer." He focused his beam on the frightened buck. It froze a moment, too. Without warning, it turned and leapt over a fallen sycamore tree and disappeared into the woods.

"This time of year, I'm more worried about snakes," Sabrina said, continuing on up the hill.

"If we were closer to the swamp we'd have to worry about alligators, you know?"

"Alligators?"

"Might be a Bigfoot out here, too," Jon chuckled, with bemusement in his voice. Sabrina paused and took a step back.

"So that's what that was," she muttered, stopping.

"Huh?" Jon bumped into her again.

"I've had the feeling *someone* was watching us," Sabrina said. "*Something.*"

Jon stepped back. "You mean to tell me you have a psychic connection to Bigfoot?"

"Jon," she said, eyeing him with trepidation. "I'm joking." She laughed trying to lighten the mood. "Besides, I'm not technically a *psychic* and you know it. I'm a *clairvoyant empath.*"

"Iceberg, Goldberg." Jon shrugged. "What's the difference?"

"Just trust me," she said. "There's a difference."

There was a snap in the trees beyond them, and they both froze. He grabbed her and pulled her close, not sure which one he needed, his gun or his flashlight. There was a growling sound that echoed from a distance.

"Mountain lion?" she whispered. "Or bear?"

Jon put a finger to his lips and reached for his weapon. He moved quietly, placing her behind him—putting himself between her and danger. Her hand snaked around him, her palm spreading across his stomach as she clung to him, trying to see over his shoulder into the darkness beyond the beam of his light. Hers was dying.

"More likely a bear," he said softly. "Both dangerous."

The crackle of dried leaves and pine litter told of heavy footfalls in the darkness as the growling and grunting continued; moving closer. Sabrina's hand wrapped into Jon's shirt, and he could hear her panting in his ear. "It's okay," he assured her. "I'll protect you."

He'd protected her before; saved her from *The Handyman*. He took a deep breath and lifted his light, piercing the darkness. The grunting beast before them ran into the beam of Jon's flashlight and froze. The bear lifted onto its hind legs and made a bawling noise before dropping back down and pawing at the ground. "Get out of here, bear!" Jon shouted. "Go on! Get!"

The bear grunted and whined, then turned and rambled off. Jon felt Sabrina's hand slide off his stomach as she leaned her head against his back. "That was close," she said. At the same moment, a much more distant howl lifted above the trees from across the mountain. This one was high pitched; like a woman's scream.

Jon spun around, lifting his light into the distance, but it was futile. "Holy hell!" Sabrina panted. "What was *that*?"

"I've watched enough of the *Exploration Channel* to know what that is," Jon swallowed hard. "That was a *sasquatch*."

"You believe in Bigfoot?"

"*You're* the one that said you felt like you were being watched."

"Doesn't mean I thought it was Bigfoot," she smirked.

Jon chuckled. "Come on," he said. "The clearing where the bodies were found is just up here."

As they inspected the scene, he told her the details of his observations; observations that had been confirmed by the medical examiner and the crime scene unit. He was just about to cover his interview with Nate when she stopped and caught his arm. "What?" He asked.

"They're here ..."

Sabrina's eyes grew wide and even in the dim light, he could see her skin go pale. He glanced up as a bright light reflected in her frightened eyes. He turned to see the meteorites ablaze against the dark velvet sky. Then the sky went white as they were enveloped by a blinding light. There was a piercing noise and the smell of ozone filled Jon's nose. The world tilted—and then, there was nothing.

Sabrina wasn't sure what happened, or how she came to be laying supine in the middle of an open clearing. The sky above her was as clear as glass, with meteorites raining down with a fury she'd never seen before. Her head throbbed. Her body ached. She felt as if an unseen force was pressing down on top of her, making it hard to breathe.

She could hear moaning, but it took a moment to realize she was the one doing it. Then, she thought about Jon. She forced herself up onto her elbow, and realized she wasn't alone. A little girl lay curled up a few feet away, crying and trembling.

Sabrina managed to crawl over to her. "Hey," she said, putting a hand on the little girl's back. "It's okay. You're safe. My name is Sabrina. I came to help you." The little girl sniffed and seemed to relax. "What's your name?"

"A-a-a-amber," she shivered one more time. Sabrina pulled off her jacket and lay it over the little girl to warm her. The night had gone chilly, but she knew the child was most likely in shock.

"Amber!" Sabrina tried to say the name brightly, though even she could hear her own relief. "We've been looking for you."

She glanced up as she heard a shuffling nearby, seeing two more little girls walking her way, pausing to help up another. "You came for us!" one of them cried.

"We did," Sabrina got to her feet, rushing over to draw the girls in. "I'm so glad to find you."

"Me, too?" Another little girl appeared from the woods, followed by another.

Sabrina stood with the girls huddling around her as more and more came into the clearing. Her mouth dropped at the sheer number of girls that gathered around her. She had come for a few, but ... more than two dozen assembled, looking lost; relieved to be found.

"Jon?" Sabrina called out. "Jon? Are you out there?"

One of the little girls tugged on her pant leg. Sabrina dropped to one knee to meet the child's gaze. "Boys aren't allowed at *Sunshyne Camp*. Aunt Sunny doesn't allow it."

"Oh?"

"No," the little girl—who couldn't have been more than six—said. "Miss Talana's brother came to visit, and Aunt Sunny got so mad she fired Miss Talana and her friend."

"Fired her?"

"She sent her away and we never saw her again."

She didn't have to be an OSBI Agent for a statement like that to get Sabrina's gears spinning. Speaking of OSBI Agents ... *where was Jon*?

Jon could hear the pulsing hum of something just beyond his ability to comprehend. The space he occupied was like something off of *Star Trek*—a dimly lit room, with the platform he lay upon in the middle. There were no other furnishings; no windows, no visible light fixtures, just a dim glow that seemed to emanate from the walls. An eerie sense of foreboding washed over him, and his body began to tremble in response; his teeth chattering beyond his control. He took a deep breath, trying to will himself to still. The air around him did have an unusual fragrance; like a new car smell—or a science lab.

Jon struggled to rise from the surface beneath him but found his body unable to respond though he was not physically restrained, at least not by visible means. He struggled against the force that held him, but it was of no use. He couldn't break the ties that held him down.

The sensation of being restrained caused Jon's pulse to race and he felt anxious and afraid. That feeling was intensified when there was a whooshing noise above his head, and he couldn't turn to see what it was. The presence of the beings in the room, however, was readily plain. He knew *they* were there.

The *beings* moved to the side of the bed and Jon found himself frozen in terror. They had large metallic glowing eyes with no lids. The heads were elongated, hairless and too large for the proportions of their bodies. What should have been hands were more insect-like, with two sets of pincers on each.

There were four of *them*, though one was clearly in charge. It made a series of clicks and hums from deep in its chest. One of the creatures—Jon suspected as being female—stepped forward and eyed him a moment before it began to prod him, tugging on his clothing, lifting up the hem of his t-shirt, peering at his body beneath. It lifted his arm and rolled up his sleeve, studying the skin beneath. It seemed particularly interested in the hair on his arms. It moved up his body to his face. An alien hand moved to his hair and seemed to tousle it as the inspection continued around to the other side.

Jon bit his lip, and pinched his eyes shut trying to will this horrible dream to go away. He tried to wake himself up, but it seemed in vain. "No!" he ordered flatly when the female began prodding lower down his body. The being lifted its head and gazed unblinking at him. She started to resume her inspection, but he repeated, "No!" He struggled again against the force that held him, but it was in vain.

The creatures clicked and hummed between them and the one that was the leader moved closer, while the others stepped away and disappeared into the void beyond where the light could reach. This one was much larger than the others. Its brow was more pronounced; jaw more square. The emphasis of the beings elongated head made Jon think of a silverback gorilla. It reached for Jon's shirt, as the other had but Jon snapped, "No! Don't touch me!"

The being's eyes darkened, and it did not follow the command. When its hand—if you could call it that—touched him, a bolt of lightning seemed to pass through his body, and he yelped in pain. It didn't dissuade the being from continuing its inspection. It lifted the waistband of his jeans and peered beneath the fabric. Without so much as a how-do-you-do, it moved on, rolling up his pant leg, lifting the edge of his sock.

It made a few deep clicking noises, and Jon found himself rolling over onto his face, and the inspection continued. It didn't hurt, but not being able to see what they were doing was terrifying. His plaid shirt lifted, and he could feel its hand moving up his spine, as if counting each vertebra. When the being completed its inspection, Jon was rolled back over, and found himself sitting upright; his feet hanging off the platform. What appeared to be a machine was brought over and opened, Jon's hand placed into the middle of it before the lid closed. He wanted to protest; wanted to fight and try to escape, but he still was restrained, even as he sat upright. The machine hummed to life and his hand grew warm, as if it were being scanned by a copy machine or a CT scanner. Prickles of energy sparked through his flesh, and he flinched despite himself. The female moved back in to take the machine, and Jon realized the back of his hand was bleeding, and a pool of his blood remained in the bottom of the machine. He suspected they had run some kind of a blood test on him, though how or why he thought that escaped him.

Without any effort he was lifted to his feet, though they didn't seem to quite touch the floor. The leader moved to stand in front of him and made noises that sounded threatening. Jon swallowed hard. "Look, dude," he started to say, but the creature's lipless mouth opened to show two rows of razor sharp, triangular teeth, and the hum turned into a growl. Jon's jaw locked and he kept any snarky comment to himself as he recoiled. The being's breath was fetid. Its tone harshened further still and the volume of its growl crescendoed. It was terrifying and Jon felt his blood rush into his feet. The room spun around him. A series of bright lights flashed in his eyes, and then, there was nothing.

Sabrina used her cell phone to call the county sheriff. He sent EMS and his deputies to collect the girls and have them taken for medical evaluation before Child Services took them for processing and reunification. "Are you okay?" he asked Sabrina.

"I'm not hurt," she said, still sitting on a log by the fire she and the girls had built to keep warm while they waited for help. The night had gone unseasonably cold, and it felt good on her face. "Though I am a bit shaken up."

"And you don't have any idea where Agent Bowen went?" She'd already explained what had happened to her—or what she thought had happened. She couldn't be sure. She had seen the meteor shower; been blinded by a bright light. The next thing she knew she was lying in the meadow. What had happened in the hours between, she couldn't be sure. She wasn't even sure how many hours it had been.

"No," Sabrina said. "I'm scared something may have happened to him, but … but I can't be sure. I don't think he'd have gone off and left me of his own free will."

"You realize we've had four young men murdered in these parts, don't you?"

Sabrina blanched, swallowing hard. "I can't let myself think something like that would have happened to Jon."

"And can you tell me what your relationship to Agent Bowen is?"

She expected this question. "He's my ex-fiancé," she said, honestly.

"Ex?"

"It was an amicable split," she explained. "No animosity between us, if that's what you're thinking. He called me to help with his investigation."

"And why would he call you?"

"Well, because I'm a novelist," she said. "I helped him with one of his cases a year or so back. I am also … I'm a *clairvoyant empath*."

The man's eyebrows slowly crept up towards his flat brimmed hat. "A what?"

"A psychic," she sighed. "Though that's a simplified explanation. Jon thought I might be able to help his sister remember what happened to her thirty-five years ago."

"And did you?"

She pursed her lips, suspecting she couldn't tell him what she knew without him thinking she was a complete crackpot. The look he was already giving her was enough evidence of that. "No," she said. "Not really. That's why we decided to take another look. He thought I might be able to read the scene and come up with something."

He scratched his chin, eyeing her. "That kinda nonsense don't hold water around here, Miss Bishop."

"I get it," she said, not willing to fight with him. She knew there was no way she could win him over, so why bother? "Uhm, Sheriff, do you know the woman that runs the Sunshyne Girls' Camp?"

"Aunt Sunny? Sure," he said. "Everyone knows her. She's practically a legend in these parts."

"One of the girls said she doesn't allow men at the camp," Sabrina said. "Is that right?"

"She's asked if I ever have to send the law out there that I send one of my female deputies," he said.

"You have a female deputy?"

"Used to," he said.

"Used to?"

"Victoria Brown took a job with the Choctaw Tribe," he said. "'Bout three years ago."

"So you've had to send your male deputies out there?"

"I have not," he acknowledged. "She runs a good camp. Has her own team of security folks. Never had any cause to go out there."

"What about after the girls went missing?"

"Well, it wouldn't have done any good to go out there. The girls weren't *there*," he said. "I did my interview over the phone."

"Hm," Sabrina huffed. "Interesting."

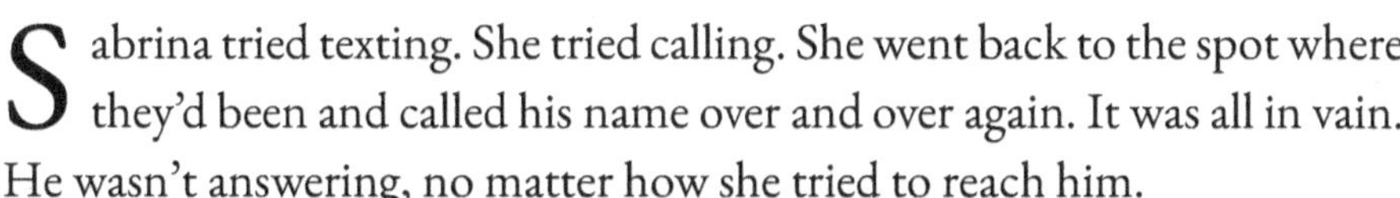

Sabrina tried texting. She tried calling. She went back to the spot where they'd been and called his name over and over again. It was all in vain. He wasn't answering, no matter how she tried to reach him.

A nagging feeling had been swirling around in her mind since her conversation with the Sheriff. Sunshyne Gaylord was the central pivot point in all of this, and he'd just talked to her over the phone. How could that be considered good police work?

She hiked back to the car and drove to the camp office. The gates were closed, locked from the inside, but Sabrina was not dissuaded. Gates were to keep cars out. Fences were to keep people out. Apart from a couple of sections of decorative wood fence, designed to give the camp a rustic Colorado vibe, Sabrina found the fence ended where the woods began. There was a yellow sign with brown print that said, "*Girls Camp: No Boys Allowed.*" *Hmph. Some security system*, she scoffed to herself.

It wasn't hard to gain access, and she walked nonchalantly back to the path on the other side of the fence and right up to the Camp Office.

She knocked, but no one answered. She knew someone was there. Her sixth sense told her to try the knob and she found it unlocked. The door railed a high pitched squeal as it swung open on rusting hinges; the wood floor beneath her feet creaked. The aged wood held the aromas of the decades, including an overt aroma of stale cigarette smoke.

The entry took her through the kitchen where it appeared dishes had been recently washed. The kitchen's collection of knives had been laid out, a whetstone and leather strap lay beside the cleaver, chef's knife, paring knife and filet knife; as if ready for sharpening. Sabrina recognized the stale perfume of fried liver and onions. She turned up her nose at the thought. She'd never cared for that dish when she was a kid; didn't care for it now either.

"Hello?" she called. "Anyone here?"

"We're closed!" A gruff old voice called faintly from upstairs. Sabrina came around the corner and found the steps leading up. Without hesitation, she climbed them. The landing at the top took her to the hallway where she could see four doors, one of which was open. A woman sat by the open window smoking a cigarette through the stoma in her neck. Seeing Sabrina, she covered the gaping hole with her palm. "I said we're closed!" Sabrina realized now why the voice was so gruff. This woman had undergone a medical procedure; emphysema or cancer had been her undoing—which one was hard to know for sure.

"I'm looking for Sunshyne Gaylord," Sabrina said, forcing a smile.

"Are you a reporter?" The woman coughed and returned to smoking her cigarette.

"No," she said. "I'm ... I am a writer," she said. "But I'm a novelist."

The woman covered the hole. "No story here. Go away."

"Are you ... Sunshyne?"

"Sunny," she said, then was overtaken with a wracking cough. The rattling in her chest told Sabrina enough. It didn't appear she was going to live much longer. The fact that she continued to smoke, even after lifesaving efforts, was proof of that.

"I'm a friend of Jon and Maddie Bowen," she said, still standing in the doorway. "Jon asked me to help him find out what happened to his sister."

"You didn't bring him here, did you? No boys allowed!!" She shrieked as loud as she could, which wasn't that loud. "No ... boys!" The coughing resumed and continued for a long moment.

"No," she said. "He's gone missing."

"You *did* bring ... him," she choked. "Big ... mistake."

"Miss Gaylord," Sabrina started.

"Aunt Sunny," the woman corrected, glaring at her. Sabrina realized one of her eyes was clouded over with a cataract.

"Do you know what happened to the young men? The ones that disappeared?"

"They were warned," Sunny grunted. "No boys allowed!" The coughing resumed and the woman doubled over. "Not my rule ..." she gasped, her lips tinging blue as she struggled for a breath of air.

Sunny was in trouble. Sabrina recognized the fact at once. "Do you have oxygen? Can I help?" Sabrina stepped into the room looking for anything that might provide the woman with some comfort. A flailing hand pointed toward the table by the bed. Sabrina saw the inhaler and grabbed it, taking it over to the woman, holding it to her mouth. Sunny snatched it away, and pressed it to her throat, activating it as she wheezed for breath; then activated it again. It didn't seem to help. The wheezing continued. Her lungs seemed to be filled with fluid.

"You need help," Sabrina said. "I'll call 911."

Sunny grabbed her arm and shook her head.

"The aliens don't like them," she grunted, wheezing.

"What are you doing here?" A woman's voice startled Sabrina. "You can't be in here!" The new player rushed over to the struggling woman.

"Who are you?"

"I'm Bethany Jordan, I'm Sunny's assistant," she said, trying the inhaler again. "Sunny, take a deep breath." Bethany gave her another dose. Then another.

"They don't ... like ... the boys ..." Sunny repeated between coughing fits. "And neither ... do ... I ..."

"What?" Sabrina recoiled,not sure she'd heard right. "What are you talking about?"

"The boys," Sunny choked. "Can't ... use them. Don't want ..." The woman's voice trailed off, and her grip on Sabrina's arm loosened.

Sunshyne Gaylord gasped and drew her last breath.

"You killed her!" Bethany sobbed.

"No," Sabrina started to protest, but the woman spun on her, a knife appearing from nowhere. "No!" She jumped back, the blade just missing her.

"You don't belong here! You don't belong here any more than those horrible boys did! You shouldn't have come! Now you will pay!" Bethany slashed repeatedly with each statement, backing Sabrina up into the hallway. "The gods might have use for you, but they'll have to take you in pieces!" The maniacal woman made a running start at her; Sabrina danced and parried, avoiding the assault.

Sabrina had learned a thing or two in the time that she and Jon had been dating. She knew that a knife raised the odds from '*someone might die*' to '*I am going to make you bleed*.' Her goal was to avoid the pointy end at all cost. The attacker's goal was not to lose their weapon.

She'd written a whole series about a sadistic serial killer with a penchant for cutting up women, so she also knew a few '*defense against the sharp arts*' techniques, thanks to Agent Bowen. She knew she needed to stay out of range of the blade until she was ready to commit. She also knew she needed to keep her eye on the knife. If she looked away—even to make eye contact with this psychopath—she might not see it coming.

"Take your time," Jon had told her, "but don't *mess* around." He'd used a more *colorful* word.

"I didn't hurt your boss," Sabrina insisted.

Distance.

Jon had told her the best defense was distance and a lot of it. Sabrina backed up, but the woman charged. In the time it took for Sabrina to dance past her attacker, the blade caught her in the upper arm and burned like holy fire. She could feel the blood welling up and running down her arm—hear it dripping on the wooden floor. Sabrina knew she had no time for any more nonsense. She needed an improvised weapon or something to divert her attacker. A half-dead potted plant on the hall table was the first thing she caught. She grabbed it by the leaves expecting the pot to come with it as she swung, but just the dried up root ball flew at her attacker, disintegrating into a wad of roots and a cloud of dirt, peat, and vermiculate.

The attacker blinked, her eyes filled with grit and dust. She coughed as she inhaled it. The woman staggered as she coughed harder, folding. The knife fell from her hand and clattering down the stairs. Sabrina lunged, knocking the woman off balance, sending them both tumbling. Sabrina grabbed the woman's head and slammed it against the wall before leaping to her feet and backing up.

Nonplused, the attacker jettisoned herself towards Sabrina, but already on her feet, the author side-stepped the assault, and the aggressor missed. Bethany catapulted herself into a roiling ball, down the steps with a wicked *ka-thunk-ka-thunk-ka-thunk*, and finally a gut-wrenching *snap* as she landed with her head at an awkward angle and didn't move.

Staggering over to the stair rail, Sabrina's eyes were fixed on the scene below as she fell back onto her rump on the top step, her hand going to her injured arm, applying pressure a moment before turning loose to inspect it. Blood gushed down her arm. She let it flow as she fished in her pocket for her cellphone and held down the red button, activating the emergency call for help.

"911. What is your emergency?" the operator on the other end of the line asked.

"I need an ambulance," she said, pinching her eyes against the blurring world. "And tell the Sheriff to bring his *men* ... and the medical examiner."

Sabrina sat on the back step of the ambulance as the Sheriff took her statement. Paramedics had her bandaged up until they could get her to the hospital so doctors could stitch up her arm. She told him what

Sunny had said, and what had happened. "And then she just ... died. That's when her assistant came in."

"We ran facial recognition on Bethany Jordan," he said. "Her real name is Eleanor Gaylord. She's Sunny's daughter."

"Her daughter? I thought she never married."

"She didn't," he said. "She had an affair with a boy in college and ended up pregnant. When he wouldn't marry her, she left school and had the baby in secret. She founded this camp not long after. She raised her here ... like mother, like daughter ... both bat-crap crazy."

"Sheriff," one of the deputies approached. "You need to see this."

"What is it?" he asked.

The man nodded at Sabrina, tipping his hat in a polite Southern greeting, but he turned his attention back to the Sheriff. "I think we found your primary crime scene," he said.

Sabrina started to get up, as if to go with them. But, the Sheriff put a hand on her uninjured arm. "You did what you could," he consoled her. "Don't worry about this. We'll take it from here. You need to get that arm tended to."

"The main thing I'm worried about is Jon. Those two were the only ones who might know what happened to him," Sabrina sniffed, a hot tear peeling down her cheek. "Just tell me he wasn't ... *here*."

"No, ma'am," the deputy said. "He's not *here*. No sign of him."

"You said he told you the *details* of the case?" the Sheriff asked, lifting a brow.

Sabrina nodded, not wanting to think about the condition of the bodies they had found. She'd seen the photos, even the ones that had been removed from the original case. Those young men had faced the same fate as the men Jon had seen. She understood how serious it was by how Jon felt. She could read him like an open book.

"Look," the sheriff said. "If Agent Bowen is *out there*, my deputies will find him."

"But what if ... he isn't?"

"You let me worry about that," he answered.

When Jon came too, he found himself lying on an empty two-lane road. The asphalt beneath him was cold and a bank of mist rolled from the trees around him. The petrichor flooded his nostrils and he could taste the damp on his tongue. It seemed to take every ounce of strength he had to push himself up to a sitting position. Getting to his feet was damned near impossible, but he tried. As he feared, he stumbled and lost his balance and went over, landing flat on his face.

He lay there for a moment, trying to figure out where he was. How he'd come to be there. There was a rumble beneath his hands as the road began to vibrate. *Why would the road vibrate?* he wondered to himself.

John caught a flash of something in his peripheral vision as a form came running behind him. Without any effort it scooped him up just as a large truck appeared out of nowhere. The lights blinded Jon as he tried to use his own feet to escape, but his friend—whomever this was who had just saved his life—had him up and out of the way before he knew what was happening.

Jon found himself lying in a pile of leaves and pine needles, breathless but alive. "Thanks, man..." he panted, rolling over to see who had saved him. But, there was no one there. A dark, lumbering shadow disappeared into the fog, leaving Jon to wonder what in the hell had just happened. *Wait! What?* He glanced down at the damp ground and saw the massive print pressed deep into the soft soil. Jon placed his hand in the depression and spread his fingers, barely able to reach the outer margins of its width with his thumb and pinky.

The blaring refrains of a Jimmie Hendrix guitar riff startled him. He rolled over and reached into the hip pocket of his jeans and found his phone. "Sabrina?" He could hear the trembling in his own voice.

"Oh, my God! Jon! Where are you?"

"I ... I'm ... I'm not sure," he muttered.

"Are you hurt?"

"I ... I don't ... I don't think so."

"Does your phone have a geo-locator?"

"Yeah." He seemed to snap to his senses.

"Share your location with me," she ordered. "I'm coming."

Jon sat on the edge of the gurney in the ER with a sense of *déjà vu*. The lights in his eyes didn't help ease the anxiety or the sense that he didn't belong here—had somewhere else to be. "Agent Bowen?" He popped up to his feet when his boss walked in, but the room spun, and she caught his arm and helped him sit back down before he went over.

"Karen," he panted, catching her sleeve. "What happened? What am I doing here?"

"Your girlfriend and I were wondering the same thing," she said.

"My ... *girlfriend*?"

"Sabrina found you passed out in the woods near the Sunshyne Girls' Camp," she explained. "She said you were babbling something about being abducted by aliens and saved by Sasquatch."

"Sabrina was here?"

"She's out in the lobby filling out an incident report," Karen said, pulling up a stool, taking his hands. "Jon, do you remember what happened?"

He shook his head and regretted it almost at once. "No. It's like ... my brain went blank for a while."

"That's an understatement," Karen shook her head. "You've been gone for three days."

His mouth dropped open. "Three? Three days?"

"Mr. Bowen," a nurse came to the curtain and peeked in. "Miss Bishop is asking if she can see you."

"Yes." Jon's head snapped up. "Please, send her back."

The curtain flew open. Sabrina froze when she saw another person in the room. "Jon?"

He started to rise, but she put a hand up. "Sabrina," he said. "This is my boss, Karen."

Sabrina nodded.

"We've met," Karen said. "Nice to see you again."

"Likewise," Sabrina said. "Jon, can we ..." She hesitated, glancing first at him, then at his boss. "I want to talk about ... the case."

"Anything you want to say, you can say in front of Karen. I trust her," he affirmed.

Sabrina's brows lifted. She could read him even from the entryway and knew what he meant. Karen stood and let her have the stool. She moved to the other chair.

"Did you tell him? About the girls?"

"The girls?" Jon looked to his boss. Karen shook her head.

"They're all home," Sabrina said. "Thirty-five years later and ... and it's like a day never passed. They're still ... little ... if you can believe it."

Jon puzzled over this a moment; the confusion written on his features. "They're home? All of them?"

"All of them," Karen said. "Jon, we need to know what happened to you."

"Maybe we should tell him about ... about the boys," Sabrina suggested.

"And what we found at the Sunshyne Girls' Camp..." Karen said, as if giving Sabrina permission.

"What's going on?"

"We've solved your case for you," Sabrina admitted.

"Sabrina solved your case," Karen pointed out, giving credit where it was due.

"Huh?" He looked at Sabrina.

"Well, CSI helped," she added. "When I put two and two together, no matter what axiom I began with, it always came back to the Sunshyne Camp—to Sunshyne Gaylord herself. One of the girls told me that boys weren't allowed at the camp—a fact further confirmed by the Sheriff who told me he took *Aunt Sunny's* statement over the phone. When I went out there, the woman I met wasn't at all what I expected. I had some aging earth-mother-hippie in mind, but what I found was a chain smoking and bitter old woman who held a grudge against men because a man got her pregnant and left her to raise the child alone."

"What?" Jon gasped.

"This camp was her way of *sticking it to the man*, so to speak. The boys from the 1977 case, and the ones from this most current case, weren't the only ones to die. The CSI team found the remains of more than a dozen men—presumably most of whom either wandered on to the property from the nearby state park or snuck onto the property to visit a friend or, more likely, a girlfriend."

"That woman's basement ... looked like some kind of dark temple," Karen explained. "It was a temple to the sky gods ... effigies painted in blood on the walls ... aliens. Forensics found her prints in the marks. They found foreign DNA in her shoes and on the knife her daughter used to attack Miss Bishop here."

Jon's jaw dropped. "Sabrina? Are you okay?"

"Just a scratch." She pushed him away as he reached for her.

"Sixteen stitches is hardly a scratch," Karen retorted.

"Sixteen ..." Jon looked horrified. "Come here. Let me see."

"There's nothing to see," she said. "It's all bandaged."

Jon pulled her into him and made her sit down beside him. "You remember what I said about knives and fighting."

"Every word." She leaned against him. "That's why I'm here with just sixteen stitches. Could have been a lot worse."

"The crime scene unit found Sunny's journals and ledgers," Karen continued. "She rambled on about *sacrificing* the men she caught on her property and leaving what was left of their *purified* remains for the gods, if they wanted them. The fact that the bodies weren't taken seemed to suggest—they didn't."

"They didn't want me either," Jon said, "unless I was hallucinating."

Sabrina leaned into him and put her hand on his chest, closing her eyes and taking a deep breath as she did when trying to read a victim ... or a suspect. He'd seen her do it plenty of times. He closed his eyes and tried to open himself to her; not sure if he could do anything to help.

"Protect the younglings," she muttered. "Protect from evil." Sabrina's eyelids fluttered and she sat back, taking a deep breath. She looked at Jon with an expression of relief. "*They* believed they were saving the girls from the evil woman's grasp. *They* took them ...but *they* brought them back when *they* were sure no harm would come to them. *They* gave *you* back when they knew you were not part of Sunny's evil scheme."

"So I was right? *They* didn't want me."

She pursed her lips into a smile. "You're right," she said. "No Boys Allowed."

Epilogue

Jon glanced down at the little girl holding his hand, then looked at Sabrina. He knocked on the door, and listened for the footfalls on the hardwood floors, then the locks clicking as the tumblers turned, and the door swung open.

Maddie stood looking at him, then turned to Sabrina, a look of surprise on her face. They hadn't called. Then, she looked at the little girl. "Maddie?" the child asked.

"Amber?" Her voice cracked. She looked at Jon, stunned. "Is that ... is that really you?"

"Uh huh," she stepped in and wrapped her arms around her friend. Maddie returned the hug but turned loose of her long enough to drop down and hug her properly.

"All this time? I thought ... I thought you were lost forever."

"For Amber, it doesn't seem like a day has passed," Jon said.

"Come in," Maddie said, drawing Amber into the house, sitting on the sofa, studying the face she knew so well from her childhood. "Are you hurt?"

"No," she said. "I'm fine. I brought cookies." She pointed to a shopping bag Sabrina held. Inside were the Oreos the girls had loved as children. "We can have a tea party."

"Of course we can," Maddie beamed. She hugged her friend again and looked to Jon for answers.

"Amber's parents passed away some years ago," Jon said. "Family Services is looking to find any remaining family that might take her in, but they haven't had any luck. She has no one."

"Of course she has someone," Maddie insisted. "She has me." Amber's face lit up. "Why don't you go in the kitchen and get a glass of milk to go with those," Maddie suggested to her friend. "It's right in there." She pointed toward the kitchen.

"It's not an easy process," Sabrina said. "Amber may have long-term psychological and emotional effects from her ordeal."

"If anyone can understand what she's been through," Maddie said. "It's me. I've always wanted kids of my own ... maybe ... maybe I was saving that place in my heart for her."

Jon's sober expression softened into a smile. "I'll vouch for you myself," he said, "for whatever good that will do."

"Me, too," Sabrina added. "There's no one better to care for her."

Kinvarra

GOTHIC HORROR BY JB CAINE

Ivy Burke watched the red-tinged tap water circle the shower drain, mingling with her tears. She wouldn't make that mistake again.

This time, she leaned her head out of the shower stall rather than bringing the wineglass inside and thus sloshing her self-pity-laced pinot noir across her body and onto the shower floor.

She'd never been fired before. They could call it "laid-off" if they wanted to, but it amounted to the same thing. Well, almost. They'd had to give her six weeks' severance pay. But it was still rejection, and it still hurt.

And so, she'd sniffled and snuffled all the way home, dragged herself up the three stories to her boring little apartment, grabbed the wine from the kitchen, and left her clothes wherever they fell on her way to sit in the scalding water. She could hear her phone ringing from her coat pocket, which lay sprawled in the hallway with one forlorn arm reaching in through the bathroom door. She ignored the trilling ringer and let the call go to voicemail. One and a half glasses of wine later, it rang again. Ivy reached up and turned off the water, which had turned tepid.

The phone kept ringing.

"Fine!" she yelled, setting down her wineglass and crawling out of the shower. She grabbed the arm of the coat and yanked it inside the room, causing the phone to fly out of the pocket and go skittering across the floor until it whacked into the base of the toilet. Ivy howled in frustration and dragged herself across the tile, leaving pools of water in her wake. She snatched up the phone and looked at the notifications.

All three calls were from her friend Laura, as were five text messages saying simply, "CALL ME!"

With the fire of her rage somewhat doused, Ivy hit the callback button without listening to any of the voicemails. Laura picked up on the first ring.

"Oh, my GOD, Ivy, why didn't you answer your phone? Are you okay? Do I need to come over?"

"I guess you heard." Ivy felt a fresh surge of tears rising.

"Hell yes, I heard. Eva called me. Tommy told her as soon as the memo about the layoffs came out. The question is, *why didn't I hear it from you*? I can't believe you got laid off after three years in that bullshit company. Seriously, they're stupid, and you're going to be better off. I'm coming over."

Before Ivy could protest that she was a drunk, naked, soggy mess, Laura hung up and was probably halfway to her car. Ivy hiccuped through her sobbing and smiled just the tiniest bit.

Twenty minutes later, she was sitting on the couch wrapped in her robe and the fluffiest blanket Laura could find.

"Isn't ice cream a more traditional depression food?" Her fingertips had a precarious grip on the plate of angel food cake her friend had thrust into her unsteady fingers.

"Only when you haven't downed a whole bottle of wine. Believe me when I tell you that you don't want dairy on top of that. As your friend, it is my job to make sure you're hydrated and filled up with something that can absorb some of that alcohol."

"Oh. Thanks." She knew she should show more gratitude, but her whole face felt numb from all the crying. "You're a good friend."

"I *am* a good friend. And we'll talk all about this tomorrow, but for now I'm just here to make sure your hangover is minimal. It's a triage situation."

"I got fired."

"You got laid off," Laura corrected her. "It's not the same thing. You didn't do anything wrong. It's just how business works."

"Business sucks," Ivy grumped, putting a comically large bite of cake in her mouth.

Laura looked at her friend critically. "When was the last time you took a vacation?"

"What? I don't know. I went to Cancún ..."

"Ivy, you were 15 when you went to Cancún. When in your ADULT life have you gone on vacation?"

"I ... um ... I went for a weekend to Hilton Head two years ago."

"Wasn't that a conference that narcissistic asshole Dave dragged you to? And then you sat by the pool for two days because he didn't think you should go to his work receptions? Girl, are you telling me you've NEVER been on a real vacation?"

"This isn't making me feel any better, Lolz."

"This, my friend, is a call to action. When you get your shit together tomorrow, here's what you need to do: You need to take half of that severance money and go on vacation somewhere you've never been."

"All by myself?"

"Yes, all by yourself. Because one, I can't afford to go with you. And two, you are a strong and capable woman, and it's time you reminded yourself of that."

Ivy woke up face down on her bed the next morning with no memory of how she got there. At first, she jolted awake because the angle of the light told her it was at least 9:00. But then she remembered that she had no reason to get up early, so she flopped over and sighed at the empty phone charger on her bedside table. She may have made it in here at some point during the night, but the phone hadn't.

She tightened the belt on her robe as she shuffled out of her bedroom, searching for the device. She found it on the charging pad next to her TV alongside a note from Laura.

Ivy,

I stayed for a while after you fell asleep, just to make sure you weren't going to Jimi Hendrix yourself, and then I let myself out and locked the bottom lock on your door. Two things, just in case the wine fogged up your memory. Thing one: it's not your fault you lost your job, so stop trying to tell yourself it is. Thing two: pick a place for your vacation. Where is somewhere you've always wanted to go? Eva and I are coming over tonight with her magic spring rolls and we are planning your fucking vacation. You've earned it.

Love you,

LOLZ

A week later, she found herself standing in the Shannon Airport in Limerick, Ireland, waiting for her cousin Colm to pick her up. She'd only met Colm Burke once, at her grandmother's funeral a decade ago, but he'd found her on social media a few months after, and they'd liked a few posts back and forth over the years. He always told her that if she wanted to see where the family had come from, she was welcome to visit the Burke Farm anytime. This was that time, as it turned out.

Atlanta had been a balmy 80°, but the weather in Limerick was 57° with light showers. Colm had told her to bring "jumpers", "Wellies", and a "Mac" to battle the Irish springtime. It had been good advice.

"Hey! Hey, Ivy!" She turned to find a fair approximation of the few photos of himself that Colm had posted online. His black hair was an unruly mop, and he was a bit taller and thinner than she'd remembered, but the half grin that belied secrets and mischief was unmistakable.

"Colm, hey!" They hugged briefly then stood in awkward silence for a beat, neither sure of what to say to a family member who was, for all intents and purposes, a total stranger.

"Well, then," Colm broke the silence, "let's get going! Can't wait for you to see the place. I usually Airbnb the cottage out this time of year, but the market's been a bit slower than in years past. Lucky for you, though, eh?" He inclined his head toward the glass doors and gave an *after you, madam* gesture. She chuckled and began rolling her suitcase in the direction he'd indicated.

"Very lucky for me. Are you sure you don't want me to pay you something to stay there? I don't want to take advantage..."

"I wouldn't hear of it. You're family come home! Our ancestors would drag me through the streets if I charged you to stay on our own land. Don't be absurd."

"Okay, if you say so."

"I do."

"I really do appreciate it. I'd probably like to rent a car, but is it okay if I get settled in for a couple of days first?"

"Yeah, sure. You can hire a car anytime. If you want, we can stop at the grocer on the way and you can pick up some things. I did get you a few staples, but I didn't know what you like. Seems like Americans either eat burgers or sushi, and I didn't want to presume which you lean toward."

She chuckled. "Probably both. But not at the same time, of course."

"Yeah, of course. That would be sheer lunacy."

A couple of hours later, Colm slowed his VW Golf and turned right onto an ungated driveway edged with low whitewashed concrete walls outside of the town of Kinvarra. A similarly whitewashed two-story house with tiny windows came into view after they'd passed through some raggedy privacy hedges, but Colm kept driving past it toward a smaller cottage in the distance.

"This is where I'll be if you need anything," he explained, referencing the large, boxy house. "The cottage was built in 1901, but the family has made a lot of modernizations and improvements over the years."

"Like Wi-Fi?" Ivy asked hopefully, only half-kidding.

"Oh, certainly. We've even gone for indoor plumbing. Most of the time, you'll even have electricity."

His dry tone indicated sarcasm, but she had to glance over just to be sure. His smirk reassured her, and she laughed out loud.

The cottage looked to her like something out of a storybook. It appeared to be constructed entirely of gray stones of varying sizes, with a wood-framed door along the right side and shuttered windows every few feet. "Our great-great grandparents built this place, and Burkes have owned the land even before that. The house I'm in was built in the '60s." He rolled to a stop near the door. "Let me give you a hand with your things, and then I'll leave you to settle in. One word, though, you're welcome to wander about, but be mindful that the ground will likely be a bit boggy."

"Awesome. Thanks." Something in her chest started to loosen a little. Maybe it was a return to her ancestral home or simply the green expanse of the property, but she let herself entertain the notion that maybe—just maybe—everything would be alright and that things were looking up.

She grabbed her luggage from the "boot" of the car while Colm grabbed the groceries and unlocked the door. By the time she made it inside, he'd set the shopping bags on the wooden table in the center of the small kitchen and had started unloading their contents. "Now, there's no landline phone here, and cellular can be a little spotty, but the front of the house gets decent reception. We don't have central air, but there's a small radiator in each room." He pointed to a white contraption on the wall of the sitting room. "I've got them set to keep the place at around 20° ..."

"Twenty?"

"Celsius, love."

"Oh, right."

"But if you're chilly, there are extra blankets in the chest at the foot of the bed. As I told you, I got you a few staples ... coffee, tea, microwave popcorn. Anything else you need right now?" He gestured to a tray of cellophane packages in a basket on the counter.

She inspected the contents and picked up a small red box of Folgers packets. "You call this coffee?" she smiled.

He smirked back. "Well, you are American, after all."

"It'll be great. Thanks for being so thoughtful, and for letting me come."

"My sincerest pleasure. And now, my dear cousin, I must positively leave you. There's a football match starting in half an hour, and I have a friend meeting me up at the pub. I hope you don't find me rude for not inviting you along ... it's just that it's sort of a brothers-in-arms thing ..."

"Nope ... not at all. You enjoy yourself. I'm going to get cozy and possibly make some tea and read, assuming I don't pass out first."

"Right, right, tiring journey. I'll check in on you tomorrow, yes?"

"Absolutely. Thank you again."

Colm nodded curtly, then slid out the door and into his still-running car. He beeped the horn twice, then made a three-point turn and drove back up the hill.

Ivy went back inside and found the kettle to make herself some tea, and jumped through a quick shower to wash off the day's travel while it heated up. The feeling of the fleece jammie pants and hoodie was like a comforting hug, and she poured the hot water over the chamomile tea bag, letting the gentle scent warm her up on the inside as well. She stepped out into the chill evening air as a gray drizzle *pitter-patted* on the gravel drive.

Perfect tea weather, she thought, savoring the first sip. She surveyed the green landscape before her, wondering idly where the Burke property ended. Several hundred yards away, a low hedge was dotted with spindly trees, and she guessed that was probably one of the borders. Her eyes followed the hedge around until she caught a glimpse of something that was neither tree nor hedge.

She almost didn't notice at first, but next to one of the craggy trees, a woman stood facing the cottage. Facing Ivy. *Looking* at Ivy. It was hard to tell if she was wearing a hooded coat or if her clothing was the same shade of gray as her hair. Was she stooped, or was it a trick of the light and distance? Ivy couldn't be sure. The only thing she *was* certain of was the woman's intent gaze.

Well, after all, that wasn't so unusual. If she were an elderly neighbor, she might be curious about the stranger occupying the cottage. Ivy raised her hand in greeting, and the woman's head inclined slightly in acknowledgement. Then she stepped behind the trees and disappeared.

Somewhere in the weak evening light, a screech ripped through the air. An owl, perhaps, taking off to hunt.

The entire encounter left Ivy feeling unsettled. She stepped back inside and secured the door and pulled the thin burgundy curtains over all the windows in the sitting room. She'd have to remember to ask Colm about the strange neighbor lady. Thus resolved, she finished her tea, buried herself under all the blankets in the old cedar chest, and slipped into a troubled sleep.

Bright morning light streamed through the living-room window of the apartment, and Ivy opened her eyes, still wearing her robe and snuggly blanket. The empty wine bottle was on the end table where she'd abandoned it the night before. There was the sound of rustling and banging in the kitchen.

"Laura? Is that you?"

The refrigerator door closed and a familiar and unwelcome face poked out from behind the cabinet.

"Dave? What are you doing here?"

"What do you mean, what am I doing here? I was hungry. And you were too hungover from your pity party to do anything about it, so I helped myself."

She blinked and looked around the apartment. Everything looked more or less as it should, except for Dave being there, but something else felt...off. "I didn't invite you over. You should leave."

"Psh. Women are so crazy." He opened the pantry and began rummaging around.

She stood, her feet unsteady as she moved toward the kitchen. "You shouldn't be here. Please go."

"Oh, I shouldn't be here? Ivy, you're such a mess. Look at you. One little setback and you down a whole bottle of wine?" He turned over his shoulder and looked at her in distaste. "It's your own fault I left. God, there's something in your hair."

She felt confused, scrambled. "You didn't leave. I dumped you," she replied uncertainly. That was the way it went, right? She turned to look at the mirror on the antique hall tree.—But wait, that was wrong. She didn't own antiques.—The light from the window reflected in it so that it took a minute to focus on her reflection. No, the reflection wasn't right, either.

She reached down and pinched the ends of her hair between her fingers. She'd dyed it the same chocolate cherry color since college. Ivy glanced back at the reflection. The burgundy-brown hair was still gripped in her fingers, but the hair around her face tumbled down in honey-colored waves. What was happening?

She reached up to touch the foreign curls, but when she pulled back her fingers, they were wet and sticky and red. Had she spilled wine? No, that was yesterday. She looked back in the mirror and the light faded from the room. The hairline around her forehead began to darken and she realized that it wasn't wine at all.

Rivulets of blood streamed down her face. She wanted to scream, but if she opened her mouth, she knew the blood would trickle in, so she reached up to pull the golden hair away ... to throw it somewhere, anywhere ... but even as she pulled at it, she knew she couldn't get it free. She leaned toward the mirror, trying to find a glue line, anything that might help her rip this horror away, and her eyes caught a movement in the window. Her gaze darted to the window's reflection.

Gray talon-like fingers scraped against the window, framing a gaunt gray face and eyes ... oh, those eyes, empty and red like the wine, red like the blood. The apparition opened its mouth in a soundless scream.

Ivy's eyes snapped open to unfamiliar darkness and the screeching of an owl somewhere in the distance. She tried to scream, but only a gaspy wheeze escaped. Her arms and legs felt heavy, unwilling to accede to her desire to move. Her eyes darted around the room, and gradually, her terrified and fuzzy brain began to put the pieces together. She wasn't in her Alpharetta apartment; she was in an Irish cottage. Dave wasn't here, and neither was anyone else. She was all alone, and she wasn't sure if that made her feel better or worse.

She'd had a nightmare. *Breathe, Ivy, breathe,* she thought to herself. Shaky at first, she counted *1-2-3* in and *1-2-3* out. As her heart rate slowed, her limbs began to obey her, and she shook off the heavy blankets.

It's fine. Everything's fine. It was a nightmare.

The curtains were still drawn, and there was no light peeking through. She looked at her fitness tracker ... 4:37 a.m. She drew a deep breath and sat up slowly, knowing she would sleep no more tonight. The Folgers beckoned, and she was profoundly grateful to Colm for thinking of it.

She reached over to the bedside table and switched on the small ceramic lamp. A pool of weak yellow light filled the room, and she took a deep breath, trying to shake off the last of her frightening dream. Feeling thus fortified, she slid out of bed and started toward the kitchen. Out of the corner of her eye, she caught the shape of the antique hall tree and a thrill of adrenaline rushed through her. She quickened her steps to the kitchen, turning on every light she could find along the way.

By mid-day, the day had turned into the most beautiful spring day Ireland could offer. It was still cooler than Atlanta, but the sky was a bright blue and the grass was the greenest green Ivy had ever seen in her life. Every bit of last night's unease burned away in the noontime sun.

She was still in her sweats, and gloried in the fact that she had no reason to have to be more presentable. Is this what vacations were supposed to feel like? She stood on the gravel and gazed out over the property, then she darted inside and grabbed the rain boots Colm had advised her to pack. If the ground was boggy, she didn't want to ruin her sneakers. She started toward the back of the larger house, but instead of knocking or calling to Colm, she found the beginning of the low hedge she'd seen and began following it along the Burke side of the property line.

She crested the hill that ran at an angle through the property and surveyed what lay beyond. There was a somewhat steep cut-off, but the Burke land continued down to a muddy flat which gradually became a rocky coastline. She gasped in delight. She hadn't realized she'd been so close to the water! On both sides of the little cove, small boats were tied to nearby trees, though some were resting on mud rather than water. *Must be low tide.*

The closer she got to the water, the more her rain boots made squelchy sounds with each step, and the more effort she had to put into pulling them out of the muck. Hoping to find an area with drier ground, Ivy retreated to the hilltop and walked along the edge of several small copses of trees, leaving mucky footprints as she went. When she reached the spot where she'd seen the elderly neighbor the day before, she examined the area closely to try to determine where the old woman had gone.

She must've stayed on dry ground, Ivy reasoned, noting the lack of footprints. She also observed that she was solidly in the middle of Burke land, meaning that the woman had been trespassing. *I'll have to mention that to Colm later.*

She made her way to the treeline that ran up to the back of the cottage, but hesitated to cross into the woods since she wasn't sure how far she could go without setting foot on a neighbor's private property. The back of the cottage held a couple of surprises. The first was a back door that Ivy hadn't seen from the inside of the little house. The land here was a little lower than at the front of the cottage, so three steps led down to an overgrown path leading into the forest, meaning that the property must extend at least some distance in that direction. Behind the stairway was a pair of cellar doors, padlocked shut.

Ivy rushed around the front and into the house, pausing only to strip her muddy boots off before entering. The mysterious door seemed to be off the kitchen, and she found its reverse side leading out of the back of the pantry. She hadn't seen it before because of the cleaning supplies arranged in front of it. A childlike thrill ran through her, as though she'd solved some great mystery.

She started at the sound of a purposeful rapping at the door, and padded across the kitchen and sitting room to find her cousin grinning in the window.

"Heya," Colm smiled as she pulled the door open. "How you getting on? Looks like you've been out exploring." He raised a brow toward the muddy boots beside the door.

"Yeah, I have! I had no idea we were on the coast."

"You didn't walk all the way down, did you?" He looked concerned.

"No, it looked too muddy."

"Good, good. You might have got stuck out there. That mud has a tendency to hold tight."

She shuddered at the thought of being stuck during a rising tide. "Duly noted. How far does the farm extend into the woods?"

"Not terribly far, really. Maybe ten meters."

"Oh, okay. I just didn't want to trespass. Speaking of, I think one of your neighbors was strolling around here last night. An old woman."

Colm's bushy black eyebrows shot up. "No one bothered you, I hope?"

"Oh, no, she just startled me. I'm not sure which way she came from or where she went." "Did she have a dog with her?

"No, I don't think so. I didn't see one."

"Hm. Was she carrying anything? Like a dead rabbit maybe? It's possible that someone from over that way came across my land to trap a rabbit in the woods or some fool thing. My da' used to do that when he was a kid. Of course, it was our woods, though."

"No, I didn't see anything in her hands, but then she was wearing a pretty big coat, I think. I couldn't see her all that well. She was over there." She pointed toward the spindly tree.

"Huh. That's an odd thing, but probably nothing I'd lose sleep over. If it's a neighbor, they probably didn't realize someone was in the cottage, and now that they've seen you, they'll be less likely to walk that way again.

So hey," he said, shifting topics, "I'm thinking of running into town for a couple of errands. Do you fancy joining me? We could hire a car for you if you like, maybe grab some high-quality pub grub on the way back?"

"I'd love to! I'm not sure I need a car just yet, but maybe you could show me around the town a little? And you have to let me buy dinner since you won't let me pay to stay here."

"You absolutely may NOT pay for dinner, as I'd never live down the shame of letting a guest pay for a meal. But I will let you pay for petrol," he chuckled. "I'm not too prideful for that."

"Deal."

"Might I suggest a shower and change, though? No offense intended, cuz, but you're a bit of a sight just now."

Ivy looked down at her frumpy sweats and stocking feet, then reached up to grip the messy bun she'd slept in. "What? Don't all Irish girls dress like this?"

"Not in public, love. That's just you Americans," he laughed.

"Damn, I was trying so hard to blend in. Give me about 30 minutes, and I'll get cleaned up."

Colm nodded. "I'll go bring the car around, milady."

It didn't take long to show her around the village of Kinvarra. In fact, there were really only a half a dozen streets of much size; the rest was largely residential. One thing she did note was the amount of construction all over town.

"Yeah, it's sort of a good-bad thing. The building brings in jobs and businesses, but agh ... it also brings people." Colm made a face of distaste.

"Wow. I totally get that."

"I don't dislike people, mind you. It just seems that when outsiders move into a place they don't understand, they just ruin it."

Ivy nodded in agreement, but lost her train of thought as Dunguaire Castle came into view. She leaned forward to see better through the windshield.

"You want to go in?" he asked.

"What? Really?"

"Yeah, of course. It's not huge, but worth seeing. I should see if we can book tickets at the medieval banquet while you're here. The castle was built in the 16th century, and then it was popular with some writers for a while, fell to seed, then it was restored about seventy years ago. The Shannon Heritage owns it now."

"Maybe you should be a tour guide," she ribbed.

Colm snickered in response. "Maybe I could do, at that. But you know, *people*."

They spent nearly an hour touring the small castle and Ivy burned another thirty minutes taking pictures of the breathtaking views of Galway Bay. He finally dragged her away with promises to look into banquet tickets.

After a stop at a hardware store and a pharmacy, Colm suggested dinner at Keogh's, a bar and tavern which had, he explained, a menu for every taste. They walked inside and selected a table near a stone fireplace.

"This place is great!" Ivy gushed.

"It's one of the best places to eat in town," he confirmed, nodding at the man with the graying hair and glasses who was tending bar.

"You know the bartender?"

"Kinvarra only has about 1000 people. Pretty much everyone recognizes you and wants to know your business," he laughed.

A thirty-something waitress with dyed hair and sparkling eyes approached to take their drink order.

"What can I get for ya and your lady friend here, Colm?"

"Aw, now don't get excited, Emmy. This is my cousin Ivy. She's visiting from the States."

Her drawn-on eyebrows shot up. "Well, then, welcome home to Ireland, Ivy! What would ya like to drink?"

Ivy started to answer, but then bit her tongue, realizing that asking for a sweet tea would probably blow whatever good juju she'd been afforded by being a relative of a local. "I'll take a white wine, please. Whatever type the house recommends."

"Oh, a lady, is she?" Emmy winked.

"Come off it, Em," Colm laughed. "I'll take a Harp."

"Meh, you're no fun," the waitress teased him as she bustled off to get their drinks.

"She seems nice."

"She's alright. She—" Colm's phone started to buzz and he looked down. "Sorry, Ivy, I need to step outside to take this. I'll be back in two shakes."

She nodded, and by the time the door closed behind him, Emmy was back with their order.

"I'm sorry for making assumptions, Ivy," she said as she set the wineglass down. "I was glad to see Colm had a friend. 'Course I guess having a cousin is just as good."

"No worries! Have you known him long?"

"Since he's been old enough to see over the bar," she chuckled. "Are you visiting for long?"

"Maybe a week or two. I'm staying in the cottage on the family farm, so I can afford to take my time, I guess."

"Aw, that's nice. I know he rents it out now and then, but I don't think he's had a real visitor stay there for a few years now. It was a bit of a scandal, and then it didn't end all that well, so I'm glad you're here to turn it around."

"I know I've just met you, Emmy, but you can't drop a nugget like that and not let me in on the details!" Ivy leaned forward conspiratorially.

"Augh, I guess you got a right to know. It's your family after all! But don't mention it to him, because I think he's still sort of ass-chapped about it."

"Oh, do tell."

"Well, Colm's parents split when he was a young man because his da' had another woman and had a child by her. Didn't find out about it for a few years, either, so the little girl was maybe eight at the time. Just a few years younger than Colm. His ma just left and never came back, and the boy was devastated.

"Then a few years later, the girl shows up after she finishes secondary school, trying to decide what to do with her life." Emmy craned her neck toward the door to see if Colm was coming back. "At that time, he was living there with his father, of course, and Colm was none too pleased to see her show up. I think her name was Dierdre? Something like that. Anyway, I guess your Uncle Sean let her stay in the cottage, and according to the neighbors, one night she and Colm got into a big row. A real scream fest. That night, those same neighbors saw her drive off with a flip of her blonde hair and a middle finger, and as far as anyone knows, she never spoke to your uncle or cousin again. I am sorry about your Uncle Sean, by the way. He was always good fun. Damned cancer."

"Yeah, thank you for that. I only met him the once, and I don't think anyone on the States side knew him well except my father. Weird how some families just aren't that close. Just like Dierdre, leaving like that. Must've been a hell of a fight."

"Well, it's not just the ginger Irish with tempers, love." She winked as Colm pushed the door back open. "Just between us," she whispered as he approached. "I'll be back in a few minutes to see what you want to eat." She knocked twice on the wooden tabletop and set off to check on her other customers.

"Hopefully she hasn't been filling your mind with fool stories about the fine folk or anything," Colm smirked, giving Emmy side-eye.

"The what, now?"

"Faery lore. She used to fill my head with stories when I was younger."

"I wish she had! Remind me to ask!"

"Augh, you'll never shut her up. She leans hard into that rubbish."

"I think it's fascinating. But then again, maybe I should wait. I had a terrible nightmare last night, and the last thing I need is more fuel."

He looked concerned. "Want to talk about it?"

"Oh, it was one of those nonsensical things that's just terrifying enough to screw you up in the morning. I was home, and my asshole ex-boyfriend was in my kitchen, and then my head was bleeding, and then I saw this scary face ... I don't remember most of the details, but it really freaked me out."

"This fellow must have been quite an ex."

"You can't even imagine. But I haven't talked to him in months. I'm sure it was just because I was in an unfamiliar bed and exhausted from the flight. I felt a lot better after walking around the farm a little."

"Well, I'm glad for that. Are you okay for tonight then? Do you want to stay in the big house?"

"Oh, no, I'm fine. Thank you, though." Ivy looked around the pub. "Is this where you came last night? I don't see a TV."

"Huh?" He looked startled at the question. "Oh, no. I, uh, went to the Pier Head. Keogh's does sometimes put a TV on the mantle over there if there's a big event, but Pier Head has one in the bar. How long do you fancy staying? There's a music festival coming up in a couple of weeks."

The conversation turned to life in Kinvarra and how it was changing, but Ivy's mind kept dancing back to the rift between the American and Irish sides of the family. She knew that her father and grandmother had moved to America some time in the 1980s, and that her Uncle Sean had kept the family land here. But her father never talked about Ireland much, which seemed strange. As far as Ivy knew, the only time her dad had seen his older brother since they'd emigrated was at her grandmother's funeral. And now Colm was alone ... his dad was gone, his mother was who-knows-where, and his half-sister had fled as well. It made Ivy sad.

The evening light was still quite bright as they left Keogh's and headed back to the farm, but dark clouds threatened in the distance.

"Augh, looks like a storm is coming in. You sure you're alright in the cottage on your own?"

"Yeah, for sure! I'm going to call my friends back home and chat a bit, then probably turn in early since I had a rough night. Plus, I think I'm a little jet lagged. I'm fading quickly here," Ivy smiled.

"All right, then, if you're certain. I won't be around much tomorrow, I'm afraid. I'm in charge of coordination of one of the construction projects just south of town, and I'm needed on-site tomorrow. Do you have everything you need?"

"Absolutely. Don't worry about me. I'll be aces if those screech owls don't keep me up tonight."

"Screech owls?"

"Yeah, you didn't hear them?"

"No, but then I sleep like the dead. I've heard the *hoo-hoo* sort from time to time, but not the screechy ones."

"Must be since I'm right next to the woods."

"No doubt." Colm pulled up the drive as the first fat raindrops started hitting the dashboard. "Ah, none too soon. Button up tight! I hope the storm and the owls aren't potent enough to divert you from a proper slumber."

"Thanks, Colm. Have a good day at work. I'll see you tomorrow evening!" Ivy stepped out of the car and slammed the door. She gave a quick wave as she unlocked the door and stepped inside.

Ivy changed into her pajamas and dialed Eva's number.

"Hi, friend!" Eva's bright voice greeted her. "How is Ireland? Did you catch a leprechaun yet?"

"You'll have to give me more than a day for that, I'm afraid," she laughed in response, "but it's great, actually. My cousin is really nice and I saw some amazing stuff today. I'll post the pictures before I go to bed tonight. I'm also in this great cottage that's been in my family for more than a century."

"Put me on video and show me around!"

"Okay, hold on." Ivy flipped into video mode as she walked back to the door. "So this is what it looks like if I'm standing with my back to the door ..." She proceeded to narrate the short tour through the sitting room, kitchen, bedroom, and bathroom, pointing out some of the quirky hand-made items and deliberately—and somewhat superstitiously—avoiding mention of the antique hall tree. "So that's it. Pretty cool, right? And I also found a door at the back of the pantry, here ..." She opened the pantry and pointed to the sealed latch. "It leads outside to the cellar doors, but I haven't opened it because there's too much stuff in the way."

"What's in the cellar?"

"I don't know. It's locked."

"Okay, so you're terrible at giving tours. You know that when you watch yacht tours on video or whatever, they open all the drawers and stuff to show you the storage."

"You want to see inside the empty drawers?"

"Are they all empty?" Eva pressed.

"Well, I guess not all of them. Colm says he rents the place out to vacationers sometimes."

"Okay, then. Random drawers and cabinets. Let's go!"

As the rain began falling in earnest outside, Ivy laughed and started in the kitchen, showing Eva where the flatware, dishes, and cleaning products were stored. Then she checked the medicine cabinet, and the bottom drawer of the bureau in the bedroom.

"What's that?" Eva craned her neck on camera as if that would help her see the contents of the drawer.

"I don't know. Some sort of box. Hold on." Ivy reached into the drawer and pulled out a wooden case that resembled a slim briefcase. She set it on the bed and flipped the clasps open.

"You have to show me while you open it!" Eva insisted, trilling with excitement.

Ivy flipped the phone around as she opened the case. The contents included a slick wooden palette, three small, flat canvases, a twelve-inch easel, a set of pencils and brushes clipped in a row, and small, bright-colored bottles of paint. "It's an art set!"

Eva *squeed*. "You have to make me a picture!"

"You're the artist, not me," Ivy protested, but ran her fingers over the rough surface of the canvas. "I'm terrible."

"Stop it. No excuses. Make me a painting! Please? Pretty please?"

"Oh, okay, but they might arrest me at customs if I try to bring it back. It might be criminally awful."

"I have a refrigerator covered in art from my six-year-old nephew."

"Good point. I'll give it a shot."

When they finally hung up, Ivy carried the case over to the small desk next to the bedroom window. The wind had picked up and she could hear it whistling through the shingles above her head. She pulled back the curtain to look toward the water, though it wasn't visible because of the hillside. The rain had brought darkness with it, and most of the landscape was silhouetted against a charcoal sky. She wondered what the cove looked like with the gale whipping the water amongst the rocks. She pictured the rowboat being tossed asunder, pitching with the crashing water.

Having found her inspiration, she propped the canvas up on the small easel, picked up one of the pencils and began to sketch as much as she could from memory. At first, the pencil moved slowly, shaking with her uncertainty, but as the angled lines of the coast and the trees and the rocks began taking shape, her hand moved faster, as though it knew what her mind wanted.

The storm raged outside, and she lost track of time as pencil gave way to paint. She mixed colors on the palette, and the image of moonlight reflected on water emerged. Her brushstrokes varied from long, languid lines to short, feathery and wispy ones. She forgot where she was, seeing only the scene she was creating, and the pounding of the rain and screeching of the wind became slashing lines of water in the painting. She was vaguely aware of the banging of the shutters and the cellar door, and the *whooshing* sound that was almost like the roof being torn away.

Ivy woke to the sound of blackbirds and robins heralding the morning. She didn't even remember falling asleep. As the haze of sleep left her, her eyes focused on her paint-covered hands and arms. Even her pajamas had fallen victim to her maelstrom of creativity the night before. In a moment of clarity, she jumped up and examined the duvet, but it seemed to have escaped unscathed.

She turned toward the desk. The fruit of last night's labors stood propped upon the tiny easel. Though there were some abstractions to the work, there was no question that she had fairly accurately captured the look of the cove as it would have appeared under moonlight and rain. The rocks were black against the blue hues of the water, and moonlight reflected off the water between the white-crested tips of the waves. A golden reflection at the far edge of the water reached up like delicate fingers and blended with the shadows of the trees on the far shore.

She remembered her idea for the painting, but the image in front of her was radically different in style and technique than what she remembered. Stippled swatches of color covered the lines she remembered from the night before, and these splotches had been raked through with the palette knife which now lay askew on the floor. The resulting image was beautiful, yet somehow eerie and violent. She crossed to the desk and touched the canvas, only to find that the acrylic paint was still slightly tacky, leaving blue-tinged residue on her fingertips.

Still dazed, she looked at her watch. It was nearly noon. *I mustn't let Colm come home to find that I made such a mess.* Part of her knew that there was something much more *off* here, but this, at least, was a concrete problem she could solve. She stripped off her pajamas and showered, scrubbing the paint off her skin until her forearms and hands were pink and raw.

The shower renewed her somewhat, and as she scrubbed the mostly-dry paint off the desk and floor, she tried without success to recover the hours she had lost. Once the clean-up was finished, she pulled out her laptop and searched for information about sleep disorders, particularly nightmares, sleep paralysis, and sleepwalking. She'd never been prone to any of them until arriving here. Or, her rational brain told her, until she'd had the shock of losing her job followed up by jet lag and a foreign environment.

Someone once said that the most obvious answer is usually the right one, and by the time the afternoon sun cast long shadows across the edges of the property, Ivy had returned to reason. She stood outside the cottage door as the wind whipped her hair against her face. What she really needed was rest. No adventures for a day or two. Reading, movies, rest. Thus resolved, she went inside to make herself some tea and take her own advice.

It was after seven when Colm finally came knocking at the door.

"Hey, there!" she grinned, opening the door wide and waving him inside.

"Heya! How'd you get on today? Are you wilting from boredom?"

"No, not at all. I ... slept late today, then cleaned myself up and binge watched a bunch of episodes of trash TV."

"Sounds delightful. I brought you some biscuits to have with your ... what is *that*?" He froze in mid-step, his gaze fixed on something in the bedroom.

Ivy had a flash of panic, fearing that she had missed a paint spill, but when she followed his eyes, it was clear that he was looking at the painting itself.

"Oh, that? Yeah ... I found some art supplies in the drawer in there, and I thought I'd try to paint your view of Galway Bay. You know, from that spot on the hill there."

He moved slowly toward the painting, staring at it intently. "You painted this?"

"Um, yeah ... I didn't even really know what I was doing at first, and then, you know, I got going on it and this was the result. Is it okay that I used the art set? I can replace it if ..."

"No, no, that's fine. I ... didn't even know it was here. Must have been left here by ... a prior guest. What's this part here?" He pointed toward the golden glow in the water. Though he was trying to sound unbothered, there was a tension in his voice that Ivy hadn't heard before, and his finger trembled ever-so-slightly as he extended it toward the patch of color.

"I ... um ..." The truth was that she had no idea what the golden glow was because she didn't remember painting it. "Moonlight on the water? The hint of sunrise, maybe? I don't know. I'm kind of a crappy painter," she laughed, trying to sound light, but feeling deeply awkward.

"No, it's good ... this is a rather unusual technique, though." He indicated the gashes made with the palette knife. "Something you'd see more in oils than acrylics. Have you ... seen this technique before?"

"No, definitely not. The only experience I have with art is my friend Eva letting me paint ceramic ornaments with her at Christmas."

"I see. Well, I ... hate to dash off, but I ... need to go handle some things at the house. Enjoy your biscuits." He turned on his heel and hustled toward the door without even saying good-bye.

She stood in the doorway and watched him head to the house in a near-jog. *What in the world? Maybe I'm not the only one losing my marbles around here.* She looked over her shoulder at the painting, then pulled on her rain boots and walked toward the top of the hill. What *had* those tendrils of gold been trying to reflect? She stood with her shoulder against the craggy tree and stared at the water. The light was fading, but there was no moon to dapple the water just yet. The salty wind whistled around her, stinging her eyes. She stood for another moment, watching the rowboat bob up and down as the waves crashed against the shore, spraying foamy mist across the rocks. Then she turned back to the cottage, wondering what in the painting had disturbed her cousin so deeply.

As she drew close to the back of the cottage, she noticed something amiss with the cellar door. The padlock was intact, but the hasp had been torn out of the wood. She bent to examine it, and it appeared that the wood around the screws had rotted somewhat. Perhaps something had flown against it in the storm? The wind had certainly been violent enough. In fact, now that she was right here, she was fairly certain she could hear the wind whistling from somewhere below.

Colm was already upset; the last thing she'd want was for him to also have damage to this building that was part of his heritage—*their* heritage. She hefted the door open and peered inside, but the change in air pressure seemed to silence the whistling she'd heard. She followed the four steps down, intent on checking for structural integrity, but if she was being honest with herself, she was really just curious what was down here.

She pulled her phone out of her pocket and switched on the flashlight. It wasn't nearly as mysterious down here as she'd hoped. The wind swirled around the open door, stirring up dust in the mostly-empty cellar. Next to the steps, a coal bin and shovel hearkened back to an earlier age. Against one wall, there was an old bicycle with flat tires, and wedged beside it, a heavy oil cloth covered what looked to be a frame. She lifted the fabric and shined her light under the edge.

It was a painting of the front of the cottage. There wasn't a wide array of colors … mostly shades of brown, green, and white. Simple, but beautifully done. Even the grass seemed to have depth and movement.

The grass … so many subtle shades of green … but each blade was distinguished from those around it with swipes of the palette knife through the pigment.

Ivy gasped, dropped the oil cloth, and stepped backwards, nearly stumbling on what appeared to be a manhole cover.

What is that? She stared at the hatch, her curiosity in high gear. What could it be? A bomb shelter? An underground passage? She grabbed the heavy metal handle and pulled, steel shrieking on steel as it slowly gave way, releasing an acrid stench she recognized as mildew and rot. She had expected to find a ladder within, but it was just a hole. A crossbar with a chain hanging from it spanned the two-and-a-half-foot diameter. Ivy shined her light into the darkness and caught a glimpse of a wooden bucket floating a dozen feet below. A well. She almost laughed at her foolishness.

But then she saw the orange and pink stripes peeking out from under the bucket. She felt a knot form in her stomach, and her hand shook as she reached for the chain. The water below stirred as she lifted the bucket a few inches.

The stripes were part of a sleeve.

Extending from the cuff, a skeletal hand bobbed along the surface of the water.

Ivy yipped and leapt backwards, her mind racing. Was the well somehow connected to Galway Bay? Had some poor person drowned and then been sucked here by the current? Or had …

"What the … FUCK!" Colm's voice rose above the wind and within seconds, he burst through the cellar door and down the steps, a ring of keys in his hand. He was backlit against the sky for a moment.

"Colm! Oh, my God, I think someone drowned and they're down here and …" She raised the light so she could see him without blinding him.

Instead of the shock and horror she expected to see on his face, she saw … anguish.

"Why, Ivy? Why did you come down here?" He took a step toward her then stopped. "You don't understand …"

Understanding and fear dawned in her. *Run. Just run.* "What don't I understand, Colm?" *Keep him talking. Buy time. Then get past him and run.*

"You don't understand. It wasn't my fault …" His face was lost in memory, twisted in pain.

She had to get outside. Maybe run into the woods to a neighbor. But as long as he was next to the steps, she'd never get by him.

"Oh, Ivy, you weren't supposed to come down here …" There was genuine despair in his voice as his hand reached back for the coal shovel. Ivy's heart thundered against her ribs, partly in fear of her own life, but in the light-dappled dust behind him, she found a new reason for terror.

From the recesses of the cellar corner to his right, the darkness began to move, and a smoky apparition began to emerge. The indistinct mist began to sharpen and take form.

The blood-red eyes from her nightmare, the gaunt features that had terrorized Ivy in her sleep had pierced the veil and clawed their way into the waking world. Gossamer rags clung to gray skin, and skeletal arms reached out of the dim corner of the basement.

But the ember eyes weren't fixed on Ivy. They were fixed on an unknowing Colm.

The grim phantasm floated behind him even as his hand found the shovel's handle, and as he raised the makeshift weapon, the spectral maw opened next to his ear. An inhuman shriek split the air and Colm stumbled and spun around, startled and searching for the source of the sound. Ivy wasn't sure if he could see the terrifying visage nose-to-nose with him, but she wasn't going to stay for curiosity's sake. She bolted up the cellar steps and fled across the lawn.

She ran up the hill and toward the treeline, only then registering that she had no idea where she was going.

"Ivy! You don't understand!" Colm's voice was pleading, but she didn't dare turn around. She could hear his footfalls running after her, even over the whipping wind.

As she neared the crest of the hill, she looked around for a destination, knowing he was just seconds behind her. She ran toward the edge of the cove. Maybe she could run along the coastline until she found another house?

Then she spotted it—the rowboat. If she could just make it to the boat, she could at least get far enough out into the water that she'd be safe from her cousin. She would take her chances with the currents.

"Ivy, STOP!" But she didn't stop. Even as her boots began sinking in the muck, she kept moving. Slower and slower, but still moving forward toward her only means of escape.

"I didn't kill her, Ivy. I swear I didn't!" He was close. Not close enough to reach her, but if he could fight his way through the mud better than she could, she might not make it to the boat.

"Oh, yeah? Then why is her body in the fucking *well in your cellar, Colm?*"

"We had a huge argument and she fell and hit her head! I didn't kill her!"

"Then why didn't you call an ambulance?" She could barely move forward through the mud's vice-like grip on her boots. She hazarded a glance over her shoulder. He had tried to follow in her footprints, but the mud was holding him back as well.

"Because she was *dead!* Cor, there was so much blood, Ivy."

"So you just dragged her to the well and chucked her in? She was your *sister*!"

There was a second of stunned silence. He hadn't realized, of course, that Emmy had told her about Dierdre. "No one would have believed it was an accident. Especially not my father. Can't you understand? They would have blamed me for her death!"

Ivy's feet had sunk nearly to the edges of her boots, and she might as well have been trapped in concrete. In desperation, she tried pulling her feet out, and sent herself pitching forward as she lost her balance.

"Do you think this is what I want, Ivy? I really liked you! It was so nice to finally have family again ..." His voice broke, and she could tell he was crying.

"What if I promise not to say anything?" She crawled forward as her knees and arms began to sink. The rocks were so close ... close enough that the crashing waves sent stinging salt mist into her eyes. If she could just get that far, maybe she could run along them to the boat.

"I wish I could believe that. I truly do. But I'm afraid I just can't take that chance, Ivy." His words were laced with sadness and resolve: a deadly combination for her.

Her clawing fingers brushed a half-buried rock the size of her head and she tried desperately to get a grip on it, hoping to pull herself forward. Water smashed on the rocks ahead of her and she had to turn her head to avoid swallowing part of Galway Bay. When she spotted Colm's legs, she screamed. She'd run out of time, and she knew it. There was no hope of reaching the boat now, even though it was only twenty feet away.

"I'm not a bad person, Ivy. I'm not. I didn't kill her. I hated her, yeah. And I wasn't going to have my father hate me because she had shite balance. It was her own fault!"

"It will be your fault when you kill me," she spat back at him.

He thought about that for a minute, his brain trying to rationalize the shovel in his hand. "I suppose it will."

Her mind rebelled against the inevitable. *Keep him talking.*

"How'd you get a neighbor to say she left?"

"I ..." He paused here, as if he didn't want to say too much. She took that as a good sign ... maybe she could convince him to let her live. "I moved her car up the road a bit and then walked home. Then I moved it to the airport the next day."

"Make me understand, Colm. Maybe it doesn't have to end this way. You're not a killer." She rolled into a sitting position, hoping he couldn't kill her if he was looking her in the eye. The surf roared behind her as the tide came in, crashing hard against the craggy rocks and soaking her hair and shoulders.

"I wish it didn't." He started crying again as he raised the shovel and the voice of the sea rose to a fevered pitch. Then the voice changed from the hollow roar of water to a wailing shriek that would have been terrifying if it hadn't become so familiar to Ivy over the last few days. She wondered how she could ever have confused it with the screech of an owl.

The sound intensified behind Ivy as though it was riding in on the waves, and Colm's face contorted into a mask of terror. She didn't need to look over her shoulder to know what he was seeing. She felt the water suck back the way it does before a big wave hits, and she braced herself for impact.

When the hit came, it wasn't water she felt. It was stabbing electricity. Ivy's limbs seized and her head jerked backwards as the creature passed through her, feeding her a lightning strike of jumbled visions as its arms reached for its true prey.

Deirdre's body on the cottage floor, her head haloed in a growing pool of blood ... blood dripping from the marble shelf of the hall tree ... a bloody knife falling from Colm's hand as he grabbed Dierdre's arms to drag her back to the cellar ... Colm's bloody hands gripping the steering wheel of Deirdre's car as he waited for a neighbor to pass by, walking their dog ... blood seeping through Colm's hair and dripping down his forehead as he turned his head so that all the neighbor would see was honey blond hair as he passed by ... Colm in the rowboat, tying blond hair around a rock and tossing it into the bay ...

The electric shock passed, but her body still thrummed with the charge as Ivy returned to full consciousness. The shrieking of the woman-beast was echoed by a high-pitched scream of pure terror erupting from Colm's throat.

The Gray Lady's arms jolted forward and grabbed him by the forearms, sending the shovel flying backward. Her fingertips frayed as bloody blond strands grew like vines from beneath her claw-like nails. The golden hairs wrapped around his arms, neck, and torso, and as the wave that carried her receded, the Lady held tight to Colm, dragging him with her toward the sea.

"Ivy! Ivy, help me! Please help me!"

Despite the fact that he'd been about to bash her skull in, Ivy reached for him as he was dragged past her. "Colm!"

He reached toward her outstretched arm, closing an iron grip on her wrist. "No!" she screamed as he held tight, hauling her with him out to sea.

The apparition dissolved as it moved through the crashing water until all Ivy could see was a vaguely shaped sea spray pulling them forward. Ahead, the tethered rowboat rocked in the agitated water, and again Ivy hoped it might be her salvation. If she could get a grip on it somehow ...

The vengeful mist seemed to be moving directly toward the boat, and the image of Colm dropping his grisly package overboard played on the edges of Ivy's mind. As the amorphous shape of the Gray Lady passed through the bow of the boat, the golden tendrils jerked Colm forward, knocking his head against the wood with a hollow *thunk* and rendering him temporarily senseless. He released Ivy, and she was able to catch the edge of the rowboat as it rocked forward.

She found footing on a rock beneath her and pushed herself up enough to see over the bow just in time to see Colm's twisted expression topped with a black mop of hair sink under the turbulent waters.

The Gray Lady was nowhere to be seen.

Weeping, Ivy dragged herself along the edge of the boat toward the shore, where she saw a middle-aged couple running along the treeline to try and reach her.

"Hang in there, girlie, we've got you!"

The man reached the rope which tethered the boat to the tree, and the woman picked up Colm's shovel and stretched the handle forth to try and hook onto a cleat and bring the boat and Ivy to safety.

When she was close enough, Ivy grabbed the handle of what would have been the weapon used to murder her and pulled herself to shore.

The couple grabbed her arms and helped her into the grass and she broke down, sobbing a mixture of horror and relief. "We've got you. We've got you."

Two days later, Ivy stood inside Shannon Airport, waiting for her flight home.

"Honey, I can't believe all this happened to you," Laura gushed on the other end of the line. "He seemed so nice. I'm so sorry."

"Yeah, it's awful," Ivy mumbled, still numb. "The coast guard guy said the currents can be pretty bad sometimes."

"What were you guys even doing out there?"

"We were ... digging for razor clams." Ivy had run the lie through her head a thousand times, knowing no one would ever believe the truth. "Or at least that's what he told me. I think he was just trying to get me out of the cellar when I was poking around."

"Because of the body?" Eva's voice shouted from the background. "I told you you should always search everything!"

"I ... I didn't know about the body. I didn't know why Colm wanted me out of there. But yeah, that's what he said: razor clams. I found the body later when I went back for my phone." To her ears, the story sounded preposterous, but the police had bought it without question.

"God, what a nightmare. I'm glad you're okay. We'll come and get you from the airport, and then buy you whatever drink you want."

"Thanks, guys. I've got to go through the security line. I'll text you when we land in New York."

"Okay. Listen, Ivy, I'm so sorry your dream vacation turned into a nightmare. I know you'll be so glad to be home."

"Thanks. Love you. 'Bye."

She hung up and reached into her carry-on to retrieve her passport, and her fingers brushed against the canvas she'd tucked into her bag. She traced the honey-colored lines of paint stretching skyward from the acrylic water. A reflection of the setting sun ... that's what she'd tell anyone who asked.

Holmes for the Holiday

HORROR BY JENNY SIMARD LABRANCHE

Part 1: The Cabin

Tonight, the outside world was just a few iron bars away. The damp chill of the cell had long since seeped into H.H. Holmes's bones, but he barely noticed anymore. For days, he had been imagining the moment that awaited him, savoring it as one might savor a rare vintage, slowly uncorked and poured with relish.

A thin smile ghosted across his lips as he leaned back on the hard cot, his mind spinning with elaborate plans. He had been an exemplary prisoner to those around him, biding his time, apologizing with proper remorse when required, and playing the humbled man's role. He knew how to convince others that he was innocent. And the fools had believed it. This time, he thought he wouldn't squander his freedom on simple pleasures. There were bigger, far grander schemes to accomplish, all waiting for him outside these walls.

He heard footsteps down the hall and rose, straightening his collar. The guards were coming as they had every night, but tonight felt different. Tonight, the metallic echo in the dim corridor sounded like a victory march.

The guard's keys rattled against the iron bars, his heavy sigh filling the silence. "Well, looks like it's finally your time, Holmes," he muttered with a note of resignation.

Holmes flashed his most charming smile. "I believe it is, officer," he replied smoothly, relishing the moment. He couldn't help but feel a rush of satisfaction as he walked through the cell door, a phantom shiver of victory running down his spine. Soon, he would be able to indulge in all the things he had missed for so long.

Holmes was led down the long corridor, his gaze sweeping over the other prisoners with a detached sort of amusement. In their eyes, he saw awe, jealousy, even a hint of fear, and it was all like music to his ears.

The last metal door clanged shut behind him, and he emerged into the cool night. He took a deep breath, drinking in the night air, filling his lungs with freedom. He felt an exhilarating rush. Outside of these walls, anything was possible. And Holmes had never been a man to let an opportunity slip by.

A sleek carriage sat waiting for him just beyond the wrought-iron fence, its polished brass features glinting in the fading light. The dark lacquered wood was so flawless it reflected the world around it while thick velvet curtains hung inside, drawn tightly over the windows to keep prying eyes away. The faint hiss of steam escaped from a hidden vent, a reminder of the cutting-edge technology powering the vehicle from within.

Holmes adjusted his collar, straightened his cuffs, and made his way toward it with a confidence that bordered on arrogance. He had always known he would be set free. It was only a matter of when, how, and who would help him. He had made it this far, after all. His mind had played the long game, a series of manipulations and subtle moves.

The driver's door swung open before he reached it, the woman who stepped out was nothing short of arresting. She was tall, poised, with raven-black hair coiled neatly at her nape, and green eyes that watched him with a mixture of amusement and something darker, something unreadable. Her fitted black dress clung to her frame, paired with a slim blazer that exuded an air of effortless elegance. Her heels, sleek and black with red soles, flashed like blood against the gray of the road with each calculated step.

"Mr. Holmes," she intoned, her voice smooth, almost musical, with a cadence that felt both foreign and familiar. She extended a hand, her fingers long and slender, gloved in deep black. "I'm Miss Holiday. I'll be handling your ... housing needs."

Holmes took her hand, noting its coolness, her grip surprisingly firm. The sharpness of her touch lingered, sending a strange thrill through him. "Miss Holiday," he replied, unable to hide the curiosity and something darker creeping into his voice. "It's a pleasure."

The pleasure was all his, of course. As he watched her, he couldn't help but imagine how satisfying it would be to bend her to his will, to shatter that composed exterior. He could already feel the twisted satisfaction that would come from wrapping his fingers around her slender throat, feeling her pulse thrumming against his hand as he squeezed the life from her.

Those vibrant green eyes would widen first in surprise, then slowly cloud with terror as the realization dawned that there would be no escape.

But even as the thought flickered through his mind, he stopped. He had always been good at reading people, and something about her, something about the way she stood there, unfazed, not the least bit intimidated, aroused him. She was an exquisite specimen, a creature of grace and refinement, and yet there was something else about her. Something ... untouchable.

She tilted her head slightly as if considering him, studying him with an unnerving focus. Holmes felt an odd flicker of annoyance pass through him, but he quickly suppressed it, forcing his usual composure back into place. He had never been intimidated by anyone, least of all a *woman*. He had made his living outwitting others, playing games in dark corners, and always, always coming out on top.

"Shall we?" she inquired, her voice smooth like silk, wrapped around a straight razor. She gestured as she opened the passenger door, her eyes still locked on him.

Holmes hesitated for a fraction of a second, his hand twitching at his side. The air between them seemed to ripple, heavy with something unspoken, as if her words carried weight beyond their meaning. He brushed off the feeling with an inward scoff. Nerves. Nothing more.

"Of course," he said, his lips curling into his practiced, disarming smile. He stepped forward, his polished shoes crunching on the gravel driveway, and slid into the passenger seat.

Miss Holiday closed the door behind him with a firm click, the sound ringing louder than it should have in the still night. She rounded the car with an unhurried grace, her heels tapping out a deliberate rhythm. Holmes found himself watching her reflection in the side mirror, the way the faint light caught her sharp features.

As she slipped into the driver's seat, the car's interior seemed to grow smaller, the air cooler. She turned the key, and the engine purred to life, but she didn't shift into gear right away. Her hands rested lightly on the steering wheel as she stole a brief glance at him.

"I understand you're looking for a place with ... privacy," she said at last, turning her gaze back to the road ahead.

"Indeed," he replied, keeping his tone even, though his pulse quickened. "Privacy is key."

She offered him a smile. "I've selected a few properties that should meet your standards. Places where no one will disturb you, no matter what you're doing."

Her words carried a subtle edge, a hint of something that made his skin prickle. Still, he felt his excitement grow. She understood his needs, the way he thrived in the shadows. She would make an excellent accomplice, or, he thought with a chill of anticipation, an even better victim.

As they pulled away, the prison behind them seemed to vanish into the shadows, as though it had never been there at all.

As they continued through the deserted woods, she began listing the rivers they passed, the towns they skirted. He recognized many of them from maps, from memories, until she mentioned one he hadn't heard before.

"The Styx," she told him, her tone casual. "Renamed not too long ago."

He chuckled, amused by the irony. "I always did have a certain affinity for myths."

She smiled but said nothing, her gaze fixed on the road, her fingers gripping the steering wheel with an intensity that belied her calm.

They passed through more trees, more winding roads, and he let himself sink into thoughts of what he would do to her once he'd made his choice of a house. He had no intention of harming her immediately; no, she was a delicacy best savored. He would let her think she was safe, let her feel as if she held control. And then, at the perfect moment, he would strip it all away.

For now, though, he'd play along.

"You strike me as a man who doesn't frighten easily," she said, her tone conversational yet laced with something he couldn't quite place. "Am I right, Dr. Holmes?"

He chuckled softly, leaning back in his seat as he adjusted his hat. "Fear, Miss Holiday, is a tool. One I wield, not one that wields me."

Her lips stretched into a small smile, but her eyes, dark, fathomless, remained fixed on him. "How fascinating," she murmured.

Holmes forced a smile. Yes, he had always appreciated a challenge. And Miss Holiday, with her unbreakable poise and untouchable demeanor, would be his most satisfying masterpiece yet. He did not doubt that, in time, he would break her. Her calm, controlled presence would unravel before him, like a delicate thread coming loose.

She was no ordinary woman, of that much he was certain. Holmes had seen countless other rich women, desperate women, those who had lost everything to his machinations. But Miss Holiday? She didn't fit any of the categories. She didn't seem to fear him. In fact, she looked entirely unbothered, as though he were just another piece in her own game. And that thought thrilled him. She wanted to toy with him, but she had no idea *she* would become *his* toy.

She glanced at him then, her green eyes meeting his with unsettling clarity. "You're wondering about me, Mr. Holmes," she said, her voice laced with a knowing amusement. "Maybe you're wondering why a woman would help you purchase a home after all you were accused of."

"Accused, not convicted," he corrected, "Are you worried about being with me?"

"You should know that I'm not the one who needs to be worried," she said with a sensual smile and a wink that almost stopped his cold heart. Then she laughed, and the sound aroused him.

Holmes's smile turned devious, but he quickly masked it. He couldn't afford to show his hand, not yet. "I assure you, Miss Holiday, I'm not worried about you."

She didn't respond. Instead, she turned her gaze to the window, watching the passing landscape with a quiet intensity. The carriage rumbled softly beneath them, the wheels moving along the road in a steady, almost rhythmic pattern. Holmes was left to contemplate her words, the unsettling nature of their exchange hanging between them like a thick fog. Why was she toying with him? Was she having a bit of fun because of who he was?

Whatever she was, Miss Holiday was not someone to be taken lightly. As the carriage carried them into the unknown, Holmes felt a gnawing sense of anticipation build in his chest. This was not simply a ride to freedom. No, there was something much darker, much more complex, at play here. And he couldn't help but wonder what role he would play in it all. Might she require his skills?

The world outside grew darker with each passing mile, and Holmes believed that she had underestimated him. And that, he decided, was a mistake she would never have the chance to make again.

The carriage rattled through the winding path, flanked on both sides by dense, dark woods. The forest grew thicker as they ventured deeper, branches curling over the path as though reaching to encircle them. Holmes felt an odd tightness in his chest, an almost imperceptible pressure from the canopy above. Despite his resolve, he found his fingers tapping impatiently on his knee, the shadows outside weaving into unsettling patterns.

Miss Holiday observed him quietly from her seat across the carriage, her posture still and serene, the lamplight casting an ethereal glow over her sharp features. She seemed to absorb every minute movement, her eyes watchful and curious, in the way a predator sizes up prey.

"Have you always been ... drawn to dark places, Mr. Holmes?" she asked, breaking the silence in her smooth, almost musical voice. "Your preference for remote locations caught my attention."

Holmes raised an eyebrow, her question catching him off guard. He smiled, but it didn't reach his eyes. "You could say I appreciate the solitude and privacy of the shadows, Miss Holiday," he replied, attempting to keep his tone light. "They have a way of revealing things people would rather keep hidden."

Miss Holiday's lips curved slightly, though her expression was inscrutable. "Indeed. But shadows do not conceal forever." She paused, her gaze unwavering. "They have a habit of shifting, revealing things one would rather leave untouched."

Holmes's jaw tightened involuntarily, but he forced a smile, refusing to let her odd manner unsettle him. "That sounds like a philosophical stance, Miss Holiday. A bit grim for my taste."

She chuckled, the sound soft, as though she alone understood some private joke. "Life has a way of acquainting us with grim truths, Mr. Holmes. Sometimes it is wise to acknowledge them."

Holmes's anger deepened as he turned his gaze to the window, but the forest revealed nothing beyond the deepening shadows. Miss Holiday's words had a peculiar way of piercing through his carefully maintained armor, pricking at corners of his mind he preferred to keep locked away.

"We'll be arriving soon," she said, her tone calm, almost soothing. "Our first destination is the most isolated, but I trust you will find it ... suitable."

The carriage jolted to a stop, and Holmes peered out to see a gloomy cabin nestled at the edge of a clearing. Its weathered wood seemed to absorb the dim light, the shutters slightly askew, as though they hadn't been disturbed in years. The forest beyond was dense and silent, an unyielding wall of ancient trees.

Holmes stepped out, the stillness pressed against him; not a bird, not a rustling leaf, only the faint whisper of the wind weaving through the pines.

It was an oppressive quiet as if the woods themselves were holding their breath, waiting.

Miss Holiday appeared at his side, her gloved hand gesturing toward the cabin. "Shall we?"

With a nod, Holmes followed her up the creaking steps, watching as she produced a key from her coat. The lock gave a reluctant groan as it turned, and the door swung open to reveal the cabin's dim interior. Miss Holiday entered first, lighting a lantern that cast long, flickering shadows against the rough wooden walls.

The cabin was sparse but impeccably clean. A simple table with two chairs stood in the center, a narrow bed tucked neatly into one corner, and a large stone fireplace dominated the far wall. The air carried a faint mustiness, mingled with the earthy scent of damp wood and the faint tang of something metallic.

Miss Holiday moved with practiced ease, her fingers trailing lightly over the table's surface, brushing the back of a chair, and finally coming to rest on the windowsill. Holmes noted her deliberate movements, as though she was reacquainting herself with every inch of the space yet assessing it anew.

"It's ... rustic," Holmes said, his voice dry, though his unease was palpable. "Not quite what I expected."

Miss Holiday smiled a serene yet inscrutable expression. "Think of it as a threshold, Mr. Holmes. A place where the past and present meet."

Holmes's eyes narrowed slightly. "An interesting choice of words. You speak as though this cabin holds some particular significance."

"It holds only what you bring to it," she replied, her voice soft but firm. "Perhaps more than you realize."

Holmes turned his attention to the fireplace, running his hand along the cool stone. "And what exactly do you expect me to find here?" he asked, his tone edged with impatience.

Miss Holiday's smile widened ever so slightly. "That depends on you, Mr. Holmes. Some places reflect the truths we carry within. Others ..." She paused, her eyes glinting in the lantern light. "Others reveal the truths we've tried to leave behind."

Holmes straightened, his gaze sharp. "I've no time for riddles, Miss Holiday. If this is some elaborate game—"

"Patience," she interrupted, her voice like silk over steel. "All will become clear soon enough." She stepped toward the door, her movements graceful and deliberate. "Shall we move on?"

Holmes glanced around the cabin once more, noting its unsettling stillness, the weight of the silence pressing down on him. Whatever this place was, it was not meant for lingering. With a final look, he adjusted his coat and followed Miss Holiday back into the night.

The forest loomed around them as they walked, the path barely visible beneath the tangled roots and fallen leaves. Holmes cast a glance at Miss Holiday, her figure cutting effortlessly through the shadows ahead. Her presence was both a comfort and a challenge, a guide through this strange, shifting world.

The cabin quickly disappeared behind them, swallowed by the darkness. Holmes felt the weight of the unknown pressing in, but he pushed forward, determined to uncover the purpose of this peculiar journey.

Part 2: The Mansion

The mansion rose before them, its silhouette like a jagged wound against the twilight sky. Deep within the forest, the house was isolated, as though the earth had conspired to swallow it whole and failed. Vines clawed at its crumbling stone facade, and the darkened windows reflected no light, giving the impression of a soulless, unblinking stare. The gnarled trees surrounding it swayed in the cold wind, their skeletal branches whispering secrets Holmes couldn't hear but felt crawling under his skin.

As he stepped down from the carriage, Holmes adjusted his coat against the chill, though the cold air was not the source of his discomfort. It was something else, a prickle at the nape of his neck, an unshakable sense that the house itself was alive, observing him. He dismissed the thought with irritation. It was absurd. It's just her playing games, he thought. She was well aware of who he was.

Miss Holiday stood beside him, her slender frame straight and still, her face calm as if the oppressive presence of the mansion meant nothing to her. Her gaze lingered on the house, but something was unsettling in the way her eyes glimmered in the dim light, as though she saw something beyond its crumbling exterior that he could not. What was he missing?

"Shall we go inside, Mr. Holmes?" she asked, her voice quiet but firm, carrying that infuriating air of control she seemed to wear so effortlessly.

Holmes gave a curt nod, his jaw tightening. He refused to show hesitation, not to her, not to anyone. The wind howled briefly as they approached the front doors, a low moan that seemed to carry a warning, though he dismissed it as a coincidence.

Miss Holiday reached for the heavy, iron-bound doors, her gloved hand pressing against their warped wood. They creaked open slowly, groaning as if in protest. The sound reverberated through the entry hall, a cavernous space where shadows danced on every surface.

Holmes stepped inside, his shoes clicking on the marble floor. Dust swirled in the weak light filtering through the high, grimy windows, and the stale air was thick with the scent of mildew and something faintly sweet, like decayed flowers. The hall stretched out before them, its grandeur faded but not entirely lost. Ornate moldings adorned the high ceilings, and a massive chandelier hung precariously overhead, its crystals dulled by decades of neglect.

Miss Holiday moved ahead, her movements fluid, her heels clicking against the stone. She seemed to glide through the space, untouched by the oppressive air. "This place has history," she said, her voice reverent, almost wistful. "It was built for those who sought freedom from the prying eyes of the world. A refuge, if you will."

Holmes let his gaze wander, taking in the faded opulence of the mansion. It reminded him of certain aspects of himself, shrouded in shadows, a veneer of civility hiding something more sinister. Yet the thought irritated him. The house was too presumptuous, as though it thought itself equal to him.

Miss Holiday glanced over her shoulder at him, her expression unreadable. "It's said that those who come here are searching for something," she continued, her voice soft. "Even if they don't know it yet."

Holmes felt a spark of anger at her words. What was she implying? That he, of all people, needed something? He clenched his fists momentarily, forcing himself to relax.

They moved through the halls, past towering portraits of dour-faced figures whose painted eyes seemed to follow his every step. Holmes's irritation deepened as he felt their gaze linger on him, as though they judged him unworthy. He imagined ripping the canvases from their frames, tearing through the painted faces until there was nothing left but tattered remnants.

Miss Holiday led him to a room at the end of a long, dark corridor. The door was heavy and scarred, its wood weathered by time. She paused, her hand resting on the handle. "This room," she said, her voice quieter now, almost conspiratorial, "belonged to the mansion's last resident. A man of peculiar tastes."

The door creaked open to reveal a study, colder than the rest of the house. The walls were lined with shelves, each crammed with books whose spines were cracked and titles faded. Strange artifacts cluttered the room: a small, intricately carved skull, an hourglass filled with shimmering black sand, and a jar containing something that floated limply in cloudy liquid. The air was dense, and Holmes felt a sudden, sharp unease.

"This room was his sanctuary," Miss Holiday said, moving further into the space. "A place for privacy, to surround himself with objects that spoke to the depths of his mind."

Her words grated against him, the insinuation cutting too close. "Privacy," he repeated, his tone sharp, "or isolation?"

Miss Holiday turned to him, her eyes meeting his with that maddening calm. "Perhaps both. For some, they are one and the same."

Holmes' irritation boiled over into anger, a dark and violent anger that he could feel simmering just beneath his skin. She thought she understood him, as if she had unraveled him with a few carefully chosen words. He wanted to show her how little she knew.

The fantasy came unbidden, vivid and intoxicating. He imagined her standing just as she was now, serene and composed, but with his hands on her throat. He would shatter that calm, watch her confidence dissolve into panic. He imagined the way her breathing would hitch, as realization emerged that she had underestimated him.

The thought sent a thrill through him, a surge of power that he quickly buried beneath his composed exterior. She was testing him, toying with him, and he would not let her win.

Miss Holiday moved to the window; her gaze fixed on the dark forest beyond. "This house," she said, her voice distant, "has always been drawn to certain kinds of people. Those who think themselves in control. Those who believe they are the hunter, not the hunted."

Holmes's mind flickered with violent fantasies, each more vivid than the last. How satisfying it would be to watch that calm façade shatter, to see fear replace the smugness in her eyes. His imagination conjured scenes of her delicate neck beneath his hands, her composure finally cracking as her breath came in short, panicked gasps. He would enjoy the struggle, the moment she realized her error in thinking she could toy with him.

He envisioned the slow, meticulous unraveling of her control. Perhaps he would bind her in one of the mansion's many forgotten rooms, leave her to the whispers she seemed so fond of. Let her hear them as they clawed at her sanity, let her learn what it meant to be powerless. Or maybe he would take his time, drawing out her fear until it was palpable, until she begged for mercy she would never receive.

The thought sent a dark thrill through him. She believed she understood him, but she had no idea of the darkness she was inviting. He had spent years perfecting his craft, turning cruelty into an art form. And if Miss Holiday insisted on playing games, he would show her just how dangerous a game with him could become.

She paused ahead, turning to look at him with that same infuriating smile. "Is something troubling you, Mr. Holmes?" she asked, her tone light, almost mocking.

Holmes met her gaze, forcing his expression into one of cold neutrality. "Not at all, Miss Holiday," he replied smoothly. "I'm merely ... enjoying the atmosphere."

Her smile widened slightly, as though she could see the storm brewing behind his eyes. "Good," she said, her voice soft but laden with hidden meaning. "The house thrives on those who truly *feel* its presence."

Holmes suppressed a laugh, dark and hollow. *Feel?* Oh, he felt plenty, and soon enough, she would feel it too. Let her keep smiling, keep thinking she held the upper hand. The moment would come when he turned the tables, when he made her understand the depth of his cruelty. The whispers seemed to urge him on, their unintelligible murmur growing louder, feeding the shadowed thoughts swirling in his mind. "Yes," he murmured under his breath, his voice almost inaudible. "Let's see how long that smile lasts."

Miss Holiday turned back to him, her smile faint but unshaken. Holmes forced his lips into a thin smile, hiding the storm within.

"This house," she said, stepping past him toward the door, "has a way of showing people their true selves."

As they moved on, Holmes trailed behind, his gaze lingering on her silhouette. His mind swirled with plans and dark possibilities. She believed she had him figured out. Soon, he would show her just how dangerous that presumption was.

Part 3: The Victorian

It was the third house, however, that ensnared him completely. A grand, decaying Gothic Revival tucked far from any prying eyes, its air thick with the scent of old wood and cold stone. The sight of it stirred something familiar within Holmes. Its brick walls, darkened by age and cloaked in ivy, spoke of secrets long buried, and the faint, musky scent that wafted from the open door was almost comforting.

Crossing the threshold, Holmes felt not uneasy but an unexpected sense of belonging. The heavy, dust-laden air carried a weight that matched his own, and the shadowed corners of the house seemed to beckon him forward, promising whispers of things unseen.

The rooms, filled with relics of forgotten lives, felt like an echo of his own mind, places where shadows lingered, secrets were tucked away, and control could be exerted. He found himself trailing a hand along the dark wood paneling, appreciating its sturdy craftsmanship and the way it absorbed light, creating a cocoon of dim intimacy.

Each corridor, narrow and pressing, felt purposeful rather than oppressive. The labyrinthine design was most pleasing, as if the house had been built for someone who understood the art of concealment and control.

Miss Holiday moved ahead, her silhouette gliding through the gloom like a phantom. For the first time, Holmes felt no inclination to scrutinize her. The house itself demanded his attention, its creaking floors, its groaning walls, and its peculiar, knowing quiet. He could already imagine how easily he might navigate its halls, how well it would serve his purposes.

"This place," he murmured, his voice low and almost reverent, "has a character of its own."

Miss Holiday glanced back at him, her expression inscrutable but edged with the faintest hint of approval. "Indeed, Mr. Holmes," she said softly. "It's a house that rewards those who know how to use it."

Holmes's lips curved into a thin smile. Yes, this was a place where he could thrive.

"Quite a collection here," Miss Holiday remarked, her fingers brushing an old, dust-laden vase on a side table. She traced the cobwebs as though savoring their texture, her glance back at Holmes lingering with an expression he couldn't quite read. "Some might say it's haunted by its own memories, filled with stories that refuse to rest."

Holmes smiled, but this time, it wasn't tight or forced. It was genuine, curling at the edges of his lips as his mind began to race. The house, dark, heavy, and steeped in shadows, felt less like a trap and more like a sanctuary. The air was thick, almost suffocating, yet he found it oddly invigorating.

This was a house that understood him.

His gaze flicked to the relics scattered about the rooms: dusty trinkets, tarnished silver, a faintly glinting blade tucked into the corner of a cabinet. The stories Miss Holiday spoke of did not trouble him; they intrigued him. No, this house was not a prison. It was a canvas.

"I can see that," he said softly, running his fingers along the edge of a side table. The wood was solid beneath his hand, unyielding, perfect. His smile widened as his mind began to wander.

Miss Holiday moved ahead, her steps light, almost floating, and Holmes found himself studying her with interest. She was an enigma, yes, but she was also an opportunity. The way she spoke, the way she moved, it all felt carefully rehearsed, as if she expected him to feel uneasy. Instead, he felt excitement bloom in his chest.

He pictured it easily. The way her calm, composed demeanor might falter under pressure. How her confidence would crack when her perfect, knowing smile met his scalpel. His fingers twitched at the thought, his mind painting vivid pictures of her terror, the way she might beg, how her voice would break.

He followed her through the house, his attention half on her words and half on the surroundings. The mirrors caught his eye again, their gilded frames glinting faintly in the dim light. His distorted reflection pleased him, fragmented, shifting, like a predator moving through shadows.

In one, he saw her reflection just behind him, her face pale, her dark eyes watching him intently. But instead of fear, it ignited a spark of anticipation. He turned, pretending to study the hallway, but the wheels in his mind turned faster. He would bide his time, let her lead him through this labyrinth. She had chosen this house to unsettle him, but she had no idea what kind of man she was dealing with.

"It's almost like they never left," she said, brushing her fingers over a dusty, gilded mirror. The glass rippled under her touch, a trick of the light he assumed. She looked at him, her expression cool.

He tilted his head, meeting her gaze with a smirk. "Memories are a powerful thing," he replied, his tone smooth. "Sometimes, they linger longer than the flesh they belonged to."

She smiled, but Holmes thought he saw the faintest flicker of unease. It thrilled him. *Finally.*

As they moved deeper into the house, he took a mental inventory of the tools at his disposal: heavy candlesticks, sharp-edged relics, even the shadows themselves seemed complicit. Each step deepened his sense of power, the house's oppressive atmosphere feeding his imagination.

In the basement, he discovered something that nearly took his breath away: an iron maiden, a rack, and other medieval devices of torture. Holmes trailed his fingers over the cold, cruel metal, envisioning their use, the screams they might elicit.

"I can tell you like this place," Miss Holiday said. She approached the iron maiden, and to his surprise, stepped inside, closing it nearly all the way before letting out a scream so piercing, it thrilled him to his core. She opened it a second later, laughing. "Just like yesterday's tour," she said, wiping a mirthful tear from her eye.

The scream echoed in his mind, teasing him. Now he knew it was all just a game to her. This house would be perfect, he decided, even if Miss Holiday was dangerously clever. He could wait. He'd get her soon, he thought, and he'd make her regret every sly smile mocking laugh she threw his way.

"Well then, Mr. Holmes," she said as they walked through the dark, winding passages. "There's one more room here I'd like to show you. I think you'll find it ... special."

They descended another staircase, deeper than the last, into a hidden chamber. Here, under dim, flickering light, he could see that Da Vinci's *Vitruvian Man* was carved into the stone wall, a hauntingly precise etching, complete with arm and leg holds that looked designed to fit someone perfectly.

"Go on," she said, her eyes alight with an invitation. "Try it. After all, I stepped into the iron maiden," she laughed again. It thrilled him.

Something in him hesitated, but his arrogance won over. Holmes stepped into the etching, and kept his eye on her to make sure she kept her distance, stretching his arms and legs to fit the outline. He felt the cold press of stone around him and heard a click as iron clamps snapped shut around his wrists and ankles, binding him in place. He struggled, pulling against the restraints, but they didn't budge. What locked them?

Holmes' breath caught in his throat as the iron clamps bit into his wrists and ankles. He felt the cold press of metal digging into his skin, unnervingly tight, as if forged precisely for him. His initial shock quickly gave way to anger, a hot, consuming fury that someone had dared to trap him like an animal. He tugged hard against the restraints, but the steel held him fast.

His heart thundered, and for a fleeting moment, a feeling he hadn't known since childhood clawed its way up from the pit of his stomach: fear. But pride was quick to stamp it down, and he struggled, snarling. "Miss Holiday!" he spat, twisting his neck to glare at her. "Release me this instant, or I swear you'll regret it."

Her silence was his only answer as she approached, her face still framed in that strange, composed smile. She circled him like a vulture, her eyes glinting with a knowing chill that unsettled him. He tugged again, feeling the iron bite deeper, but the binds didn't yield. This wasn't just an accidental restraint; it was a trap. Designed for him.

"Mr. Holmes," she finally spoke, her voice as smooth and icy as the stone walls surrounding them. "Do you know why you are here?"

His anger flared. "I know I'm here because of *you*," he hissed, trying to summon the cold command he'd used to cow so many before her. But his voice sounded small, hollow, bouncing back from the walls like a mockery.

She raised a single dark brow, her expression impassive. "No, Holmes. You're here because of every foul, twisted act you committed. Every scream you silenced, every soul you stole."

The words made his skin prickle with dread. He shifted against the iron restraints, feeling the cold seeping into his bones. "You think you're the first person to try and make me feel remorse?" he scoffed, though his voice was weaker now, threads of doubt winding through his mind. "You're no different than the rest. Self-righteous, bleeding-heart—"

She leaned in closer, her breath cold against his ear. "Oh, no, Holmes. I am not here for redemption. I am here to collect."

The words slithered down his spine like ice. He'd never believed in spirits, in punishments beyond the grave, but the way she spoke made him wonder if he had been wrong.

"I think you'll find your arrogance doesn't hold much weight on this side of the river," she whispered, her lips twisting into a cruel smile. "Did you notice, Mr. Holmes, the Styx? The river you crossed with such blithe arrogance, as if it were any other stream?"

He felt his throat tighten, the certainty that usually braced him slipping away like sand through his fingers. The Styx. It had been a joke, he thought. A clever renaming. Nothing more.

The realization dawned on him slowly, chilling him to his core. The River Styx. The restraints. She was Death. It was all a grotesque, intricate trap that he had willingly walked into, lured by his own vanity and longing for freedom. And now, bound and helpless, he was completely at her mercy.

"No—" he rasped, the fury draining from his voice, leaving only a small, panicked whisper. "You ... this is some kind of sick joke."

"Not a joke," she replied softly, almost pityingly. "A sentence."

Her words settled into the air, thick and suffocating, each one slicing through the shreds of his confidence. She took a step back, watching him with a detached curiosity, like one might watch a moth trapped under glass. "You'll stay here, trapped in this very room, for all eternity. And with each passing moment, every one of your victims will come to you, visitors from beyond, their silent faces reminders of what you've done. They will be your only company."

He twisted again, pulling frantically against the binds, and this time he felt something give, the faintest, bitter taste of hope. But as he yanked, the metal tightened, slicing into his skin. A searing pain radiated up his arms, and he bit back a scream. His panic rose, his vision blurring as he struggled, but the iron held fast, a vise of eternal punishment.

"You can scream, Mr. Holmes," she said, her voice low and cold. "But no one will hear. No one will come. This prison is yours alone, and your agony will go unheeded for as long as you exist."

"Please," he whispered, all the power drained from him, the arrogance crushed under the weight of her words. "This isn't real."

She tilted her head, a shadow of triumph ghosting across her features. "You think you can charm your way out of this, like all the others here before you?

What does she mean by the others before me?

I assure you, Mr. Holmes, your charm means nothing here."

She stepped back, her green eyes glinting with satisfaction that chilled him to his bones. "Enjoy eternity," she whispered, and then turned, her heels clicking softly as she walked away. The heavy door creaked, and his voice broke in desperation.

"Wait!" he screamed, his voice raw, but the door swung shut with a deafening finality, sealing him in the cold, silent darkness.

Holmes yanked and pulled, cursing and screaming, until his voice cracked and his muscles burned. His breaths grew shallow, his screams turning into pathetic whimpers. Alone, encased in darkness, the faint echo of his own breathing and the chilling memory of her final words were all that remained.

Holmes sagged against the restraints, his wrists and ankles raw where the metal had bitten deep into his flesh. The room was suffocatingly dark, the silence so thick it felt alive, pressing in on him from all sides. Panic gnawed at him, a frantic animal clawing at the last remnants of his mind, and he began to pull and thrash wildly, his skin tearing as he tried to wrench himself free.

Then, from somewhere in the blackness, he heard it, a low, wet sound, like footsteps in thick mud. The sound echoed slowly and deliberately, drawing closer. His breath came in shallow, broken gasps as he strained to see something, anything. "Who's there?" he rasped, his voice a cracked whisper.

In response, the footsteps grew louder, the unmistakable scrape of something heavy dragging along the floor. A faint, sickly glow began to pulse around him, casting an unnatural, deathly light across the cold stone walls. Emerging from the shadows were hollow-eyed figures, their faces pale and drained, as if all life had been siphoned from them. They watched him with expressionless stares, each gaze weighted with silent accusation.

But it was the wounds, raw, brutal reminders of his own sadistic genius, that paralyzed him with terror. Jagged lacerations, twisted fractures, and burns marred their flesh in horrifyingly familiar shapes. His stomach twisted as he recognized each unique, calculated mark, as though staring into a mirror of his own cruelty. These weren't just corpses; they were his creations, grotesque specters of his art, clawing back from the depths to confront him.

He felt the bile rise in his throat, his hands beginning to shake as the first figure stepped closer, its skin sloughing away to reveal the carnage beneath. The heavy, dragging sound grew louder, joined now by the wet slap of torn flesh against stone. They were coming for him, all of them, drawn by the same dark artistry that he had once found such pleasure in. Now, in the sickly glow, he could see it for what it truly was: the haunting shadow of his own monstrosity.

One by one, they advanced, their footsteps pooling blood across the floor, leaving crimson trails that gleamed in the dim light. The smell of iron filled the room, thick and cloying, and Holmes's throat closed in horror.

"Get away from me!" he shrieked, his voice cracking as he struggled harder against the restraints. But they only tightened, the metal biting down to the bone. Blood streamed down his arms and legs, warm and sticky, mingling with the trails of crimson inching across the floor toward him.

The figures stopped, just close enough for him to see their vacant, glassy eyes fixed on him. A short woman with a slashed throat leaned close, her cold breath brushing against Holmes's cheek as she mouthed soundless words. Another, a woman with a jagged wound across her torso, lifted a bloodstained hand and pressed it to his chest, her touch freezing his skin, paralyzing his breath.

Then, one by one, the figures raised their hands and fingers curling into claws. Without a sound, they tore into him, flesh ripping from his arms, his legs, each jagged tear sending a flood of searing pain up his spine. His screams filled the stone chamber, echoing off the walls in a cacophony of terror and agony, but his voice reached no one. Each wound burned with unnatural heat, but he couldn't pass out, couldn't escape the reality of their punishment.

As his blood pooled beneath him, staining the etching, he felt the cold touch of Death at his shoulder, watching him with serene satisfaction. His cries grew weaker, fading into whimpers, as he realized with dawning horror that this wasn't the end. Every drop of blood, every torn fragment of flesh, would regenerate, only to be ripped away once more by the silent, unblinking souls of those he had condemned.

And he would feel it, every bloody, screaming moment, again and again ... forever.

His cold blue eyes widened first in surprise, then slowly clouded with terror as the realization dawned that there would be no escape.

Peach Blossom Pink and Bloody Red

HISTORICAL FICTION BY BETSEY KULAKOWSKI

1: Into The Fray

April 2, 1862

Every young man believes they'll never grow old. I never thought I'd die so young. I took up the Blue when so many of my brothers bled Gray. I suppose I should have expected what was to come.

I was just a boy, not even a man. I should have stayed home with my mother and sisters, but I couldn't abide the way things were. I knew I had to fight, no matter what the cost. So, in the cold hours before dawn while the house slept, I packed a few belongings, took a side of dried salt pork and a dozen apples from the root cellar, and snagged a handful of cold biscuits from Auntie Phaedra's kitchen and left my home outside of Ripley, Mississippi. It was the only home I'd ever known. I'd never even traveled outside the county, but I had heard Union forces were in Tennessee, and I had a mind to join them.

It wasn't an easy journey. Rain and thunderstorms hampered my efforts to reach Pittsburg Landing. Rebel forces were already on the road to meet them, and I had to keep to the animal trails and back woods to avoid them. I most certainly didn't want to run into my older brother, Holman.

He served in the Army of Mississippi under the *Creole Napoleon*, or so he'd said in his most recent letter to our mother. He spoke of the Confederate General, Gustave Toutant-Beauregard who was born on a sugar plantation in Saint Bernard Parish, just outside of New Orleans. His family was old, wealthy, aristocratic.

However, I often heard him referred to as a *Creole bastard* by his detractors, and I didn't know enough about him to contradict them. I heard he graduated second in his class from West Point, which told me enough not to second guess his military expertise. From Holman's letters, I knew my brother admired him, which made me abhor the General.

It was late the next day when I found myself walking along the railroad tracks. There was a town ahead, but I knew better than to go anywhere near it. Holman's early letters spoke of him meeting up with the Confederate Armies in Corinth. No, I needed to turn and go north toward the Tennessee River, which I would have to cross, one way or another.

That night, I made camp beneath an outcropping of rock, where the rain didn't quite reach me, but the cold curled down off the rock walls like a ghost. I couldn't remember ever having been so cold and afraid. I slept beneath a tattered bedquilt I'd taken from home, wrapped around my father's rifle. I had my uncle's Damascus steel-bladed knife tied in a sheath on my right leg. It had come home with his body after the Vidalia Sandbar fight in 1827. Our family didn't have a dog in the fight between the two wealthy families who were feuding over financial interests, allegations of vote-fixing in a sheriff's election, and bad bank notes. My uncle, William, had been traveling from Natchez when he met with his fate, a victim in the wrong place at the wrong time.

Too fearful of rebel scouts to make a fire and cook the salt pork, I ate a dried biscuit and surrendered to exhaustion. It was a long and restless night. I woke several times to the sound of voices, though whether they were soldiers or nightmares I couldn't say.

At dawn, I woke to the distant sounds of drums, and realized fifes were playing *Dixie*. The Rebels were close, I surmised. That urged me to get moving. I walked all day, hearing the sounds of canons echoing in the distance.

At sunset, I reached the edge of a river so wide, I knew I could not cross it. I could see and smell the gun smoke and hear the shouts and screams of soldiers. Their bodies and weapons were silhouetted against the backdrop of the setting sun, the sky painted a bloody red.

I had not arrived before the conflict began, but the promise of battle urged me on in the hopes I wouldn't miss out entirely. From the cover of the trees as I went the opposite direction in search of a bridge or a ferry. The smaller munitions began to sound like woodpeckers, then mosquitos. Then, something clicked behind me.

"Hands up, boy." I froze and dropped my gun and ruck sack. Terrified, my hands crept up even with my ears. "Name, rank, and unit."

"My name is Thomas ..." I swallowed hard, my mind trying to think quick enough not to give myself away. "I'm just hunting. I ain't no solder."

"Turn around?"

I did, and realized they were Union soldiers. There were at least half a dozen of them. The relief I felt must have been visible as it washed through me. "Thank God," I muttered under my breath.

A weary looking man in a blue wool coat festooned in gold braided epaulettes stepped out of the line of soldiers. "You sound like a rebel, son."

"I'm from Mississippi, but I don't side with the Confederates. I was hoping to join the Union and fight for my country."

The man gave me a long inspection before he spoke. "How old are you, boy?"

"Nineteen," I lied, my voice cracking.

"Sounds more like fifteen," one of the other soldiers laughed.

"So you wanna join the Army, do you?"

"Yes, sir," I swallowed hard.

"If you were smart, you'd go shoot some rabbits and head home." He leered at me, then started to turn around.

"A man don't gotta be smart to fight," I said. "I came to fight."

“A man has to be smart if he wants to live,” the man said and turned back, considering me another moment. “Surgeon Major Reeves?” he called to one of his men. “You need a boy to help you out?”

“Yes, Captain Goodwin. I could use all the hands I can get,” a man stepped out of the crowd, his white apron was smeared in dark red hand prints and spatters.

“If you can’t be smart, I’ll be smart for you, son,” the man stared me down. “You can fight Ol’ Nick with the medical corps. Private Childers, you are hereby commissioned into the US Army of the Tennessee.”

“Come on, boy, you just joined the Army. Time to get to work.”

At dawn, we joined the Union forces encamped at Pittsburg Landing. They’d already engaged the enemy but had been lacking needed supplies and reinforcements. Major Reeves ordered me to follow him across the field to the tents where soldiers lay on litters, lined up like lambs from the slaughter. The perfume of blood and peach blossoms lay heavy in the still morning air. A dense fog obscured the fields, but the eerie sound of drums, bugles, and marching feet preluded the first crack of musket volleys, then the waft of gun smoke joined the nauseating miasma.

Other doctors worked on wounded soldiers as I stood, frozen, staring into the true face of war as I realized many of these soldiers had been wounded from the fighting I had heard the day before. For some, it was too late. Their faces and hands were blue, masked by death.

“Childers,” Major Reeves barked, and I snapped out of the rigor that held me frozen. I hurried over to him. “Don’t worry about the dead. Let’s focus on the ones we can save. You do everything I tell you, when I tell you. Understood?”

“Y-y-yes-s, s-s-sir,” I responded, feeling the blood rushing from my face into my feet.

He stood at a table that was dripping blood, the damp green grass around our feet equally sodden with gore. “Next patient!”

A wounded boy, hardly older than me, was brought forward on a litter. Bandages wrapped his mangled leg as he sobbed, gripping the edge of the bed. Major Reeves assessed his injuries quickly. “That leg has to come off,” he said. “Bone saw.”

"No!" The patient wailed. Major Reeves ignored his cries.

I glanced at the weapons on the table beside me: blades and saws of all kinds, all covered in filth and flesh, dulled by countless hours of use. "Childers, hand me the bone saw!" he snapped at me, and I jumped, reaching for what looked like the right one. "The other one," he said, pointing.

Another medic came over and held out a stick in front of the boy's mouth. "Soldier, bite down on this. Dr. Reeves will be quick and you'll be home eating your mother's cooking before you know it." The boy cried and begged, but when he opened his mouth wide enough, the medic moved the stick into place and looked at me. "Hold him down. Don't let him move." I glanced at the boy, and felt sick. Tears streamed down his panicked face as he tried to protest, but Dr. Reeves was already ripping open his pant leg, up to his thigh, taking the bone saw from my hands.

"Hold him!" the doctor ordered.

I did, and realized quickly it would take all my strength to keep him pinioned in place. I all but lay atop him, as tears flooded my own face. I wept for this young man I didn't even know, and for the other men and boys screaming on the battlefield that lay beyond the fog. I cried for those who lay dead and dying. I cried for my mother and wished I'd stayed home. I cried for my brother who could have been out in the fog, for all I knew, maybe he'd even shot this boy. As the boy struggled, the sound of the saw cutting through flesh and bone was sickening. It was everything I could do not to vomit.

"Dr. Reeves?" The medic holding the stick in the boy's mouth said with urgency. "It's too late." I realized the boy had stopped fighting. *He must have passed out*, I assumed. It would be a small mercy, no doubt.

I looked up and realized the doctor was holding the boy's severed leg, then looked at the medic, whose face had gone pale. He shook his head. I saw the boy's placid face, and realized he was gone. He'd died with me holding him down, crying.

I took a step back, stumbling at the grotesque vision before me. Blood dripped from the severed limb, oozed from the mangled stump. It pooled beneath him.

The doctor laid the limb back in place, and nodded. "Next patient!"

Thunder rumbled overhead, and the skies opened up as daylight waned. Dr. Reeves dismissed me and ordered me to report to Captain Goodwin. He must have known I'd had enough. I was slow to respond to his orders, and between each patient, I found myself gagging and retching in the grass outside the medical tent.

The Captain must have thought me a horrific sight. I stood before him, conveying the message Dr. Reeves had given me. "Reassignment, huh? No guts for surgery. Understandable. It's not for everyone." He stood and poured water from a pitcher into a basin. "Come wash up," he said, snatching a towel from a rope hanging on the wall of his tent.

I did as ordered, wincing as the water turned pink, then red. "Be honest, son." He put a hand on my shoulder. "How old are you?"

I didn't hesitate. "I'll be fifteen next month."

"I thought so," he said. "While other commanders might, I don't send boys into battle. That doesn't mean you can't be useful." He turned to the entrance of his tent. "Lt. Colonel Webster," he called out. I washed my hands and scrubbed at my face, until it was raw. I took the towel he offered and dried off, leaving smears of red on the white flannel cloth.

"Yes, Captain?" Another officer stepped into the tent.

"A new recruit joined us last night," he said. "He spent the morning assisting in medical care, but the doctor asked to have him reassigned."

Lt. Colonel Webster pointed at me with a questioning glance. "Can you play the drum?"

"No sir," I said.

"Fatigue detail?" Captain Goodwin suggested.

"If you can't mend the belly of a wounded soldier, maybe you can help feed them. A steamboat with supplies arrived not a quarter hour ago." Webster said. "Excellent suggestion, Captain. Assign Private ..."

I swallowed and found my voice. "Childers, sir. Thomas Childers."

"Assign Private Childers to the quartermasters corps," the Lieutenant Colonel said. "And once everything is unloaded, you can help serve dinner in the officers' mess tent."

Captain Goodwin sat back at his desk and took out a sheet of paper and a quill, along with a bottle of ink. He drafted my commission and orders, and handed them to me. "Make sure the coffee is strong and hot. General Grant doesn't abide weak coffee."

The steamboat was already unloaded when I reported for duty, the supplies staged in the barn that had been commandeered by the Union Army. General Grant and his high command had taken over the farm house, and a tent had been set up nearby where fires were stoked and the perfume of bacon fat melded with the horrific odors of war.

At first, I was grateful I'd been assigned the task of gathering firewood rather than butchering a deer carcass that was now spitted over one of the open fires. I had seen enough butchering for an entire lifetime that morning, and was certain my stomach couldn't take any more.

As I was feeding hickory wood into one of the cooking fires, I glanced up as a rider came racing in camp and pulled up in front of the hastily constructed platform where the General sat under a canopy. He was observing the battle, the rider threw himself off his horse and raced up the steps. The General rose from a chair on the platform and accepted the message.

Steam rose from the horse's flank as the rider stood at attention, allowing the General to read the message. "What are your orders, General?" I heard him ask.

The man folded the paper and tucked it into the pocket inside his jacket. He paused for a moment, then spoke softly. "Tell them to hold the line."

"Private Childers!" one of the cooks shouted. I glanced back at the fire and realized an ember had ignited my pant leg. I jumped back, swatting at my leg, burning my hand as I snuffed out the flames. "You okay, son?" The cook was an old freed man, serving in the Union forces.

"Yes, sir," I managed.

"Don't call me *sir*. Name is Jessup." He took my hand and inspected it. "Looks like that might blister." He held onto my wrist, leading me over to one of the wooden crates where his supplies were stored. I watched as he took out a small vial of oil and poured a few drops into my hand, gingerly massaging it over my stinging skin. The perfume of flowers filled my nose, and I thought of Ellie Belle, my little sister. She liked to play in the herb garden and often came in smelling of lavender or rosemary, sometimes both.

"Lavender oil?" I asked.

The old man nodded. "My granny was a yarb doctor," he said. "She swore by oil of lavender for burns. It draws the sting out, and keeps the rot from the wound."

"It feels better already," I admitted.

"We'll put some more on it in an hour," he said, wrapping a piece of cloth he tore from a muslin flour sack, around my hand. "Keep it clean and dry, if you can." He finally turned loose of me. "Now, how much do you know about cooking?"

"Nothing," I admitted. Auntie Phaedra, my mother's cook, never allowed us into the kitchen. My mother wouldn't have allowed it either. It wasn't *proper*, she'd say.

"Then I'll teach you," he said. "First lesson, biscuits."

I learned a lot from Jessup in a short period of time. He patiently explained how to feed an army and the importance of a hot meal when times were hard. "These boys have been out there fightin' for their lives and ain't eat in days," he explained as he split open a hot biscuit, slathered it in butter, added a slice of bacon right out of the skillet and handed it to me with a nod. "Taste that." I did and it was wonderful.

"It's delicious," I said, but I knew I didn't have to. He could see the expression on my face, and the joy exuding from me.

"Now, imagine you been out there dodging bullets and trying not to eat a bayonet." He lifted an arthritic hand in the general direction of the battlefield.

I got the point.

"Jessup!" the quartermaster called from the back of the tent. Jessup stood and turned. "General Grant's orderly has taken ill. Who can serve the General tonight?"

Jessup turned and considered me for a moment. "Private Childers can do it." I stood, prepared to protest, but Jessup turned around and put up a hand. "They don't let us freemen serve the General. Usually his orderly does it, but if you do a good job, you could end up replacing him."

"I been in the army all of two days," I protested. "Surely there's a more experienced man than me."

"Does your father have a valet?"

"He did," I said. "Before he died."

"You ever watch him serve your father?"

"All the time," I said. "I didn't like the way my Pa spoke to him. How he treated him."

"The General isn't like that," Jessup said. "He's stern, but he's a good man. It's not like you'll be a slave to him. You just make sure to fill up his coffee cup when it gets empty, and bring him his food. When he's done eating, you bring his plate back here."

I hesitated, watching as Jessup moved from the biscuits cooling by the fire, to a pan of beans he'd cooked up with bacon and onions. The perfume of it reminded me of Auntie Phaedra, who served in our family's home since she was a little girl. Her mother had served before that. She was an excellent cook, and I 'd enjoyed many happy meals around the table with Phaedra watching from the corner to make sure everything was exactly right.

"Here," he said. "Eat this, quickly, then report to the cooking tent outside the Officer's tent. The General got his own cook. He'll tell you what to do."

I ate as fast as I could and raced to report, as ordered. Lanterns hanging from three crossed poles flickered in the pouring rain. Thunder competed with canons to shake everything as lighting flashed and cannonballs flared from the ends of their weapons.

The General's cook was dissatisfied with my state and sent me to wash up, comb my hair and change my apron to one that was cleaner. After a second inspection, he determined I would just have to do, and ordered me to take the General a cup of coffee on the front porch, and let him know dinner would be ready in ten minutes.

With the cup filled too full, perched atop a heavy silver tray, I moved through the house slowly, careful not to spill it. I fumbled with the door, and nearly did upend the cup. But the General's aide-de-camp, a Captain named Bennett, came to my rescue and offered his handkerchief to sop up the spilled coffee.

The General sat at a table on the front porch. He was mud-spattered, silent, studying a map by lantern light, while his aids bustled around him. When I offered the cup to him, the General accepted it with thanks, hardly noticing me. I stood, as instructed, and waited to be dismissed. He wrapped his hands around the cup, and inhaled the steam that rose from it. When he sipped, he offered a contented sigh and said, "How are the men eating?" His question caught me by surprise, but his concern for the troops was a feather on my heart. I hadn't expected any concern for the plight of the men who lay bleeding across the peach orchard, where the blossoms came down like rain with each cannon blast. Even in the rain and fog, it painted a colorful picture in my young traumatized mind. It was an image I would not soon forget.

"A steamboat arrived today with provisions, sir," I answered. "The cook is preparing beans and biscuits for their meal."

"Good," he said. "The men have earned it today ... those who survived."

"Yes, sir," I said, not sure what else to say.

The General took another sip of his coffee and nodded, "That will be all, Private. You are dismissed."

Even inside the farm house, which was probably half the size of my family home back in Tippah County, I could hear the thunder fighting with the cannons, and the constant barrage of gunfire as it echoed over the rain-soaked field.

Dinner was long but uneventful. The General ate little, his mind still on the battle, the map spread out before him. He reminded me much of my father in his mannerisms. Captain Bennett, the General's aide-de-camp who'd held the door for me, came into the kitchen where I washed the pots and pans in a tub of steaming hot water, and announced that the Confederates were retreating and our forces would send a moderate pursuit the following morning.

"Childers," the cook turned. "Go give aid to Jessup and the commissary team. Soldiers who can return to camp will be hungry."

Jessup ordered me to serve the returning soldiers who began lining up at the tent. Tin plates rattled as the soldier next to me slopped beans onto them. I added a biscuit to the plate, while another soldier filled cups with bitter coffee that had already begun to go cold.

The men hovered under a tent to eat, sitting on boxes, tree stumps or the few chairs that could be found. Some were wounded but refused medical treatment, but all were weary, and quickly disappeared to their tents to rest while they could.

Jessup and the rest of the commissary detail remained at their posts, and I returned to my job of stoking the fires that now heated water to wash the plates, spoons, and cups used to serve the men.

It was late when Jessup finally dismissed me with a pat on my back. "Well done, Thomas," he said. "Be back here before sun up. We'll send them back into battle with full bellies and pray they all return for supper."

They didn't. Nearly 2,000 Union soldiers lay amidst the peach blossoms where they fell. Beside them, another 2,000 Confederate troops bled the same color. In all, there were over 13,000 Union casualties, and 12,000 Confederate casualties when all was said and done. There were the injured and the captured to feed. I watched as my fellow soldiers combed the field for survivors, and began the arduous task of collecting the dead.

Within a few days, order for all hands to take a turn on mortuary detail came down the chain of command. When we weren't feeding soldiers, we were burying them. With bandanas soaked in lavender oil wrapped around our faces, Jessup and I worked side-by-side, digging a mass grave for the dead Rebels. No one spoke ill of the dead, and I confided in Jessup that it was possible my brother might be among the casualties. He didn't ask questions as I checked each corpse to see if I recognized him among the bodies we buried. I didn't.

The Tennessee River ran thick with blood and debris, and men around me began to fall ill from infection, dysentery, or sheer exhaustion. Jessup did his best to keep the commissary team healthy, relying on his mother's remedies to care for them.

We were sustained by molasses hard tack and bone broth made from captured Confederate horses that were injured. Peach blossoms from the remnants of Sarah Bell's peach trees provided a nutritious tea, but no peaches would come from the orchard this year, if ever again. The family who owned the land where so many men died and ghosts now walked would be appalled at the devastation wrought on their land.

When orders came down from General Grant that we would be marching south to Corinth, I was relieved and worried. That day we surrounded the small town I had avoided in my bid to join the Union army. It lay just forty miles south, and here, the conditions grew worse. The heat of an early summer sun burned down, and was unbearable. More men became ill, including Jessup.

I ended up back in the medical tent, trying to aid the sick and provide comfort and encourage them to eat, but it was often a futile effort. Malaria and dysentery were cruel weapons.

There was no glory in war, only the gore of rot and flies and fever.

The Confederates finally withdrew, leaving us with another haunted ground we could occupy, but couldn't control.

Days later, Jessup succumbed to dysentery and died with the soldiers he served, leaving me in charge of the box of medicines from his mother's pharmacopeia, what little was left. I had enough knowledge to scavenge the countryside for what I could find, but there was little left by armies in retreat and those who advanced after them.

2: The March to Memphis

I turned fifteen on the day we marched out of Corinth, heading toward Memphis. That was also the day I was promoted to corporal. Now in charge of guarding supply lines, I realized that soldiers weren't the only ones suffering. I saw the faces of the citizens left behind, their cheeks sunken, their bellies as hollow as their eyes. Crops were burned and the fields that should have been lush and full of grain lay fallow. Men hung from trees, holding signs that declared them as traitors or spies.

In one town, I was ordered to take the Commissary unit through the houses and businesses to scavenge for whatever supplies we could find. Anything useful to an army was to be taken, as our own supplies were running low.

In one house, we encountered a woman, barely older than I was, armed with a rifle too big for her small frame to manage. But she appeared ready to defend her property at all costs. "I'm just following orders," I told her. "Stand aside. We are acting under the authority of General Ulysses S. Grant."

"He has no authority here," she said. "This is my house. My family. I protect what's mine." She raised the weapon and leveled it at me, her finger hovering over the trigger. I stared her down, our eyes locked. In another place and time, she might have been a beauty, but war had done its worst, and she looked like a faded flower, as much a victim of war as the peach blossoms at Shiloh.

"Lower your weapon, ma'am," I spoke softly. "No harm will come to your family."

"Without food and supplies, my family will starve. You got no right to bring this damned war into *my* house," she trembled as she spoke. Her finger curled around the trigger and I lifted my hand to plead with her to lower her weapon.

Before I could speak another word, a gunshot rang out, echoing through the foyer of what might have been a once-lavish home. The woman fell to the ground in a heap. I turned to see who fired, and found Captain Charles, one of the commanders of another unit, with his pistol drawn, a cloud of smoke curling from the barrel. "We don't negotiate, Corporal. Carry on."

I stood frozen, my gaze returning to the woman who lay on the floor as one of the men wrestled the gun from her hand, then riffled through her petticoats, finding a handful of bullets in the threadbare pocket of her homespun cotton dress. He groped her salaciously, and the other soldiers laughed. My lips went numb, my hands cold, but fire burned in my belly and rose into my cheeks. I clenched my fists and fought the urge to strike a higher ranking officer.

"That's enough," I snapped at the men in my command, and they paused, glaring up at me, then gave up their game and moved along.

There was almost nothing in the house of much value. What little food stores we did find were infested with worms. A barrel of pickled cucumbers in the root cellar provided the unit with a welcome snack, and even I gave into my hunger and devoured several of them.

Then I made my way upstairs, finding a door that seemed out of place blocked by a chair. I moved the chair and tried the door. It didn't give at first, and I thought for a moment I felt it tug back. I hesitated, inspecting it, then grabbed it and yanked hard. A small child tumbled into the room, and rolled into a ball in the corner, trying to hide behind a table.

Inside the void, a dark face hid, but moved into the dim light where I could see her. "We don't want no trouble, Mistah." The woman, dressed in rags with her dark hair wrapped in tattered strips of cloth, came out, and moved past me cautiously. She walked calmly over to the child, collecting him before she moved back to the attic space. She paused at the door, sending the child back into the darkness. "Take what you can find, and move along, if you please." I realized there were other children taking shelter in the attic with the servant. "Ain't nothin much, but don't matter now. We all be dead by spring, most likely."

I said nothing, and stood there a moment after she closed the door. I could hear children sniffling, as her deep warm voice tried to calm them. Then, I moved the chair back in front of the door and went back down stairs.

"Leave it," I said to the men in my unit as they bundled up what little they found to take. "It's infested. We don't need to contaminate the rest of our stores."

If they wanted to argue with me, they didn't. "We need to bury this woman before we move on. Private, form a burial detail. Put her in the back yard."

"Yes, sir."

We wintered over in Memphis, and in that time, I grew even thinner. I missed Auntie Phaedra's cooking, and wondered how my mother and sisters were doing. I'd written letters home but had received nothing in return. I could only assume they considered me the enemy.

I had no idea where my brother was stationed or if I might encounter him in combat. I dreaded the thought, and could only hope he was fighting somewhere to the north. It would be cold there, but it would be less miserable than the lice-infested barracks where the Union Army awaited the coming spring. It snowed the night before Christmas, and one of the reconnoiter teams returned from the woods with a moonshine still they'd found, along with crates of glass jugs of homemade liquor.

I'd never been one to drink, but the Lieutenant Colonel ordered the booze be distributed among the men, calling it a Christmas Gift from the Rebels. If we'd been attacked Christmas morning, the war would have been over. None of us were fit to stand, much less brandish a weapon. Fortunately, the liquor didn't last long, and word of it never reached General

Grant, who didn't imbibe except on extremely rare occasions and only in moderation.

In early January, I became ill with influenza. Dr. Reeves tended me in the medical tent, where the fireplaces were stoked almost all night and all day, the firewood rationed as dry lumber became scarce in the winter rains that blanketed Tennessee. For a number of days, I thought I might be dying. A week into it, I was sure I *wanted* to die. I burned with a fever that left my head throbbing. Wracked with coughing fits that doubled me over, my body ached.

One night, in a fit of delirium, I managed to crawl out of my bunk and slip out of the tent into the snowy night. One of the guards found me laying in a snow drift and called on the medics to collect me.

The next morning, my fever broke. Two more weeks passed before I was strong enough to be dismissed from medical. Back in my barracks, I noticed a number of bunks were empty. "Where's Private Simpson?" I asked.

"Deserted," Corporal McNabb said. "Absent without leave. And he's not the only one. There isn't any food, no water. What are we supposed to do? Hang around here and wait to die? Half tempted to go home myself."

"What will happen if they catch you?"

"Shoot me, or string me up, depending on whether or not they wanna waste a bullet or a length of rope," he whispered. "Best not to think about it."

He must have thought about it, because McNabb was gone the following morning. I hated him for being a deserter, but I prayed for him to make it home safely. That's all any of us wanted. For me, however, the job wasn't done.

Fortunately, General Grant agreed. The next objective for our unit was the Vicksburg Campaign. After wintering over around Memphis, we began the push south, along the river.

Just after dark on the tenth day of our march, Confederate troops made a desperate attempt to raid our supply lines. We were already starving, but the worst of it was seeing the devastation as both sides tried to burn out the other, destroying farms and crops in their wake. I lost three of my men in the skirmish, and took a bullet in my upper arm before we repulsed the Rebels.

Medics carried me back to camp where I was stripped of my coat and shirt. They wrapped my wounded arm in strips of linen bandages—most likely torn from the clothing of the dead—and left me to lie on a litter in the cold. The shivering sent shockwaves of pain through my arm, and finally someone had the mercy to cover me with a tattered blanket.

"You're lucky," Reeves said, tending to my injuries in the aftermath. "A few inches to the right and it'd hit you in the chest."

"Don't feel lucky at the moment," I winced as he probed for the bullet.

"Hold him," he instructed the assistant. It was bad enough having the doctor cutting in to find the bullet, but to be held down while he did it was brutal. Finally, he announced he'd gotten it, and I glanced up as he held up the bloody ball, much larger than I expected it to be.

I didn't remember passing out, but when I came to, I was burning with fever, once again. I heard the doctor talking about infection and debating amputation, and in my delirium the memories of seeing other soldiers butchered under the guise of saving their lives came flooding back. I decided there was no way I was going to lay still—or worse, be held down—while he cut off my arm.

When I found myself alone, I rolled out of the cot and managed to get to my feet, swaying as the world spun around me. I found a coat in a pile of uniforms in the corner. There was no way I could get my injured arm into it. I had the blanket over my shoulders, and struggled to pull the coat over it. Then, I slipped off into the cold night and staggered from the hospital tent, bypassing patrols and anyone who might stop me.

I don't know how long I walked, but it was near dawn when I finally decided I could go no further. The woods were quiet, unnaturally so, but I found shelter under a stand of sand plums. I collapsed there. Either I would die below the plum blossoms, or the fever would run its course. At this point, either would be a relief.

In and out of delirium, I heard the voice of my mother calling to me. I envisioned Auntie Phaedra bringing me soup and mopping my brow with cool water. "Auntie, have you ever dreamed of being free?" I asked her.

"Dreamin' ain't never did nobody no good," she said. "Ain't nobody free. Even you."

Her words resonated with me in and out of the fevered dreams. I was as much a servant to a war as she was in my mother's kitchen. Damn this war! I prayed to God I would see it end, and to see Phaedra and the others freed.

There were those who said the charge that the South went to war to preserve slavery was a slanderous accusation. But in my mind, that was the only reason for this whole conflict. Even within my own home, the debate had raged in the days leading up to the war. My brother supported it, and didn't see the problem with it. When I spoke out against him, he glared at me and said, "I don't see you out picking cotton in the fields, but if you have your way, we'll both be out there breaking our backs to keep this farm afloat."

Yes, my own family contributed to the problem. We relied on the economy of slavery, our plantation ran on forced labor, and I seemed to be the only one who hated the whole concept. I loved Auntie Phaedra, probably more than my own mother. She made sure I was fed, and she was the one I was sent to when I fell and scraped my knee. I thought she loved me as much as I loved her, but I was coming to realize that probably wasn't true. She just did what she had to do to stay alive. Her plight was better than the others who toiled under my father's thumb. He was not a kind task master to those who worked our fields. Cotton and corn were our primary crops, but we also grew wheat, oats, sweet potatoes, and peas. There were hogs and cattle as well as chickens, and my mother was most proud of her peach and apple orchards.

Our farm wasn't the biggest, but our family never went hungry. We had nice clothes and our family donated money to build the local church in town, enough to get our name on the brass plaque over the door. I was more than willing to work the land, if I ever made it home.

Home. It seemed like such a distant concept. I'd been gone over a year, and now, the fear of never seeing home again was ever-present in the back of my mind. I had plenty of time to think about home, and war, and contemplate Death there in the thicket. I should have died, but the fever broke and the burning fire in my arm abated.

When I had the strength, I made it to a small spring where clean cool water bubbled up from the ground and I drank as much as I could manage. Once my thirst was sated, the issue of food became the next priority. It was too early in the season for sand plums, but I found a patch of wild strawberries that were ripe, and I feasted. I couldn't remember a strawberry ever tasting so good.

I found wild amaranth and persimmons that were edible, and I gathered as much as I could carry, using the blanket as a bag. I knew I would be in trouble when I returned to camp, but I had nowhere else to go. I could only hope that the ravages of fever and fear of being permanently maimed would be enough to earn me some mercies.

I wasn't wrong. I reported to Dr. Reeves who looked at me like he'd seen a ghost. Then he took my arm and led me to his surgery, but I protested. "You're not taking my arm."

"It's probably gone gangrenous," he said. "You could be dead in a week."

"Then they'll bury me in one piece," I stated. "You're not taking my arm."

He shook his head, and promptly peeled me out of the coat and took off the bandages. He was quiet for a long moment before he put a hand on my chest. "I'm not going to take your arm." Those were the sweetest words I'd ever heard. "But you have to be the luckiest bastard in Grant's army. No gangrene. No blood poisoning. You may not be able to use it for a while, but it's not going to kill you."

"Thank God."

I rejoined the Commissary Unit a week later, and no one said anything about me being a deserter. For all I knew, my commanders thought I'd been in the medical tent the whole time. What genuinely surprised me was the reception I got from the men in my unit. They hailed me a hero and said I led a courageous defense against the enemy, taking out a half dozen Rebel forces armed only with my uncle's knife. I didn't remember killing anyone, and I had no idea what happened to my knife.

Word must have reached the General because I was summoned to his tent a few days later. Private Spencer brought me a clean uniform and an ewer of water so I could wash up before reporting, and once properly attired, I went to find the General by the fire outside his tent. There was no coffee, as we hadn't seen any since before Christmas, but a cup of steaming tea perfumed the air.

"Corporal Thomas P. Childers, reporting as ordered," I spoke to his aide and stood at attention and waited to be addressed.

"Come join me by the fire, son." The General spoke in a deep voice. I locked eyes with the aide, who tilted his head toward the head of the Union Army, indicating I should follow his command. "Have a seat."

I sat down on the crate across from him, sitting stock straight, not sure what to expect. "I understand you were injured in the raid on our supply wagons a few weeks back."

Had it been that long ago? "Yes, sir. Took a Confederate bullet in the arm."

"And how is it mending?"

"Quite well," I said, swallowing hard. "Dr. Reeves is a skilled physician." Neither statements were lies. I could never lie to a General, least of all *the* General.

"Your men said you saved our supplies, and probably many of their lives."

"Did we lose anyone, sir?"

"Nine wounded, including yourself, but no one died. No inventory lost, I might add."

"That's good," I said, not sure what else I could say. "I don't need to tell you. Hard times aren't over. We're down to a handful of rice and peas for each man per day. Drinking water is being rationed, too.

"I found a spring," I added. "It's not far. Near a thicket of sand plums."

The General looked me straight in the eye for the first time. "Sergeant, form a detail. Take every container we have. Bring back as much water as you can."

I stood there a moment, confused. Was he talking to me? I was just a corporal. "What are you waiting for, a medal? Sergeant Childers, go resupply the water."

"But, I'm ... I'm just a Corporal."

"Not anymore," Grant said, waving to his aide. "Get this boy some stripes. I'm promoting him to Sergeant."

"Yes, sir," the aide nodded.

"One more thing," the General stood and went to a trunk. "I believe this belongs to you." He returned my Uncle's knife. "You may need it yet again." He laid it in my hand, patting my uninjured shoulder as he did.

"Thank you, sir."

If I thought the promotion was a gift, I was sorely mistaken. We made camp in the spring of 1863 in a place called Hard Times, Louisiana. A month before my sixteenth birthday, I marched with the infantrymen to rendezvous with the Union navy, in the hopes they had supplies. They didn't have much more than we did, but we had to make do until steamboats could bring more supplies.

On the night of April 15th, our army marched south through Louisiana as part of the Union fleet, commanded by Rear Admiral David Dixon Porter, prepared to run by the Vicksburg batteries. We took to the water just after 9:15 pm, with our engines muffled and lights extinguished. As our boats rounded DeSoto Point, we were spotted by Confederate lookouts who sounded the alarm. Bales of cotton soaked in turpentine and barrels of tar lining the shore were set afire by the Rebels taking away the cover of darkness we'd hoped to protect us.

The miasma of burning cotton, turpentine, and tar was made even more nauseating as they fired upon us. The vessels, including the one I took cover in, were riddled with bullets as we were bombarded. Still, we fought to make our way past the Confederate batteries.

Blinded by smoke and desperate for a breath of fresh air, I was shuttered as our steamer was struck repeatedly and began listing badly. "Abandon ship!" I heard the order go out, but in all the confusion, I wasn't aware that it was directed at me specifically. I watched as my shipmates rose from their hiding spots and leapt over the port side of the vessel.

"Sergeant Childers," one of my men grabbed me by the lapels and hoisted me to my feet. "Abandon ship, sir!"

The boat was on fire, and I hadn't even realized it. One minute I was dodging flames, the next, I was fighting against the current of the murky Mississippi River. It wasn't like I couldn't swim. I'd played in rivers and ponds all over Tippah County, but none of our rivers were anything like this. I found myself underwater, struck by debris and flotsam, presumably from my own supply ship. I fought the current, trying to get my head above water. My body screamed for oxygen and my arm, still recovering from taking a bullet a month or so before, ached with the effort as I clawed the debris trying to gain a hold that would get me a breath of air.

One moment, I was swimming toward the surface... the next, it felt like I was being dragged down. Before I knew it, I couldn't tell which way was up or down. Just as I was certain I could endure no more, a hand grabbed me and hoisted me to the surface. The would-be rescuer lost his grip and I plunged into the dark waters. That was my only chance at survival, I was sure of it. My young life flashed before my eyes once again. I'd faced death beneath the sand plum thicket, now I faced it beneath waters of the Mississippi River.

"Childers," a voice brought me from the darkness. "This is the second time you've outfoxed ol' Nick." I forced my eyes open and realized I was laying on the deck of one of the supply ships. There was no more gunfire. No more smoke. Only Dr. Reeves kneeling beside me. "I believe you must have been born under a lucky star."

"What happened?"

"Corporal Stewart pulled you out of the river," he said. "You looked like a drowned muskrat, but then you coughed up the water and took a breath. Stewart and the men started calling you the *Soldier Who Wouldn't Die*."

"I'm very much relieved to still be alive."

"Don't get too used to it," Major Goodwin appeared over the doctor's shoulder. "We're going to lay siege to Grand Gulf and make our move on Vicksburg as soon as we can get there."

Grand Gulf was the first battle we lost. It was too well defended, and we suffered heavy damage in the attempt. Moving an army wasn't an easy task, even with boats to cross the river. General Grant had no choice but to continue on to find a more favorable crossing.

We made it at Bruinsburg, under cover of dark, unopposed. It opened wide the path to Vicksburg.

Vicksburg wasn't just one battle, though. It was an intense campaign to draw out the nail that held the South's two halves together. The town sat on high bluffs overlooking the great bend of the Mississippi River.

Instead of a frontal attack, General Grant utilized multiple approaches. We began digging canals to bypass the rebel artillery attacks. It was dangerous work, and until we dug deep enough into the red clay, we were targets for the enemy. I watched with horror as one after another, the men in my detail were picked off. By the time we got to the end of the canal, we had to turn around and retrieve the bodies. Then began the burial details.

Then we marched the swamps trying to maneuver around to more favorable positions, but the Rebels knew the territory better than we did, and they took advantage of our weaknesses. We lost men not only to Confederate snipers, but alligators and snakes.

For eighteen months we maneuvered troops to split the South in two, to sever vital Confederate supply lines, and to effectively doom the Confederacy. We'd tried everything that didn't work, but once the General had the enemy figured out, he began the march inland, cutting off the Confederate reinforcements. We fought and won five battles between Port Gibson, Raymond, Jackson, Champion Hill, and Black River, just to reach the gates of Vicksburg. That's where the real siege began.

Here, we began a campaign of starvation and demoralization. I watched the General from my post as Union artillery and gunboats pounded the city day and night. The trenches crept closer each week as we began tunnelling to try and breach the Confederate fortifications.

Our forces now held the entire Mississippi River and supplies for our troops were easier to obtain. We didn't have the finest cuisine, but we were fed twice a day, and the doctors had medicine and medical supplies to treat the wounded.

It didn't make life easy. Night bombardments shook the ground like thunder, and I slept in the trenches with the smell of rot permeating my psyche. I dreamt my brother was behind the stockades. I could envision him coming over the wall, charging me with our father's pistols drawn. His bullets pierced my flesh and the horror of his wild eyes haunted me as he came to finish me off. He considered me a traitor, and I supposed I deserved that, but I felt I had the moral high ground.

One night as I was on tunnel detail, deep beneath the war raging above with little more than a small oil lamp to light my way, the soil ahead of me began to collapse. I heard the crying of a child as the muddy face of a woman appeared in the candlelight. Her face was caked in mud, but her blue eyes were bright in the lamplight. She stopped when we locked eyes, and I realized she had an infant in a sling on her back. Her hands were caked in mud, her clothing just as filthy. I had my knife in my hand, and I raised it, ready to strike, but I froze.

I remembered the woman in Memphis, trying to defend her children, her property. I remembered her lifeless eyes as I carried her out of the house and laid her in her grave. I had watched as the detail tossed dirt over her. I had said a prayer under my breath, as much for my own soul as for hers. I wanted to think I could have saved her, but I hadn't been the one to pull the trigger. Maybe I could save this one.

I reached over with my knife and began cutting in a new tunnel for her, "Go this way, it'll take you past the road to the north. Dig until you hit rock then come up, and hope you're far enough away to avoid the Union Army."

Tears ran through the mud on her face as she thanked me softly, and made the turn, continuing on, leaving me with a direct route to her hiding place. The bunker she'd been hiding in had collapsed in her wake, and I only assumed she'd done it on purpose.

That night I dreamed about her eyes, about the child strapped to her back. I dreamed of mothers dying to protect their infants, buried in collapsed tunnels, shot by Union soldiers, molested by faceless men who laughed at their own savagery. The dreams became the nightmares that haunted my waking visions as well. I dreamt of children with swollen bellies, hungry for even a scrap of bread. I had known hunger and the familiar ache of it. I knew the fear of war and the agony of taking a life. I fought alongside my fellow soldiers knowing that if I didn't kill my enemy, they would not hesitate to kill me. I still dreamt of my brother, and feared for him. If he wasn't in this battle, he was in one somewhere else, if he still lived and breathed.

Maybe it was the not knowing that did me in. I'd have given anything for a letter from my mother or sisters. Just to know if the farm survived, if my brother survived, if life continued in Tippah County or if the war had come to our doorsteps—if my family still had a roof over their heads, or even a single ear of corn in the fields.

The morning of July 4, 1863 dawned hot and still; by afternoon the air was stifling, full of powder and the smell of the wounded. There had been a brief thunder-shower the day before that washed the dust from the trenches and left the air thick and close. Our uniforms clung to us like second skin, and even the river seemed sluggish.

As the days turned into months, the horrors of war grew. The stench of death was a constant companion and it wasn't until the gunfire and bombardments ended that I realized what silence felt like. Rumors began to spread between men, spoken at first in whispers and then with hopeful expectations. Were the Rebels going to surrender?

We were summoned to the front lines and ordered to muster our lines behind General Grant at a spot called the Third Louisiana Redan, a ravine that had seen brutal fighting in the earlier weeks. After brushing off the dirt and mud from my uniform, washing my face and hands, and running a damp cloth over my weapon, I reported as ordered, ensuring my men were as presentable as possible.

Just before 8:00 am, General John C. Pemberton rode out to meet General Grant as we stood in formation behind him. The two men met under an old oak tree. Pemberton wore his full dress uniform—proud to the last—while Grant appeared as I had never seen him before. He was rumpled, but unceremonial as usual. They spoke briefly, discussing terms of surrender.

Pemberton wanted his men paroled. Grant, aware that holding 30,000 prisoners would strain our resources, agreed. They shook hands and returned to their own lines. We stood in rank-and-file order until the buglers sounded along the siege lines. We marched into Vicksburg, but rather than being greeted with cheers, we were met with silence. Gaunt, hollow-eyed defenders stacked their rifles in neat piles, and many of the men collapsed as they walked away.

Old Glory was raised above the courthouse, and I'm sure it was a slap in the face of the already broken Rebels, some who sat in silence, others weeping, some too numb to feel anything at all.

I realized that this is what victory looked like, but it didn't feel triumphant. It was Independence Day, but the air smelled of death, not freedom. The gray men laid down their rifles. "Can we not at least offer them a morsel of food, sir?" one of the commissary men asked me. "They must be starved."

I reached into my own pack, and drew out a cotton flour sack filled with hard tack. "Start with this," I said. "I'll talk to command."

3: Discharged

In the months that followed the Confederate surrender at Vicksburg, I was given the rank of *Acting* Lieutenant, though it was an unofficial appointment. It wasn't because I earned it, but because there was no one left. The stripes were stitched onto a jacket that still smelled of the man who'd worn it before me—his blood dried into the seams. I haphazardly stitched up the bullet holes myself.

My commanding officer called me *steady under fire*. Truth was, I'd gone cold. Numb. I could load and shoot and march and bury without thinking, which made me useful. Small-boned and long, I was the perfect tunnel rat, though I never mentioned the woman and child I helped escape. I never saw her again.

When they told me I was being discharged, I felt nothing at all. Only the weight of home pressing down on me, like a grave waiting to be filled. I seriously considered reenlisting, though by all rights I'd done more than my share for the Union Army. I'd battled the *grippe* as well as *swamp fever* that still came on from time to time unexpectedly. I'd been shot and nearly died of fever in the aftermath. I'd killed more men than I could count. I was complicit when women and children were murdered or starved so the armies could eat.

Could I go home after what I'd done? Would my family forgive me? I had a long journey home to pray for reconciliation. The war was over. Now was the time to make peace, and by God, I would certainly try. I had nowhere else to go.

Major Bennett printed out my discharge papers, then handed them to me. I studied the paperwork, noting the remarks on my character. *Attentive to duty. Exemplary under fire. Steady. Sober and obedient. Courageous beyond his years.* Bennett must have known what caught my eye. "General Grant instructed me to include that last one."

"Thank you sir." My eyes went to the next line. "Discharged for disability contracted in the line of duty."

"You're sending me home because I have malaria?" I asked, not expecting that. I assumed the Army was done with me. I was more than ready to be done with it.

"You'll be eligible for a soldier's pension," Bennett said. "That and the disability caused by the bullet in your arm. You just need to stop by the medical tent and have Dr. Reeves sign your medical discharge forms."

Something else at the bottom of the paper caught my eye. Right next to a smudge of ink where someone hesitated before writing, it said, *unfit for duty*. I felt the blood in my face drain into my boots.

"It's no mark against your character, son. You may have been a strong young lad when you enlisted, but the war has taken its toll. This *swamp fever* will be something you carry with you your whole life. With any luck, and proper doctoring, your years may be many. Focus on the top of the page."

My eye went to the beginning. "Discharged with Honor."

"Nothing for you to be ashamed about. You answered when your country needed you. Now, go home and take your much needed rest." He sat back down and reached into a metal box, and took out a handful of coins. "I'm issuing you a month's pay in silver," he told me, "along with a note of credit for the back pay you are owed. You are also allowed to take a horse from the stable, and any supplies you need for the journey."

"When can I leave?"

"Whenever you want," he answered. "I'd recommend you take your leave as soon as you can. It's a long trip back to Ripley, and you'll want to see home before winter arrives."

Then, the Captain did something I never expected. He rose, standing at attention, and saluted me. "You're a good soldier, Childers. It's been an honor to serve with you."

Stunned, I somehow managed to straighten and return a proper salute. It probably wasn't by-the-book for him to do that, but for that one brief moment, I felt like what I'd done mattered. That there was a purpose for it. That somehow, I'd made a difference in the war.

The euphoria didn't last long.

I left early the following morning, taking the best horse offered to me, with a bed roll and saddlebags full of food. Thirteen dollars in silver, a month's wage for a Lieutenant. At least if I had to pay the boatman to row me across the River Styx, I'd have a coin to pay him. I thought a lot about the story of Odysseus as the road slowly passed by. I passed other ghosts—soldiers— like me. Wandering restless spirits in search of a mythical land known as *home*.

The scars of war blanketed the south. I passed what must have been mansions laid to ruin, fields burned and left fallow. The cries of the Furies haunted my dreams as I bedded down in the remains of a half-collapsed barn. The smell of acrid smoke lingered in my nose night and day.

I came to realize that war was a labyrinth—twisting, impossible—filled with darkness. But I was not Odysseus. I was Theseus, sent to slay the Minotaur. The beast had fallen, the war won, but the battle was not yet over.

The October sun hung heavy over Tippah County as I made the turn towards home. The golden orb cast long shadows along the red-clay lane that led to my family farm. My boots were worn clear through, my horse having been abandoned weeks before when it went lame on the road from Vicksburg. Despite the season, the day was warm, and dust clung to my sweat-soaked collar. The last perfume of honeysuckle and smoke drifted from the barren fields. If there had been a harvest, there was no sign of it now.

As I came around the curve to the house, I could see a man sitting in the old cane-bottom chair. His hat tipped low. Holman Childers—older by two years, sat with a wool blanket over his lap. He looked gaunt, his coat hanging on shoulders and I glanced down at my own coat, my hand wiping away dust as I paused, swallowing hard.

"Well, I'll be damned," he said, rising slowly. I recognized immediately something was wrong. He took a staggering step forward, leaning on the rail as he leveled his gaze at me. "If it ain't my little brother, come home from fightin' on the wrong side."

I stopped at the gate, gripping the post to steady myself. I'd been dreading this moment since the morning I left home. "Ain't no right side in hell, Holman. Just men dying for no good reason."

He spat in my general direction, his brow furrowed. He looked like our father more now that the war had aged him. "You got a lot of nerve showin' up here in the colors of the enemy."

"The war's over, Holman. Let it end."

"You turned your back on your kin, your land. Your mother. You think you can come back here and we'd welcome you back? Your damned Yankee army burned our fields, took all the livestock, left your mother and sisters to starve."

I could see the stubborn expression of the woman in Memphis, defending her home and her children. My mother could have that same determined look. But then I saw the blue eyes of the woman in the trench, frightened, desperate. She reminded me of Ellie Belle, my little sister.

"I took a bullet to defend my home," Holman continued while I gazed into the eyes of ghosts.

"You fought for a lie. For men who keep others in chains and call it honor," I said, not sure where the words came from, then remembered something General Grant had said. "War is a cruel thing, brother. Let us have peace. Here. Now."

Holman's face darkened, jaw tight. "You don't know nothin' about honor."

"I know it ain't measured by the color of a coat, or the color of a man's skin," I lowered my voice. "I seen the price of hate. You just paid for it with a limp. Some men paid with their souls."

The air was thick with swirling leaves and tension. Then Holman reached under his coat for the pistol he still wore on his hip. His eyes went black as night, and I could see the darkness that reached into his soul. "Best keep walkin', Tom." His voice shook. "Before I do somethin' I'll regret."

"You already have," I said. I could see that darkness spreading through him.

I heard the shot as it rang across the valley—sharp, final. I didn't feel the bullet, only the force of it as it hit me in the center of the chest and sent me staggering backwards. I saw the spray of blood—my blood—and heard Holman's boots coming down the stairs. Somehow, I kept to my feet.

Holman limped toward me, breathing hard. One minute I was staring into those wicked eyes, the next, I lay flat on my back, gazing up as golden yellow stars swirled around me. The leaves of the sweet gum tree we climbed as children reminded me of the peach blossoms outside the meeting house at Shiloh. My brother's shadow fell over me as he knelt beside me, hate and sorrow twisting his features.

"You shoulda stayed gone," he growled.

I found our uncle's blade in my hand, and without thinking, I struck. My hand moved slow, steady, the knife flashing in the sun. The blade found its mark. Holman gasped, clutching his side, surprise washing over his face.

From the porch came a scream—our mother's voice, raw and breaking. "Stop it! Both of you! For the love of God!"

But it was too late.

Holman collapsed beside me, our blood—the same color—blended on the red-clay Mississippi dirt, and the war was at last over. The last thing I saw was my mother's face, damp with tears. She cried my name and pleaded with me not to die. "I've been waiting so long for you. Tom. Don't leave me again."

"I tried, Mama," I gasped, hearing the gurgling in my chest. "For peace."

In every battle, there comes a time when both sides consider themselves beaten; then, he who continues the attack wins. The words of General Ulysses S. Grant would never be engraved on my tombstone.

My mother, however, being the wise woman that she was, ensured my stone spoke of my legacy.

Lt. Thomas Pleasant Childers
Beloved Son & Brother
Born May 16, 1847
Died October 30, 1864
He fought for the Union, and for what he believed was right.
He fought the good fight, finished the course, and kept the faith. —2 Tim. 4:7

My brother, beside me, even in death, was no less memorialized.

Corporal Holman Fletcher Childers
Beloved Son & Brother
Born October 1, 1845
Died October 30, 1864
He fought for the South, and the home he loved.
Judge not, that ye be not judged. —Matthew 7:1

Line of Succession

MYTHOLOGICAL REIMAGINING BY JB CAINE

"What are you talking about? Where is his body?" Grief raged through me like a storm. Orin couldn't be dead. Seth had to be lying.

"We couldn't get it out of the mine shaft, Isa. Not without sending someone else into the rattlers' nest. Somehow, he must not have noticed the rotted boards ..."

"It's absurd and you know it. Orin would have smelled a snake nest of that size." Even in human form, shifters have excellent senses. Whether he was in his human skin or his wolf pelt, he would not have missed the stench, and probably not the sound either. It wasn't quite cold enough for the snakes to be hibernating yet.

"Isabeau." Seth spoke softly with great sadness in his eyes, but I wasn't buying it. This was all one of his elaborate tricks. It had to be. "I wish it were untrue. No one mourns my brother's death more than I do."

He laid his hand on my shoulder, and I shook it off, wailing in my loss. "Do you think I'm a fool? You hated him. He was too tender-hearted to see it, but ..."

"You wound me, Isa. Never would I wish harm on my brother."

"We both know that isn't true. So does half the clan."

"You Sky People. Always looking for the invisible. You know I adored Orin, and I never begrudged him his good fortune. I supported him as Clan Leader, just as I will support you as his mate until a new Clan Leader is chosen."

I stared at him, venom in my eyes just as potent as what Seth claimed had killed the love of my life. I placed my hand on my belly, only barely swollen with Orin's and my first child. "If you loved him so much, where are your tears?" I spat as my own flowed freely down my cheeks. "Where is your mourning? And how dare you leave his body behind to rot in a hole rather than to be buried properly by his clan?"

A fresh wave of hysteria bowled me over, and I found myself on my knees. He's lying. Orin's alive and being held somewhere. The thought gave me the thinnest sliver of hope.

"We tried, Isa. We did. But there was no way to pull him from the pit without endangering more of us. He would not have wanted us to lose another clanmate just to retrieve what must already return to the earth. Please. I owe it to him to care for you and for the child." He smiled his smooth and toothy smile, and my pain morphed into rage. No doubt he thought to take Orin's place as Leader.

Grabbing onto the wispy strand of hope, I fought my way to my feet. Seth reached out a hand to steady me, but I swatted it away. "Where were you hunting?"

"In the Bighorn National Forest, near Walker Mountain. A little outside our usual hunting grounds, but not by much. Look, there are probably dozens of old mine shafts left over from the Gold Rush. It was an accident, Isa." He reached out for me again. Perhaps he wanted to claim more than just Orin's place as leader. Fear for myself and my unborn child pumped adrenaline through my system.

"You're lying!" I turned from him and fled, though I had no destination in mind. Somehow, jumping into the Jeep and driving back to our house in Sheridan seemed impossible. Staying here at the clan's lodge seemed equally impossible. All I wanted was to have my husband back, and I didn't know where on Earth I could make that happen.

I had to start with the tiny light of possibility which had pulled me from my agony. Maybe he wasn't dead at all. By his own admission, neither Seth nor the other two members of the hunting party had gone into the viper pit to try and save Orin. Perhaps he had just been unconscious. It was all I had to hold onto.

Wyoming is rough to travel in by car. Not so much because of the condition of the roads, though sometimes that was an issue, but more because there were so few roads compared to other places. It's what made it ideal for our little shifter community to live safely and undetected among the humans. Privacy took the form of vast plains, dense evergreen forests, and craggy mountains. No, if I wanted to get to Walker Mountain quickly, I needed to fly.

I stretched out my arms and summoned the ancestral spirits of the Sky People, giving them a prayer of honor, and shivered as the feathers burst forth and covered my shrinking form. I leapt into the sky and gave an owlish cry as I soared into the fading daylight, just one more owl on the hunt.

It was late into the night when I reached the cabin our clan owned on the outskirts of the National Forest. It was yet another practical choice on our part ... all sorts of animals made their homes in the National Forests of the Rockies, and having easy access to federal land meant vast areas where any shifter could run free with minimal chance of encountering a human. In our animal forms, we hunted in the National Forests as well as in and out of hunting season, making it easier to avoid the risks of human hunters and their guns.

I called back my human skin, retrieved the key from its hiding place, and let myself into the well-provisioned cabin. It was evident that Seth and the others had recently been here, and I closed my eyes and wept at the thought that only the memory of his scent would remain before long. My human nose was far better than my avian one, and soon this last sense of him would be gone. But no! I couldn't afford such thoughts until I had proof he was dead.

I opened a can of soup and ate it cold, lacking the energy to cook it but knowing I needed the nourishment, and so did the tiny life growing in my belly. When I finished the soup, I found the bunk where Orin had slept, and crawled beneath the woolen blanket, wrapping myself in the traces of his scent. I cried myself to sleep, praying to the Old Gods that my hope was not in vain.

A few short hours later, I woke as the first light of dawn crept across the floorboards of the cabin. Now the search could begin in earnest. Forcing myself to eat an entire tin of canned peaches, I planned my search. A small desk sat in the corner of the cabin with pens, paper, matches, candles, and—perhaps most importantly—a map of the region.

I surveyed the area and devised a search pattern, cursing my owl form because it was no good for tracking the scents of the hunting party. Oh, to be a wolf like Orin! I would have to rely on sharp eyesight to try and find the mineshaft with the broken boards, but I had a sizable area to search.

I began my search in the town of Wolf, because there was an outfitters shop where our clan often went if they were hunting in human form. It was also close enough that I could drive the ATV, which looked like the offspring of a golf cart and a pick-up truck. As an owl, I would not need such things, but as an owl, I would not be able to ask questions or gather clues.

"Can I, uh, help you, miss?" The young clerk in Wild Side Provisions eyed me with a mix of suspicion and alarm. How wild and desperate I must have looked with my puffy eyes and haggard appearance!

"I hope so," I began, trying to calm my voice somewhat so he wouldn't suggest I call the police with my inquiry. "My family came through town on a hunting trip a few days ago, and I was hoping to catch up with them. Four men. Two of them were a little above six feet, and two of them were maybe a little shorter ..."

He interrupted before I could finish my description. "Yeah, I saw 'em. Not from around here. They sorta stood out, even though we do get a few outsiders once elk season opens."

"Stood out? In what way?"

"Oh, I dunno. Mostly when folks come through, they're jokin' and joshin'. But your bunch seemed downright stern. Guess they're pretty serious about huntin'."

"I suppose they are. Did they happen to say anything about where they might be hunting?"

The young man scratched his peach fuzz of a beard and thought about it. "I don't reckon they did. The tall brown-haired one, though, he bought a prospector's map. I remember because we sold a few of those in the summer, but it's been a while. Hunters usually aren't too interested in searching for mines and whatnot. It might be a little early to stumble into a den of bears hibernatin', but you can't be too careful, you know?"

"Of course. Was there a lot of prospecting around here?" What was Seth up to, buying a prospecting map? Perhaps looking for a place to hide his brother?

"A fair bit, sure. Especially over into the Park, around Walker and She-Bear Mountains. Not easy going, but the hunting would probably be pretty good out that way. You'd have to go off the Prairie Trail, but once you get into the hills ..." He shrugged, indicating he didn't have a lot more information for me. "I don't think I'd head out to that area alone, though, miss. If they're out that way, you aren't likely to find 'em just on happenstance."

"I'm sure you're right. I'll keep looking around and see if I can figure out where they chose to stay. They might even be camping. Do you happen to have any more of those maps?"

The young man sold me one, and I looked over it as I gassed up the ATV. It was meant to be more of a novelty with historical information than an actual guide to the area, but I suspected it was sufficient for what Seth had in mind. I mentally noted areas that looked most promising for mining.

With each passing hour, I was more sure my brother-in-law had had nefarious intentions from the outset. He had seemed to support

Orin as Clan Leader to the public eye, but privately, he often criticized and belittled my mate, hinting that Orin's live-and-let-live attitude belied weakness. A handful in the clan shared this view and believed it was more natural for us to be ruled by strength rather than led in peace.

I folded the map and put it in the glove compartment of the ATV. I checked the other gear I had brought: rope, an oilskin tarp, water, a sleeping bag, a first aid kit, and a smoke flare. Then I fired up the ATV and headed south/southwest toward Walker Mountain and the Prairie Trail. I drove as far as I could on established trails, then pulled the vehicle off into some dense trees and prepared to take to the sky to further my search.

I called forth my feathers and lit into the sky. I couldn't fly too high, since I wanted to be able to search well, but it would be much faster than searching on foot. Mid-day was an unusual time for humans to see an owl, to be sure, but my presence in this form would do little more than raise an eyebrow or garner a photo on someone's phone. Besides, the sun would set around 5:00, so I had to make the most of my time.

My eyes were focused mostly on the ground, but I couldn't help noticing the already-snow-capped crags of Cloud Peak to my south, rising high out of the ocean of trees. Small prairies nestled themselves among lower mountains, bursts of light green amid the deep and varied shades of spruce, pine, and fir, dotted with the occasional aspens, their leaves glimmering like gold in the autumn sun. In some other time, I would be inspired and awed by the beauty around me, but today, I sought a lone figure or a hole with broken boards at its mouth.

The day wore on and I fought the rising wave of hopelessness as the futility of such a task began to set in. Once, I felt a flare of hope when I spotted a lone hiker, but when I saw the long black braids on either side of his backpack, my heart broke yet again. It was entirely possible Seth had completely lied about where Orin had been lost, knowing full well that I would insist on finding him. It was nearly 3:00, with the shadows lengthening along the eastern ridges before I found what I sought.

Just west of the mountain, near a rocky outcropping circled by lodgepole pines and Douglas firs, the setting sun revealed an irregularity in the landscape. I swooped in to investigate and found a squarish hole framed with logs that were riddled with dry rot. Immediately, I realized that, if this was the shaft entrance I'd been looking for, there was no way Orin would have accidentally fallen into that darkness. Not only were the logs resting very visibly above ground, but it had been at least partially boarded over. He could not have missed the sight of it.

I crept to the edge of the chasm and peered within, my strigine eyes cutting through the shadows. I spied a human-like form below, and my heart thumped within my chest. It would not be an easy descent, even for my avian form, as owls were not built for diving into close-quartered caverns, but hope propelled me forward.

Nearly thirty feet down, I dug my talons into the layer of dirt covering the floor of the tunnel. Even my limited sense of smell detected the stench of decay over the acrid aroma of guano. An agonized *hoo-hoo-hoo-hoo* escaped me, and I wished I could screech like some of my smaller cousins.

Orin's body lay at the bottom of the shaft, limbs akimbo and neck at an alarming angle. I didn't even have the momentary respite of being able to imagine that he was simply unconscious as I took in the grisly sight. I had tried to steel myself against this, but the reality of his death shredded my very soul. If not for the life growing within me, I would have dashed myself against the rocks so I might lay beside him in death.

Even in my maelstrom of grief, I noted one thing: the complete absence of snakes.

The truth of Orin's murder—and murder it was—lodged itself within me. If he had fallen by accident, there would have been no issue in retrieving his body. No, that was not what had happened. If he had been alive when he stood at the mouth of the mine shaft, the fall had certainly killed him. And Seth, the lying bastard, had left my love here to rot.

Just as the sun was setting, I managed to return with the ATV and the rope, my eyes nearly swollen shut from crying. But I could not fail Orin in this last act of love and respect. I tied one end of the rope to the ATV, then shifted and flew back into the hole with the other. I was grateful now for an owl's weak sense of smell. I shifted back into human form and gently touched Orin's wavy black hair.

"Orin, I'm so sorry ..." The tears came again, and I let them flow for a moment more before screwing up my courage to do what needed to be done. Gently, I lifted Orin's head and shoulders and wound the rope under his armpits, tying a bowline knot against his back. Then I shifted again and soared back out of the hole.

I turned the key on the ATV and the engine sprung to life. Slowly, I urged it forward and away from the shaft, drawing my beloved's body out at the end of the rope. Once Orin had been pulled onto the surface, I untied both ends of the rope, laid out the oilskin tarp, and rolled the body of my beloved onto it. Then, taking my time, I wrapped him in the heavy cloth, tying seven knots tightly, offering prayers to the spirit of the Great Wolf. I was no priestess, but no prayers were ever more heartfelt.

Maneuvering his body into the passenger side of the vehicle was difficult, particularly since I was trying to be as delicate with Orin as I could. It took me nearly forty minutes, but eventually, I had him buckled in safely. I wished I had thought to bring a spare jerrycan of gas, since I would not be able to travel back through Wolf when I returned to the hunting cabin.

I had made it maybe two miles in the deepening darkness when it occurred to me that returning to the cabin might not be safe. Clearly, Seth's two cronies were loyal to him, and had agreed to cover up Orin's death. I would be a fool not to expect him to know where I had gone, and more foolish still to think he wouldn't do whatever it took to silence me. I pulled into the shelter of a few sparse trees, keeping a keen lookout for late-returning horseback riders from one of the local ranches.

Where could I possibly go? The simple answer was: Not far. At least not with Orin. I didn't want to leave him unprotected. It was only a matter of time before Seth returned to the scene of the crime, and with his lupine senses and hunting skills, he would have some ability to track me if I stayed off the paved roads. It was a conundrum, because paved roads meant more people, and an increased likelihood someone would question the wrapped figure in the seat next to me.

Taking his body to a police station was an option, but there would be so much to explain, and I couldn't risk the exposure it would bring to our clan. It was impossible to make it all the way home in the ATV ... it was just too far. And the worst part ... I wasn't sure who in our clan I could trust. Who else had been in on the plot to depose Orin as Clan Leader? Frustration and helplessness welled up within me yet again.

Think, I chided myself. *You don't have the luxury of failure.* I wracked my brain, desperately trying to come up with even one person who was privy to the shifter community and could be trusted not to call Seth if I showed up. Oh, and someone who lived within ten miles. In this terrain, and given how far I had already driven, I wouldn't make it much farther.

Then a single name came to me: Therese Worland. Her father had been a shifter, and her mother had been a Shoshone woman with a great gift for medicine. Therese had no ability to shift, but the magical blood in her veins seemed to amplify the mystical gifts her mother possessed. Therese had been a friend of Orin's father's, and had performed our Joining ceremony three years ago.

I could not bring Orin's body to her house, since it was considered tremendously bad luck in her culture. But there had to be some way she could help me. She lived outside of Dayton, only a few miles away. It would take some finesse to reach her without interacting with people, but hopefully my ancestors would watch out for me.

I headed north toward the only chance I had.

I stopped the ATV a respectful distance from Therese's house and shone the headlights toward her windows. A rustle at the curtain showed that she had noticed my presence, and I stepped out into the weak electric light that illuminated her front yard.

The door opened and a solid woman of fifty-some-odd years stood silhouetted in the light from within. "Who's there? Can't see a thing with those headlights in my eyes!" She sounded mildly annoyed, but I couldn't really blame her.

"It's Isabeau Gillette. I'm sorry to come here uninvited and so late, but something has happened, and I desperately need your help. I don't know who else I can trust." My voice broke as I spoke the last sentence and Therese moved down her front steps toward me.

"What's happened, Isa?"

I found myself unable to speak as the promise of help and safety washed over me. My knees buckled and I found myself sobbing, clutching handfuls of gravel from her driveway.

I didn't even notice her approach, but when I felt her strong arms around me, my last bit of strength ebbed away and I collapsed, unconscious, against her.

I heard the crackling of the fire before I had the will to open my eyes. Somewhere in another room, I heard the clinking of cups and the sloshing of water. I stretched out my fingers and felt rough fabric beneath me as I heard the soft padding of Therese's slippered footsteps moving closer. I forced my eyes open and found myself staring at a textured ceiling. The light from the flames gave everything a golden glow.

"Ah, good, you're back with me." Therese set down two coffee mugs with the telltale strings from tea bags hanging out of the sides. I sat up slowly, and she sat beside me, taking my hands in hers. "Is that Orin in your tiny truck?"

I nodded, unable to speak, and she sighed.

"Oh, my dear girl. Tell me what's happened."

I summed up the facts and shared what I suspected, and my heart felt hollow as a drum. "It's not safe for me to go back, but I have to find a way to warn the Clan. They must know what he's done, or they'll likely make him Clan Leader in Orin's place."

The woman nodded slowly, her mind working on the problem. She seemed to decide something. "Well, we can't leave him out in the yard, or some scavenger is likely to ... well, you know. We'll have to put him in the shed for the moment." I slanted my eyes toward her. "Don't look at me like that, Isa. I can't bring him in here. I love you both, but I can't have his ghost infecting my house. We'll put him in the shed for tonight, then tomorrow we'll take care of business. Once we're done, I'll destroy the shed so his ghost won't be trapped here."

"You've seen his ghost?"

"No, of course not. And I'd like to keep it that way. But it seems it isn't meant to be. Doesn't mean I have to keep him here, though."

I tried to work out what she was trying to say, but it made no sense. "What business are we going to take care of tomorrow?"

"Tomorrow, my dear, we ask him what happened. And then we figure out what to do about Seth. Tonight, however, you're going to drink this chamomile tea, nestle down in that fleecy blanket, and get some rest. You'll need your strength for what's coming."

The next morning, Therese woke me at sunrise. I wasn't sure how she'd managed it, but she'd crept past me, out into the yard, and dragged her gardening equipment out of the rickety wooden shed that now housed Orin's body.

"What now?" I looked at her, confused by what I was seeing.

"Now we find out exactly what happened. We only get one shot at this, but if it works, you'll have the ammunition you need to go back and depose Seth. That is what you want, yes?"

I nodded. The morning was cold, so Therese wrapped me in a parka and a blanket and directed me to sit in the lawn chair she'd pulled out from who-knows-where. She disappeared back into the house for a minute, then reappeared with a steaming cup.

"You must go on a vision quest, and if he is waiting for you, you will see Orin and get to speak to him one last time in this life. I don't know how long the vision will last, so you must not let yourself get distracted by all the things I'm sure you want to tell him. If you want answers, this is your one chance to get them."

"Why only one chance? Couldn't we do this again if it doesn't work the first time?"

"No, Isa, that's not how it works. In order for him to speak to you, I must release his ghost. He must be separated from the physical bonds that hold him here in this world so that he can move on to the Land of the Coyote."

My eyes widened, and I turned and looked at the pile of garden tools next to the house. "You mean to burn him. Burn the shed."

"It must be done. His spirit must be set free, and the building is now a tether for him."

"But that would be burning all of the evidence against Seth ..." My mind spun. I wasn't expecting a solution with such finality.

"Were you planning to take him to the human authorities? Then why did you bring him here at all?"

I tried to think clearly, and of course, she was right. It would be a huge mistake to expose our entire clan in some hope of human justice. We had to handle things our own way, as it had always been. I took a deep breath. "No, you're right. Your way is the only way."

"We must begin the ceremony before the sun has fully risen. Drink this." She handed me the cup. "I will say the necessary prayers, and when you seem to have slipped into the in-between place, I'll start the fire. Do you wish to view his body one more time?" She added the last question as an afterthought.

I shook my head. I had already seen the damaged shell of Orin that Seth had left behind. I didn't need any more memories of it. I took a deep breath and drank the hot liquid, which tasted of spices and earth. I sat back on the chair as Therese circled the shed, chanting in a language I did not know. For a moment, I thought she called my name, but as I trained my ears on her tapestry of sound, I heard the word ***bia'isa***—the Shoshone word for wolf and one of the only words in her language I knew—woven into her song. She trailed scented smoke from the bundle of herbs in her hand.

As I watched her, the scene before me began to slowly morph into a blend of colors like a watercolor painting. If I had stood enough distance away, I was sure I'd be able to make out the middle-aged woman, the shed, and the growing fire, but as it was, I only saw a mass of oranges, browns, blues, and whites.

From the center of the cloud of colors, a figure began to take shape. I didn't need the sharpness of my owl sight to recognize the form of the man who I held close to me for six years of my life, three as his lover and three as his wife. He moved forward and the details of his features took shape. I tried to rise and go to him, but my limbs would not respond.

"My sweet Isabeau. I am so sorry to leave you."

His eyes were sad, full of dreams that would never be for the two of us.

"Orin ..." My voice broke. I wanted to hold onto this vision forever, to be with him even in this place.

"You must raise our son. Tell him stories. Make sure he knows me through your love."

I wanted to wail, to cry, to protest the unfairness of the fate that had befallen us, but I also didn't want to waste these precious last few moments on wishes that would never come true.

"Tell me what happened to you, my love. Tell me what vengeance I must take."

His expression grew serious as he stood above me, his form haloed in the rising sunlight. *"Seth came to me as we waited for the deer to come, told me that Mathias had fallen into a mine shaft, and that he needed help. Of course, I followed him at once. We leaned over the edge of the hole together, and then Mathias and Evan rushed toward us and pushed me in. I don't remember anything after that except emptiness and then the hooting of an owl. I knew then that you had found me."* He smiled at me then, his eyes full of love, knowing that I had not failed him.

"Seth seeks to be Clan Leader." It wasn't a question. That had been his motive all along.

Orin nodded. *"He will destroy our Clan if left to lead it. He has no loyalty, except to his own selfish interests. The power of leading a small Clan will not satisfy him. Soon, he will lust for wider territory, even wage war with other Clans to increase what he believes he possesses. This cannot happen."*

"How can I stop him? He is stronger than I am. The Earth People are stronger than the Sky People. Even with my relatives, I cannot defeat him, especially not with others at his side."

"With the exception of Mathias and Evan, the others who follow him do so out of fear. You must give them something greater to believe in. The Earth People will follow you if you can expose and humiliate my brother."

The sun had risen so that it touched the top of his head, and something in my soul told me that our time was short.

"Is there anything else you can tell me that will help me bring justice?" Orin shook his head sadly. "Then sit with me, and we will watch one more sunrise together."

He sat on the edge of the lawn chair and took my paralyzed hands in his. "The sun can rise, but I will watch its reflection in your eyes. *"I believe in you, Isabeau. You have it within you to lead our Clan, and our son will be strong and good. My spirit will always be near you, even if you cannot see me. It will be as if I was only away on a long hunting trip, and someday you will come to join me on the hunt. Live your life knowing that your happiness and safety and that of our son is the greatest legacy I leave behind."*

Just then, one final question sprung to mind, one that I hadn't thought to ask before. "What shall I name him?"

"His name shall be Harlow, and he shall be of the Sky People like his mother." Orin's eyes overflowed with pride and love as the rays of the sun grew bright and strong, like the son he would never see. He leaned forward and kissed my forehead gently. I closed my eyes, drinking in the feeling, and when I opened them again, he was gone, lost in the rays of the sun.

The Earth People were far more gifted at cunning than the Sky People, but sometimes, cunning went hand-in-hand with wisdom, which was the Sky People's strength. I had spoken the truth to Orin ... I did not have the physical strength to battle Seth and his followers. Mathias and Evan were both Earth People, bear and fox. Most of Seth's other loyalists were likely to be Earth People, too, as Sky People rarely cared much for the philosophy of ruling by might. My best bet was to reach out to the Sky People before returning home, trying to win them over to my side and having them work amongst the remainder of the Clan to persuade whichever Earth People could be persuaded to listen.

I used Therese's phone to call my mother's people, who consisted mostly of owls and hawks. The first call I made was to my grandmother, who was far too old to fight on any side, but who was revered among the races of the Sky.

"Hello?" Her voice was cautious, probably because she didn't recognize the number that came up on her caller ID.

"Grandmother? It's Isa."

"Isa! My little one! Where have you been? Everyone has feared for your safety!"

"I'm safe, Grandmother, at least for now. I assume you heard about Orin?"

"Yes, my dearest. We feared you might take your life out of grief. Seth has gone to search for you. He will be most relieved ..."

"You mustn't tell him anything! I know that you are wise, Grandmother, and I beg you to hear me out before telling anyone that I've called you." I went on to tell her of Seth's betrayal, of finding Orin and verifying that Seth's story had been a lie. I then told her of the vision quest and what Orin's ghost had told me before he passed into the Other World. I feared that she would think me mad with grief, but she listened patiently and asked a few pointed questions as I spoke.

"You say the Medicine Woman assisted you in this vision quest?"

"Yes, Grandmother."

"I was acquainted with her mother before her. She is wise and has great gifts. If she says it is as you say, then I know it is not your broken heart speaking with your voice. I will send whispers among the Sky People and learn what I can. Orin was much beloved. I am certain there are those among the Earth People who will fall in beside you. This is a dangerous road you travel, child. Are you certain that you wish to make this challenge?"

"It must be done, Grandmother. I have no passion to lead, but I love my Clan, and I cannot let it be ripped apart by one with such a deceitful soul."

"Those with no passion to lead make the best leaders," she told me. "Give me until sunset to speak to the Sky People and find out who your other allies are."

"Thank you, Grandmother."

"And another thing, Isa. You must not come here. If it is as you say, then no doubt Seth will have my house under watch. You must come in a way they will not expect. There is a Sending Away Ceremony for Orin at dawn tomorrow. Perhaps that is when you should come. Seth is searching for you now, but he will be back in plenty of time to show himself as a respectful brother to try and gain the loyalty of those who supported Orin. The ceremony will be at the clearing at sunrise. Come early, then watch and wait for your opportunity."

"Thank you for your wisdom, Grandmother. May the Old Gods bless you as you walk today."

"I love you, Isabeau. Be careful."

One of the benefits of being a nocturnal creature is the ability to make my way to familiar places at night. I arrived at the clearing hours before dawn and positioned myself carefully downwind to the in-routes, but close enough to see who was coming and when. Seth might be a fratricidal monster, but he was no fool. He would have returned to the mine shaft and found Orin's body missing. He would have seen the ATV tracks and been able to follow them as far as the paved road. I hoped he would not have guessed where I had gone, and that he would be banking on me returning here with the evidence of a non-snake-bitten corpse. He would have been watching our house in Sheridan and any route that would bring me to our Clan's home lands east of town.

I was relying on the idea that he would have assumed I would not abandon Orin's body, and that I would insist on returning it here to our Clan.

I knew that my confrontation with him would be a huge gamble, and that there was no way to know how many of the Clan would be on my side when it began. He would not kill me in front of the Clan, no matter what

I accused him of, because everyone knew I was pregnant. But he could banish me with the intent of hunting me down later.

As dawn approached, our people began arriving in the clearing, each carrying an armful of wood. Ordinarily, this would have been for a great pyre where Orin's earthly body would have been burned and his spirit released into the Wild. Without his body, they would make a smaller bonfire as a ceremonial gesture. I clutched in my talons the Medicine bag that Therese had given me, containing sacred herbs and a scoop of Orin's ashes. She had spoken many blessings over it, and I had added prayers to the Old Gods and some of my own tears and blood.

The morning was a misty one, and the first gray light of day gave the trees and the clearing an otherworldly glow. I counted forty-two of our people in attendance, including Seth, his cronies, and my own grandmother and cousins. Seth assumed the northernmost point of the circle, the place that rightfully was his brother's. He wore a mask of solemnity, but his eyes were shifty, expecting a disruption. I imagined he was quite frustrated that he hadn't found me or the ATV.

As the light touched the treetops, Seth began his eulogy. "It is with great sadness that I face you today, friends. Not only do I mourn for my lost brother, but I fear the worst for his mate. No trace of her has been found by our scouts. Many of you witnessed the extremity of her grief. We shall continue to search, but we must all prepare for the worst.

"My brother believed in the harmony of all things, in the balance of the Earth. And as such, we mourn his loss to us, but celebrate his return to the bosom of the Earth Mother."

At this invocation, everyone stepped forward and added their bundles of wood to the

log frame erected in the center of a shallow indentation, ringed by stones like a giant fire pit.

"I will miss Orin all the days of my life," Seth continued, his voice rising in strength. "He was an inspiration to all who knew him, and I would not hesitate to take his place in death." Seth's hypocrisy turned my stomach. He lifted a torch high and stepped toward the woodpile, setting it alight and stepping back outside the stone circle.

This was the moment. Owls were known for silent flight, and when I dropped out of the trees into Seth's sight, it was far too late for him to stop me. I swooped low over the fire and dropped the Medicine bag into the flames. The copper powder within it would burn a green-blue when the contents were consumed, an unnecessary bit of drama, perhaps, but I felt like my beloved deserved at least that moment among his people.

There was no doubt that all had seen me, and there were gasps and murmurs of my name as I circled back and landed before the fire, outside of Seth's reach, but within the sight of all.

I shifted into my human form, knowing that I must use my words now to persuade anyone I could to turn against this usurper.

"You wish to trade places with him?" I asked, my voice laced with acid. "Sadly, I can't push you down a mine shaft as you did with him, but please feel free to leap upon his funeral pyre and join him!"

"Isabeau! Thank the Old Gods that you're safe!"

"Spare me the theatrics, Seth. I have come to expose your betrayal, as you knew I would. Hear me, friends! Many of you know that Seth disagreed with Orin's leadership and felt that the mantle of Clan Leader should be his instead. What none of us could have known was the lengths he would go to take that mantle for his own!"

"Isa, my sister, your grief has twisted you ..." In the shadows of the firelight, I saw Mathias, Evan, and a handful of other Clan members melt into the trees, no doubt to try and flank me and grab me from other directions.

"Orin did die in a mine shaft, as he claims, but there were no snakes to be found. When I found Orin, his neck was broken from the fall. There were no bite marks. The shaft was not hidden or hard to see. Orin had been lured there with the story that Mathias had fallen and needed help, and then, on Seth's command, Mathias and Evan rushed Orin and pushed him in."

"That is ludicrous, Isa. I would never do such a thing. What possible proof do you have of this? Not Orin's body, clearly. These are horrific accusations."

I had expected him to challenge me this way and knew that I could not produce what he asked. It was only my faith in the wisdom of my Clan that gave me any hope at all.

"I took Orin's body to the Medicine Woman and she released his spirit in fire. Before he crossed to the Other World, his ghost told me what you had done, which only gave detail to what I had already pieced together when I found his broken body at the bottom of the mineshaft."

"Do you hear yourself, Isa?" His voice boomed out the question to fill the Clan with doubt. "His ghost? My dear sister, you've been through such a shock. I'm sure everyone understands your rage and grief. But wanting to blame me doesn't make it the truth."

"The Medicine Woman has seen his body." My grandmother stepped forward, putting her own life at risk alongside mine. "She verifies that there were no bite marks. She watched over Isabeau during the vision quest and lit the funeral fire herself. She has nothing to gain by taking a side here."

A sizzling sound from the fire told me that the Medicine bag had caught aflame, and I saw the burst of color out of the corner of my eye. Mathias and Evan emerged from the crowd behind me and grabbed my arms, restraining me.

Sylvie, another of the Earth people, a fox when she was in animal form, stepped forward and held one knife to my throat and another to my belly. "Don't try to shift," she hissed at me.

Seth approached as the others held me fast. "The Medicine Woman is not one of ours. She may have any number of reasons to lie for you."

"Is it the Medicine Woman's imagination that your associate here holds a knife on your unborn nephew?" There was mumbling among the crowd. My point was well-taken, as children were sacred to us, and threatening one with harm was cause for exile.

"She did not do so on my orders."

There was a pop in the fire and the blue-green flame burnt out, its supply of the mineral powder spent. Sylvie bared her human teeth savagely, and for a moment I feared the worst. But then she whipped around, pulling the knives away and turning her rage on the leader that had betrayed her to the Clan's justice to keep his own name clear of blame. I hazarded a look around, and noticed that the Sky People had moved forward, tightening the ring of people so that the betrayers could not run.

"Everything I've done has been on your orders," she spat. "That and the promise to take me as your mate when you became the Leader. You treacherous bastard!"

Seth was caught in his own web. The Earth People began tightening the circle as well, and the expression on Seth's face twisted into a mixture of panic and rage.

Sylvie did not look away from his face, but shouted over her shoulder to Mathias and Evan. "Do you think he won't betray you, too? He will run away and leave us to die a traitor's death! His promises mean nothing!"

"I don't need promises," he growled. "Our Clan will follow the strongest among us, because that's how Nature works. Throw her in the fire!" he yelled to the men who held my arms. "Let her join her beloved. Do the same with anyone who opposes me, starting with this one." His eyes dripped venom at Sylvie.

She lunged at him with both knives slashing, but he had expected her attack and parried, spinning her around and pinning her wrists to her sides with his powerful arms. Pandemonium broke out amongst the Clan, and some of the People shifted into their animal forms. Animals and humans alike advanced on those of us in the center of the circle. The cries of hawks, wolves, owls, and a handful of other creatures split the air with their chaos.

Mathias and Evan, knowing a fight was coming, tensed their grip on me, preparing to shove me into the flames. I fought and struggled, but was no match for their combined strength. From across the flames, a streak of white slammed into Evan, throwing the three of us off balance and sending us crashing to the ground. Recognizing a momentary advantage, I broke their grips and leapt toward the safety of the mob.

Many hands found me and forced me to the outside of the circle, where my baby would remain safe. Grandmother found me then, and cradled me in her arms, stroking my hair and weeping. I did not see what happened next, but the snarling and screaming told me the story. When the crowd parted, bloody claws and muzzles and talons and beaks painted a gory picture of the Clan's justice for my treasonous brother-in-law and his goons. Sylvie was restrained by human hands, but she did not fight because they had allowed her to live. At least in exile, she would survive.

What was left of Seth, Mathias, and Evan was thrown into the fire, and the stench of burning meat filled the air. The screech of hawks and eagles, the howls of wolves, and the yips of foxes filled the sky.

And off in the distance, the familiar howl of a lone wolf in the Wild caressed my ear, the wind carrying the sound far away into the Land of the Coyote.

Allegory of the Castle

SPECULATIVE DARK FANTASY
BY JENNY SIMARD LABRANCHE

Parker Laine had never belonged.

At college, her voice was quieter, her clothes darker, her ideas stranger. She wore thrift-shop jackets and carried notebooks full of sketches and half-finished poems, while others wore designer sneakers and filmed each other for TikTok. At first, the gap wasn't cruel, just there, like a crack in the sidewalk nobody paid attention to. But over time, it hardened into something Parker carried like a bruise. To them, she was weird, aloof, or worse: invisible.

The film club was the only event she attended every week, even if she stayed in the corner and let others do the talking. She enjoyed the buzz of people debating about movies, the way light from the projector sliced through dust in the air, and how the world felt smaller when the room went dark.

The announcement came at the end of a Wednesday meeting. Professor Alder closed his laptop and produced a stack of applications, fanning them out across the desk like a magician about to reveal a trick.

"An opportunity," he said, voice deliberate. "Rare. Extraordinary. A residency in Romania, at Castle Bran, better known as Dracula's Castle. One student from this group will be chosen."

The room erupted. Phones lit up instantly, notifications firing like sparks. Someone shouted, "We'll get so many views if we go!" Another laughed, already Googling flights.

Parker felt her heart lurch. The castle was a cliché, sure, but not to her. She thought of shadows and screens, of stories whispered against stone.

"The application is simple," Alder went on. "One page. Write what you hope to gain. Deadline: Tomorrow at midnight. That's all."

Parker gathered her things slowly, careful not to look too eager. She knew how this went. Programs like this always went to the bright kids, the popular ones with references stacked like poker chips. The ones who had professors on speed dial and parents who could buy them tickets to anywhere.

Still, that night, she sat at her desk and wrote.

She didn't write about vampires. She didn't write about horror movies or gothic architecture. Instead, she wrote about shadows. About film as a cave wall, flickering light against stone. She wrote about how stories could free us or trap us, and how truth and illusion blurred until you couldn't tell them apart. She wrote about being an outsider, about watching the world from the dark edges of the frame.

It was raw. Strange. But it was hers.

Two weeks later, Professor Alder called her into his office. The letter was waiting on the desk. She had been accepted.

The fallout was immediate.

Jealousy turned classmates into enemies overnight. Kayla, her once-best friend, laughed so loudly in the cafeteria Parker felt the whole room pivot.

"Of course she got picked," Kayla said. "She probably wrote something creepy. Who else would they send to a haunted castle but a freak?"

The words sank deeper than Parker wanted to admit. She folded into herself, shrinking smaller, but inside she carried a stubborn ember. For once, something had chosen her.

At dinner, her parents reacted with confusion.

"Romania?" her dad asked her. "By yourself?"

Her mom frowned. "Do you even want to go, Parker?"

Parker nodded. "Yes. More than anything." She hesitated, then added, "I won't be alone. Some of my ... friends from class are coming, too." The word *friends* caught in her throat, but she let it stay.

The flight was long, a blur of airports and stale coffee. Parker stayed quiet, earbuds in, eyes fixed on her notebook. She sketched mountains, even though she'd never seen the Carpathians before. She wrote lines she didn't understand but couldn't stop: *the cave is not a metaphor; it's a place.*

The shuttle climbed switchback roads into the mountains, pine trees thick as walls. When she stepped off, the cold cut through her instantly. The mountains rose like dark shoulders, forests crouched heavy at their bases. And then she saw it.

The castle.

Its pale stone towers clawed at the sky, its walls jagged and bone-white, as if it had grown out of the mountain itself. It looked like a fortress and tomb, myth and memory all in one.

Something in her bones whispered she had been here before.

A man waited at the gate, tall and still. His coat looked too thin for the weather, his face pale but not fragile, like marble cut too precisely. His eyes, black and deep, caught hers and held them. For an instant, she thought she saw herself reflected back, but not as she was now. Another self. Older. Dressed in silks. Her hair was braided into heavy ropes.

"Welcome," he said, voice smooth, unsettling. "At last, you've come."

Parker froze, suitcase dangling. "You ... you're with the program?"

He smiled, but his eyes stayed cold. "You could say that."

Inside, the entry hall swallowed her footsteps. The ceiling rose high with heavy timbers, tapestries sagging on the walls, their colors faded to bruises. A chandelier of antlers glowed with beeswax candles, though no one seemed to have lit them.

A curator in a wool blazer appeared, ledger in hand. "Miss Laine? You're our first arrival. Your room is in the scholars' wing. Tea is available in the library. Breakfast at seven." His tone was matter-of-fact, like someone used to refereeing old arguments about authenticity.

Parker thanked him. She wanted to ask who else was coming, but the memory of the man at the gate was still a sharp weight between her ribs. She followed the curator up stairs hollowed by centuries of footsteps.

Her room was small: an angled roofline, a narrow window framing a slice of mountain. A writing desk waited under the glass. On the bed lay a folded gray sweater, sleeves stretched from another person's elbows. A note beneath: *For the cold, E.* She checked the staff list in her packet. No one had a name starting with an E. The sweater fit perfectly, but it didn't smell like detergent, more like rain on stone. She told herself it was tradition, part of the residency. Still, she shivered. Beside the sweater lay a small hand mirror, its silver handle cool and slightly tarnished. The glass was splintered, with fine cracks webbing across its surface. She picked it up carefully, turning it in her palm. Her reflection fractured, each shard showing the room in impossible angles, as if the ceiling and window refused to align.

The library filled the north tower. Shelves sagged with leather spines. A spiral stair twisted upward into a frost-glazed dome. She pulled a medieval chronicle at random, its Latin glossed by a nineteenth-century hand. The handwriting was equal parts skeptical and enchanted, like someone trying to believe.

She read until her eyes blurred, wrote until her wrist cramped.

Dinner that night was set for three: herself, another scholar "delayed by weather," and a third place laid for a host who never came. The extra plate, the older goblet with a nick in the rim, unsettled her more than she admitted.

When the steward brought bread, Parker asked, "Do people live here year-round?"

He paused. "The staff live in the village. We tend the fires, mind the gates. The castle keeps its own counsel."

Later, Parker stepped into the courtyard. Night fell hard and sudden. Stars crowded close, the mountains crouched darker than dark. She notices a plaque engraved with a language she did not recognize. And at the far edge of the courtyard: the man who picked her up. Still as stone until he lifted his head.

His face was handsome but severe, grief carved into every line. His pale eyes fixed on her until she felt pinned in place.

"I didn't see you at dinner," Parker said, trying for casual. Her breath didn't fog. Neither did his.

"I ate," he said simply. Then, "You read in the north tower."

"You watched me?"

"The tower watched you."

She should have laughed. She didn't. "Are you with the foundation?"

"I've been with many foundations. Temples. Armies. Museums. Now, I stay with the mountain." He stepped closer, just outside her warmth. "You wrote that film is a cave. Do you still believe it?"

Parker's mouth went dry. "I think we mistake shadows for truth when it's comfortable. And when someone turns us toward the light, we call them villains because it hurts."

He smiled with half his mouth. "Most travelers don't quote Plato in courtyards. The mountain prefers silence."

"Are you the mountain?" she asked. "It's caretaker?"

"I'm its echo." His gaze followed a bat flickering against the stars. "Tomorrow, the others will come. They'll tell you shadows are only shadows. Let them. Talk is rain on a closed window. It never gets in."

"Others?" she asked.

He didn't answer. But she could already imagine them: Kayla, loud and laughing. The film club boys with their expensive sneakers. Ashley with her restless energy.

"Why me?" Parker asked finally.

"Because you know the cave isn't a metaphor," he said, voice almost tender. "Because you're already underground. And because you know who I am."

The name echoed in her head. *Dracula.*

And then he was gone.

The next morning, Parker ate breakfast alone. The steward had tried for pancakes, though they were thin and rubbery, edges singed, drowned in a jar of jam that tasted faintly of smoke. She forced them down, her stomach tight with nerves. Halfway through, the shuttle pulled into the courtyard. Voices spilled out before the door even opened.

Kayla.

Her laugh cut through the morning air, bright and sharp as ever.

"Park!" she shouted the second she saw her, swinging her arms wide, as though nothing had passed between them in months. A coat worth more than Parker's entire laptop hugged Kayla's body. Sunglasses glinted. And behind her came Henry, broad-shouldered, already recording himself with a flexed arm in the shuttle window. Ashley, her hair tucked under a knit beanie, earbuds dangling. Parker stood frozen, a piece of pancake still heavy in her mouth.

Kayla rushed forward and hugged her. "Oh my God, look at this place. It's so *you*."

Parker stiffened. "Why are you here? This wasn't your residency."

Kayla leaned back, eyes wide in mock innocence. "Support. And content, duh. I wasn't going to let you be stuck here all alone."

"Support?" Parker's voice cracked, sharper than she meant. "You humiliated me in front of everyone. You called me a freak. And now you show up acting like we're friends again?"

For the briefest moment, Kayla's smile faltered. A flash of something crossed her face, guilt, or maybe just irritation at being called out. "That was just ... college stuff. You know how it is. Don't be so dramatic."

"It mattered," Parker whispered. Heat rose in her throat, not anger but the sting of betrayal. "You mattered. And you made sure everyone knew I didn't."

Henry clapped Parker on the shoulder, oblivious. "Don't be salty, Park. It's a castle, dude. We're all about to blow up on TikTok. Chill."

Ashley rolled her eyes at Henry but didn't defend Parker either. She was already framing the castle in her phone camera, narrating in a half-bored voice. "Day one, Bran Castle. Apparently, it's haunted. Subscribe for updates."

Kayla looped her arm through Parker's as though the conversation was finished. "Come on. Show us around. You've been here, what, one night? You're basically the expert."

Parker let herself be pulled forward, her anger softening into something quieter, heavier. It settled behind her ribs like a throb she'd stopped pressing on but could still feel. The warmth of Kayla's arm would once have been comforting, but now it only reminded her how far they'd drifted.

She thought of the bathroom years ago, how Kayla had held her on the cold tile floor, whispering promises of loyalty, of always. Parker could still remember the steadiness of her voice, the way her fingers had tangled in her hair like an anchor.

Parker wanted that girl back, the one who had stayed through the worst of it, who hadn't yet learned how to look away. But when she glanced at Kayla now, she saw only a stranger wearing familiar features. The laughter came too easily. The warmth felt borrowed.

Parker forced a smile and let herself be led on, wishing grief didn't have to feel so much like love refusing to die.

They passed beneath the archway, their footsteps echoing against the stone. The air inside the castle was cool and hollow, carrying the faint scent of dust and extinguished candles. Tapestries stirred slightly in the draft, their colors dulled by time.

Kayla's laughter filled the corridor, bright and careless, bouncing off the walls until it sounded almost foreign. Parker followed a step behind, her hand brushing the worn banister, feeling the grooves where generations had passed. It reminded her of a touch that lingers long after the warmth has gone.

She thought of how they used to walk side by side, whispering secrets, their hands brushing without hesitation. Now there was a space between them that no echo could bridge.

When Kayla turned to grin at her, torchlight caught her face, softening her features until Parker almost saw the girl she remembered. But then the light shifted, and the moment collapsed like breath on glass.

The door closed behind them with a weighty sound, sealing the air tight. Parker drew in a slow breath, the scent of old stone and regret heavy in her lungs.

The group took over quickly. They claimed larger, newer rooms in the tourist wing. Henry tested the mattresses like he was reviewing them for a brand deal. The halls filled with noise and Wi-Fi signals, their laughter bouncing off the stone. Parker tried to feel angry, but what she felt instead was hollow. She kept imagining the man in the courtyard, Dracula, though neither of them had said the name aloud, listening to their voices with quiet amusement.

They went on a tour with the red-scarf guide. She rattled off practiced lines: Vlad the Impaler wasn't the novel's Dracula, this wasn't Stoker's setting, legends multiplied like cats. Her voice skimmed the surface of history like a flat stone on water.

Parker raised her hand. "What about the plaque outside? The old one, the script with the sharp vowels?"

The guide's smile faltered. "It's quite old and I dont really remember. Nothing to dwell on." She moved on before Parker could press further.

Kayla filmed herself posing in a crypt, captioning it *Spooky but hot.* Ashley hummed a lullaby, her voice thin in the damp air.

Parker followed, but the castle resisted groups. Corridors twisted in the wrong directions. Staircases doubled back. Twice she trailed Kayla into a gallery and ended up alone in a mold-stained hall. Once she descended stairs that stretched longer than the building could contain. The air shimmered with candlelight then steadied, as if granting permission.

When she rejoined the others, Kayla leaned close, perfume heavy. "You good? You keep disappearing."

"I am here," Parker said.

That night, the steward extended the table. Another arrival had joined them: the archivist, a woman with iron-gray hair pinned neatly, eyes sharp as chisels. She carried herself like an engineer who had built half the castle herself.

"I'm Emma," she said simply.

Parker's eyes flicked to the sweater folded in her room. To the card marked *E*.

Emma noticed. "You found my things. Good. They're for the work, not for keeping." She ladled more stew into Parker's bowl before she could protest. "Eat. You'll need it."

The conversation drifted into inventories and manuscripts, into soldiers' journals and villagers' myths. Parker let the words blur, her attention snagging only when Emma's gaze landed on her.

"You wrote about caves," Emma said suddenly, her eyes on the gaps in the shelves. "I read your application."

Parker swallowed. "I did."

"You said stories are caves we mistake for daylight. That some people never leave."

"Yes." Parker's voice came out thinner than she wanted. "I still think that."

Emma nodded. "Leaving is a myth. What we do is carry fire." She tilted her head, as though listening to something Parker couldn't hear. "Have you spoken to him yet?"

Parker froze. She didn't need to ask who. Her silence was answer enough.

"Good," Emma said. "He usually waits longer. When he's impatient, it means something."

"Dangerous?" one of the grad students asked, laughing nervously.

"To patience. To certainty." Emma's gaze returned to Parker. "He thinks you're someone you can't be."

The words slipped from Parker's mouth before she could stop them. "His wife."

Emma sighed. "Echoes are harmless, until you follow them." She reached into her pocket and pulled out an iron key, heavy and black. She pressed it into Parker's hand. "Don't go below the kitchens. If you get curious about the cisterns, don't. The mountain eats scholars who go thirsty."

The key pressed cold into Parker's palm.

Later that night, Parker stepped outside again. The courtyard was empty, stars tight above her, the mountains hunched dark around the castle. The air was sharp, metallic, the kind that made breath visible and thoughts seem louder. Each step on the stone tiles sounded like a shout, echoing off the ancient walls, hollow and accusing. Her pulse thudded in her ears, a reminder that she was alive, even if part of her felt suspended in disbelief.

And then he was there.

Dracula.

He did not move like a man, or like a ghost; he moved like a thought made flesh, inevitable and eternal.

"You know who I am," he said, his voice smooth, resonant, carrying the weight of centuries.

Parker swallowed hard, her throat dry as dust. "You're a story. A myth. Vlad the Impaler. Dracula."

He gave the smallest shake of his head, a gesture that seemed almost fragile in its subtlety. "I was a hammer before I was a man. The gods made me their hammer. They dressed me in flesh and sent me to bring order. I brought order the way hammers do: I mistook people for nails. For that, they punished me. Left me hungry for what I had spilled."

"Blood," Parker whispered.

"Life," he corrected softly. His gaze swept over her, deep and steady, as if searching for something buried beneath years and lies. "Names followed me, Vlad, Impaler, Dracula. But names are only shadows. Do you see? You are not the first to believe in shadows."

Her mouth was dry. Her hands twisted at her sides, her fingers brushing the hem of her cloak as though grounding herself in the fabric could anchor her from what was happening. "And me? What do you see when you look at me?"

He stepped closer. The air between them tightened, each breath a tether of unspoken memory. Parker could feel the pull of him, cold as the night but heavy with the weight of all that had been lost and forgotten. Her heart fought against it, a small, futile rebellion.

"I see the one who once stood beside me," he said. "The one who begged me to stop. The one I lost when the gods turned their faces away."

Parker shook her head, though the motion felt weak, like a futile attempt to escape a tide she could not hold back. "I'm not her."

His gaze didn't waver. It held her in place like the stone of the castle itself. "Then why," he murmured, "does the castle remember you? The stones whisper your name when you pass."

The wind rose, carrying a sound that might have been leaves, or the echo of something ancient remembering. It wound through the arches, threading around the towers, curling through the shadows like smoke. Parker shivered. Not from cold. Not entirely. Something inside her ached, a dull, persistent throb that made the night feel heavier than it should.

"You speak in riddles," she said, trying to keep her voice even. "The stones don't speak. The castle doesn't remember anything. It's just walls."

"And yet it does," he said. "Everything leaves a mark. Even you. Even now. Even when you tell yourself you are not who I knew, who the world knew." His words were measured, precise, each one weighted with centuries of regret and longing. "Do you think the earth forgets the footprints it has carried?"

Parker looked away, toward the edge of the courtyard where the stone balustrade fell away into shadow. Her hands clenched into fists at her sides. She wanted to run, wanted to convince herself she could escape the past she was somehow attached to simply by walking faster, by breathing harder, by not looking at him. And yet she couldn't. There was something magnetic in his presence, something that demanded acknowledgment, even if it terrified her.

"I'm not her," she said again, more firmly this time, though the sound of her own voice betrayed her doubt. "I'm me. I've lived my life. I've made my choices. Whatever you lost ... whatever you're holding onto ... it's not me."

He tilted his head slightly, a motion so small yet so deliberate it carried the weight of ages. "Perhaps," he said. "Perhaps. But loss has a way of echoing beyond what it touches directly. You carry shadows of her ... or she carried shadows of you. Perhaps it is the same thing. Perhaps it is why you are here."

Her chest tightened. She had to fight the urge to flee, to step backward into the cold embrace of the night air. But she stayed, because something inside her, a stubborn, trembling piece, wanted to understand, wanted to hear him out, wanted to see if truth could exist in this place of memory and myth.

"Why now?" she asked, her voice breaking slightly despite her efforts. "Why appear to me? After all this time?"

He stepped even closer, until the moonlight traced the sharp lines of his face. "Because the past never leaves quietly," he said. "Because I am bound to it, and so are you. Because the gods, in their strange ways, set the pieces on the board, and the game moves even when players are unaware. You are part of the game, whether you wish it or not. And I ... I am here to see if you remember."

Parker swallowed, her throat dry, her pulse hammering in her ears. She did remember. Every fear, every hope, every echo of the girl she once was, the one who had been beside him, was buried beneath layers of years and lies, but it was there, stubborn and painful.

"I remember," she said, finally. "I remember enough."

A flicker of something softened in his eyes, almost imperceptible, like a candle fighting the wind. "Then perhaps there is hope," he murmured. "Or perhaps there is only truth. Sometimes, that is the same thing."

The courtyard stretched around them, vast and empty, yet alive with memory and shadow. Parker felt the weight of centuries press against her shoulders, yet in that weight, she found clarity. Whatever he was, monster, man, myth, he was tied to her in ways that went beyond fear or disbelief. And she ... she could not walk away, not yet.

For the first time, she realized the night was not silent. It whispered, it breathed, it remembered. And in that remembering, Parker and Dracula stood, two figures caught between what was lost and what could never be recovered, bound together by echoes and shadows, by names and memories that refused to fade.

She took a slow, steadying breath. The stars above seemed sharper now, pinpricks of light that reminded her she was alive. And still, he watched her, pale eyes unblinking, as if he had been waiting for this moment across centuries.

The wind rose again, carrying a faint scent of old stone and iron, of something long forgotten yet impossible to ignore. Parker shivered, not from cold, but from the weight of truth pressing down, heavy and inexorable.

She realized then that the courtyard, the castle, the night itself, they were all witnesses. And in that witness, the past and present coiled together, fragile and dangerous, waiting for her next step.

By the third night, Parker had stopped expecting sleep. Kayla had begged to share Parker's room, and she did not deny her.

When the lights flickered out, the castle seemed to shift, stone creaking as if it had joints. Doors that had been locked earlier swung open into halls that weren't marked on any map. Windows gazed at each other across courtyards; reflections layered like whispers.

Later that night, Parker heard a sound.

At first, she thought it was the wind, threading through cracks in the stone. But when she sat up, she realized it was a voice, Kayla's voice, soft and unsteady, like a prayer spoken through clenched teeth.

Parker turned. Kayla's bed was empty, the quilt dented with her shape, still warm.

Parker shoved her feet into her boots and followed.

The corridors had grown wrong. A stair that should have led toward the kitchens bent sideways into a hallway Parker didn't recognize. Her phone's flashlight barely touched the dark, bouncing off damp walls. The sound of Kayla's voice tugged her forward, too faint to catch words, but insistent.

At the end of the hall stood a gallery Parker had never seen before.

Its walls were covered in broken mirrors.

Some leaned; others hung, cracked, in golden frames. Every shard reflected her differently, older, younger, crowned, buried. Some warped her into grotesque shapes, others made her too thin, too tall. And in some shards, she saw her classmates.

Henry stood in one, posing shirtless. His reflection multiplied until the glass became an army of Henrys flexing back at him, each one more exaggerated, more grotesque.

Ashley appeared in another, cradling a baby. The child turned to ash in her arms, re-formed, then crumbled again with every blink. Ashley wept each time, but she didn't let go.

And Kayla, Kayla twirled in a smoky gown, an audience roaring from nowhere. Her smile grew wide, wider, until the corners of her mouth cracked. Applause thundered through the gallery, which was empty.

Parker pressed her palms to her ears, but the sound sank through her skin anyway.

"Kayla!" she shouted.

A dozen Kaylas turned toward her from different shards. Only one, deep in the glass, met her eyes.

For a breath, Parker saw the girl who had once held her in the bathroom at twelve, whispering promises that they'd survive middle school together. Kayla's eyes were wet, real.

Then the vision snapped. Kayla's grin returned, brittle and blazing.

"I like the shadows," she said. "They love me back."

Parker reached for the mirror, but a hand seized her arm.

Emma.

Her hair was loose from its bun, her nightclothes plain, but her eyes were sharp as ever. "Don't look too long," she warned. "That's how he keeps them."

"Kayla's in there," Parker said, her voice breaking.

"I know." Emma's expression softened, but not with pity. "They all wander here eventually. The castle doesn't build cages; it only paints the bars. They bring their own fears. He ... illuminates them."

As if to prove her words, Henry flexed harder, straining until his muscles tore. Blood streaked the mirrored floor, though his real body stood intact, mesmerized. Ashley rocked her vanishing baby, sobbing quietly, each cycle of dust leaving her more desperate. Kayla kept dancing, bowing to a crowd that didn't exist.

"Help them," Parker whispered.

Emma shook her head. "Can you help someone who loves their cage? He only provides the stage. They write the script. Wait until morning."

The next morning, Parker found Kayla in the courtyard, sipping coffee as though nothing had happened. The sun glinted off her oversized sunglasses, hiding her eyes, but Parker could still see the exhaustion in the way she held herself, shoulders drawn in, one hand trembling slightly as she stirred her drink.

"You disappeared last night," Parker said, her voice sharper than she intended.

Kayla didn't flinch. She tilted her head lazily, lips curving into that same camera-ready smirk. "You disappeared first."

"No." Parker crossed her arms. "I followed you. Into the mirrors."

For the briefest second, something flickered across Kayla's face, a crack in the perfect performance. Then she laughed, too loud, too bright. "God, you're dramatic. You probably dreamed it."

"I saw you." Parker's voice trembled, but she pressed on. "I saw you dancing. I saw how badly you wanted the applause. I saw you smiling so wide it hurt."

Kayla's jaw tightened, her coffee cup pausing midair. "So what if I like being seen? At least I don't hide in a notebook, waiting for the world to come knocking."

The words hit like a slap, and Parker had to bite the inside of her cheek to keep from reacting. "You used to see me," she said quietly. "You were the only one who did. And then you turned on me, Kayla. You humiliated me in front of everyone. You made sure I was alone."

Kayla lowered her sunglasses. For the first time in years, Parker saw her without the armor, just Kayla, raw and cornered. "I was jealous, okay?" she said, voice cracking. "You got picked. You, with your weird thrift jackets and your creepy poems. I hated that it wasn't me. But I never stopped being your friend."

"Yes, you did." The words came out like broken glass. "You left me when it counted."

Kayla flinched, her mouth opening as if to argue, but no sound came. The silence between them stretched taut, broken only by the soft gurgle of the coffee machine and the faint laughter drifting from inside.

Henry strolled past, phone in hand. "Breakfast montage, let's go!" he called, turning his camera toward the mountains. Ashley followed, quiet, her eyes dark as storm clouds.

Kayla slipped her sunglasses back on. "We'll talk later."

Parker watched her go, knowing they never would.

That evening, Dracula invited them all to dine in a vaulted chamber lit by torches that should have suffocated in the stale air. The room smelled of iron and wax, of damp stone and something faintly sweet beneath it all, like the ghost of spilled wine. Shadows swayed on the arched ceiling, making the frescoes of angels and beasts writhe and shift as though alive.

The long table was set with unsettling opulence: platters of roasted meats glistening with juices, bowls of dark stewed fruit, loaves of black bread steaming faintly as if fresh from some unseen oven. Pewter flagons of spiced wine caught the firelight and shimmered red as blood. But no servants appeared, no footsteps echoed from the corridor. The meal existed ... waiting.

Dracula sat at the head of the table, hands folded as if in prayer, his posture perfect and unmoving. He did not eat. He did not drink. He simply watched. His eyes traveled the table slowly, deliberately, like a shepherd counting his flock.

Henry and the others were too charmed, or too drunk on novelty, to notice. Cameras clicked. Laughter echoed. Kayla raised her glass high and called for a toast to "the Count who knows how to host."

Dracula inclined his head with the faintest of smiles. "To life," he murmured, his accent curling around the word like smoke. "And all its beautiful illusions."

Henry laughed, clinking his goblet with Ashley's. "That's deep, man. You should have your own podcast."

Dracula's eyes flicked toward him, just once, and Henry's laughter stuttered, faltered, then resumed a beat too late.

Parker didn't eat much. She pushed food around her plate, her stomach too tight for appetite. Every time she glanced up, she found his eyes waiting. She told herself it was a coincidence, the trick of torchlight and nerves, but the feeling that she was being weighed, measured, and remembered would not leave her.

Kayla, meanwhile, thrived under his attention, or what she believed was his attention. She leaned toward him, her laugh soft and deliberate, her hand grazing his sleeve as she told some story about modeling in Milan that no one at the table believed.

"You must have seen so much," she said, voice coy. "All these centuries of castles and royalty and mystery. It must be lonely, though. Being surrounded by all that history."

Dracula smiled, slow and patient. "Loneliness," he said, "is a mirror we all pretend not to see."

Kayla blinked, unsure if he was flirting or philosophizing. "That's ... poetic," she managed.

"I have had much practice pretending."

Laughter fluttered around the table again, thin as the torchlight.

Then his gaze turned, deliberate and absolute, to Parker. The air shifted, thickened. Every torch flame seemed to lean toward her, drawn by an unseen current. Parker swallowed hard, her throat dry despite the wine she hadn't yet tasted.

"You dream of caves," he said softly. His voice didn't rise above a whisper, but it carried across the room as though it had been spoken beside her ear. Yet no one else reacted. Henry was filming his plate. Kayla was scrolling through her phone. Ashley stared into her wine as if it contained secrets.

Parker's pulse quickened. "What did you say?"

"You already know," he said. "You dream of caves. You already know what it means to live in shadow."

Her lips parted. "And you?" she asked before she could stop herself. "Do you dream of light?"

His smile was terrible in its tenderness. "I dream of the day I mistook people for demons," he said. "That light burns hotter than the sun."

The torches hissed, as though a sudden wind had passed through them. Parker felt heat rise to her face, a prickling that wasn't embarrassment but recognition. Something inside her, something old and instinctive, understood him, even if her mind refused to.

Kayla noticed their silence and leaned in, her tone playful but edged. "Careful, Parker. He might be trying to hypnotize you."

"I don't think he needs to," Parker said, eyes still locked with his.

Dracula tilted his head, his expression unreadable. "No, Miss Laine. She sees clearly, even when the others prefer the dream."

Kayla bristled. "What's that supposed to mean?"

He regarded her, the corners of his mouth curving. "It means, Miss Kayla, that the mirror shows us not who we are, but what we fear."

Henry laughed uncertainly. "Man, that's so true. That's like ... deep psychology stuff."

Dracula did not look away from Parker. "Would you agree?"

She hesitated. "I think ... I think the mirror shows both. Fear and truth. Sometimes they're the same thing."

His gaze softened, almost approving. "Spoken like someone who has already looked."

The table had gone quiet. Even the torches seemed to wait.

Kayla forced another bright laugh. "Okay, this is officially the weirdest dinner I've ever been to. Can we talk about something normal? Like, I don't know, where do you even shop for all this Gothic decor?"

Dracula turned to her, his composure unbroken. "It was here long before I was," he said. "I only borrowed it for company."

Kayla's smile faltered. "Borrowed?"

"Yes." He lifted his goblet, though he did not drink. "From those who came before. From those who will come again. We all borrow, Miss Kayla. Time. Breath. Warmth. Until someone comes to collect."

Henry gave a nervous laugh. "Okay, now you sound like a horror movie villain."

Dracula's eyes glimmered. "Do I?"

Parker's fork clattered against her plate. She hadn't realized she was shaking until she saw the tremor in her hand.

"Excuse me," she muttered, rising from the table.

The torches flickered as she passed, each one bending subtly toward her, as though following her movement. She felt his gaze like a hand on her back, cool and weightless but inescapable.

"Miss Laine," his voice followed her. "Be careful when you dream tonight. The caves remember."

She turned at the doorway, heart pounding. "Do they remember you, too?"

He smiled without showing his teeth. "They never forget what they shelter."

Parker stepped into the corridor. The air was colder there, and for a moment she thought she could hear something beneath the laughter from the dining hall, something deep and rhythmic, like the slow beating of wings against stone.

Back inside, Kayla laughed again, too loudly, filling the silence Parker had left. Dracula listened, that faint smile still hovering, and raised his glass in a mock toast.

"To those who cannot see," he said. "And those who will not."

He drank nothing.

And the torches burned a little lower.

That night, the mirrors claimed the others again.

Henry's fists bled from punching the mirrors as his reflections mocked him, bigger and stronger each time. Ashley's cradle rocked endlessly, her phantom child crumbling and reforming, her sobs growing rawer with each cycle. Kayla twirled until her gown shredded into smoke, applause echoing in her ears.

Parker pressed her hand against the glass. "It's not real," she begged. "Kayla, please, it's shadows, just shadows on the wall!"

For a heartbeat, Kayla's eyes softened. The bathroom girl again. The friend who had once promised never to leave her.

Hands clamped Parker's shoulders.

Dracula stood behind her. His voice slid around her like smoke. "Don't take their illusions. They will hate you for it. They are not ready to see the fire."

"Then why show them at all?" Parker demanded, spinning on him.

"Because truth and prison are often the same thing," he whispered. His eyes held hers, steady and patient. "And because you need to learn the difference."

That morning, the castle seemed to be holding its breath. There was no bird song, no rustle of wind under the eaves. Even the usual hum of tourists in the distant wing had died out, leaving a silence as thin and distant as sound trying to pass through a barrier of felt.

After Parker got dressed, she walked quietly down the corridor toward the north tower. The gray sweater Emma had left for her was soft and warm, but nothing special. It hung from her shoulders. She paused at the landing and pressed her hand against the cold stone. Somewhere beneath and beyond these walls, someone was counting, not aloud, not with numbers, but with a steady, patient pace that felt like the weather.

He was waiting for her in the courtyard, as if the castle had softly pushed her down its steps and placed her at his feet.

"You know my name," he said. Not a question. A calibration.

"Everyone knows the name," Parker answered. "The book. The movies. Halloween costumes. I know the story you got stapled to you."

A line of amusement creased his mouth. "And the real one?"

"Fragments," she said. "Warlord. Impaler. Terror as policy. Maybe a patriot, depending on who writes the script. And then the fiction that ate the man." She swallowed. "But you told me last night you were a hammer before you were a man."

He nodded once. "Walk with me."

They crossed the yard without touching. He took her to the wall, to a place where the stone met the mountain as if there were no seam at all. The wind came up the cliff in a long exhale and pressed their clothes to their bodies, but he didn't shiver.

"Once," he said, "the world had too many stories and not enough order. People begged the sky for a conductor. The sky sent an instrument instead. I was made to be a straight line through the noise. I was not given a soft hand." He glanced at her and added, "Do you understand?"

"I understand tools," Parker said. "I understand what happens when someone decides other people are problems to be solved instead of ... people."

"The gods called it necessary," he said. "I called it work. Villages burned more slowly when I rode through them. The roads got safer. Merchants were able to count their sons on both hands at night. I made sure it all came out even, Parker, blood for peace, loss for order. I did it the way hammers do." His voice had gone flat, not defensive, not proud. Fact.

"And then?" she asked.

"The gods required balance," he said simply. "They make their favorites pay. The punishment fit the crime: I was made to thirst for what I had spilled. To hunger for the thing I had wasted, the thing I had reduced to accounting. History gave me Vlad to wear like a coat. Later, when history felt ashamed of itself and wanted a prettier failure, it called me Dracula."

He let the name sit there. It didn't echo. It didn't need to.

"People made you a monster," Parker said. "Because it's easier than admitting we asked for the things you did."

He tilted his head in a way that read as both yes and no. "People like patterns. They call them prophecies after they happen. They draw circles and pretend the circles were already there."

"And your wife?" Parker said, quieter. "The one you think I am a reincarnation of."

Something loosened in his face and then held. "She was small and stubborn. She talked like a bell that expected to be heard. She had hands that looked like they had never done anything hard, and somehow they had done everything hard." He breathed, or pretended to. "She asked me to stop. She asked me to give the gods back their hammer and then teach them how to live without it."

"What did you do?"

"What hammers do," he said, and in the space after the words sat oceans of regret.

He looked at Parker and didn't blink. "I tell you this not because I want confession, but because I do not want confusion. You know the popular story. Keep it. It entertains the tourists. But you must also know the other one, the one with no capes and no fangs, only choices and what those choices make of us."

She thought of her notebooks. The scenes she'd written where nobody got out clean. "I get it," she said. "I think."

"Not yet," he said. "But you will."

They didn't return inside by a door. The wall admitted them where stone should have refused. Parker swallowed the reflex to ask how. The castle had been offering answers she wasn't ready to understand since she arrived.

He led her past the kitchens. Emma's warning flashed across Parker's mind like a hazard light: do not go below. The iron key in her pocket throbbed with its own cold.

"Wait," Parker said. "Emma told me, "

"She told you true," he nodded. "And still you should come."

He didn't touch the barred door. The chain sank obligingly as if set in water instead of metal. The padlock swung in a slow circle and stopped with the keyhole facing her like a pupil. Parker slid Emma's key into a smaller, hidden slot in the wood. The interior bar sighed and lifted. She glanced at him, but he was watching the doorway the way one watches a stage before the curtain goes up.

They descended.

The air cooled and thickened. Sound became a thing that gave up halfway and turned around. Parker's phone light made a tight circle on wet stone and then bounced back; beyond the circle, the dark felt textured, like the painted side of a wall. She thought she could hear their feet contacting the steps, but only the idea of steps reached her ears.

"What is this place?" she asked.

"Storage," he said. "For water. For grain. For mistakes."

They reached the cisterns. Great stone bowls. Water flat as glass, colorless and awake. The arches held the world up with the cheerful denial of architecture older than its own plans.

"Why bring me here?" she asked.

"Because you asked to know," he answered. "And because you already do."

Her throat tightened. "I know stories."

"You know caves," he corrected. "You know what happens when the same picture plays so long it feels like weather."

He led her past the first bowl and the second. At the third, he stopped. He didn't look at the water. He never did.

"Parker," he said, and the name felt like a precise instrument in his mouth, "your friends drifted to the mirror room because it called them by their favorite names. You are not immune. Your room is different. Come."

He turned left into a tunnel Parker would have sworn wasn't there. The stone narrowed. The ceiling pressed down until she had to bend, then tuck, then fold. Her heart sped and her lungs raised their small protest. He moved with the patience of a glacier.

"Stop," she said. It wasn't a command. It was a confession.

He stopped. His voice came back to her from ahead, unraised and perfectly clear. "You know the myth of the cave," he said. "You know the people chained facing the wall and the puppet show and the man who went out to the light and staggered back in, annoyed that eyes are parts of bodies and not lanterns."

"I teach it to freshmen when Alder lets me," she said. Her knees were damp. Her palms were dirty.

"What does the myth forget?" he asked.

She swallowed down her panic. The tunnel had become a thought that wanted to be a throat. "It forgets how the chains feel. It forgets how scared people are when the person they trusted turns on the lights. The myth also pretends you can just walk out once. Like it's a door and not a habit."

"Good," he said. "You can breathe."

"I'm trying," she said, and wanted very much to laugh, or cry, or put her head down on the rocks and sleep like an animal that doesn't remember beds.

The passage widened suddenly, as if the mountain had been holding its stomach in and decided it had nothing to prove. A chamber opened around them, no cistern this time, no columns, just a blank bowl of space with room for a voice to do whatever it wanted. Torches sparked the way they always did here, a convenience Parker refused, on principle, to find convenient.

Shadows moved on the walls, but they weren't cast by the torches. They assembled themselves from memory. Her father at the kitchen table, reading an email and not hearing her when she said she'd been published in the campus journal. Her mother setting down a stack of laundry and saying, *I just want you to be normal, Parker*. Kayla in the cafeteria, the laugh hammerized. Henry filming everything because if a thing wasn't content, it wasn't real. Ashley practicing apologies she never said out loud. Every small betrayal Parker had downgraded to "not a big deal" because to name them honestly would make her life require more courage than she felt she had that day.

"Make it stop," she said, not to him. To it. To the room. To the compiled record of micro-cuts.

"They are shadows," he said, "and they are knives. Both can cut. But only one can be put down."

He gestured. The pictures sped up: classroom back rows, empty texts, Kayla's arm hooked through Parker's at a party where Parker hadn't wanted to be; then release, Kayla sliding her arm out again five minutes later when someone cooler arrived. Parker watching the holes people made and then called *growing up*.

"Why are you showing me this?" Parker asked. "What do you get from it?"

"I get nothing you do not give," he said. "The mountain is not a vending machine. You do not put pain in and get absolution out. I am not a god anymore. I am a man who remembers being one. Memory is not mercy."

She turned on him. "Then why help me?"

He studied her the way he had in the courtyard, the way a builder looks at a beam and calculates the stress it can take. "Because you are the right shape for a door," he said. "Because the castle sent for you. Because I, " He stopped, impatient with himself. "Because I am tired of watching people drown in shallow water."

"And because you think I'm her," Parker said. She didn't make it an accusation. She laid it down like truth, the piece that made everything else fit.

He inclined his head. "And because of that."

She stood there, breathing hard. She expected to cry, but no tears came. "What now?"

"Now you climb," he said. "I will not lie: it will hurt. You do not need my permission to do difficult things. You will, however, take my lantern."

"I thought eyes aren't lanterns."

"They aren't," he said. "But a hand can be."

He set nothing in her palm. Still, something rested there, a steadiness, perhaps. A refusal to panic that wasn't entirely hers.

The chamber shuddered, and the back wall became a slope. Not a staircase. Not a ladder. A slick shoot pocked with shallow holds, wet with the collected breathing of the mountain.

Parker reached up and got her fingers into a seam. The first pull wrung sound out of her. Her forearms lit with heat and white noise. She planted her boot in a notch not quite the shape of boots and levered up. The rock sloped again at an angle that changed the calculation of what counted as possible.

Shadows wrapped her ankles. They didn't seize; they suggested. *You could rest. You could sit. You could slide down and say "I'll try again tomorrow," except you won't.*

"No," she said to them, and to herself. "No."

Her shin scraped and left a wet line. She didn't look. Looking turned pain into theater. She didn't have the budget for that show today.

Halfway up, a shelf promised to be a ledge. It wasn't. When she put her weight on it, it behaved like an apology instead of a plan. Her left hand slipped. Her right hand held. She swung in the air and banged her hip so hard her ears hissed.

You are not strong enough, the darkness said in her voice.

"I'm not," she said through her teeth. "I'm stubborn."

She found new purchase by bruised instinct. She counted three breaths, then five, then forgot counting and made bargains with herself instead: just to that crack; just to that seam; just to that memory of light that might be real; just to where you can stop calling your fear by clever names and recognize it as what it is: weight.

She tried to think about Professor Alder, the good feedback, and how it felt to finish a shot and know it worked. She tried to think about freshman year when Kayla sat with her on the library floor and traced plans on the carpet with a capped pen, listing the films they would make, the cities they would live in. But memory made her hands loosen, not tighten.

So she thought instead of the page. Of a pen in her hand that no one could take away or grade for likability. Of every late hour she filled with words when there was no audience but the quiet piece of her that demanded to exist.

Her left knee bled through the denim. Her fingertips stung, pads burned thin. She put her forearm in a crack and hugged rock and dragged. The low sound she made belonged to animals and engines.

When she looked down by accident, the ground she'd left hadn't moved at all. The dark loves to keep score with different numbers than you do.

She didn't look down again.

Time got weird. You couldn't call what was happening minutes. You could call it tries. She tried. And then she tried again. And when that failed, she found a slower verb and tried that.

When she made the lip of the slope, it wasn't triumph. It was the sudden absence of effort. The light above wasn't golden or holy. It was thin, a stripe of morning that had barely begun to mean it. It touched her face and didn't ask questions.

Below, he waited where she had started, the negative of a shadow.

"You've chosen," he said. "But light always makes a shadow. Remember that."

She lay there, chest burning, face wet with sweat and whatever else had finally agreed to become tears. She didn't answer him. She didn't have to. The answer was under her. The answer was the cut on her knee and the raw moons of skin where stone had taken tithe.

She breathed until breath went back to being air and not a project.

"Why didn't you help me?" she asked when she could speak.

"I did," he said, and for once did not make it a riddle. "I did not carry you."

"That's the part I noticed," she said, and pushed herself upright with a laugh that sounded like broken glass and relief.

You are not done, the dark said, but more politely now.

"I know," she told it. "But I'm not where I was."

When she stood, her legs argued. She bribed them with the promise of floors and chairs later. He stepped back as if to make room for her to decide which direction meant up.

"Your friends," he said, as if reciting an appointment. "They're still anchored to their cages."

"They're not cages," Parker said, surprising herself. "They're mirrors."

He acknowledged the distinction with the smallest nod. "Will you go to them now, or later?"

"Now," she said, and the word didn't feel brave. It felt like the only available option.

"Then take this," he said.

He put nothing in her palm again. This time, nothing felt like a key.

She found Kayla by sound before sight. Not applause now. Breathing. Fast and ragged, like someone trying to walk off a panic attack and pretend it was cardio.

The mirror room had rearranged its bodies. Henry's reflections had gone sullen. Ashley's cradle rocked itself without her hands. Kayla stood in the middle and had put her phone face down on the floor, which was how Parker knew something had changed.

"Don't," Kayla said without turning when she heard Parker step into the room. "Whatever speech you've got. Save it."

"I don't have a speech," Parker said. "I have a hand."

Kayla laughed once. It wasn't funny.

"That is not true," Parker said, and the courtesy of saying it aloud, clean and direct, steadied her. "I didn't. But I have one now."

Kayla turned. There was no performance in her face. What Parker saw there made room to be both anger and grief at once. "You left me," Kayla said.

"And you left me first," Parker said. "And before and after that we took turns calling it survival."

Kayla wiped her eyes with the inside of her wrist, the way you do when you're tired of smudging mascara with your fingers. "If I step out of there," she jerked her chin toward the glass, "and I'm still nobody, "

"You won't be nobody," Parker interrupted. "You'll be somebody who isn't hungry the way that room needs you to be."

"What if I like being hungry?" Kayla asked, and meant it like a dare and a confession.

"Then you'll go back," Parker said. "You always can. It's a door. It pretends to be a destination."

Kayla stood still a long time. The mirror nearest her flexed as if exhaling. Parker didn't move, didn't plead. She offered her hand and let the offer be mortal: limited, shakable, real.

Kayla took it.

The mirror nearest them cracked, just a hairline, like ice making a decision. Kayla flinched, but she didn't let go. The applause that wasn't playing anymore thinned into memory.

"Okay," Kayla said. "Okay."

They left the gallery together. Henry and Ashley's illusions didn't pop with a neat sound effect. That wasn't how this place worked. Henry would need to find a mirror that showed him small on purpose and decide he liked that view. Ashley would need to hand a lullaby to silence and accept that it counted as a song. Parker could not do either for them. It felt inadequate and honest at the same time.

Emma waited in the corridor with a thermos and a towel and the face of someone who had been right about something she wished she'd been wrong about. "You did it," she said, not congratulating, just acknowledging.

"We did a version of it," Parker said. "There will be sequels."

Emma's mouth tipped in what might have been, in a different life, a smile. "Everything worth doing is a series."

Kayla drank from the thermos and coughed when it turned out to be tea with a personality. "We should go home," she said to no one in particular, which in Kayla-language meant: I am starting to understand that staying has costs I can't charm my way past.

Parker nodded. "Soon," she said. "Not yet."

"Why not yet?" Emma asked, though she knew.

"Because he needs to hear me," Parker said. "And I need to hear myself say it."

Emma tightened the cap on the empty thermos. "Then go back where you promised you wouldn't."

Parker looked at Kayla. "Do you need ..."

Kayla shook her head. "I'm going to find Ashley," she said. "And then Henry, because otherwise he will die posing like a Greek statue in front of a water barrel."

"Reasonable," Parker said.

They both knew that meant: be careful.

He was where she expected him to be: the cistern chamber that turned an absence of movement into a kind of authority.

"You enjoyed the climb," he said without turning.

"I did," she said. "And I'm going to keep doing it, since apparently it's a subscription service."

"That is what it is to be alive," he said. "The mountain charges daily."

"You should raise your rates," she told him. "Maybe fewer people would sign up to suffer."

He looked at her and the smallest amused line found his mouth again. "If only I were the billing department," he quipped.

"Listen," Parker said, and the word came out steadier than she felt. "I understand you better now. Not all the way. Enough to be dangerous. You were made a function and nobody asked you if you wanted to be a person first. Then somebody did ask. She asked you to stop. And you didn't. And then you lost everything. Now you think I'm her, and maybe the castle thinks so, too, and maybe part of me likes how it feels when you look at me like that, not because it's romantic, but because it means I matter in a place where I've always felt optional."

The room listened.

"I am not her," Parker said. "I don't owe you her answers. I owe you mine. Here they are. I won't be worshipped or used. I won't be a replacement part. I will not love you for your ruin. I will not hate you for your history. If I walk beside you, it will be as someone who can choose to leave. And I will leave if I have to."

He received the words like a letter that would need time to answer. "Then why are you still here?"

"Because I'm not done," she said. "Because my friends are still stepping into pictures they think will save them and I know the exit better than they do. Because the cave is my major and my minor and my hobby and my problem. Because you told me the gods made you a straight line and I don't like the way that sentence ends."

He nodded. He didn't argue. "Do you want your sweater back?" he asked, as if remembering late in a meeting that somebody had asked for coffee.

She laughed despite herself. "You didn't give it to me," she said. "Emma did. The castle did."

"It belonged to the last scholar who insisted on making me answer questions I had not scheduled," he said. "She is not dead."

"That's a weird way to say 'she left.'"

"She is not dead," he said again, and Parker understood he meant: the castle keeps more than stone.

"Good," Parker said, and the word surprised her by being true.

"Parker," he said, and the way he said it made the sweater warmer. "You said once the light hurts. I say also that it humiliates. It shows you you are not centered in the picture. People hate that. They prefer applause. You will not always be thanked for being the person who turns faces toward the flame."

"I am rarely thanked now," she said. "Might as well do something useful with it."

He looked past her shoulder the way a person does when they hear a car arriving long before anyone else. "They will try the cisterns again tonight," he said. "Human curiosity is a patient river."

"I'll be there," Parker said. "I know the way."

He inclined his head in that formal way he had, the one that felt like a door opening but not necessarily to the room you thought you were asking for.

"Parker," he said, when she had already turned to go.

She faced him.

"I am not afraid to climb," he confessed. The words were quiet, true. "I am afraid to stop."

She considered that, considered him, considered herself. "Me too," she said. "We'll practice."

***

They didn't leave the next day. Tours kept coming. The red-scarf guide kept rehearsing her script and avoiding Parker's questions. Henry found a window ledge that made his angles look mythic and spent an afternoon filming sets of pushups. Ashley slept late and woke with her voice raw and no explanation. Kayla posted a carousel of photos with a caption about supporting her "dear friend Parker Laine, the realest artist I know," and Parker didn't have the energy to be angry at how sincere and manipulative that sentence managed to be at once.

That night, the cisterns called again. This time, Parker was waiting at the barred door when the others arrived, pretending they were just exploring.

"Ground rules," she said. "Nobody goes alone. Nobody stares. If you hear anything that sounds like a compliment from the dark, it's a trap. If you hear anything that sounds like the truth from the dark, it's a trap with better taste."

Henry snorted. "You're not the boss of the basement."

"Correct," Parker said. "The basement is the boss of the basement. I'm the one who knows where the stairs cheat. Pick your leader accordingly."

Kayla laughed, a real one that wasn't aimed at an audience. "Let her run point."

They went down together. The air met them with that familiar, careful chill. When the walls started to hum like the mirrors, because that's what they did before they performed, Parker clapped once, loud.

"Don't look," she said. "Look at me. Or look at your feet. Or look at your phone and read a text chain from last year and remember how boring being alive can be. Boredom is an excellent anchor."

Ashley trembled. "I keep hearing the song," she whispered. "And I know it's not real, but what if it is? What if it's telling me..."

"It isn't," Parker said. "It's telling you what you would tell yourself if you were trying to hurt yourself in a way that looked like love. Sit down." She pointed to the driest patch of stone. "Name three things in your bag right now."

Ashley blinked. "What?"

"Three things. Now."

"My, my charger. A granola bar. My mom's stupid saint necklace."

"Good," Parker said. "Open the granola bar. Eat it. That's your god now."

Kayla snorted again. It turned into a choked sound and then a muffled laugh and then, finally, a slow exhale. "That's actually ... smart."

"Write that down," Parker told her, and Kayla did, thumbing a note into her phone with a seriousness that made Parker's throat ache.

Henry hovered near a reflection of himself in a puddle that had found his best angles once already. It called to him again, but softer, less urgent, like a friend who had learned manners. Parker stepped into his line of sight.

"Do you know what you look like when you're not working so hard to be looked at?" she asked.

He bristled. "I look small."

"You look possible," she said. "Come try that."

He hesitated. It was a long, ugly five seconds. Then he nodded and sat next to Ashley on the floor.

The images dimmed without theatrics. The room didn't surrender. It just got tired of being interesting. The castle, which had always wanted weight more than attention, let them be.

When they climbed back up, Parker's legs shook the way they had on the mountain, but this time with effort distributed across more bodies than hers.

They ate the kind of dinner that gets described as "simple" in expensive cookbooks and tasted better than any of them deserved. Emma pretended to be surprised they'd all survived and then slid a folder toward Parker filled with photocopies she said she had "forgotten" to file. Inside were letters written in a slanted hand, dated a century earlier, from a woman whose name was smudged out in places but whose voice came through anyway: *The water under the castle pretends to be still. It is the busiest thing here. Do not let it choose what you remember.*

"Is that your scholar?" Parker asked.

Emma shrugged a shoulder. "Never ask an archivist to commit to one version of a story."

Parker slept. When she woke, she didn't reach for the cracked mirror on the desk. She reached for a pen. The first sentence came like something owed. The second like payment. The third because two lines make a path and three make the start of a map.

She wrote about the cave, yes, but not like a professor. She wrote it like a person who had rocks under her nails and a bruise on her hip the shape of a decision. She wrote Kayla and did not make her a villain. She wrote Henry and did not make him a clown. She wrote Ashley without the baby because Ashley had to exist without the baby to get out of the room. She wrote him, too, not a monster, not a husband, not a god. A man who had been used as a tool and had learned late he wanted to be a hand.

When Parker took breaks, she and Kayla walked the halls and didn't talk about followers. They talked about freshman year and what they'd hoped would happen if they looked hard enough at the future. They compared stupid things they'd said to people they wanted to like them. They compared apologies they still owed.

"Why are you forgiving me?" Kayla asked once. "I don't deserve it."

"I'm not," Parker said. "I'm remembering you. The forgiving will have to be a thing we do repeatedly. Like laundry."

Kayla nodded, eyes bright and not ashamed of it. "I can do chores," she said.

On the last evening, the steward, Dracula, Vlad, the hammer, the man, stood in the courtyard as the light dropped out of the sky like a curtain ending a long play. The others packed or pretended to. Emma argued with a radiator that had been winning for a hundred years.

"You will go," he said.

"Yes," Parker said.

"You will come back."

"Probably," she said. She stepped closer, not into his cold, but into a range where people talk to each other instead of to the air. "I meant what I said. I'm not her."

"And I meant what I said," he answered. "The castle remembers. I remember. Both can be true and still you can be not her and also the right shape for the door."

Parker nodded. "Then you have to do something for me."

He waited.

"When people come here, tourists, scholars, idiots, we both know what this place does. You don't have to make it kinder. But you could make it clearer. Less ... seductive."

"You would have me change the pitch of gravity," he said, almost smiling.

"I would have you put better signs on the stairs," she said.

"Done," he said, as if she had asked him to move a chair. "And you?"

"I'll finish something," she said, stunned to hear the sentence come out without a lie baked into it. "A film. Or a book. Something that turns and looks back."

He inclined his head, and for a moment she saw the king the stories wanted him to have been, not because he ruled anything, but because he could recognize a promise and hold it without squeezing.

They stood there, and the moment demanded no kiss and no oath. It demanded only grown people remembering they were not myth and deciding to act like it anyway.

When Parker turned to go, he said her name once more. She faced him with the ordinary patience you give someone you respect.

"Light casts a shadow," he said, putting a period on the old warning. "Remember also: shadows prove there is a light."

"Sometimes," she said. "Sometimes they only prove there's a shape."

He considered that, genuinely, and then nodded. "Bring your fire," he said. "I will bring the room."

They left early the next morning. The shuttle made the castle small between trees. Kayla fell asleep with her head against the window and her phone off. Henry posted a long, uncharacteristically quiet video about how sometimes the coolest thing is not to film a thing. Ashley ate two granola bars and didn't mention babies.

At the airport, Parker texted her mother a photo of a mountain and didn't wait for approval. She started a note for Professor Alder titled *Exit Strategies for Caves 101*. She wrote the opening voice-over for a short: *We mistake shadows for truth when it's comfortable. We mistake comfort for kindness. Here's what it looks like when you turn around slowly, so no one gets hurt on the way.*

On the plane, she took the cracked mirror out of her bag. The glass held her in fragments. Somewhere among them, a shape that could have been his smile waited and didn't. She turned the mirror face-down on the tray table and wrote instead.

Back on campus, there were inevitable reactions, some petty, some warm, some pretending to be one and meaning the other. Parker didn't shrink the way she would have before. She didn't grow, exactly. She set her shoulders and made room for herself like a person opening a door into a crowded room without apologizing.

She met Kayla for coffee and, after four minutes of awkward, they found a laugh that belonged to both of them. She found Ashley texting her at midnight with an edit and texting again at one to say *never mind* because she'd figured it out and was proud. Henry asked if she wanted to run in the mornings. She said no and didn't feel bad, then added, *ask me next week* and meant it.

Emma emailed: scanned letters, a photograph of the plaque Parker wasn't supposed to dwell on, a line in the body of the message that read simply, *Good. Keep the sweater.* The subject line said: ARCHIVE/ACTIVE. Parker saved the file in a folder with that same name and smiled.

Epilogue

She did go back to the castle, months later, with money from a grant that felt like a vote of confidence and smelled like bureaucracy. She brought a better coat and worse shoes. She brought a camera that didn't want to be a phone. She brought a plan that had holes in it large enough for surprise to climb through.

He was there. He was not waiting. That turned out to be okay.

"Bring your fire," he said, when she gestured to the gear and the script and the folder of permissions Emma had bullied out of reluctant administrators.

"I did," she said. "You bring the room."

They did not say *action*. The mountain did. The film did not look like anyone else's idea of the castle. It was too bright in places and too quiet in others. People in Q&As said the ending lacked closure. Parker nodded and agreed with them out loud because she was polite and had become strategic. Inside, she let herself be pleased.

On the night of the first screening back home, she took the cracked mirror out of her bag again. The room behind her in the reflection was a classroom with ugly carpet and poor lighting. The girl in the mirror was tired and proud and not finished. In one corner of one shard, something that could be a smile waited and might always.

She put the mirror away and held the page she'd written her credits on. *Directed by Parker Laine.* That was a kind of light. That, too, cast shadows. She was learning to live with both.

When the Q&A ended, a freshman waited until everyone else left and then said, "I think I've been watching the wall. How do you turn around without falling?"

“You don’t,” Parker said, and didn’t soften it. “You fall and then you climb. And then you do it again. It’s ugly. You can DM me when you need someone to count for you.”

The student nodded like that was oxygen.

On her way out into a night that was only night and not a gothic anything, Parker felt the familiar tug in her chest that used to feel like loneliness. It felt like something else now. Like a tether. Like direction.

She walked home. She didn’t look for shadows. They would find her; they always did. She had hands. She had light. She had a story that wasn’t finished and didn’t need to be.

The castle was far away and also where she stood. The mountain charged daily. She paid and kept the receipt.

And somewhere, in a courtyard made of stone that remembered and forgave as much as it could, a man who had once been a hammer and had learned to be a hand stood still, not waiting, exactly, simply holding his post in a world that required it of him, while a set of better signs on the stairs pointed more honestly toward up and down.

She went back to the castle. Not because she was pulled, not because she was unfinished, but because she had learned the difference between leaving and abandoning. He was there, unchanged in the ways that mattered. She stayed a while. Then longer.

City of the Dead

HORROR BY BETSEY KULAKOWSKI

"Heroes always get remembered but you know legends never die."

Panic! At the Disco – "The Emperor's New Clothes"

Prologue

The Curse existed before the days of Gilgamesh. It began in the days of the Sumerian gods who wrote their histories on clay tablets. They told the story of the first man, Adam, and his first wife, Lilith. In these tales she refused to be subservient to her husband. She left Adam to become the *Queen of the Demons*. Thus the gods banished her from Paradise.

Some believe that Hebrew law forbade the eating of human flesh or the drinking of blood because of Lilith. But she is not the only one to suffer *The Curse*. In Babylon, there was Lamashtu, the daughter of the Most High, Anu. As a *Daughter of Heaven*, she was often depicted as a terrifying blood-sucking creature with a lion's head and the body of a donkey. New mothers prayed for mercy as she came for their infants, taking life and creating only mayhem in her wake.

In ancient Greece, they described Hecate—the undead daughter of the goddess Asteria—as a demonic, bronze-footed creature. She feasted only on blood by transforming into a beautiful young woman—a seducer of men—sleeping with them before taking their lifeblood.

In Hebrew tradition, *Alukah*—literally translated as *leach*—is synonymous with those who suffer *The Curse*, the *Motetz Dam*. *The Blood Sucker*.

The Curse persists today, but as the legends of old do not tell, there is more to *The Curse* than simply living an undead life, drinking blood, and wandering the streets at night. *The Curse* is ruled by the *Black Commandments*, said to have been handed to Lilith, or perhaps *Lamashtu*, by Anu himself.

Thus my tale begins.

PART ONE: Lessons Learned

The First Commandment

Nu poate fi decât unul.
The Earth may suffer only one.

Paris, France – October 2001

I was dying when *The Curse* was brought upon me. I turned eighteen a week before I arrived in Paris to study at the Sorbonne. Not well acquainted with Parisian life—born and raised in Iowa—I knew more about fried chicken and sunflowers than I did *escargot* and *fleur de lis*. Paris was wonderfully romantic, but little did I know the dangers that lurked there.

The first inkling of illness came just after I arrived. Indigestion. Nausea. Fatigue. Night sweats. Aching back. Nothing big enough to raise alarms, but as the weeks passed, I found it difficult to get through long hours sitting in on lectures or hovering over a microscope in the lab.

I discovered *Death* is a patient hunter. It is stealthy and quick to anger. I saw doctors who said I was working too hard, not eating right, or getting enough exercise. What was I supposed to do? Did they expect a college student on a fixed budget in—a country that didn't believe in Ramen noodles or Kraft Macaroni & Cheese Dinner—to live off quiche and ratatouille? When I could tolerate food, my go-to meal was salad niçoise, made with canned tuna. Occasionally, I would pair a baguette with a chunk of stinky cheese and a handful of grapes, or fresh pears. Not exactly a well balanced meal, but it wasn't anything like what American college students were eating in Iowa.

I walked everywhere, or rode a borrowed bicycle to classes. I drank red wine almost daily, and never went to keggers or smoked pot. I should have been in the best shape of my life, but my health continued to decline.

And so it happened late in the fall of my junior year. I had been assigned to a rotation at *Le hôpital américain de Paris.* Here, I would observe last-year residents-in-practice to prepare for my own first-year residency that would follow in the spring.

The department of Neuilly-sur-Seine was a lovely urban commune in the west part of Paris. The neighborhood of quaint, but immaculate residential neighborhoods, housed corporate headquarters, and a handful of foreign embassies. It was one of the most affluent areas of France, and the most expensive suburb of Paris.

My health continued to falter, but I was managing to hold it together, despite having lost the entire *freshman fifteen*, and then some. My healthy American figure fell away, and I looked more like a Paris fashion model—gaunt, rail thin.

One dark and stormy night, a patient came into the emergency department screaming and covered in blood. He cried out that the *Night Walker was after him,* and he would be dead before dawn.

The Director of Residents paired me with a gifted surgeon. Like most French men, God blessed him with a head full of thick black hair, pale white skin, and ice blue eyes. He was charming, as are all Parisian men. He was also cocky and confident, declaring the patient on the verge of a nervous breakdown. He ordered the nurses to restrain him while we assessed the man's injuries, instructing me in the process.

"BP is 150/94. Pulse is 144," the nurses started the assessment as soon as they could get to the patient. The doctor stood back watching, his arms folded across his body. "In English we would say, O.M.I., or *Oh, my!* Oxygen, Monitor, IV. This is not a time to take a leisurely history. You know your ABCs?"

"ABC stands for airway, breathing, circulation," I said, as I began to look for the signs that would confirm an issue.

"Because he is screaming, I am not concerned about his airway or his ability to breathe. The goal at this moment is to ensure it stays that way, while calming the patient. He took the man's restrained hand. I could see the pumping of blood at his wrist where the doctor pressed his middle fingers. "He has a pulse. It is elevated. Now what?"

The man continued to struggle and cry out, convinced the *Night Walker* was coming for him. "Start an IV," I said. "Check his pulse ox. Would you medicate?"

"Tell me of his color," the doctor spoke calmly.

I turned to study him. With blood all over him, I couldn't tell for sure, but I thought he appeared pale. His pupils were dilated to pinpoints. "We need to determine if this is his blood," I realized. "*Monsieur*? Have you been injured? Are you taking anything? Heroin, maybe?" I raised my voice.

"You're dying!" he screamed. For a moment I wondered if I heard him right. I wasn't the one in distress, after all. "You're dying! *You're* dying!"

"We're all dying," my mentor said, waiting for me to continue.

I don't know exactly what happened at that moment, but somehow, the patient freed himself and leapt at me. I fell to the floor with him on top of me, his bloodied hands around my throat. His grip tightening. "You're dying! You're dying!" he screamed, as the medical staff tried to pull him off me. His hands tightened around my throat.

I couldn't scream, even if there had been time. The man's eyes locked on mine, and I felt a terror unlike any I had ever known. The irises were red, like a demon's. They burned with rage, almost spinning with madness as dots began to dance in my eyes. I could hear the pandemonium that overtook the room as the medical staff panicked. The doctor ordered him sedated.

As his hands tightened he lifted my head from the floor, and I could feel my hands going numb. My lips tingled and my vision narrowed. "*The Curse* that is mine is now yours," he whispered in my ear. He pressed his lips over mine, his hands coming loose. I gasped my last breath as his lips clamped over mine.

Then, it was over.

The Second Commandment

Călătorul trebuie să învingă inamicul ca plată a tarifului.

The Traveler must vanquish the enemy as payment for the fare.

When I woke up in the morgue, I knew there must have been a mistake. I shivered, cold and naked. I sat up and found a tag tied around my toe with a cotton string. A thin white sheet had been draped over my form. As I sat feeling numb, my hand found the stitches that ran down the middle of my body, the mark of the coroner who performed my autopsy. My brain wasn't fully processing the magnitude of the situation, but I put the pieces together and surmised I was dead.

I wrapped the sheet around me and climbed off the cold metal gurney. No one was in sight.

"What was your name, girl?" a voice behind me asked.

I spun around and found a tall shadow in the corner, similarly clad. He moved where the light could touch his features. It was the patient who had killed me, but—something was different. Eyes that once burned red were now yellow and cold.

"Ileana," I answered, my voice trembling. "Ileana Brendan."

"Pleasure to make your acquaintance, Ma'amselle," he bowed his head, weakly.

"Wh-who are y-you?" I asked.

"Once, they knew me as Peter Blagojevich," he said. "When I lived in Serbia. Today, I have no name, save *Death*."

"Y-y-you k-k-killed me."

"I saved you," he said. "Just as you saved me."

"I don't understand."

"You were cursed. Death already had its hold upon you. I simply *expedited* your transformation," he said, pausing to consider me. "There is a curse upon me, too." He moved and wrapped the sheet around his waist. His toe also had a tag tied to it. It had no name written on it. "My curse is now your curse, until it is time to travel."

"What does that mean?" I asked.

"There isn't time to explain now," he said, rummaging through one of the cabinets and fetching a pair of scrubs for each of us. "Put these on. I've prepared a refuge. There, I can properly instruct you in the little time we may have. No one can hurt us, but we must move with haste. Dawn is coming."

I wanted to protest, but he moved so quickly. One moment he moved cautiously in the shadows, the next we were racing through the rain-soaked streets. He avoided the brightly lit streets, hovering close to the buildings. In one particularly dark alley, I realized I had no trouble seeing the cracks in the pavements or the rodents that scattered as he approached. Normally night blind, I reached for my glasses and found them gone. "You don't need glasses," he said. *Did he have the power to read my mind?*

"Yes," he answered, turning into an arched entryway, forcing the door open with a shove. "You will never be breathless or feel your heart pounding in your chest."

"But ... I took your pulse. I saw your veins ..."

"Something I have learned to control," he said. "Once you adapt, you will not be cold, nor will you feel pain. The only thing you will know is an insatiable hunger."

"So, I am ... *dead*?"

"Worse," he said. "You are *undead*. And you must do only two things."

He led me into the catacombs beneath the city. I had come here on a tour when I first arrived. It had given me chills when I entered. I felt no such fear, nor dread. It felt like ... like ... like coming home.

"What two things?" I asked.

"You must feed." He paused. "And you must kill. The dark gods decide your fate, and when you can travel."

The Third Commandment

Pentru a-l ucide pe stăpân, trebuie să-i iei capul și să-i străpungi inima.
To kill the master, you must take his head and pierce his heart.

"It is the *Kiss of Death* that gives us life," he said. "The blood of mankind is the path to destruction and ruin."

"I don't understand," I said, as he led me into a burial chamber. Shelves carved into the earth were stacked with the bones of men and women who had died long before.

"It was your dying breath that made you. We are bound together, you and I."

"How ... how did you know?" I asked, trying to make sense of it all.

"Cancer is not hard to detect," he said.

"Cancer?" The words hurt. In my heart I had suspected it, but none of the tests had identified it as the source of my declining health. I always thought I'd have time to find the problem once I became a doctor myself. Time no longer had meaning.

"Am I suddenly your *paduan*? Are you my *Jedi Master*?" I asked.

"No," he replied with a mirthless chuckle. "I am your Creator ... and your Doom."

"What do you mean?" I found myself face-to-face with one of the skulls, drawn to its delicate features. Perhaps it was that of a young woman, like me.

"I made you for one simple purpose," he snapped. "To destroy you."

"What? I don't understand."

"There are rules to our existence, scribed in ancient texts. Unbreakable laws carved into unbreakable tablets. The first commandment of our kind is *The Earth may suffer only one*.

I still didn't understand, and I said as much.

"*The Curse* demands there can be only one," he said. "I made you solely for the purpose of killing you. I have lingered here too long, and I fear the dark gods have forgotten me. If I must live for an eternity, I do not wish it to be here. Or now."

I puzzled on that thought for a moment, noticing his fists flexing as if another instance of insanity might come over him. I moved closer to the way we had come, in case I needed to escape.

"There is no escape, child." He turned. "A life for a life. That is how it has been since the dawn of man. Since Anu made us from the deception of his sons, and the hatred of his daughter. When all good was destroyed and the heavens were at war, Anu cursed us and cast us into the shadows. We are Cursed to hunger, but never be sated. To war with ourselves and never rest. We fight for a life we are guaranteed never to have, and yet, we fight all the same."

"So, how do you *kill* a ... a ... someone like us? What are we?"

"We are *The Cursed*, no more ... no less."

"Oh," I managed.

"We are born when we die," he said. "Only when we are pinioned to our coffins may we truly understand death. It is only final when there is but one."

"You're talking in riddles," I insisted.

"Commandment number three," he said. "To kill the master, you must take his head, and pierce his heart." That is how it has been done since the days of Adam and his bride Lilith. So it remains."

"So, wait." I shook my head. "Let me get this straight. Cut off our heads and we die?"

"No," he corrected me harshly. I sensed he grew impatient with my questions. "The earth may suffer only *one*. Only then is it finished."

The Fourth Commandment

Moribundul trebuie să hrănească morții.
The dying must feed the dead.

"It is the dying that feeds the dead," he explained.

"You killed me so that you could stay dead?" My confusion seemed to surprise him.

"I am and am not dead," he said. "As are you."

"That makes no sense," I insisted.

"I took your last breath, so that I might continue on," he said. "I can feed on the blood of the dying, but it is the *Kiss of Death* where the true power lies. When the time for battle comes, I will take your life again, so that I may be reborn into a new world."

"You will take my life ... *again*?"

"Unless you think you can defeat me," he said, lifting a brow. "You do not understand the torment, child! Even when your head lays in your arms and a spike pierces your heart, *The Curse* is not broken. The earth may suffer only *one*. *One*!"

One, huh? I considered him for a long moment. He wasn't much bigger than me. He'd gotten the drop on me in the ER because I wasn't expecting it. His hands had been strong, but I had a skill that I suspected he didn't.

In my youth, I won the hog-tying contest at the Iowa State Fair, twelve years in a row. My father had put me in charge of slaughter day as a result. I'd butchered my own pigs, without a tear. I didn't need my brothers to help me. I counted on that skill to make me a surgeon. I would be able to cut out a cancer like the one that doomed me. A scalpel's blade pierced no flesh without the surgeon's hand to guide it. Now, it would seem, I needed it to save my own bacon.

"I'm not sure I have the strength," I feigned.

"The irony of it all is, when I am at my weakest, you will be at your strongest. It's the tenuous tango we must dance."

"Then what makes you think you can defeat me?"

"Because of what I am, Miss Brendan."

"And what is that?"

"I am a cold-blooded killer," he smirked.

"And why do you think that gives you an advantage over me?"

"Taking the life of our kind is nothing like slaughtering a pig."

The Fifth Commandment

Dacă masa ta supraviețuiește, ei îți iau locul.

Those that survive, replace.

It took some time for me to contemplate the four commandments he'd given me. Fortunately for me, he climbed into his crypt and pulled the stone slab over his resting place, leaving me to wonder what would happen when he awoke.

Everything in my gut told me I should be afraid. If what he said was the truth, I knew what I would become ... what I already was.

I wanted to deny it. Vampires were a myth—fanciful legends to explain something uneducated people could not comprehend by logical means. I was a scientist, a doctor. *Almost.* I couldn't possibly be dead. *Could I? Why wasn't I more afraid?*

Yes. I needed to be afraid. I should run. I wanted to. Instead, I sat in the darkness. As the hours passed, I became aware of my senses growing stronger. I could see everything in the shadows. I could hear the rats moving among the bones. I could smell the rotting flesh. I began to hunger.

When the grating of the stones signaled his rising, I froze like a rabbit, sensing his hunger. It came as an odor, like that of singed flesh, burning with desire to feed.

"The flesh is willing," he said, licking his lips as he considered me. "But better to teach you to fish."

"P-p-pardon me?" I knew now how the gazelle felt when the lion approached.

"You will serve me, for a time," he said. "Serve me well, and that time will be long."

"I-I-I-I don't even know your name." I could barely get the words off my frozen tongue. After I said it, I realized he had given me a name, but I could not remember it. Memories came and went like the setting sun, and I wanted to panic. I fought to remember the frightened little farm girl who stepped off the airplane at the terminal of the *Charles de Gaulle* airport in her ripped overalls and tube top, only three years before. I remembered the smell of my mother's apple pie resting on the window ledge. I could remember my father's face, and my brothers' teasing tones.

"In this life, I have taken the name Damien Betancourt," he said.

"I will not forget my name." I decided at that moment, I would not give up my name, if I could avoid it.

"The person you once were? She is dead," he said. "You have been reborn, and you've awakened hungry. I will teach you to hunt. You will feed yourself. You will find your own name when it is time. Any name your bear will be one those we hunt will come to fear."

I realized at that moment, he did not intend to destroy me. Not yet. I dared not ask about the first commandment, for fear he might enforce it.

Over the nights and weeks that followed, he educated me on the lifestyle of a *vampire*, though he never referred to himself by such a title. He only called our kind *The Cursed*.

In a wealthy city like Paris, one might have thought our kind would starve, but where there is wealth and privilege there is poverty and pestilence.

"That is the buffet on which we will feast."

The Sixth Commandment

Atâta timp cât există două, blestemul nu poate fi rupt.
So long as two exist, the curse cannot be broken.

"How many of us are there?" I asked Damien one morning as we retired to the catacombs. Over long nights of hunting and feeding, I had come to know him as a mentor. He had been a teacher in his past life. He taught physics and mathematics at the same college where I studied medicine. His maker had taken his life, and he'd been given no chance to learn the rules. The battle began for him, almost as soon as his heart stopped. "*The Cursed*?"

"In this place, there are two. You and I."

"But you said the earth may only suffer one." I knew I shouldn't press, but in the past few weeks, I had learned much about *The Curse*. I still felt the most important information was withheld from me.

"I have been alone for so long; I could not bring myself to challenge you when I made you. I may pay for that sin."

"If your master was destroyed, how do you know everything you've taught me?"

"When I am not hunting, I seek answers in science, and myth."

"How long can we exist like this?"

"Not long," he said. "Perhaps I'm trying to give you more of a chance than my maker gave me."

"You said, in this place, there are two," I realized. "Are there others somewhere else?"

"Not some other place, but some other time," he smiled wistfully.

"I don't understand," I puzzled.

"Time has no master, but there are those of such tremendous power that time has no command over them. I had hoped I might harness such power when I took you, but ... alas. I have grown weak."

"But you've done it before?" I pressed, sensing there was something he wasn't telling me.

"Yes," he said. "I am not of your age, as you may have already guessed."

"Damien, when were you born?" I asked, not sure I wanted to know the answer.

"1350," came his reply.

"*The Black Death*," I muttered.

"Yes," he said. "That was when I was born into this death. I fed on the corpses of the dying. We feasted like never before. I made my first kill within days of my birth."

I was beginning to put the pieces together. I had to feed this growing hunger, in order to gain my strength. I would never be able to defeat him otherwise. As a doctor, I abhorred killing, but my hunger over took my better judgement. I made my first kill. It proved I had become the monster he made me, whether I liked it or not.

He continued. "The time will come when the last of our kind will remain. Any fool can see ... it will not be me."

I wasn't sure what to say to that. "This is hard to take in," I admitted, when I could find the words.

"I now hope that a being of my making might know these ultimate powers. We cannot change what we are, child. This is a truth we must accept," he said. "Each day, you grow stronger. I know the time will come when you will seek dominion over me, and I must either submit or we fight."

"I could just leave," I told him.

"You could try," he sighed, pushing back the stone lid of the crypt. "But Fate will not allow us to avoid what must be."

"Why must there be only one?" I demanded as he climbed in, and sat, studying me.

"So long as two exist, the curse cannot be broken," he said. "When there is only one, it will end, and we will all be free."

The Seventh Commandment

Când poruncile îți greșesc, amintește-ți prima poruncă.

When the commandments fail you, remember the first commandment.

I began my own research. On the nights I hunted alone, I went to the library, the church, and the hospital, seeking answers. He did not permit me to talk to those who were not like us. Damien insisted that the wolf did not talk to its dinner, nor should we. I found tomes of ancient lore, myth, and science, but I found no explanation. I wondered where he had found such answers, but he would not say when I asked.

The summer night when Fate came for me, I hadn't been expecting it. Looking back I see how foolish I was. I returned from hunting before dawn to find his crypt empty. A sword and hammer lay on the stone lid to the sarcophagus, with a gopher wood pike beside them.

I turned at a rustling behind me, as he charged through the darkness, tackling me. My hand found the hammer's handle as I went down, and I got a blow in on him as I hit the compacted ground. I wasn't sure who got the better shot, but I was on my feet before he could rise, and turned to find the sword gone from the crypt.

I sensed the sweep of the blade as he made to sever my head from my body but moved more quickly than humanly possible. The Curse gave me strength and speed I lacked before and I knew my enemy had it, too.

Dodging the blow, I put the hammer into his gut, and he doubled over, giving me time to snatch the pike from the crypt. The battle raged and I had the eerie sense that this was some twisted version of *Mortal Combat.*

I had never been much of a video game player, but I had seen a few martial arts movies. Watching Jackie Chan and Bruce Lee didn't make me an expert in combat, but I surprised myself when I found I had the ability to envision the move I wanted to make, then execute it with near perfection. It further reminded me that I was no longer human.

"You have grown strong," he said, as he assaulted me from behind, the blade catching my upper arm, peeling flesh from bone. "Hunting must have been good tonight."

No blood dripped from the wound, and no pain found its way to my brain. My arm, however, hung limp at my side, It refused to answer when I tried to raise it.

"I could say the same," I said. The pike was now the only option for me, or so I thought. As the battle raged on, and I side-stepped another blow, the wound healed, almost as if by a miracle. It was at that moment I felt a spark of brilliance come over me. Putting the butt of the pike against the head of the wooden mallet, I used the two weapons as one, and came around on him, aiming low.

The pike found its mark. The hammer drove it home.

The piercing scream of unholy agony deafened me. He fell to his knees, dropping the sword. I took a step back, feeling regret for having to destroy him. He'd trained me well in the rules, and I knew the job was not yet done.

I picked up the sword.

"There is yet but one more rule you must learn," he said, as I hesitated.

"And what's that?"

"When the rules fail you," he continued, "remember the first rule."

I raised the sword to strike and bit my lip as I did.

As I prepared his body to return it to the crypt, I had to wonder if I had done things right. I expected some miraculous epiphany, a flash of blue light enveloping me and sweeping me to another life, to another time. No fanfare accompanied my victory. No cacophony of fallen angels appeared to herald the day. No smoke or blood erupted from my fallen mentor. He died as much as one of our kind possibly could, and my hand assured it.

I placed his head in the crook of his arm. I made sure the pike pierced the bottom of the crypt, finding a niche that seemed to fit the stake perfectly.

Just as the corpse was pinioned to the crypt, I noticed something at his knee. A book lay hidden in the depths of the sarcophagus. I reached for it and turned it in my hand as I stepped back. I lifted the cover to see a neatly printed cover page.

Livre des morts. La vie et mort du Professeur Bartolli.

That's when the flash of green lightning surrounded me. It crackled on my flesh and made my hair stand on end. I felt something boiling in my core. It spread out into my extremities. Then the world went dark, and I fell into oblivion.

PART TWO: The Journey

"Ask not for whom the bell tolls. It tolls for thee." —John Donne

New Orleans, 1853

Some people say New Orleans is home to voodoo priests and witches. Others say it is filled with vampires and ghosts. I say it's a city with a macabre history, bathed in blood. It is not so much a city of serial killers or monsters, though at times, those creatures had their due. As I came to it—this time— *The Crescent City* was painted yellow.

By this time, I had seen many lives, and many deaths. I'd seen history and a future that had not yet been written in ink, only sketched in chalk.

I had battled to save my own head on more than one occasion. I knew there were others out there. I could sense one in particular. I thought perhaps an escape from Paris would offer respite, but I sensed his presence all the same.

The earth shall suffer only one.

This wasn't my first time in New Orleans either. I had come to *The Big Easy* once before, almost a quarter of a century after my own time. The city had undergone a transformation after a wicked hurricane ravaged the region in 2005. Like Hurricane Betsy before it, Katrina had laid waste to not just the city, but a good portion of the central Gulf Coast. The name Katrina would be retired, and never again be used in the World Meteorological Organization's naming convention. They did this when a particular tropical cyclone became so deadly and/or damaging that future use might be considered insensitive or confusing.

"*Bon soir mam'selle*," a young man greeted me as I stepped off the ship and onto dry land for the first time in months. "Do you have accommodations? May I arrange for your luggage?"

Some things never changed. Just like con artists tried to pick up women at the airport in my own time, this young man offered to see me safely delivered to my hotel, for a small fee, and perhaps a shilling or two for his pocket. Small fee indeed. I knew his sort. He might have been a con artist or peddler of human flesh, but the chances of both of us being a dyed-in-the-wool killer might be slim to none, and I knew which of us could be most lethal.

I'd already been run out of Paris. I got careless in my hunt, taking for granted the fact that this was the same city that spawned a revolution against its own royal class. *What might they do to a monster like me?* Nothing I couldn't survive, but it made the hunting difficult, and I recognized it as a sign to move on. The journey on a slow boat to Haiti took an ungodly month, followed on an even slower boat to New Orleans. I survived by feasting on the abundant colony of rats, along with one careless deckhand. He stumbled into the hold one night, finding me particularly ravenous. I'd been able to convince the captain he'd fallen overboard, but it had been a close call.

"No thank you," I replied, side-stepping him. I had no such accommodations. I had no money. Yet.

The streets of *The Crescent City* were nothing like I remembered from my last visit to *The Big Easy* so many centuries ago. That was more than one hundred years in the future. When one was not bound by time, it made the future a memory, and the past became something to look forward to.

As it stood now, New Orleans was more than a one-hundred-year-old city. I expected to find it filled with French, Spanish, and Haitian traders, trappers, and adventurers. Tonight, the streets were empty.

From the harbor, I found my way to Charity Hospital. The brick and mortar edifice wasn't the massive building I remembered from my own time. It still served the indigent, many of whom lay in the streets. The hospital was overwhelmed. Many of the patients died. My suspicions were confirmed when the nun tending the sick occasionally lay a scrap of cloth over the victim's head. It spoke to the poverty and devastation in the region. There weren't enough shrouds to cover the dead. There were no blankets for the dying—little hope for the living.

"Pardon me," I interrupted her somber work. "I've just arrived from Paris. I'm looking for the physician in charge."

"Dr. Samuel Choppin," she said in a thick French-laced accent. "You'll find him inside."

"Merci."

"Madam, I do not intend any offense, but can you not see I am up to my eyeballs in the dying? We've already lost a thousand men, and nearly half as many women." Dr. Choppin sat behind a desk in an office on the third floor of the pauper's hospital. Run by the Sisters of Charity, the hospital was stately for a building of its day. I remembered a modern building that towered alongside the Quarter, flanked by the Super Dome. During the dark days of Hurricane Katrina, the building had been flooded, while patients who could not be evacuated before the killer storm were kept alive by any means necessary. It wasn't easy and not everyone survived. Days of no water, no electricity and no air conditioning had been bad enough. The lack of flushing toilets and adequate food supplies made it a living hell.

"Dr. Choppin," I insisted. "I'm not asking for anything. I'm a doctor. I came to help. I am Dr. Marie Betancourte, your servant, sir."

The man eyed me from beneath his brushy brows. "A woman *doctor*? *Pshaw*."

"I am a graduate of *Sorbonne Université*," I said. It wasn't a lie. I had not finished my degree in life, but over the course of my travels in time, I'd managed to complete several other degrees. I just didn't have the paperwork to back it up, only the forged documents I carried tucked in my bag. "I have a specialty in communicable diseases and public health."

This gave him a moment's pause. "And what do you know of *le fièvre jaune*?"

The Saffron Scourge? I knew plenty.

"I know that this is not the first summer there has been an outbreak like this, but I know this has been the worst," I said, building my case on a layer of empathy. "Unacclimated newcomers have contracted the disease by the thousands, and with refugees coming from Haiti, and the influx of ships arriving from Hispaniola, Cuba, Guadeloupe and Barbados, the sword of pestilence cuts the masses down like lambs at the slaughter. Symptoms come on fast. Fever. Jaundice. Black vomit. Delirium. Many die the following day."

"And what is the treatment for the fever, madam?"

"There is no cure," she said. "Not presently. I believe, however, to know the source."

Now, I had his attention. "This pestilence *can* be treated, madam. Blister, bleed, or purge. That is how it is cured. We received a fresh shipment of Swedish leeches only a month ago. They are the best in the world for bleeding a patient and removing the pestilence."

"I am sure there are plenty of leeches in the swamp," I observed without admonishment.

"Perhaps. There is also a *hoodoo doctor* who swears by a bath infused with meadowsweet and willow bark. But it must be taken beneath the light of a blue moon, in the open air, with the victim unclothed." His words told me he considered the concept scandalous, at best.

"And how is that working out for you?" I snipped, tartly. "Have you seen a reduction in the fatality rates?" That shut him up, but his face reddened. "Is it not better to prevent than cure?" I added.

"If there's anyone yet who has not been infected," he said, and I sensed his ire cool. "How do we prevent infection?"

"Yellow Jack is caused by a mosquitos bite," I said. "Vector control is the first step to prevention." The second step was vaccination, but I had yet to perfect a vaccine. I'd come close in one time, when I'd charmed a virologist and coaxed him to teach me how to create a vaccine, but he died before he showed me the full process. Heroin over-dose.

"Vector control? Mosquitos? Madam, surely you must be joking. Even if you're correct, *Doctor* Betancourt—which I seriously doubt—mosquitos are ubiquitous. That means they are everywhere."

Mainsplaining. Seriously?

I had given him my creator's name. Any other name I might assume could have been out of place in this age. The name Betancourt carried some weight. An ancient family name, it could be found in the records as far back as the Middle Ages, in Artois, a former province in Northern France. Jean de Betancourt was a French explorer who led an expedition to the Canary Islands, earning the title *The King of the Canary Islands*. Before that, Augustin de *Béthancourt* led armies of Templar crusaders into the Holy Land where they slaughtered the forces of Saladin. It was a magnificent battle—one I had been fortunate to observe, and to celebrate with a banquet of my own.

"They swarm in the millions. How do you propose we keep them from biting?" He brought me out of my thoughts.

"I have several techniques designed to interrupt their reproductive process. It isn't going to be easy, and it will take some time, but with a city-wide effort, we should be able to at least slow the infection rate."

He considered me for a long moment. "You intend to keep the mosquito from ... ehem ... mating?"

"No, but there are things we can do to interrupt their larval stage," she said. "We begin by removing areas of standing water. Then, we must make any standing water inhospitable to the eggs and hatching larvae."

That made him roll his eyes and let out an exasperated breath. "Madam, you realize we are living in a swamp that is held back only by the levees? Yes?"

"I am aware of the challenges, Doctor," I said. "We will need the able bodied to begin the effort within the city. I can't do much for the swamp, but I can affect the local mosquito population. There are plants that deter the insects, and I know some remedies to prevent them from biting. In the meantime, I also know some treatments to support the ill. Bloodletting, purging and blistering the skin with nettles are archaic and barbaric. We must provide fluids. Intravenously if necessary. We also can treat with willow bark tea to reduce fever and discomfort. Adding sugar and minerals to water, for those too weak to eat, will also help."

I wasn't sure if he considered my idea crazy and planned to throw me out on my ear. But he was at least considering my proposal. "There aren't many able-bodied people left."

"I'll see who I can enlist," I said. "I've only just arrived, and it's late. I'll need some supplies, too."

"Of course you will," he said, rolling his eyes. "Like what?"

"Kerosene," I said. "For one."

"Are you going to torch the little bastards?" he blanched, realizing his language might be too harsh for a Parisian lady.

"Well, if my plan doesn't work, that might be an option," I responded. "Let's hope it doesn't come to that. No, treating standing water with a film of kerosene over the top prevents the larvae from being able to take wing when they do hatch. It increases the surface tension of the water. They essentially drown."

"Curious," he said, nonplused. He reached for a sheet of paper and his ink pot and quill pen. "We already tried burning all the infected clothing in tar. It didn't do anything except stink up the city."

So that's where the vile smell came from.

"Here is a letter of recommendation. Give this to Monsieur Gagnon at *Le Château Creole* over on Clio Street. If he doesn't have a room, he'll be able to recommend somewhere nearby."

"There is one other small matter," I said, hesitation intentional in my voice. The doctor's brow lifted again. "I do hate to have to be so bold, but I've arrived with only a letter of credit. I have no cash to pay for a room."

"My note should ensure he trusts you," he said. "I can offer you a wage of fourteen dollars a month while you work here. You will be expected to tend patients in addition to your public health duties."

"Only fourteen dollars a month?" I asked. I had no idea what constituted a living wage here in *The Crescent City*, but as in my own time, I suspected a wage gap of at least fifty percent, if not more. "For the work of two physicians? It hardly seems fair."

He pursed his lips and narrowed his eyes at me. "Very well." He let out an exasperated breath. "You have a point," he said. "Twenty is as high as I am allowed to offer without board approval."

"I'll take twenty-six, pending board approval." I took the letter he held out and smiled, though he looked as if he'd been punched in the throat. "I'll be back in the morning."

Once settled at *Le Château* I unpacked my bag. I didn't own much, but what I had fit in the armoire, with room to spare. I glanced down at the mud-caked skirts and reminded myself to ask about laundry services. By morning, I would need it.

The buffet, which lined the streets around Charity Hospital, remained unattended. The dying outnumbered the living when I arrived. Tonight, moving silently through the shadows, I wore a gray travel dress and jacket, the perfect camouflage in the foggy streets. I knew now how *Jack the Ripper* had been so successful. I considered myself more tidy than *Saucy Jack*. While he eviscerated his victims, a simple bite to break the skin allowed me access to my favorite meal. Better yet, it might be easily confused for a physician's attempt at bloodletting.

I debated the wisdom in encouraging the head surgeon to avoid bloodletting, but I knew if I had to be around it, I might lose any control I had. It was hard when I was hungry. In this place in time, the practice had become so commonly accepted, I supposed there would be physicians who might reject my theory. Tradition and training were hard for anyone to overcome.

It took a long time for me to become accustomed to this undead life, and the necessities of survival. I learned quickly that I couldn't sustain myself on just any prey. My food had to still be warm, but so close to the verge of death that hope abandoned my victims. It allowed me the luxury to think of myself as more of an *Angel of Mercy* than the *Angel of Death*. If I ended their suffering by even a few minutes then I considered it a favor of reciprocity—the tango of life and death.

It didn't mean I always slipped silently back into my room, sometime between midnight and dawn, unscathed. Sometimes the dying didn't go willingly. Some lashed out in their death throes but were too weak to do much damage. Most wounds healed by the time I rose. Cursed flesh mended easily.

Unlike the one who made me, the daylight held no fear for me. In the dreary morning, I bundled up my hunting clothes and donned the blue dress and white smock of a physician. The owner at the desk offered me a cotton flour sack to bag my laundry in and informed me the servants would have it returned to me the following day.

A foggy night yielded to a rainy morning. The drizzle wasn't enough to require an umbrella, but it was enough that my hair became sodden, tugging against the pins that held it out of my way.

I found Dr. Choppin in his office when I reported for duty. He appeared unchanged, and I wondered if he'd sat at his desk working through the night. "Dr. Betancourt." He eyed me dubiously. "You're practically drowned. Could you not get a covered carriage?"

"I walked." I shook the rain from my hair and smoothed it back with a cold hand. "I'm anxious to see to my duties. How would you like me to proceed?"

"See Sister Marie-Claire," he told me. "She is in charge of triage. We're setting up tents near the potter's field to the east for the most serious of the indigent patients."

I stood firm, my brow drawn down over my eyes, considering what he'd just said. It seemed insensitive to place critical care patients so near their ultimate destination. I'd seen for myself upon arrival, work crews digging a mass grave.

It wouldn't serve the dead well, anyway. Graves in T*he Crescent City* were often above ground to prevent the caskets from floating up. New Orleans, already well below sea-level, had a high water table, and even without a box for each of the dead, the corpses would again see the light of day. It might just take a little longer. That also meant the corpse would be in an advanced state of decay.

"Yes, Dr. Betancourt?" he inquired without looking up from his work.

"It would be better to burn the dead," I pointed out.

"In this downpour?" he asked dryly.

"Maybe not today, but ... the bodies will come back on us if we don't. Along with the pestilence."

"I thought you said mosquitos carried the plague, madam?" Now, he looked up. "Allow me to worry about the dead. Your job is to see to the living and try to keep them that way."

If he only knew.

Weeks passed as I did what I could for the *City of the Dead*. A team of Hungarian immigrants were assigned as my work crew, and I put them to it. Our first order of business was to find all bodies of standing water in the city and drain them or cover them. Cylindrical wood cisterns were as common as the wrought iron balcony rails and shotgun houses. Most were elevated on plastered brick piers that rose three to six feet above ground.

Used to collect rain water, every house, factory, and palazzo had one. They were just as common in the ghettos as they were along Esplanade Avenue in the Garden District. Most were unapologetically in plain sight, but others were more discreet. Locals were so accustomed to them that when asked, no one seemed to know what—or where—they were. As a result we found them on rooftops, some hidden in open-top sheds. As we identified one after the other, all crawling with mosquito larvae, the words of Mark Twain came to mind. "*One even becomes reconciled to the cistern presently; this is a mighty cask, painted green, and sometimes a couple of stories high, which is propped against the house-corner on stilts. There is a mansion-and -brewery suggestion about the combination, which seems very incongruous at first.*"

"Why don't people have wells here?" I asked one of the few workers who spoke English. Béla György. In his mid-thirties, with a strong back, he accomplished more work in a day than most did in a week. I'd learned in our time together the man recently lost his entire family. He remained, alone in the world.

Béla considered me for a moment. He answered in a thick clipped accent. "Is true. The water table here is high. Water is only few feet down, but is murky. It tastes like turtle." His manner of speaking reminded me of Boris from the *Rocky & Bullwinkle* cartoons I watched as a child. "Is not good for *drinking*."

Hmm. Good to know. I decided in the long hours of work that perhaps the cisterns were a better option. Ground water could be easily contaminated by the raw sewage created by thousands of residents. Yellow fever might be easier to contain than dysentery, cryptosporidiosis, campylobacteriosis, E. coli, giardiasis, leptospirosis, and Hepatitis A—to name a few.

The Contender

"I do not fear death. I had been dead for billions and billions of years before I was born and had not suffered the slightest inconvenience from it." — Mark Twain

One evening as I sat on the veranda above the street, thinking, I came upon a problem I hadn't considered. Gutters ran along the building across the street, gutters clogged with moss and leaves from the live oak tree that hung over the street.

As I contemplated the thought of sending Béla—a mountain of a man—up a rickety ladder to clean out the gutters on the *Cathédrale-Basilique de Saint-Louis*, I felt something twinge in the back of my brain. The sensation sent lightning bolts flashing in my eyes and I suddenly lacked the ability to draw in breath.

I had experienced this feeling twice before and I knew what it meant. It was a sign that a new contender had entered the proverbial Thunderdome.

Two men enter, one man leaves. The earth may suffer only one.

Now the only question that remained, how long before he—or she—found me.

The answer came much sooner than expected. A few nights later, as I walked the moonlit streets of the Garden District, returning from my evening meal, I sensed eyes burning into my soul. *Creatures of the Night* recognized kindred spirits and it came as no surprise when a shadowed figure stepped out into the moonlight, blocking my path.

The man stood barely taller than I, but robust, barrel chested, with his hands in fists. He wore blue jeans, a white t-shirt, a black leather jacket, and boots. I suspected he came from a more modern time, perhaps even something closer to my own.

"Took you long enough," I said without introduction.

"Where are we?" he asked. His accent reminded me of the Bronx. "What is this place? What is the date?"

"Where did you come from? *When* did you come from?"

"I'm back from the future, baby," he snarked. *Yes. Definitely the Bronx.* "Ever heard of that movie?"

"Hasn't everyone?" I mused. "Michael J. Fox, Christopher Lloyd, Lea Thompson. It's a classic."

"Well, that's where I started," he said.

"1985?"

"Aw, hell no. When I left it was 2020. What a mess! Be glad you're *here*."

He took a step towards me, but I took a step back, keeping ample distance between us as I sized him up.

"I left in 1989," I said. "But this wasn't my first stop."

"So, where are we? Charleston? Savannah?"

"New Orleans," I answered him. "1853."

"Whoopty-freakin-doo," he said, peeling out of his jacket. "Let's get this over with. I hate New Orleans." He reached into his hip pocket and pulled out a switchblade, flicking it open. The moonlight glinted off the blade and shined on his teeth as he charged.

I skirted his assault but caught the heel of my shoe between the cobblestones, and fell hard, rolling back onto my feet. He turned and prepared to charge again. "How many have you defeated?"

"More than enough," he sniped. "This ain't my first rodeo."

The second charge left me scathed, a slash across my face cut into my mouth so deep I could taste the tang of the blade. There would be no blood, unless he eviscerated me. I had fed less than an hour before, and the blood in my gut would not congeal for some time.

"What? You too scared to fight back?" he taunted me, as I waited for the wound to heal. The flesh knitted together neatly and efficiently.

"Who says I haven't?" I asked as I circled him, drawing him into a tango of life and death.

Though I fought battles like this before, I didn't let my guard down. This dance was not without purpose. I had a weapon, but it wasn't presently in my hand. It didn't need to be.

On the third charge, I jabbed my fist into his shoulder, finding the brachial plexus nerve, knowing it would send shockwaves down his arm. The knife clattered to the cobblestone streets as it fell from his flexed hand. I turned and charged him before he could recover. I hoisted him from his feet with every ounce of my strength. He kicked at me as I attacked, but it was too little, too late. He was born aloft. I could hear the scrape of wrought iron against bone as his body impaled itself on the Apache pickets of the gate to one of the immaculately maintained gardens. I heard the crunch as it fractured the sternum, thus impaling the heart. He flailed, kicking, and screaming, trying to free himself.

I had his knife in my hand and considered it a moment. This would be a messy job. Still, I was a trained surgeon, and I strode confidently toward the gate, avoiding his kicking feet as I reached for the bloody latch. Skirting his desperate assault I swung it open and came around. With my left hand, I grasped his hair. His knife in my right lay against his throat.

"This ain't my first rodeo either," I said, then finished the job. "*Yippee-kai-yay.*"

The sky above split in two as the familiar perfume of ozone pierced my senses. The green fingers of lightning engulfed me, filling my vision. I hated this part. It felt like my body might be ripped apart as time and space fell away around me.

PART THREE: Les Revenants

"*But a wild creature will always go back to the wild, in the end.*"

— Susan Cooper, *The Selkie Girl*

This particular leap—I didn't know what else to call it—felt worse than my initial dying. The acrid sting of the lightning twinged in my salivary glands but left me unable to swallow. Weak from the shock alone, the journey disoriented me much more than I had been in my previous travels. I lay staring up at swirling clouds with bolts of lightning crashing around me.

The worst part came from never knowing where I would land—or when. Imagine my chagrin when I pushed myself up onto my elbows and found myself in front of a large Victorian home with a wrap-around porch on a corner lot. A wrought iron fence—like the one I'd impaled my enemy upon—enclosed the property, but there were subtle differences.

The trunks of giant live oak trees that once shaded the yards remained, amputated stumps. The home stood in disrepair, a shadow of its former glory. The gate hung on its hinges, swaying in the vortex of wind that picked up leaves and debris and sent it tumbling across the empty streets.

Most of the houses in this neighborhood were known as a *shotgun* style. They were smaller, narrow, built with efficiency in mind. Most were only one room wide, twelve feet or so. Some were three or four rooms deep with no hallways—all the doors lined up. In the more elegant neighborhoods, they might have spacious gabled front porches, perfect for an afternoon cup of tea with the neighbors, or an evening brandy with family and friends. Here, some barely had a stoop.

As I pushed myself up to my feet, I had to wonder if Armageddon had come to pass. There were no cars, no buses, no horses in the street. Surrounding buildings were shuttered; abandoned. Powerlines swayed in a growing breeze and in the distance I could see the stacks from dormant power plants.

The smell told me everything. The perpetual funk of New Orleans had become familiar. One never got accustomed to the odor. Had I been un-cursed, I might have vomited at the continuing onslaught of the miasma. Even in the gusting winds, the stink lingered, ever-present.

This was not the Garden District, though. Still, I knew it by its reputation. The Lower Ninth Ward in my own time, had been a neighborhood known for refineries, and abject poverty. In 1965, Hurricane Betsy—a category four hurricane—struck this area hard, overtopping the levees and leaving a swath of destruction. My father had worked with the Army Corps of Engineers then, years before my birth. His team worked to rebuild the levee on the Industrial canal.

Before I traveled, this area had been little more than a swamp. The military seemed determined to build on what solid ground they could find, and the new barracks would house infantry and included a magazine to store powder and ammunition.

I turned my face to the wind, my hair tossing behind me, as I gazed into the darkening sky. In the distance a somber cry pierced the night, like a wolf howling at the moon. I knew it couldn't be a wolf, though. I hadn't heard the familiar sound since leaving my own place in time—since *The Curse*. Rain came down in sheets, as my brain analyzed the situation, and I knew it meant certain danger.

A hurricane was coming.

I dashed to the gate and had to force it back against the rusted hinges. The sidewalk to the porch was overgrown with weeds and I saw movement to my left. A cat dashed out from under the house, disappearing into the knee-high grass.

I had to break a window to get inside. I didn't feel bad about it. If a hurricane was coming, it would be unlikely the unshuttered panes would survive. I was surprised to find the residence unoccupied, at least at present. The sirens whining in the distance suggested they'd headed the evacuation orders that would have been issued hours or days before.

I had no option. As the wind and rain beat against the loose siding I inspected the decor, which might best be described as *post-apocalyptic*. The chairs were worn and moth-eaten. Black mold grew in the corners of the ceiling where water dripped and began running down the wallpaper in rivulets, creating puddles on the floor.

In the kitchen, yellowed linoleum peeled up at the entryway. The floorboards were warped. A rat sat on its hind legs in the corner, munching on what appeared to be a saltine cracker. A coffee pot sat on the counter. A red can of Folgers coffee sat beside it. I guessed not everyone liked the chicory coffee made famous at the local landmark, *Café Du Monde*. A thick coat of fuzzy green mold hovered over the surface of the coffee. That would not be *the best part of waking up*, if you asked me, I decided.

With the coffee company's jingle running through my head, I opened the cabinet doors, taking inventory as if any of its contents would do me any good. I wasn't a vegetarian, nor a carnivore—technically—so the cans of green beans or Spam weren't the least bit appetizing. The Heinz Ketchup made me pause, but as a hemovore, tomato paste mixed with vinegar, high fructose corn syrup, salt, onion powder and spices held no sway with me. The rat, on the other hand, might be a tasty treat. I decided to name him Kevin.

I snatched the box of crackers from the pantry, and discovered the corner of it gnawed open, confirming my suspicion. Ripping open the box, I tossed the rest of them out for my new friend. I meant it as a peace offering, but also *bait*.

Normally I could be a patient hunter, but having just traveled, I was ravenous. Just as I was about to pounce on the juicy morsel a snake appeared from beneath the warped floorboards and snatched the rat. It was a brief battle. The snake disappeared in the void with my snack. *So much for Kevin.*

Resigned to my fate, I continued my search of the house, picking my way over swollen floorboards and discarded waste that covered almost every surface.

A grand staircase beckoned me to the second floor, but I passed with tentative steps, afraid the rotting treads could give way at any moment. Cockroaches scurried as I entered the bedroom where a stained mattress lay on the floor surrounded by dirty clothing.

In the inky darkness, the storm raged as I inspected the closets for something fitting to wear in this modern era. I found a pair of blue jeans hanging on a peg in the closet. They were men's jeans, but they were cleaner than anything else I found. I used a strip of cloth, torn from my nineteenth century dress, to make a belt. The clean-ish t-shirt hung past my knees. I found a tear near the bottom and ripped it, before taking the tattered ends and tying it in a knot. It wasn't perfect, but it would do.

I had bigger things to worry about. I needed to feed. With the difficult leap, I felt drained. It made me vulnerable, and I knew it. Of course, with the city seemingly abandoned, I anticipated the predators might be held at bay, if there were any. The tingling sensations I'd experienced in the presence of others—who were cursed like me—were absent. That gave me some confidence that I had time to find a meal. Perhaps when the storm abated, I could find a tasty floater in the flood.

As night fell, the fury of the storm intensified. I took shelter on the lower floor, fearing the wind would rip the roof off the aging structure.

I could no longer hear the sirens and I wondered if it might be because of the intensity of the storm or if it no longer functioned. The house had no electricity, and I could no longer see the lights of the city around me.

My ears popped as the pressure of the air around me fell lower and lower. Water began to seep through the doors and from under the floor boards. I moved to the staircase, hoping the added lumber made for stronger construction.

I ended up moving higher and higher up the staircase with each passing quarter hour. Seven steps up, I heard something large crash against the building. Everything shook. Water inundated my shelter. I scrambled higher, the water soaking my ankles and then my knees. By the time it reached my waist, I'd found the access to the attic, but knew better than to try and go higher. I didn't want to be trapped with no way to escape.

Instead, I swam to the bedroom where the windows seemed to undulate with the force of the wind and water pressing against it. Before I could conclude how to best break through, the force of the storm did it for me.

Drowning was not a clear and present danger, not for *The Cursed*. It wasn't pleasant, but it was temporary. I didn't need oxygen to survive. It didn't keep my body from aching to take a breath. The contaminated water filled my lungs, burning. The reflexive need to breathe had me gulping in water, as my autonomic system still struggled to fulfill its function.

I coughed up the nasty water as I broke the surface. Grasping at everything, catching nothing, I struggled to find something—anything—to hold on to. The current pulled me one direction while the wind blew me another. Like a small boat in an angry sea, I rode the roiling tide, struck repeatedly by debris both on and beneath the surface.

Just when I thought I might be sucked beneath the surface a second time, my feet contacted something solid. I tried to stand, but the current pushed against me. It was of no avail. Still, I tried again, snagging my foot on something.

Before I could react, I was hopelessly trapped, my ankle torqued as the water rose over my head, pressing me down. Growing frantic, I struggled to free myself. Once again, my body betrayed me. Fighting for a breath I did not need, I sucked in the rancid water, filling my lungs again with *God-knows-what*. The inky blackness came for me and took me down.

For Whom The Bell Tolls

"Everybody is going to be dead one day, just give them time."
— Neil Gaiman

I don't know how long I spent being cast under by the storm surge. It overtopped the levees, washing them away. The Mississippi River flooded the city that was foolishly built beneath sea level.

When I came back to myself, and coughed up the brine, I lay on a crumbling brick crypt. My foot had caught in the wrought iron arc of a fence that stood around the grave to protect it from looters.

With some effort, I freed myself, and sat up, feeling the bricks beneath me shift, threatening to give way. I froze, but the mortar failed, and the crypt collapsed.

I landed atop the remains of some poor soul who knew the finality of death but had not been allowed to rest in peace. The bones might have turned to dust as I moved off him, except for the humidness of the murky grave. Water remained in the tomb; several feet deep.

"Ah, there you are." A voice from above startled me. I looked up but saw only gray skies and swirling clouds. I had a momentary flash of a scene from the movie *Ladyhawke*. Matthew Broderick's character, Phillipe Gaston, believed he heard the voice of God. I thought maybe I had, too.

I could still remember snippets from my past life, and movies I saw or books I read. Such things seemed so trivial now.

Then, a thought chilled my heart and iced my very soul. Perhaps this leap had been different because I just arrived, and my competitor already existed in this place in time. I searched the void around me for a weapon, anything I could use to defend myself.

A marble angel stood at the back of the tomb holding a sword. I surmised the piece might be copper due to the patina of age that tinged it blue-green. White powder flaked from it as I ran my hand down the rough blade. It took me a moment to decide how to best remove it from the angel's hand, but if there really was a God in heaven, He smiled upon me now. The blade lifted effortlessly from the carved grasp of the holy being. A beam of sun seemed to pierce the tomb as I turned and gazed up at my foe. I felt like Arthur retrieving *Excalibur* from the stone.

The woman looking down at me was also *cursed*. Her black eyes and black soul cast a shadow, blocking the holy light. I felt true fear for one of the few moments in my undead life. *Was this the one who would take my head and pinion my heart to the tomb next to this rotting corpse?*

As she licked her lips and glared wickedly at me, I got the sense she was sizing me up, just as I sized her up. I sensed no fear in her.

"You survived the storm, *Cursed One*," she said, a blond curl tumbling over her shoulder, her hands on her hips. She brandished no weapon, but only a fool would believe she didn't have one.

I was no fool.

I glanced at my feeble excuse for a weapon and reconsidered. Perhaps I was.

I gazed back up at her and knew she had the advantage. Having just traveled, and not having fed, my strength waned. I never experienced anything like it in all my days, which were many.

"Will you fight me, sister?" She turned and seemed to look to the horizon.

"Now?" I asked, a chuckle in my voice. "I've recently drowned." The words made me cough and the sludge congealed in my throat. I spat and sputtered, coughing up the nasty gunk. "Have *you* been drowned today?"

"No, but ... the day is young. Do you know about the storm?"

"Know it? I rode it out."

"Yes, but this storm is one for the ages," she said, taking a step back. A brick fell from beneath her feet, and I raised a hand to shield myself. "They named her Katrina, and there won't be a storm like her again ..."

"Yes, I have seen the aftermath of this storm before," I cut her off.

"Can you taste the dying on your palate?" She inhaled like someone in a fine restaurant. "Doesn't it make you hungry?"

"All I smell is Uncle Joe down here," I snarked. "Cold leftovers that have started to draw flies ... and maggots."

"Ah, more's the pity," she mused. "Come up and join me. This may be the cleanest I've ever seen this city. This storm purged the worst of humanity out of fear, or Death. It makes no difference."

"They'll return," I pointed out. "Like cockroaches coming out of the woodwork."

"Too bad," she said, clucking her tongue. "Too bad."

"How long have you been in this time?" I asked, moving to test the door, finding it barred from the outside.

"Too long," she said. "I much prefer my own lifetime."

"Tell me," I stalled.

"I was born into my undead life in 1243," she began. "In the Carpathian Mountains of Romania. My family were followers of Radu Negru—*The Black Prince of Wallachia.*"

"Wow," I said. "You must have known Dracula." Our kind were feared and fictionalized around the world. In my time, only Sherlock Holmes appeared more times in movies, television, and literature, than the *King of the Cursed*, Vlad Dracula.

"The *strigoi* are not unknown to me," she said. "But we are the *Daughters of Lilith*—you and me. It is our fate that we are the last of our kind." *The last? Could that be true?*

"Do you have a name?"

"No, but I will have a title. One I have battled centuries to earn. I will be crowned *Queen of the Demons*," she said. "The only thing standing between me and my crown ... is you."

"Oh, well then."

"I do not wish to be confined when we take arms, so I implore you again. Join me here, in the *City of the Dead*, so that we may fulfill our destinies."

I glanced at the rotting corpse, then back up at my foe. She must have lived a hundred lifetimes and battled a hundred enemies. She would not be easy to defeat, of that I was certain. "Very well," I said. In the time we'd wasted in getting to know one another, I'd figured out my best means of escape. If I did manage to climb out, she could attack me before I had my feet beneath me. My head could be severed as it cleared the crumbling crypt, then *Uncle Joe* and I would be cozy bedfellows for all of eternity.

The crumbling bricks were my best means of escape. Without a word. I stepped out of sight and charged the opposite wall, where the mortar appeared weakest, and the bricks were already crumbling. Like the *Kool-Aid Man*, I broke through the walls, sending bricks flying. The wrought-iron fence on that side, much to my good fortune, had fallen, so my path was clear.

Once I escaped from the tomb, I recognized this place as the Saint Louis Cemetery No. 1, or *Cimetière Saint-Louis.* The oldest and most prominent graveyard in all of New Orleans, I'd taken a tour here once in my own time. I knew it was founded in the late 1790s. The Mississippi River lay eight blocks away, which explained the brackish water I'd coughed up from my lungs. I also knew the corpse of the Voodoo Queen, Marie Laveau, rested nearby. I hoped—if God had no love for me—perhaps she might.

"Impressive, sister," the strigoi said. "I made a wise choice not to underestimate your strength, or your cunning." She strolled between the once-white crypts that were now stained — polluted by the mirk and mire that collected at our feet. The quagmire was slick and sucked the shoes from my feet with each step. I slipped them off, knowing they would only hinder me.

I could hear the twang of her blade as it slid from its sheath and knew I shouldn't underestimate her, either. The very ring of it between the graves echoed and told me it was sharp.

My sword weighed more than I one I might normally wield and was not designed for fighting. To say it was ornamental might have painted a disingenuous picture. It wasn't overly pretty. There were no inlays of gold, or filigree. Nor was it exactly functional. The blade was dull, flat, and weak. One strike of her steel might shatter it into a thousand pieces. I knew I would have to find better.

I mimicked her movements, sliding silently along the narrow path, opposing her. The dance was as important as the battle, and I used the effort to search for an alternate weapon.

"You are not an ancient being," her voice seemed distant.

"No," I said. "This is beyond my time, but only because of *the Curse*. I would have lived to see this storm ... if I had lived."

"Aw, poor baby," she said, clucking her tongue. "To die young is a tragedy, to die young a second time is Fate. I hope you find this second death a relief from your suffering."

"In a city like this, the suffering is minimal," I said. "I owned this *City of the Dead* during the Yellow Fever Epidemic. The dying lined the street like a feast before a battle. I never hungered, I never languished in misery. Everyone was too busy dying to notice a killer in their midst.

"How fortunate for you, sister." Her voice came from behind me, and I turned, weapon raised, prepared to defend my life. I sidestepped, and just in time as she landed with a squish only inches from where I stood. Startled, I fell back, landing in the muck. Her blade came down over me, but I deflected her blade. It sparked as it slid off my weapon and stuck the wrought-iron behind me. The ting of it echoed as I scrambled to my feet and backed away.

She stood, pausing to inspect her blade for damage. It gave me time to position myself where I had room to maneuver. If she wanted to attack, I knew it would be quick. I positioned my own sword, so it felt like a natural extension of my arm. I struggled to keep my wrist straight against the heft of it. I could charge while she studied the steel, but I sensed that's what she wanted. She wanted me to make a mistake.

"Tell me your name," I commanded. If I were to die once and for all, I figured I at least needed to know the name of my doom.

"I have had many names." She glanced up, allowing the weapon to fall to her side. "None of any consequence to you, though."

She charged, slashing then turning with a quick riposte. My Achilles tendon screamed as the blade severed it, just below my calf muscle. I stumbled, blocking as she turned and made to chop at my head. My blade held fast, protecting me from the strike.

In the time it took for me to get to my feet, she pounced. My style of fighting was much less polished. I hacked and slashed in a forward attack. It was direct and vicious, but also easy for her to defend.

I knew I would not be able to wear her down. I could not continue such futile assaults and still walk away from this day with my head perched upon my shoulders. Timing would be crucial.

While the confines of the crypt had been tight, the cemetery itself wasn't much better. The rows between the graves were narrow, and the wrought iron fences added to the claustrophobic conditions.

I struggled to defend against her attack, backing up and dodging, ducking beneath her blade, forcing her to pivot. Then, using her momentum to charge backwards, I countered. I got one or two good hits on her here and there, but she gave better than she got. Every slash and stab left me wounded and weak.

Still, our blades clashed in a flurry of motion, violent and intense. My will to survive was every bit as strong as hers, even though I was weakened by my recent travels.

A skilled swordswoman, she aimed for my heart, but I parried, and counterattacked, bringing my blade up under her armpit, piercing flesh. A vicious scream erupted from her chest as I drove the blade in. At the same moment, she struck with her elbow, knocking me to the ground, leaving me reeling from the blow.

She turned, an angry scowl on her wicked face. "No one can defeat me," she spat the words. Rage danced like flames in her eyes as her blade hung in her limp hand. If the injury was as bad as it appeared, I knew it wouldn't last long. If she was faking it, I still needed to act.

Catching sight of something out of the corner of my eye, I realized my salvation lay at my feet. A shard of shattered wood stuck up from the piles of debris that had been washed in when the levees failed. I grasped it and found the long shank of a nail protruding from it. It had to be at least twelve inches long. With a vicious blow, I spun, going low, but aiming high. The force of the blow lifted her from her feet. The section of wood might have been part of a landscape timber, before the storm tore it from its place in someone's yard. The nail wasn't particularly sharp, but my aim hit true, and the force sufficient to pierce her heart, impaling her as it imbedded into the plaster crypt behind her. She hung from it, her feet kicking as her blade fell at her feet. It clattered on the stone.

I took a moment to catch my breath but knew I couldn't tarry. I took up her sword and turned to address her. A spew of blood and profanities flew from her lips in every language one could imagine. A creature as old as her had lifetimes to learn such vile words, words I could only guess at their meaning. I took her sword—much lighter than the one I'd used—between my sticky hands. "*The earth may suffer only one.*"

Her head landed at the foot of the grave, and only then did I realize exactly where we were. Thousands of X marks had been scratched into the plaster, drawn on the surface of the mausoleum with magic marker, or chalk. That was my sign that the Voodoo Queen did indeed care for me. I dropped to one knee in respect. "*Mèsi anpil,*" the words came to me, even though I had never heard them before. It was a Haitian Creole prayer of thanks for her intervention.

The door of the crypt swung open, the hinges grinding and squealing as they did. A dark swirling cloud enveloped the corpse and in the blink of an eye, the contender's body was received in the grave. The door closed, slamming shut. I could hear the mechanism of a lock latching from inside. The *defeated* had been welcomed to her final resting place, and left me to question what would happen next.

If I expected lightning bolts or a heavenly host singing my praises, I was sorely disappointed. I could feel the ripples of excitement at the prospects waning as the realization washed over me. The battle was over. I was the last of my kind.

Or was I?

The Hit

HORROR BY JB CAINE

Death made theirs a very convenient relationship. Neither asked where the other had been, what they'd been doing, or who they'd killed. She was a vampire. He was a hit man.

They strolled along the Riverwalk, holding hands and watching the boats bob in the current. His was a face that was easy to forget. Average height, average weight, brown hair, brown eyes ... everything about him could fade into the scenery, and that was a great asset in his line of work.

She, on the other hand, was very distinctive. Her shiny black hair was cut in a stacked bob with chunky curls flipping up at the edges, stylish in a unique way that claimed it wasn't an accident, but you'd also never see anyone else with that same look. Something about her spoke of worldliness, maybe the cut of her jacket, her Italian sandals, or the way her hazel eyes seemed to survey everything with just a touch of jaded disinterest. Her hand was warm, though, and he squeezed it.

"I guess you had a successful hunt last night?" he inquired. He often wondered how she chose her prey, but he never asked. *No questions asked* was the agreement, and it had served them well.

"Clearly," she smiled, squeezing his hand back. She did not elaborate, though she knew he was dropping conversation bait.

He wasn't surprised that she didn't answer, but he was disappointed. His jobs were sent to him in zipped files via the dark web. It was a straightforward process. He got the information on the target, sometimes he got context for *why* the person ended up in his inbox, and sometimes not. But the information came, he handled the job and provided confirmation via burner phone, and he got paid.

But what about her? Did she pick her targets based on some sort of criteria? Maybe pick them up in clubs and lure them out back for what they thought would be a hot and dirty quickie? Or did she stalk her prey for nights in a row? Curiosity would consume him if he let himself go down the rabbit hole.

"I was a little worried," he continued. "You barely made it home by daybreak."

She chuckled, a throaty sound that thickened the air and hinted at secrets. "It's sweet of you to worry, but I've been hunting a long time. I wasn't in any danger." There was so much about her he didn't know, that no one else knew, and that was how her life had been for as long as she could remember. It was safer for everyone that way.

"But what if you couldn't make it back? You know I'd come get you anywhere, right? You could ride home in the trunk. I put moving blankets back there so I could carry you in if I had to."

She was on the fence between amused and annoyed, but she kept her tone light. "You watch too many monster movies, babe. I wouldn't burn up in the sun. I'm just nocturnal. I might fall asleep somewhere I shouldn't, though, and I'd be hard asleep till nightfall. So I'll always make it home to you or call and tell you where I am; don't worry."

Though her words were affectionate, there was something in her tone that indicated that the conversation was over. So he led her over to the railing overlooking the water and turned her to face him. He drew her to him and kissed her, gently at first, but then more hungrily as his passion grew. She could feel his need as they pressed against each other, and she was glad for it, because it meant there wouldn't be much more talking tonight. Less talking meant fewer questions. They were only a few hundred yards from their apartment overlooking the river, and they closed the distance in record time.

The next morning, he woke to a room artificially dark thanks to the blackout curtains he had put up for her. He pressed the button on the side of his smartwatch: 10:37 a.m. He yawned and stretched, hearing a satisfactory *pop* from his back. and then rolled over to see her sleeping deeply beside him, wearing one of his old Van Halen tee shirts.

He wondered if she'd ever seen them live, and which line-up of the band she might've seen. That led him to wonder in which decade she might have seen them ... might she have even seen them back in the 70s when they were barely adults themselves? He knew he wasn't supposed to ask her how old she was, but he made a note to ask her about the concert.

He rose from the bed and headed toward the front room to check his email, but he paused by the window, thinking about what she said the night before. He reached out hesitantly, knowing that his next act could have consequences, but his curiosity won out over his better sense. He drew back one of the curtains just far enough for a thin beam of light to fall upon her bronzed skin and braced himself for her reaction.

There was none. Her smooth thigh remained unblemished, and she did not stir.

He stood there for another minute, pulling the drapery even a little farther and studying how her skin looked in sunlight. Then he let the fabric fall and began humming "Running with the Devil" as he slipped into the living room, closing the bedroom door behind him.

He made himself a cup of coffee and logged into his fake flower shop account. He verified his credentials and checked the encrypted bulletin board from which potential clients offered him *employment.* His inbox flag glowed red, indicating that a message had been received. He clicked on the link to open it.

My family and I would like to purchase one of your flower arrangements. Do you accept credit cards? We saw on your website that you charge $50 and can arrange for delivery. Our number is in your customer files. Please give us a call at your earliest convenience, as we'd like to have the flowers delivered for a special occasion.

The code was simplistic, of course, but it did allow for plausible deniability in case anyone ever saved a screenshot or managed to hack into his account. The Burletti family, for whom he worked on occasion, wanted to eliminate someone they suspected of stealing from them. Probably an employee. They were offering him $50,000 to do the job and wanted him to call from his burner phone for details about the target.

He liked it when this kind of job came through. The Burlettis were excellent about payment, and if he managed to do the job within twenty-four hours, they often gave a 10% bonus. Plus, anyone they hired him to eliminate was most likely not only crooked, but disloyal. The Burlettis couldn't let such disrespect go unpunished, so they needed an example to be set. They also were satisfied with a nice, clean kill. In and out. They never asked him to do anything unnecessarily brutal or showy. They valued efficiency and discretion, and he could appreciate that.

He snagged the cellphone he used for business off the coffee table and selected a contact named "Bob". The phone rang twice.

"Nice of you to return my call so quickly," the voice on the other end said. "Hold on just a sec; my signal here isn't too great."

Which basically meant there was someone there who shouldn't overhear the conversation. A moment later, the voice was back.

"I see you got my message."

"Yeah, I did," he replied. "Do you have a name for the order? Where would you like the flowers delivered?"

"The flowers are for one Darwin Clark, to wish him a lovely vacation that he bought with his bonus money. We'd like to have those delivered very soon, as we aren't sure when he'll be returning from his trip."

"What a lovely gesture," the man said.

"Well, Mr. Clark has been one of our employees for quite some time. Are you ready for the delivery address?"

"Go right ahead." The man recognized the address as being in the Palms, a relatively upscale suburban neighborhood on the north side of town. He didn't write it down, of course. But he repeated it to himself silently three times, then said it back to the stranger on the other end of the line.

"Marvelous. We appreciate your speedy delivery. Can we send you an electronic deposit, and then complete payment once they're delivered?"

"Of course. Thank you for your business."

The phone *clicked* as the Burletti representative hung up. The man didn't like taking rush jobs, but the Burlettis were good clients. Unfortunately, that meant rush planning. A good hit required surveillance of the target, but short notice made that impossible. Ideally, a rushed hit should look like either random violence or an accident. Random violence wouldn't be common in a suburban neighborhood, and drew unnecessary attention. Staging an accident would be hard to do with no knowledge of the inside of the house.

He decided to go for a drive and think about logistics.

Two hours later, he found himself wandering through the public library, searching for inspiration. As a kid, he had been teased relentlessly by his classmates and his father about always having his nose in a book. The joke was on them, though, because it turned out that crime novels were great inspiration for the methodology of the kill.

He strolled through the fiction section, scanning titles of books he'd read, hoping a memory of a clever killer would give him an idea. Cornwell, King, Patterson ... none of the authors were speaking to him today. Until he made it to the S's. Stoker.

A smile spread slowly across his face as a plan took form.

He sat in the bedroom chair as the shadows began to lengthen, watching her as she slept. There was no point in trying to wake her until her body told her it was time to rise, so he ran through the pitch in his mind, planning what he would say to convince her.

He wondered what it would be like to see her kill, and his mind began creating scenes as he fantasized.

A twenty-something trust-fund-asshole answered the door to find her standing on his step in black jeans and a tight burgundy leather top. She looked at him through her thick, dark lashes, and his lips parted into a small "o" as he was hypnotized by her gaze. She placed her index finger on his chest and pushed him backwards until he ran into the arm of a loveseat.

"Stay," she whispered, and he sat obediently still as she circled around and climbed up behind him. She licked her perfectly-tinted lips and then slowly, teasingly, ran her tongue from his collarbone to the spot in his neck where his carotid artery pulsed.

The man's breathing quickened, anticipating the culmination of his daydream.

She whispered into her victim's ear, "Now you'll be mine forever."

"Yes," he sighed as she wrapped her right arm around his shoulders and her left arm around his torso, her breath hot on his neck. She raised her head for just a moment and smiled as two thin fangs slid out from their hidden sheaths above her human canine teeth.

As she pierced his neck, her victim spasmed and moaned, as though caught in the throes of ecstasy. She clung to him as he weakened, and eventually his eyelids fluttered and he went limp. She pulled her mouth away from his throat, her lips moist with his still-warm blood.

The man felt his own arousal growing as he imagined the moment of the stranger's death, a strange and titillating mix of sex and violence.

The October sun was minutes away from setting when she began to stir, and by that time, the man felt he would lose his mind if he couldn't spill into her all the passion he'd spent the afternoon building. He ran his hands up her legs and under the edges of the tee shirt, and she smiled through barely-open eyes as he hovered above her, hooking his fingers on the edge of her panties.

"Well, well," she mumbled, "whatever has gotten into you tonight?"

"Let's save the talking until later," he whispered in a voice hoarse with desire.

She smiled and reached down to help him undress, only to find that he was already bare from the waist down, his eagerness for her apparent. She pulled him toward her by wrapping one of her legs around him, and when their mouths met, he felt as though a trembling electricity ran through his whole body. Their lovemaking was feral and empty of conscious thought: wild, heated, and complete.

When both of their bodies had been sated and given over to exhaustion, they lay woven together, gleaming with sweat and heaving with breath.

"That was positively legendary," she remarked, making a faint pink line along his chest with her fingernail. "What brought all that on?"

"Are you complaining?"

"Definitely not! I want to know how to make it happen at will!"

He gave a throaty chuckle. "You know what you mean to me. I thought I could never have an honest relationship with anyone, doing what I do."

"Yeah, baby, I know. I feel the same way."

"I've been thinking about it all day, and I thought of a way to make us even closer. Break down the last walls between us. I don't want anything standing in our way anymore."

She propped herself up on one elbow, her eyes betraying just the edge of suspicion. "What are you talking about?"

"We've been together over a year, and known the truth about each other almost the whole time, right? But yet we still keep secrets from each other, and we don't need to. We can share everything!"

"I don't think I'm liking the sound of this. There's a reason we don't tell each other everything, and that reason has everything to do with safety for both of us."

"Look," the man pleaded, "just hear me out. I'm suggesting this *for us*, to make us closer, so nothing can ever come between us, so that neither of us ever has to doubt. Don't you want that? I mean, I know we can't do the 2.3 kids and picket fence thing, but I want us to be *one*. Truly two halves of each other. How often does a guy make that kind of a suggestion? Never, right?"

"I KNOW I'm not liking the sound of this."

"Okay, listen. Here's the idea, and don't say anything till I'm done." He sat up and pulled her into his lap. "I got a call for a job today. Not a huge-payout, but that doesn't matter. I want you to come with me. More than that. I want you to be my weapon. We'll do the hit together. It'll be fun!"

"Killing isn't fun for me. It's not a game, any more than it's fun for a shark.""Okay, maybe *fun*'s the wrong word. But it will be a bonding experience."

"A bonding experience? Are you nuts? What the hell are you thinking? My life isn't an Anne Rice novel. We don't mix that part of ourselves; that was the *agreement*."

"I know, I know. But it just seems stupid. I kill for a living. You kill to live. It's what's allowed us to be open with each other. We understand each other like no one else can. Baby, it's the thing that makes us a perfect fit." He pulled her in tight, nuzzling her neck and caressing her shoulder. "I love you, and that's something I thought I'd never be able to say to anyone, not really. Do this with me."

"Living in secret is what's kept me alive for three of your lifetimes. I've never even told anyone else what I am. Now you want me to scrap the survival plan that's kept me safe?"

"You're safe with me. You've always been safe with me. Haven't I always kept people away while you slept? Haven't I made sure no one is suspicious of you being out all night? Don't you know you can trust me?"

"It isn't a question of trust," she replied, but her tone was softer.

"Isn't it? What else could it be? You trying to shield me from violence? It's way too late for that. You love me, I know you do. Don't you want us to grow toward each other, and not apart?"

"Don't do this to me. You know what you mean to me. It's not protecting you from violence; I'm just not sure I want you to see **me** as violent. I do love you, and I don't want to lose you."

"You won't, I swear. Share this with me."

She hung her head, her resolve fading, "I need a shower."

The first problem was getting into the neighborhood unseen. They dropped his car at a neighborhood park where teenagers were playing pickup games of basketball and set out along the obligatory walking trail that wound through every suburban community like this one. Individual neighborhoods, sporting themed names like *Coventry* and *Fairfield* hid behind walls and gates, insulating themselves from the outside world ... illusions of security for the upper middle class.

The target's house backed up to Coventry's outer wall, a six-foot concrete structure overgrown with ivy to make it look less industrial.

"Pretty sure I can get up that wall if I get a running start," he said.

"Hold on there, ninja warrior," she chuckled. She scanned the area for cameras attached to street lights and found none. Then she stepped behind one of the azalea bushes which had been strategically planted between the sidewalk and the wall. "Let me make sure the coast is clear." She slipped off her sandals and handed them to him.

"What are you ... oh!" He stared at her as she pressed her fingers and toes into the ivy and boosted herself high enough to see over into the target's back yard.

"No one in the pool area, family room, or kitchen," she reported. "Sliding glass doors are super helpful for recon." Then she scaled the remainder of the wall like a lizard or insect might. She held out her hand to him, and with surprising strength, helped to pull him up. Then she slid her shoes back on and dropped quietly onto the target's lawn.

The man was grinning as he dropped into the grass beside her. He had known this was a terrific idea! "That was awesome!" he whispered to her, and she smiled almost shyly in return. No human had ever seen her do any of the things that her species was capable of. Well, none who lived to tell about it, anyway. It felt nice to be recognized and even praised for being her true self.

They crept along the side of the house, mostly behind the hedges. It was a little scratchier that way, but it minimized their being spotted. There was a small garden to the right of the front door, so she crept along the back of it, then carefully placed a piece of blue tape over the video doorbell. The two of them stepped onto the porch as the chime from the warning system rang through the house.

The man cleared his throat and rang the doorbell with his knuckle.

A middle-aged man in a blue and white striped golf shirt and khaki shorts opened the door. His bushy brown-and-gray eyebrows shot up when he saw the two of them.

"Can I help you?" the target asked.

"I think so, Mr. Clark. We're associates of the Burletti family. We've been asked to look in on you."

The target looked back and forth from the man to the woman anxiously. The woman smiled brightly, and he seemed to relax. "I see. Looking in on me, eh? Probably you've come for my—eh—late payment."

"Yes indeed. We've come to collect. May we come in? It's probably better we not be seen by any neighbors."

The target's nervousness returned, and he tensed, measuring whether it would do him any good to slam the door and try to make a run for the car.

The woman smiled again. "I'm sure this won't take long. We'll be out of here in no time," she said soothingly.

The target's shoulders relaxed. "Yes, of course. I apologize for my rudeness. Please come in."

This was working out better than the man could have imagined. What other incredible skills did she possess? Not only would this bring them closer to each other, it might set him apart in his line of work. This would be a distinctive and unusual hit, and people would definitely be talking about it. Burletti might even give him an additional bonus. He touched the small of her back gently and affectionately as they stepped into the target's foyer.

"I won't be able to pay you in full, you understand. I don't keep that kind of cash in the house, and alimony is a killer. I only have a couple thousand I can give you tonight. But I'm good for the full amount. You can tell Burletti that."

"I'm sure he'll be satisfied," the man smiled, stepping aside to examine a silk floral arrangement on the entry table.

"You have a lovely home," she remarked, surveying the room. At the end of the short foyer, the house followed a typical 1980s open floorplan. The dining room on the right was the showpiece with an octagonal crystal table, accented with a mahogany pedestal and matching wooden chairs. Dim light glowed from inside matching china cabinets, glinting off of gold-rimmed china and crystal wine glasses. On the left was a formal living room, with a crisp and tailored looking blue sofa which probably never saw much traffic, and two white wing chairs. An oriental carpet extended outward toward the foyer, and she felt a twinge of guilt, knowing it would probably be ruined by the end of the night.

The man turned his attention back to the target. "When can I tell Mr. Burletti to expect the balance of your debt? He is getting a bit anxious. There's been some uncomfortable business about someone pocketing funds out of one of his accounts, and you know how touchy that makes him."

"Oh, um, yes, I think I may have heard about that. Can't imagine how anyone would be fool enough to try such a thing. I, um, I've got to go see an international client for a couple of days this week, and then I'm sure I'll be able to free up enough capital to pay Burletti back."

"International client?" the man asked. "Oh, yes, right. I remember Mr. Burletti mentioning that you had booked a flight. It's a lot cheaper to book round-trip, you know."

The target flushed pale, looking suddenly panicked. He realized too late that she had circled around behind him, and when the man nodded to her, the target realized it was much too late to run.

She blinked, and when her eyes opened, it was as though they were filled with the blackest ink. She leapt forward with an insect-like shriek, grabbed the target from behind, and opened her mouth wide. Rather than the pearly curved fangs the man had expected, two black claw-like appendages appeared not from her gumline, but from hidden sacs inside her cheeks. One mandible plunged into the target's jugular vein and the other one buried itself in his spinal column.

The target tried to scream, but the neurotoxin was spreading too quickly. He made a burbling sound as his knees buckled, the once-lovely woman still latched onto his neck. *The sound, oh God, what is that sound?* The high-pitched chittering sound was almost deafening. The target wanted to pull her off of him, but his arms wouldn't obey. In fact, he couldn't feel much other than the urine running down his leg and onto the Persian rug as she lowered him to the floor.

As the target became fully paralyzed, two hollow tentacles snaked out from behind the mandibles, each slithering into the holes in the target's neck that the ebony fangs had created. Her meal had been served, and she fervently slurped the combination of blood and spinal fluid, creating a fetid and sticky spill down her shirt and onto the expensive rug. As she drained him, she no longer felt guilt for the now-ruined decor, she felt only the ebbing hunger.

This wasn't what the man had imagined. He closed his eyes to the primal and animalistic scene, and covered his ears against the rasping trill and squelching sounds that accompanied her feeding. What finally did him in was the smell ... the sickly smell of the urine, the coppery scent of the blood, and another acrid smell he couldn't identify mingling with the plug-in air freshener from the front hall.

Thinking only of being *away*, the man bolted past the dining room and toward the kitchen, but he didn't make it two steps before doubling over and spewing sickness all over the tile floor. Over and over he retched, unable to escape the cacophony and assailing odors behind him.

As her appetite waned and consciousness returned, she thought again of the carpet and what a shame it was to destroy it. Her fangs retracted to their hidden pockets and her vision began to clear.

He was gone. The man was gone.

She stripped off her blouse and wiped the remaining gore from her mouth and chin, all the while looking for him. Might he have gone to the target's office to make sure no documents existed that might implicate his client? Had he stepped away to call Burletti and say that the job was done?

She found him in the kitchen, crouching in a pool of his own vomit. When he looked at her, his eyes, once so full of love, clouded with revulsion and horror. Somewhere deep within, her heart broke while simultaneously telling her she'd been a fool to hope that this wasn't how it would go.

Humans and their movies. She should have known he wasn't prepared for what her kind really was.

He looked away from her, trying to gather himself so he could get away. *Away, just away* ... he wanted to flee from her, from here, from everything. "I'm sorry, Clara, I just didn't expect ..."

The rest of the sentence was lost as the neurotoxin flooded his system, paralyzing him from the throat down.

Breaking News

THRILLER BY JENNY SIMARD LABRANCHE

The rain had thinned to a mist by the time she pulled over, but the street still glistened as if freshly varnished. Red and blue lights strobed against the wet pavement, their reflections stretching and snapping with each pulse. Claire Whitaker cut the engine and sat for a moment, hands resting lightly on the steering wheel, listening to the soft tick of cooling metal. Somewhere down the block, a siren wailed and then faded, swallowed by distance.

She checked the time.

Early. Earlier than she'd meant to be, though she told herself that wasn't unusual. This was her job, after all. Breaking news did not wait for polite hours.

She stepped out of the car and the smell hit her first, not blood, not exactly, but the damp iron tang that lingered beneath everything else. Wet asphalt. Ozone from the lights. Coffee from an officer's paper cup. The air carried it all together, and she breathed it in without thinking, cataloguing it the way she always did.

Police tape cordoned off the far end of the street, a bright, plastic line humming faintly as it fluttered in the breeze. A patrol car blocked traffic, its door open, an officer leaning against it with his radio clipped high on his shoulder. Two more stood closer to the alley's mouth, their silhouettes blurred by the fog that clung stubbornly to the narrow space between buildings.

She grabbed her press badge from the passenger seat and clipped it to her coat as she walked. Her heels clicked softly, decisively, on the pavement. No one stopped her. They never did, not anymore.

"Morning," one of the officers said, his voice neutral.

"Morning," she replied, offering a professional smile that didn't ask for anything.

The officer-in-charge glanced up from his radio when he saw her, recognition flickering across his face. He studied the alley once more, then nodded, lifted the tape, and let her in.

She gave a small, almost imperceptible nod in return. Years ago, when she had still worked for the police department as the Public Information Officer, she had reported to him, coordinating press briefings and managing sensitive information. They hadn't always seen eye to eye, but familiarity went a long way, and now it meant she could move through the scene with his quiet approval.

"The scene is secure," he said. "You have five minutes. Don't touch anything. Log in, and stay with Officer Marks at all times."

She thanked him and fell into step behind Marks. A clipboard appeared, names stacked tight in hurried ink. She added her own, time in recorded neatly beside it, then handed it back without ceremony. Procedures mattered, but so did knowing when you were allowed past them.

The alley was narrow and darker than the street, the light from the cruisers reaching only so far before dissolving into shadow. Trash bags were stacked against one wall, black plastic slick with rain. A fire escape ladder loomed overhead, dripping steadily, each drop striking the concrete with a faint, hollow pat.

She slowed her steps as she approached the center of the scene.

The body lay where she expected it to be.

Not because she had been told, no one had briefed the press yet, but because there was only one place it could be. The alley widened slightly about ten feet in, opening into a shallow recess where a service door sat flush with the brick. It was the sort of spot people didn't look at unless they had reason to, the sort of spot that invited neglect.

The victim lay on his back, arms angled awkwardly away from his sides, fingers curled as though reaching for something that had already slipped out of range. Blood pooled unevenly on the concrete, thinned by rainwater, its edges feathered and pale.

She stopped a few feet away, close enough to see without needing to step around the markers.

Blood always looked different outdoors, she thought. Indoors, it clung to surfaces, thick and stubborn. Outside, it ran. It followed the rules of gravity and weather, obedient in a way people never were. On concrete, it darkened the surface first, then soaked in, leaving behind a dull stain that would linger long after the tape came down.

She'd seen worse.

The thought surfaced unbidden, as familiar as a reflex. Worse scenes. Worse bodies. Worse mornings. She did not linger on it, did not feel the need to justify the assessment. Experience had a way of flattening extremes. Everything became comparative eventually.

A detective crouched near the body, his back to her, gloved hands resting on his knees as he studied the ground. He hadn't noticed her yet, or he was pretending not to. She recognized him, Detective Harris. Mid-forties, perpetually tired eyes, the faint stoop of someone who spent too much time leaning over desks and too little time sleeping.

She waited.

That was another thing she'd learned: patience was often mistaken for respect.

When Harris finally stood and turned, his gaze flicked to her badge and then to her face. His mouth tightened just slightly, a faint curve that was almost a smile.

"You're early, Miss Whitaker," he said, his tone carrying a teasing edge.

She smiled again, softer this time. "Heard it on the scanner."

He grunted, neither confirming nor denying it. "We haven't released anything yet."

"I know," she said. "I'm just getting a feel."

For a moment, it looked like he might argue, or maybe just linger a second longer in her presence. Then he sighed, the sound heavy with resignation.

"Back up about twenty feet," he said, gesturing vaguely with his chin, his eyes flicking to hers in a way that suggested both warning and something unspoken. "And don't speculate."

"I never do," she replied, and meant it in the strictest sense of the word.

She stepped back a half pace, just enough to satisfy the letter of his instruction. From here, she could still see everything that mattered.

The victim was male, late thirties to early forties if she had to guess. Well-dressed, even now, dark slacks, leather shoes, a coat that looked expensive before it soaked through. His face was pale, lips tinged blue, eyes half-lidded as if he'd been interrupted mid-thought. There was a wound at his throat, clean and precise, the kind that suggested intent rather than panic.

She noted these details automatically, assembling them into sentences in her mind. Not for broadcast, not yet, but for herself. She always did her best work before the camera was ever turned on.

Behind her, the alley filled slowly with quiet activity. A forensic tech knelt near the wall, photographing something she couldn't quite see. Another officer murmured into a phone, voice low and clipped. Somewhere, someone laughed, a short, sharp sound that seemed out of place and then vanished.

She focused on the body again, on the way the sheet fluttered slightly with each passing breeze. It reminded her of a flag at half-mast.

"Do we know who he is?" she asked, keeping her tone casual.

"We're working on it," he said. "Wallet was missing. Phone, too."

She nodded as if she hadn't already anticipated it. A robbery gone wrong would be the easy story, the one people wanted to believe. Random violence was comforting in its simplicity. It meant there was nothing to learn, nothing to fix.

But this wasn't random. She could tell by the way the body had been positioned, by the absence of struggle marks on the ground. By the choice of location.

Instinct, she told herself. Years of covering crime sharpened certain senses. You learned to read scenes the way other people read faces.

"Another one," an officer muttered nearby, not realizing she could hear.

Harris's jaw tightened. "Watch it," he snapped quietly.

Another one.

The words echoed, though she kept her expression neutral. They were already calling it that, then. A series. Patterns were irresistible to people, even when they tried to deny them.

She stepped back into the street as more press began to arrive, vans pulling up, doors slamming, cameras hoisted onto shoulders. The fog was lifting now, thinning enough to reveal the dull gray of the morning sky. Dawn crept in slowly, indifferent to the scene below.

Her cameraman, Luke, jogged up to the yellow tape just as she approached. She ducked under to his side, while he stopped short on the street side, his breath puffing white in the cold air."You beat me again," he said, grinning. "What've we got?""

"Male victim," she said, slipping easily into the rhythm of the role. "Possible homicide. Police aren't saying much yet."

"Any connection to the others?"

She hesitated just long enough to be thoughtful. "Too early to tell."

He nodded, satisfied. "You want to go live as soon as they let us?"

"Yes," she said. "Let's set up across the street. Keep the tape in the background."

They moved together, practiced and efficient. She shrugged out of her coat, smoothed her hair, checked her reflection in the dark glass of the van window. Her face looked composed, alert. Controlled.

As the camera was set and the lights adjusted, she felt the familiar shift inside her, the careful narrowing of focus, the steadying calm that came with being on air. This was the part she excelled at. This was where chaos became narrative.

She glanced once more toward the alley, now partially obscured by the growing crowd. The body was barely visible from here, just a pale shape beneath white fabric.

Another one, they would say. Another tragedy. Another story.

She picked up her microphone, grounding herself in its weight.

When the producer's voice crackled in her ear, counting her down, she lifted her gaze to the lens and let the city see her.

"Good morning, I'm Claire Whitaker, reporting live," she began, her voice even and measured. "We're standing on Mercer Street, where police are investigating what appears to be a fatal throat-slashing..."

She spoke carefully, choosing each word with practiced ease. She did not speculate. She did not embellish. She reported only what could be confirmed, what could be shown.

Behind the calm cadence, behind the steady gaze, her mind continued to work, cataloguing, assessing, preparing.

She had always believed that truth mattered. She still did. The rest, she told herself, was just instinct.

By the third body, the city had learned how to listen.

It listened in the mornings, televisions murmuring in kitchens and break rooms. It listened in cars, volume turned up at red lights. It listened with the quiet hunger of people who told themselves they wanted answers when what they wanted was reassurance, some indication that chaos followed rules.

She gave them rules.

She stood in front of crime scenes with the same steady posture, the same measured tone, the same careful distance. She reported facts, confirmed timelines, and official statements. She reminded viewers of what was known and, just as importantly, what was not.

And then, when the camera shut off, Claire replayed everything in her head.

Every scene. Every detail. Every mistake. The police were getting sloppy.

She noticed it first with the markers. On the second murder, they'd placed one too close to the body, nearly touching the bloodstain that mattered most. He was getting bolder, she thought. Or perhaps the department was simply overwhelmed.

In the newsroom, the murders became shorthand. The producer no longer needed to specify which story she was being assigned; a raised eyebrow and a tilt of the head toward the crime board was enough. Red string crisscrossed a city map, connecting dots that reporters debated endlessly and police refused to confirm.

Luke shook his head, grinning. "You're lucky your car's still in one piece with how you drive."

She smiled thinly. "I prefer to think of it as efficient."

It wasn't entirely untrue.

Claire followed the investigation obsessively, even when she wasn't on assignment. Police press conferences streamed quietly on her phone while she cooked dinner, the steady voice of the spokesperson a background hum beneath the clatter of pots and pans. Scanner chatter murmured in the corner as she reviewed scripts, fingers pausing over words, considering phrasing.

She watched every rival news channel, flipping between streams to see how each station framed the story. Graphics, camera angles, the ing of every line, nothing escaped her notice. When one anchor lingered on a particular witness statement, Claire noted it. When another omitted it entirely, she filed it mentally for later.

She read every article written by competing newspapers, dissecting the language, the tone, and the focus. Some stories highlighted panic and chaos, while others leaned on speculation or dramatic headlines. One junior reporter from a rival station referred to the weapon as a serrated blade. In her experience, serrated implied chaos, raggedness, panic. But this? This was precise, deliberate, controlled. She traced each article back in her mind, noting what was accurate, what was embellished, and what had been left out entirely.

By the time she finally set down her pen, the kitchen was quiet, the news playing softly in the background. Claire leaned back in her chair, reviewing the day's coverage in her mind, turning over every phrasing, every emphasis, every difference between outlets. The story was unfolding slowly like a puzzle, and she intended to see it whole.

At the next editorial meeting, her editor leaned back in his chair and steepled his fingers. "Ratings are up," he said, not bothering to hide his satisfaction. "Way up."

No one smiled. They all knew what that meant.

"We're becoming the authority on this," he continued. "People trust you. When something breaks, they wait for you."

Claire inclined her head, accepting the compliment without comment.

"I want exclusives," he said. "Deeper dives. Profiles. If the police won't talk, we find someone who will."

"Speculation hurts credibility," she said mildly.

He waved a hand. "We're not speculating. We're contextualizing."

She knew that word. It meant pushing boundaries just far enough to make lawyers uncomfortable but not enough to pull a story.

"I'll see what I can do," she said.

On her way out, she passed the bulletin board again. Another photo had been added that morning, a middle-aged man, smiling stiffly at a corporate event, his arm slung around someone cropped out of the frame. She paused, studying his face.

The police held a press conference that afternoon. She stood in the front row, notebook tucked under her arm, eyes fixed on the podium. Harris looked more tired than usual, *dark* circles bruising the skin beneath his eyes.

"We believe the individual responsible is escalating," he said, reading from prepared notes. "The frequency and severity of the attacks suggest a need for recognition."

A murmur rippled through the room.

"He wants attention," Harris continued, "and we will not give it to him."

She resisted the urge to smile at him.

Later, in her car, Claire replayed the footage. Harris's voice was steady, but his posture betrayed him, shoulders tense, jaw clenched. He was under pressure. They all were.

He wants attention, she thought again, tasting the words. He was careful. He chose his moments. He understood optics.

Claire's ratings climbed steadily. Social media buzzed with clips of her broadcasts, viewers praising her calm, her clarity, her refusal to sensationalize.

"She doesn't exploit tragedy," one comment read. "She just tells it like it is."

People want the truth, she thought as she scrolled past it. Or at least the version they can live with.

The arrest came on a Tuesday.

Claire was in the makeup chair when her phone buzzed, the notification lighting up the mirror. A suspect in custody. Local man. Prior record. Police were calling it a break.

Her pulse quickened, not with excitement, but with irritation. She would be late arriving, and she was always early. Claire arrived at the precinct just as the suspect was being led inside, chin tucked, hoodie dragged down to obscure his face. Cameras flashed, reporters shouted questions that went unanswered. She caught a glimpse of his face: pale, sweating, eyes darting wildly.

Claire felt it immediately, a certainty as solid as bone. He didn't move right. Didn't hold himself with the quiet assurance she'd come to associate with the scenes.

She interviewed the suspect's sister that evening, standing with her on a dimly lit porch while cicadas screamed in the trees. The woman's hands shook as she spoke, words tumbling over one another in a rush of denial and grief.

"He's not a monster," the sister said, tears streaking her face. "He's just ... he's just sick."

The camera lingered, hungry.

She nodded sympathetically, offering the practiced murmurs of understanding.

The details didn't align. The timeline was wrong. The suspect had an alibi for one of the murders, thin, perhaps, but present. The wounds described in the arrest affidavit were sloppier than what she'd seen.

Claire wrapped up the interview, thanked the woman, and stepped away from the porch as Luke cut the feed.

"You okay?" he asked quietly as they walked back to the van.

"Fine," she said.

But as she slid into the passenger seat, she found herself staring at her hands, replaying the sister's words.

He's just sick.

The suspect agreed to a jailhouse interview the next morning. Her editor practically *vibrated* with excitement as he assigned it to her.

"This is huge," he said. "Get him to talk. Get us inside his head."

She arrived early, as usual. The interview room smelled of disinfectant and stale air. A single table sat bolted to the floor, two chairs facing each other. She chose the one closest to the door.

The suspect shuffled in, wrists cuffed, eyes flicking up to meet hers and then away again. He looked smaller up close. Diminished.

She introduced herself and explained the purpose of the interview. He nodded mechanically.

"Why do you think they picked you up?" she asked.

He swallowed. "I don't know. I didn't do it."

"Didn't do what?"

His mouth opened, then closed. "I didn't hurt anyone."

The words landed wrong. Too vague. Too defensive.

She leaned forward slightly. "The police say the killer targeted specific locations. Familiar places. Places he knew wouldn't be busy."

The suspect shook his head. "I don't go out much."

"Do you follow the news?" she asked instead.

"Sometimes," he said. "I saw you. On TV."

She nodded, acknowledging the recognition without feeding it.

When the interview ended, she left with a knot of irritation tightening in her chest. The man was innocent of these crimes, at least. He didn't know where to stand, how to hold silence. He filled it with desperation.

In the van, Luke glanced at her. "You look pissed."

"I don't like it when the police get it wrong," she said. "That guy is no more a killer than you."

That night, the police quietly released the suspect. Insufficient evidence. The story pivoted, the city's attention snapping back to uncertainty.

Harris cornered her outside the station the next morning.

"You're everywhere," he observed, not bothering with pleasantries. "You know details we haven't released."

She met his gaze evenly. "I listen, and some of your men talk loudly."

He rolled his eyes in understanding.

He studied her for a long moment, his eyes sharp despite the fatigue. There was a flicker of amusement in his expression, almost a tease, as if he was daring her to admit she enjoyed being first. She gave him a steady look, letting the thought go unacknowledged.

"You ever worry about getting too close?" he asked, his voice softer now, a hint of worry under the teasing.

She bristled at the question, a flare of offense cutting through her composure. "I do my job," she replied, "well."

"I'm sure you do," he replied, a brief smile tugging at the corner of his mouth. "Just, be careful."

The next murder happened four days later.

She was on air when the alert came through her earpiece, the producer's voice clipped and urgent. Breaking news. Another scene.

She finished the segment without missing a beat, her voice steady as she transitioned to commercial. The moment the camera cut, she was already reaching for her coat.

"Where?" she asked.

The address registered in her mind before the producer finished speaking. Claire knew these streets well, and her BMW M5 rarely obeyed the speed limit.

She arrived first again.

The alley was narrower this time, the walls closer, the air thick with the metallic tang she had come to recognize. The body was positioned carefully, almost reverently, as if the killer had taken time to consider how it would be found.

She took it all in, her mind racing ahead even as her face remained calm.

This one was different. More intimate. More personal.

She straightened as footsteps approached behind her. Harris.

"You've got a gift," he said quietly. "You know that?"

She turned to face him. "For what?"

"For being exactly where you need to be."

She held his gaze, unblinking. "Someone has to tell the story."

Harris walked up, eyebrows raised. "I swear your tires were smoking when I walked by."

She leveled him with a steady look, letting a flicker of amusement pass before he nodded and moved on.

She looked back at the body, at the careful placement, the deliberate message etched into flesh and circumstance.

Yes, she thought. Someone does.

The alert came through while she was still wearing makeup.

Not the breaking-news chime this time, something quieter. A producer's voice, tight and careful in her ear.

"Stand by," he told her. "We may need you sooner than planned."

She met her own reflection in the mirror. The woman looking back at her was composed, eyes bright, mouth relaxed. She dabbed once more beneath her eyes and nodded.

Sooner than planned meant what it always meant. She was halfway through the six o'clock broadcast when the city shifted again.

"...and in other news," she said, transitioning smoothly, "police are responding to reports of— "

The words paused in her ear, rearranging themselves. A location. A name. Her breath never changed.

She finished the sentence, handed the desk off to the anchor, and stood as the camera cut away. The studio lights dimmed slightly, heat ebbing from her skin.

"Live hit," the producer said. "Ten minutes. Same format."

She was already moving. The drive was short. She took side streets, the route instinctive, hands steady on the wheel. Traffic parted easily, as if the city itself recognized urgency when it saw it.

The building was old, brick and glass, a former newspaper office repurposed into something sleeker and quieter. A media consultant now. Crisis management. Reputation repair.

She parked down the block, slipping the press badge into place as she stepped out into the cooling evening air. This one had been inside.

The lobby lights glowed warmly, incongruous against the chaos threading through the space. Officers moved carefully, their footsteps hushed on polished floors. The body lay just beyond the reception desk, angled toward the door as if caught mid-exit.

She stopped where she always did, close enough to see without interfering.

He had been kneeling when it happened. The position of the body told her that immediately. A plea, perhaps. Or an apology. The hands were folded in front of him, not clenched. The line of his clothing was undisturbed, the blood minimal and contained. Nothing about this spoke to panic or a struggle. The violence had been controlled, deliberate, intimate even. This was no random attack, no opportunistic strike. It looked personal.

By the time she returned to the lobby, the camera crew was setting up. Luke caught her eye, his expression tight.

"This one's bad," he said quietly.

"Yes," she replied. "It is."

They positioned her just outside the entrance, the building framed neatly behind her. Police lights washed the scene in alternating color, a familiar palette.

She took a breath. The city waited. The red light blinked on.

"Good evening," Claire said, her voice calm, steady, intimate. "We're breaking into programming tonight with a developing story in Midtown, where police have confirmed a fatal stabbing inside a former media office building."

She spoke as she always did, measured, respectful, precise. She described what could be seen without embellishment. She contextualized without speculating.

Her language echoed earlier broadcasts, phrases repeating like refrains. A careful listener might notice the symmetry.

Behind the camera, Harris stood watching. She didn't look at him.

"... investigators believe this may be connected to a series of recent killings," she continued. "Though no official confirmation has been made, the similarities are difficult to ignore."

She paused, just briefly. "The victim appears to have known his attacker." The words slipped out cleanly. Nothing the studio would get fined over.

From the corner of her eye, she saw Harris still. A micro-expression crossed his face, not shock, not triumph.

Claire continued without hesitation, instinctively smoothing the moment over. "... though police caution that details are still emerging."

The broadcast ended without incident.

Applause rippled faintly from somewhere behind the lights. The producer exhaled audibly in her ear. "Great work," he said. "You okay to stay if we need updates?"

"Of course," she replied. She stepped away from the camera, the city's attention drifting elsewhere for the moment.

Harris approached slowly, his steps unhurried. "You said something interesting," he remarked.

She turned to face him. "Did I?"

"You said the victim knew the attacker."

She tilted her head slightly. "It's a reasonable inference."

"Based on?"

She met his gaze, her expression open. "The lack of forced entry. The nature of the wounds."

He nodded slowly. "You're right. We hadn't released that."

"I didn't say you had."

Silence settled between them, thick but not uncomfortable. Around them, the machinery of response continued, radios crackling, officers conferring, the city doing what it always did in the aftermath of violence.

"You ever think about how stories shape people?" Harris asked suddenly. "How they decide what matters?"

"All the time," she answered.

"Then I guess that makes you the one in charge of the story," he said with a sly smile.

She considered him for a moment, calm. "Then you'd better hope I get it right."

Harris studied her face, searching for something. If he found it, he didn't say.

Later, at home, she watched the replay. She always did.

She sat on her couch, lights dimmed, the television glow painting her walls in soft blues and grays. The broadcast unfolded exactly as she remembered it. Calm. Controlled. Trustworthy.

There it was. The line. The certainty. She didn't rewind.

Instead, she let her mind drift backward, not through events, but through feeling.

The first alley. The way she'd known where to stand. The second body. The suspect interview, all flowed through her mind.

Arriving early. Always early. Never asked who found the body. Never asking how long it had been there. She hadn't lied. She'd simply curated.

The phone buzzed beside her. A message from her editor.

Viewership peaked tonight. People are glued to this.

She smiled faintly. People wanted the truth. Or at least the version they could live with.

On the screen, her image faded as the segment ended, replaced by commercials and weather updates and the comforting rhythm of normalcy.

She stood and turned off the television.

In the bathroom, she caught her reflection again. The same calm eyes. The same composed mouth. She washed the blood from beneath her painted nails.

Outside, sirens wailed in the distance, already moving toward something new.

She dried her hands carefully, methodically, and slipped the knife back into her coat before reaching for the door.

Tomorrow morning, the city would wake hungry.

And she would be there to feed it.

She had never lied on air.

She had simply never told the whole truth.

The Hidden Soul Beneath

DARK FAIRY TALE REIMAGINING BY JB CAINE

There is one knows not what sweet mystery about this sea, whose gently awful stirrings seem to speak of some hidden soul beneath. — Herman Melville

The waxing moon shone high in the sky as she waited for him.

She floated above the sandbar, where the current was the most gentle, and watched and listened. He would be here soon ... she could feel it.

Moonlight illuminated the tiny cove, making the golden sand appear to glow white. Large bits of driftwood had been pulled into a crescent facing the sea, and a firepit ringed with stones had been built in the center.

On the cliffs above the cove, a palace overlooked the ocean. It was built of shining yellow stone and had graceful marble stairways leading in and out, one of which led to the path to this beach. The path that would bring him to her.

It seemed hours had passed, though time passes with infuriating slowness when one is awaiting one's beloved. At long last, she spied four figures bounding down the flight of steps. Her heart leapt.

Lorelei rolled in the surf, careful not to jostle the eight oysters that attached to her silvery tail, a symbol of her status as a daughter of the King.

"But Auntie," she had complained when her great aunt approached with the mollusks that morning, "they hurt me so!"

"Pride must suffer pain," the matriarch said simply. "You must remember who you are, and that others do not have your advantages."

Her great aunt could not have known how useful those oysters would be today. Lorelei directed her attention back to the land and strained to hear the sound of the young prince's voice, his laughter. The wind brought it to her waiting ears, though the words were unclear. The boys' laughter was joyful and raucous, and when they reached the path, one of them pulled out a box that was cut in two, and connected by a tube. When he opened and closed it, wheezing and honking tones came out, and created a strange music. Her great aunt, who was an expert on all things human, had told her that this box was called a *concertina*, and that it only worked on land because it needed air to function, like humans did.

She slipped under the water and swam silently toward the rocks at the edge of the cove. It was one of the merpeople's highest laws that showing oneself to humans was forbidden, but on this night, she had planned carefully. Lorelei had been born with powerful gifts, as was often the case with seventh daughters. Her great aunt had been a seventh daughter, too, and now she was the court sorceress and chief adviser to Lorelei's father, King of the Sea. Lorelei was to take her place someday, and she had been studying grimoires and practicing magic with her great aunt since she was ten years old.

Unbeknownst to her aunt, she had also been practicing other spells, forbidden ones, in a secret cave at the edge of the Abyssal chasm. All around the entrance to her cave, she had grown a garden of red roses like the ones she had seen in the distance on land, planting the bushes with drops of her own blood to give the roses a purplish red hue.

Today was her sixteenth birthday, and as her present to herself, she would finally meet the boy she had loved from afar for so long.

From a small pouch round her neck, Lorelei drew forth a long white swan feather that she had managed to salvage from the beach nearer to the palace gardens. Then she reached down and pried one of the oysters from her tail. The wound stung as a thin rivulet of her blood mixed with the sea. She hoped that no sharks would approach as she enacted her plan.

Holding the oyster carefully, she rolled onto her back and used its sharp edge to make an incision below her left breast. She winced and then returned the shell to her tail. With her right hand, she held the swan feather up to the moonlight and whispered, "Do my will!" Then she took the hollow shaft of the feather and slid it into the open wound.

The magic rippled across her skin, and suddenly she felt as though she were being turned inside out. Her smooth skin erupted into welts as feathers pushed their way through from within. At the same time, she felt the end of her tail rip in two and the tips of her fins hardened and grew tiny claws. She cried out in pain as the rest of her lithe form doubled over, bones shifting. Her nose and lower jaw elongated and solidified into a bright orange bill.

And then suddenly she was floating on the water rather than in it. Her fins ... no, *her feet* ... paddled against the current and toward the land, where her beloved and the other boys had started a fire and lounged around it, singing:

It was down by Swansea barracks one May morning I strayed
A-viewing of the soldier lads I spied a comely maid
It was o'er her red and rosy cheeks the tears did dingle down
I thought she was some goddess fair the lass of Swansea town
I said Fair maid, what brought you here what brought you here to mourn
Oh I'm in search of Willie dear my bonny young sailor boy
Eight years ago he left me here for Bermuda he was bound
He said he would prove faithful to the lass of Swansea town

"Hey, look at that!" the boy with the concertina called, ceasing his playing and staring out to sea. "One of the swans from the garden has gotten loose!"

"Oh! The salt water is awful for them! Let us see if we can catch it and return it to where it belongs!" It was *his* voice, and *his* eyes gazed upon her in concern. Those beautiful eyes, the color of the sea where it drops off into deeper water.

It was still some effort to control this bulky little body, but Lorelei paddled toward the shore. She dug her webbed feet into the mucky sand, but standing on feet was foreign to her, and she stumbled and fell as she emerged onto the beach.

With a cry, the prince leapt forth and scooped her up in his arms, cooing and comforting what he assumed was a wounded bird. She lay her long neck against his shoulder, and breathed in the scent of him as he stroked her feathers. He carried her back to his friends and sat on a log, and she thought that she had never been happier in her life.

"Ah, Erick, you're always the soft-hearted one!" laughed one of his friends. "I probably would have wrung its neck and taken it home for dinner."

"Don't even say that!" Erick hissed, pulling her closer. She sighed in contentment. *Erick.* His name was Erick.

"William was only teasing you," the young man with the concertina chuckled. "No one will hurt it. Is it injured?" He got up and knelt before Erick, inspecting her feet, then her neck, then her wings. She could feel Erick's heart pounding, and it gladdened her that he was so worried about her well-being. "Huh. It seems fine. Perhaps you are right, and the salt water was making it feel unwell."

"Thank you, Liam," Erick smiled, his voice filled with warmth. "I am greatly reassured. If it will stay with us, I will carry it back when we return."

Then Liam smiled, a wide toothy grin, his dark eyes twinkling. He clapped Erick on the shoulder and returned to where he'd been sitting. He picked up his instrument and began playing again.

For an hour, the boys sang and passed a bottle between them, Lorelei clutched in Erick's arms. As midnight approached, the boys stood and poured sand on the fire, then returned to the path that led back to the palace. As they approached, she spotted the garden, and even in the moonlight, she could see myriad colors of blooms adorning the bushes and trees. So different from her garden at home, where sea grasses and elaborate rock formations blended together in varying hues of green and blue!

Erick carried her toward the garden and plopped her, somewhat unceremoniously, over the fence. "Sorry, my friend," he smiled. "Go and join your brothers and sisters in the pond. You are home now!"

Oh, how she wished that were so! But the spell would die with the dawn, so as soon as Erick was out of sight, Lorelei waddled ... awkwardly at first ... around the perimeter of the garden until she found a spot where the fence crossed a small stream which would eventually empty into the sea. It was difficult to do with such a buoyant body, but eventually she managed to dive under the fence and began swimming back to the ocean.

If she had doubted her love for the young prince before, all uncertainty was now banished from her mind.

He would be hers, no matter what it took.

Lorelei waited in the corner of her great aunt's study while the older woman finished transcribing a good fortune charm onto the smooth inner lining of a clam shell. Such talismans were highly prized among the merpeople, and were often given as wedding or birth gifts.

"Alright, niece, tell me what trouble you got yourself into today." Aunt Mathilde laid the shell aside and beckoned Lorelei over.

"No trouble, Auntie, I simply need your advice."

"No trouble indeed. Remember to whom you speak. I notice nearly all, and my intuition fills in the gaps. You got home at an absurd hour. You are missing one of your oysters, and you have a gash below your breast. Conceal nothing from me. Tell me why you have come."

Lorelei felt ashamed, not for what she had done, but for insulting her great aunt. "Auntie, I beg your forgiveness. I have fallen in love, and I need your wisdom."

Mathilde's smile widened. "I am glad that this is the problem you bring to me. Which of the lucky merpeople has drawn your eye?"

Lorelei knew that she must tread carefully. "Ah, you have hit on the problem indeed. It is not a merman, but a human prince who has captured my heart."

Her aunt hissed. "Lorelei, I always gave you credit for more sense. Loving a human can bring nothing but pain. You cannot cross back and forth between these worlds. Or is it he who has promised to give up his kingdom for you?"

"He knows not of my affection, Auntie."

"Ah, my dear, I know this is painful to hear, but you are young and foolish, and I must speak plainly and bluntly with you so that you do not understand my meaning. You are not of the land, and he is not of the sea. Whether you gave up your life and family, or whether he gave up his, both of you would most likely regret the decision, and once such a decision has been made, only death can break it. What is done cannot be undone."

"I will not regret it, Auntie. I know he will love me once I reveal myself."

"Oh, child, your heart has beaten your brain into submission. If you became human, you would lose your magic. Humans cannot harness the elements as we do. You might be able to learn to understand his language without magic, but you could never speak it. Human voices cannot make new sounds after a certain age. You would lose your voice entirely."

"A small price to pay for everlasting love, Auntie!" Lorelei pleaded.

"You have made the assumption that he would love you, my darling. But one can never be certain. He might love you only for a while, or not at all. You cannot know." The elder mermaid shook her head. "And to tell it true, you cannot be sure that you would love him forever either. That word means something different to merpeople than it does to humans. We live 300 years; they are lucky to live eighty. Did you know that?"

She had not, indeed, known that. But so certain was she of what her heart wanted, even a short time with Erick was worth sacrificing empty centuries. She sat silent, trying to figure how she might persuade her great aunt to allow her to learn the ancient magicks carved into the hundreds of stone tablets stored here in the study.

"If you will not help me, I will turn to the Abyss and seek its power! I must have Erick! I cannot live without him!"

A flash of something akin to terror crossed the old woman's face, but only for an instant. "Lorelei, stop this at once! The Abyssal magic is naught but darkness and all perversions of nature! That is never the answer, though its power is tempting. You cannot make someone feel something that does not come naturally, and you cannot force someone to become that which is counter to their nature."

"What if he falls in love with me as I am, and agrees that we must be together?"

The old woman sighed heavily. "Your father will be displeased at me for even allowing you to entertain these notions without reporting it to him immediately. But I have sympathies that he lacks, as I have at least had a human friend who knew me for what I was. Be extraordinarily careful, but find a way to speak to your prince and see if he feels as you do. You must promise me that you will not take any action until you have learned his mind. Are we agreed?"

"Oh, yes, Auntie! Thank you!" She hugged the old merwoman fiercely.

"I still say you are a fool," Mathilde said affectionately. "Now come and let me heal your tail and your breast."

The stirring in Lorelei's blood was a maelstrom of madness. With her great aunt's help, she would be able to finally be his, and he would be hers. She wanted to wait for him in her natural form, there on the beach where he had cradled her swan body in his arms. But she knew there was wisdom in Aunt Mathilde's words. She must watch and wait for the right moment: a moment when he was alone and pensive, perhaps dreaming of the beautiful white swan that had been so tame with him.

She played the scene in her mind a hundred times. Sometimes he would fall in love with her instantly, and in other fantasies, she would come to him in friendship, and their love would bloom over a series of days. But she never doubted her destiny, even for a moment.

For weeks, she watched and waited. She was in agony, aching to be with him, but when he came to the beach, he was always with Liam and his other friends, and she had no way to go to him on land, not if she wanted him to know her for what she truly was.

On the evening of the twentieth day, she hid behind the rocks along the coast and overheard him talking with Liam as they walked in the surf with the moon high overhead.

"Erick, how can you feel so miserable about your birthday? The celebration of you reaching full manhood will be the stuff of legends! The ball, the feast, the boat cruise ... it will be a riotous good time!"

"Turning eighteen comes with strings, Liam. Today, I am a boy in my father's eyes. I can be silly and carefree, and even foolish, and no one cares a lick. In two days, I become a man. And not just a man ... the next king! I shall have to become who they want me to be, not who I truly am."

"Oh, come now, it cannot be that bad. There are a good many foolish kings in the world." Liam laughed and elbowed Erick, who chuckled in spite of himself.

"I shall be alone then, Liam. No doubt my parents will seek to arrange a marriage, and I shall have to associate with courtiers and heads of state, not stable hands who can work magic with a concertina."

Liam scoffed. "We have grown up together, Erick. No one can tear our friendship asunder. We are brothers!"

"Brothers," Erick replied wistfully, and Lorelei could see tears in his eyes, causing them to sparkle like moonlight on the water. She wished that she could kiss those tears away.

"I promise you, Erick. I will be here for you forever. You can even knight me and give me responsibilities if you must. Not many, mind you, but a few would be alright." He clapped Erick on the shoulder. "Let us make a pact, my friend. When the boat leaves for your birthnight cruise, I will be on it with all your parents' fancy friends, and I will stand by your side. To hell with what they say. I say our friendship is forever!"

Erick smiled over his shoulders, but his eyes remained sad, as though he believed Liam's promise to be one that could not be kept. "You always know just what to say when I grow melancholy, Liam."

"Come on, buttercup," Liam teased. "Let us go see if we can find a lost pint or two lying around in one of the kitchens."

Erick took one more long look at the moon, then turned to follow his friend. Their voices faded into the darkness as the distance between the boys and the mermaid grew. Her heart was breaking for Erick. Oh, how she wanted to comfort him! But she was glad he had a friend as dedicated as Liam. She looked forward to becoming his friend as well. Together, they could help Erick be a strong and wise king. She rolled in the surf and imagined how happy they all would be.

It was in that moment that she made up her mind. She would find a way to reveal herself to Erick on his birthnight cruise.

Two days. She only had to wait for two more days.

The palace radiated light all evening long, and the harsh strains of human music flowed out like waves crashing on the shore. Lorelei swam in circles just inside the human harbor. The wooden ship on which her beloved would set sail was bedecked with bright and beautiful pennants, their colors rose up from the pulpit, then making circles around the mast just below the crow's nest, and then finished off at the stern. They waved madly in the wind, and Lorelei's heart felt as though it waved with them.

At long last, the revelers poured out of the palace, a group of maybe two dozen parting from the others at the dock and boarding the sailing vessel. The crew, dressed in festive livery, awaited the party and greeted each member of Erick's birthday retinue as they crossed the gangplank. When everyone was aboard, the guests waved to the partygoers who remained ashore, and the crew hoisted the sails.

The wind filled the canvas quickly and jerked the ship sharply away from the dock. There was a cry of alarm followed by laughter as the crew gained control of the vessel, tacking this way and that to match the wind and keep the sails full. The boat heeled somewhat to one side, but the humans on board did not seem bothered. The sailboat picked up speed and zoomed right past the mermaid and out into the open sea. Lorelei followed behind, hoping that the boat would stop at some point so she could try to catch Erick's attention.

Her hopes were granted only a few minutes later, as the crew cried out "Heave to!" The sails were pulled down and tied loosely to the boom, and the anchor was dropped from its housing in the bow. The boat had left the harbor, but was within sight of the coastline.

Though there was still a good bit of wind, the boat stayed relatively still now that there was no sail to pull it one way or another. The music rose up again, and the young men's voices lifted the song to the clouds overhead.

Lorelei realized that she had not reckoned how she might get the young prince alone. She swam around the back of the boat and placed her delicate hands on the stern ladder. She had never used such a device, but it's workings seemed simple enough. The difficulty came in her not having legs. Her tail was not meant to work as human legs did, and it was of no use to push her up the rungs. Still, she managed to work her way up by pulling with her arms and bending her tail where human knees might be to give her leverage and support as she ascended.

When she reached the top, she peered through a drainage hole along the deck. She was startled to see Erick leaning against the port side of the ship with his arms crossed, watching the other men sing and dance and drink. He wore a smile, but his eyes were sad. His eyes were on Liam as he worked his concertina and laughed heartily at a joke Lorelei did not understand. Her only thought was of Erick's heartache as he feared the loss of his friend. Such loyalty spoke well of him, she thought.

Perhaps I can convince him to come to my kingdom and become one of us, she thought to herself as she gazed upon him. *He does not fit in with these humans. Behold, it is his birthnight, and yet he sits alone.*

His eyes drifted away from Liam and toward the sky. A single tear slid down his cheek, and then he pitched himself backward over the rail and into the dark sea.

Lorelei let out a squeak of distress and dove off the ladder. She searched for him, but he had been on the other side of the boat, and the water was oh, so dark. What had he been thinking? Was he so distressed at having to become the man his royal family wanted him to be that he had preferred oblivion? Aunt Mathilde had been right: forcing someone to be who they are not only led to pain.

She searched the darkness desperately, knowing that she could give him the hope of a new and different life. She focused her sharp vision downward, hoping to catch a flash of his white shirt before he sunk too far, but she saw nothing. But just as she had reached desperate madness for her beloved, something tickled her face.

Bubbles!

She dove straight downward, her arms outstretched, her mind and soul praying to any spirit that would listen and take pity on her. There ... a few feet away ... a flash of white! She grabbed for it and her fingers closed around the fabric.

She nearly wept with relief, but then a new fear crashed down upon her: *how long could a human survive without air? How long had it been?* She had no idea, but she hauled Erick to the surface, re-echoing her prayers. They broke through, but his eyes were closed, and his body limp in her strong arms. She wailed aloud in her mermaid voice.

"Spirits of the sea, hear me! Help me! Bring his soul back from its skyward flight! I will sacrifice all that I have, if only to have him here with me!"

What would you give? came a rumbling from below. ***Would you give your royal blood?***

"Yes, yes, anything!" She brought her tail up to the surface, where the wounds from the oysters were mostly healed. With her one free hand, she clawed at the one that had healed the least, the one where she had ripped the oyster free with her own hands. Blood trickled from the wound, across her scales, and into the sea.

A pressure from the depths pushed Lorelei and Erick upward, as if there had been a great disturbance directly beneath them, tossing them in its wake. The mermaid clung to her prince as the turbulence passed, and when she looked at him again, his eyes were open, and looking at her, filled with confusion.

She cried out with joy and hugged him tight.

"Who are you?" he asked, but his voice sounded ... wrong.

Well, of course it does, she thought. *He's just returned from the dead.* She pulled back to gaze upon him. "My name is Lorelei ..." she began, but stopped short.

The eyes that looked upon her now were not at all like the ones who had gazed at her as a swan. They were still blue, but had a hazy film across them, as though the sky of his eyes had been filled with storms.

"You were drowning." Her heart thudded in her chest as she held him afloat.

"I was supposed to drown," he replied, looking around at the sea in confusion. "Why am I here? What have you done?"

"I have saved you, Erick! If you only knew how I have loved you from afar!"

"I feel ... strange." His words were detached and empty, and a dark fear began to well deep within her.

"You'll be alright, my darling. You have been through an ordeal, but some rest will set you to rights. Float here with me under the moonlight. You may sleep, and I will hold you up in the air so that you are safe."

He turned onto his back and laid his head against her, though it seemed more out of obedience than affection or gratitude. She caressed his dark hair and then lay back so that she could be more buoyant and support his weight as well as her own. She brought her tail to the surface, and her iridescent scales glinted under the full moon, the smoothness broken only by the thin stream of blood that still trickled into the sea.

Erick's body went rigid, and in one swift movement, he whipped his entire body around and latched his mouth on the open wound on her hip, drawing her blood from her and swallowing greedily.

"What are you doing? Erick, stop!" she shouted.

He jerked his head backward, his lips now stained red. "Why did I do that? What have you done to me?"

"I have done nothing but save you from drowning in the sea!"

"You have saved me from nothing!" He pushed himself away from her and dove beneath the dark waters. Lorelei hesitated for a moment, stunned, then dove after him. Only this time she did not have to search. He hung suspended in water but a few feet away, looking at her with horror in his eyes.

"Why do I not need to hold my breath?" Lorelei was shocked to hear him use the speech of the merpeople, and for a moment, she was filled with joy.

"Perhaps you have developed gills! Do you feel the water moving back and forth along your sides?"

"I feel nothing but the cold of the sea," he replied.

"We must go to my Great Aunt. She will know what to do. She is very wise. She can fix things, I know." She took Erick's hand, and he did not resist her as she drew him away from land, toward her father's kingdom.

Aunt Mathilde's face was unreadable as she stared at her weeping grand-niece and the man she had dragged to the city of the merpeople. She cursed her age and softness for not crushing Lorelei's dream when she had first brought it up.

"What is to be done, Auntie?" Lorelei sobbed.

"I have always been straight and honest with you, child, but it seems I should have been much harder on you than I have been. You have done an unthinkable thing. I am sorry, young man, as you will pay perhaps the greatest price for my lack of strictness."

"What do you mean, Auntie?"

"What did you promise them, Lorelei?"

"Promise who?" Lorelei knew exactly *who*, but didn't want to believe.

"The spirits of the Abyss, child. You have exchanged something for this boy's continued existence. What was it?"

"Just a little of my blood, that was all! A small price to pay to bring back my beloved!"

"Your beloved?" Erick turned to her, anger furrowing his brow. "You don't know me!"

"Oh, don't say that," she pleaded. "I loved you from the ocean, 'tis true, but ..."

"You loved your idea of me, just as my parents love their idea of me. But that isn't real. It's selfishness. You don't know who I am."

"Enough!" Matilde commanded before Lorelei could protest. "You promised the spirits your blood?"

"Y–yes. They asked if I would give my royal blood, and I did, gladly!"

"You fool," Mathilde sighed, but more with resignation than anger. She looked at the red stains that still encircled Erick's mouth, stains that the ocean could not wash away. "You have fed on her, then?" she asked him.

His eyes fell, and his shame answered for him.

"And you will again, I wager. You will not be able to resist. You are not feeding yourself, wretched boy, you are feeding *them*. They consume her blood through you."

Lorelei and Erick both stared at Mathilde in horror.

"No! I cannot ... I won't ..." Erick raced from the room, and Lorelei began to follow.

"You need not chase him, child. He will not be able to stay away from you for long. You are his only food now. And you will continue to be so for the rest of your life."

"Wha–what?"

"There is no name for what he is now, at least not among our people. But the oldest stories tell of such things. The young prince you loved lives no more. What just left here is an abomination created of ignorance, desperation, and necromancy. He will take the Abyssal spirits' blood sacrifice from you whenever they will it, as often as they will it, and he will exist in this way for as long as you live. He will try to return to his people. You cannot let him. He is a danger to them now. His madness for your blood will rip his mind apart if he is away from you, and he will seek any blood he can find, though it will not satiate him."

She fled her great aunt's chamber, and deep in the back of her mind festered the knowledge that she could never return.

There was no doubt where Erick would go.

He would go to Liam.

Lorelei swam as fast as she could, her mind searching for ways to follow Erick up on land. She had destroyed his life and hers; she could not allow her vanity to be responsible for destroying anyone else's.

She knew she could not go to the harbor and drag herself ashore in the presence of who-knew-how-many humans, so she made her way to the cove where she had fooled herself into believing she could force Erick to love her, simply because she wanted him to.

The cove was empty, and she dragged herself onto the sand, rough and grating against her scales. When she reached the staircase, she despaired, unsure if her strength would hold out. Slowly, step by step, she crawled her way to the top, ignoring the pain as her delicate, shimmering scales scraped against the stone.

Miraculously, she reached the top, but her arms ached and trembled from the strain. She had never had to bear her own weight out of the water for so long, nor was she built to do so. She rolled into the soft grass.

Perhaps I could rest here, just for a moment ...

Until the screaming began.

The shrill sound of terror rose from a small building behind the palace, and she pulled herself on her elbows and forearms across the lawn. Words became clear as she drew closer.

"Liam, please!" It was Erick, surely, but it was merspeech which left his lips, and Liam could not understand.

"Get back, demon!" Liam's voice was filled with agony and fear.

Lorelei reached the edge of the lawn, and the building lay just ahead, but the ground between was covered entirely in tiny rocks. She remembered that humans covered the bottoms of their legs and feet, and supposed that this was why. She forced herself forward, the stones slicing into the flesh of her arms and tail. She dragged herself into the building, the floor of which was thankfully covered in smooth wood.

The sight before her was a horror. Erick stood at the gate of an open animal pen, having backed Liam inside as he fled from the creature his friend had become in death. Erick's once radiant skin was wan and translucent, and resembled the flesh of a squid moreso than that of a human. His dark hair was limp and wet, and his clothes were littered with seaweed and other debris from his trek to the land. He was reaching out to Liam, who was paralyzed in terror, gripping a shovel in case the beast came any closer.

Even through his fear, Liam wept, grieving the loss of the young man he had called *brother.*

"Erick!" Lorelei cried in merspeech. "You must stay away from him! I know you don't want to hurt him, but you may not be able to stop yourself. Please, we must return to the sea!"

Erick wheeled on her. At first, his eyes were filled with pain and rage, but when he spotted the bloody ruin of her arms and tail, they became wild with the bloodlust he had first displayed in the sea. He leapt at her, devouring the blood from her arms in a blind hunger that would have no end.

Liam scrambled to his feet and raised his shovel, not sure which of the two of them to strike.

"Run," Lorelei told him in the human tongue.

He dropped the shovel and fled.

Once the blood on Lorelei's arms had been licked clean, a semblance of reason returned to Erick's eyes. He let out a wail of anguish as the realization of what Liam had just witnessed settled over him. He grabbed the mermaid around the waist and hauled her across the stableyard, across the lawn, and down the stairs to the beach. With one last longing look at the palace, he held tight to her and dove into the sea.

Once underwater, it was Lorelei that led the way, her wounds seeping into the sea and binding Erick to follow wherever she went. He vacillated between despair and blood madness, holding her hand as they swam farther and farther from what had once been his home.

The kingdom of the merpeople came into view, but Lorelei did not stop. She had taken everything from Erick, and it was only fair that she should sacrifice in return. Her selfish and childish folly had doomed them both. She led him to her cave at the edge of the Abyss, determined that it would be here that she would live out her days with Erick at her side. She had gotten her wish, after a fashion, and had learned the painful lesson of a poorly-worded bargain.

"How long must we stay here?" Erick asked her, his eyes straining in the blackness of the depths.

"For as long as I live," she answered sadly, brushing her fingers against the blood roses she had planted. "For as long as I live."

Karens in the Woods

HORROR COMEDY BY BETSEY KULAKOWSKI AND JB CAINE

Ansley Anselm was a backstabbing bitch.

Not only had she schemed behind the scenes and convinced the mucky-mucks at WKPP that Karen Hardaway was too old to be a news anchor, she was also ruining Karen's trip. How could Karen be expected to relax when her 18-year career was going down in flames?

Well, screw Ansley. Screw all of them. They didn't know who they were messing with. She'd come back stronger, and on her own terms! She'd ...

A yowl echoed across the South Baggage Claim and the humiliated ex-anchor turned toward the sound. A smile crept across her face and she felt her chest muscles loosen ever-so-slightly at the sight of the grinning blonde hauling ass across the baggage claim rolling a neon-green hardbody suitcase.

Karen raised her hand in greeting from behind the partition that separated the airport version of a popular chain restaurant from the throngs of people heading to destinations unknown. Her smile broadened as she watched Caryn Cavenaugh wind her way amongst high-top tables full of patrons and their assorted luggage. She found herself standing beside her chair by the time her best friend rolled to a stop.

They threw their arms around each other in a cacophony of *hiyeeeee!* and nonsensical squealing sounds that no one who knew either of the two women would have believed them capable of making.

But that's what the joy of an unconditional best friend will do ... turn professional, educated, serious women into gushing girlie-girls.

"Oh Mylanta, KK, when you called and said you were taking me on a surprise adventure, I just dropped *everything*!" Since their first names sounded identical, they'd dubbed each other CC and KK when they'd first met back in college at that skeevy bar outside of Dallas. Mutually bad dates and escape trips to the ladies' room made for lifelong friendships. Certainly that's where the bond formed in their case. But probably no one else knew that. CC shot a glance over her shoulder as if expecting to see someone she knew, then shook her head and hugged her friend again.

Karen's cheeks hurt from smiling, and her heart hurt out of relief to be in the company of the one person on the planet who she trusted. "I knew you couldn't resist a few days in the mountains! I've booked us the *cutest* cabin out in the woods!"

"Do you have pictures, or are you going to leave me in suspense?" CC slid into the chair across from KK and wedged her bag under the table. "Did you order already?" She indicated the menu in the center of the table and the now-slightly-watery diet soda sitting at KK's place.

"Well, I *did* order some nachos," Karen groused, "but they're taking forever to get here."

"Oh, I love nachos."

"I know! And I asked for no sour cream and extra guac, just like you like them."

"You're the absolute BEST. That plane food tastes like chicken feed. They call those *pretzels*? It's criminal."

"Girl, I hear you. All I know is that those nachos better be gooey and hot and wonderful. It's not right to make a lady starve once she's got her credit card out."

CC chuckled and inclined her head toward the approaching waitress. "Our salvation approacheth."

"Hey, y'all! Sorry that it took a minute. We had a big party all ordering at the same time. Here you go!" She slid the large plate onto the hightop, and both women's faces darkened.

"This isn't what I ordered," Karen scowled.

The server looked confused and then checked her notepad. "Ultimate Nachos," she recited.

"No," Karen snarled. "I ordered Ultimate Nachos with *no sour cream* and *extra guacamole*. This has *no guacamole* and *extra sour cream*. Clearly, this isn't my order."

"Oh, uh, I ..." the server sputtered. "I must have ..."

"You know what?" Karen had had just about enough from incompetent underlings this week. "We're going to take our business somewhere else. You should be providing excellent service to weary travelers, many of whom are arriving in your fair city for the very first time. You should think of yourself as an *ambassador* for your hometown. I'll pay for my drink, since I've already gone through half of it, but ..."

"I'll get a new order put in right away," the server protested. "It's been a crazy day, and I'm so sorry for ..."

Caryn placed a hand on her frazzled friend's arm. "That will be just fine, thank you. But please put a rush on it. My friend has already been waiting a long time, and I'm *sure* you don't want this issue escalated to your manager."

The server scooped the heavy plate off the table and bustled away, muttering under her breath.

Karen stared after her for a moment, then her expression softened. "Oh, and bring my friend a Dr. Pepper. Please." The server didn't turn around, but the pause in her retreat indicated that she'd heard the additional order. "She should have asked you what you wanted to drink."

"You didn't give her much of a chance, KK. But don't worry. She'll make it right." CC squeezed her friend's arm and leaned back. "Now why don't you tell me what's going on that's got you terrorizing waitresses?"

Two hours, some corrected nachos, and thirty miles later, CC stared at KK in disbelief. "She did *what*?"

"That little minx told Grant that I was talking to a regional network affiliate so that I'd look disloyal. She very conveniently forgot to mention that I was only talking to them because they were asking about a consumer advocacy story I did six months ago. Then they decided to let me go because they claimed they needed a *new and fresh face* anchoring the evening news."

"Why would Grant believe her?"

"If I had to guess, it's because she knocked out his reasoning with her 36-Ds. That's what I get for trying to lift up other women in the news industry, taking on an intern. I lifted her up, and she stabbed me in the eye with her stiletto heel."

"She was probably after your job." CC insisted.

"Probably, but she has no idea how this industry works. Grant wouldn't hire some intern to be an anchor. He might get rid of me, but it won't be Ansley Asshat getting my chair. It'll probably be our feature reporter. She polls well with our audiences, and Grant likes the demographic appeal of her being bilingual ..."

"So what will happen to Ansley then?"

"Oh, Grant will undoubtedly string her along with promises long enough to get into her pants, if she's that sort. If she's not, he'll shuttle her out within a month. It'd be bad for morale to keep her around."

"Because people like you, and they'd be mad ..."

"No," KK chuckled, "because they have their own agendas, and Miss Ansley is an interloper. She just overplayed her hand."

"So she'll get her due, one way or another," CC smiled. "Good."

It was at that moment that they noticed the flashing lights in the rearview mirror of their rented RAV-4 (which, by the way, was most definitely *not* the Lincoln Navigator that Karen had reserved, and Platinum Rent-a-Car would be hearing about the ineptitude with which Premium Members were treated). Karen made a sound that was somewhere between a growl and a sigh. Unfortunately, she was 1200 miles away from anywhere her familiar face might get her out of a ticket. She pulled into a fast-food parking lot and rolled down her window, keeping her hands on the wheel.

Let it never be said that a career in broadcasting can't teach valuable life skills. She put on her sweetest, most sincere beaming smile. "What seems to be the trouble, officer?"

"Ma'am, do you know how fast you were goin'?"

She widened her eyes in mock surprise. "I'm just sure I was going around 60. I know that's five miles over, but I just came off the interstate, and ..."

"Ma'am, once you pass that WalMart there, the speed limit is 45, and you blew past it goin' 64."

"Oh, no! I'm so sorry! I didn't see the sign! I just got in from Connecticut, and I've never been here before, and ..." She let the slightest hint of impending tears crack her voice. Men *hate* it when women cry.

Caryn was strategically quiet, nodding for emphasis.

"Y'all are from Connecticut?"

"My friend is from Texas. We've just flown in for a girl's weekend. You see, I just lost my job, and ..."

"Could you hand me your license, please, ma'am?"

If he called her *ma'am* one more time ... she wasn't *that* old! But she handed the card over meekly and he walked back to his patrol car to run it through his system.

"Ohshitohshitohshit!" KK swore as soon as he was out of earshot. "This is the *last* thing I need!"

"It'll be okay," CC consoled her. "I bet he lets you off with a warning."

They stared into the rearview mirror in silence while they waited for the young officer to return. After a few moments, he emerged from his vehicle and approached, scratching his dishwater-brown buzz cut. "Here you go, ma'am. This a rental?"

"Yessir," KK responded, salty as having to call someone half her age *sir*.

"Well, ladies, I'm gonna let you off with a warnin' today, but you'd be well-advised to pay closer attention to the signs and speed limits when you're in an unfamiliar area."

"Oh, yes, Officer ..." She squinted at the name badge on his uniform. "Officer Peters. Thank you!"

"I'll keep an eye on her, officer, I promise!" CC effused. "Thank you so much!"

Officer Peters shot them each one more glare of reprimand, then scratched his scalp again and turned away. Once he was out of sight, KK rested her forehead against the steering wheel and CC slumped in her seat.

"How about if we just sit here for a minute until he drives off?" Caryn suggested.

"Just long enough for my pulse rate to drop back under ninety," Karen agreed.

CC got out of the car. Her mouth hung open in complete disbelief. She had expected some run-down old log cabin in the forest, but this was practically a mansion. On top of that, the air was so cool and crisp she couldn't believe she'd left 100-degree temperatures that morning.

"I told you to trust me," KK said, grinning as she came up behind her. "The door code is 1313."

CC turned and glared at her. "You're joking, right?"

"You're not superstitious, are you?"

"I'm a little 'stitious," CC said softly as KK opened the hatchback. CC grabbed her suitcase and dragged it across the gravel driveway, struggling to keep it from twisting in her hand. KK opened the door and stood back, letting her enter first.

The cabin was even more spectacular inside. The hardwood floors gave it a rustic feel, but the course Santa Fe-style rugs provided cushion as she kicked off her shoes and left her bag behind her at the door. The main living room was spacious and the rafters above opened onto a stained glass window that looked like something out of a fevered dream. The fading sunlight shone through it and it cast rainbows on everything, and the smell of artificial pine plug-ins wafted through the tinted air.

"KK …" she said, her voice catching as she turned to look up at the loft. "It's beautiful! How did you find this place? More importantly, how can you afford it? You just lost your job."

"You let me worry about it," KK said. "I figured you'd want the loft. I'll take the room down here."

CC rushed up the stairs, her feet stomping on the hardwood that creaked as she passed. The loft was an intimate space with a small metal-framed bed and built-in bookcases with a collection of novels — everything from Asimov to Zelazny. There were fairy lights draped around the room and a window over the bed had a view of the babbling river that tossed over the rocks and down the hillside to a waterfall just below the property. There was a trail that led up the hill and around the bend and CC made a promise to herself to explore it the first chance she got.

It was a far cry from her cramped studio apartment in San Antonio, and she couldn't wait to explore the rest of the house. She found KK downstairs standing in her bedroom with her arms crossed and her hip jutted out. CC knew that look. She wasn't happy.

"What's wrong?"

"One bathroom? In a place this size? Are you kidding me?"

"Not like we're both going to use it at the same time."

"One bathroom? And it's in my bedroom?"

"KK, it's no big deal. We've roughed it worse than this before. Remember our dorm in college? We shared the bathroom with the two girls in the other suite."

"Suite was a term loosely applied at the University of Texas in those days," KK sniped, turning to her friend. "How's the loft?"

"It's perfect! Everything is perfect. Nobody would ever find us here." CC's eyes seemed distant and full of apprehension.

"As if anyone would come looking," KK chuckled.

CC blanched. "Let's check out the kitchen."

"Yes," KK agreed. "I'm starving again."

CC scanned the cobalt blue tile countertops and dark hardwood cabinets, wishing she had this much space in her apartment. She opened one of the cabinets, finding all the necessary dinnerware, including elegant wine goblets and high-ball glasses. The next cabinet was a little more barren. Several half-bottles of spices, including salt and pepper. There was a mostly-empty can of Folgers coffee, and a container of powdered coffee creamer. The next cabinet had little more than an unopened box of crackers, a jar of peanut butter, and a bottle of Worcestershire sauce.

KK stood at the open refrigerator with an expression of disbelief. "This is unacceptable."

"What?"

"A jar of pickles and a stick of butter? That's it?" KK gasped. "What's in the pantry?"

"Not much," CC went through the inventory.

A profanity-laced tirade followed as Karen threw a fit. "Given what I paid for this place, I expected to find the kitchen stocked! This is an outrage!" Karen already had her phone out, number dialed. She put it on speaker phone. "Hi, we're your hosts, Travis and Mary. Sorry we can't take your call. Please leave a message or text us and we'll check in with you within thirty minutes."

The tirade continued as KK unloaded on their hosts. CC shook her head and pursed her lips as she picked up her purse and went to stand by the door. KK's rant went on as she followed CC to the car.

She hung up and got in. "I need a margarita."

"I wouldn't say no to that," CC said. "I saw a Mexican place on the road just outside of town."

"You're in charge of navigating." That suited CC just fine, though she might have to drive back, depending on how much KK liked the margaritas.

They returned two hours later with bellies full of enchiladas and a trunk full of groceries.

"I'll take a couple of bags and put the code in," KK offered. "Can you get the rest of it?"

"Sure, no problem! I come from good farming stock, remember?" CC grinned. She watched as KK trudged up the wooden steps and through the door, then followed with her own arms laden with plastic grocery bags. She'd wished that the little grocery store had offered paper bags, since they were so much better for the environment, but at least this way, they wouldn't have to make as many trips. Then again, maybe that would have been okay, since taking more trips was easier on cracked ribs than a heavy load, especially when you were trying not to let the pain show.

CC was nudging the door open with her foot when she heard KK's shrill scream from inside. She dropped the bags and burst through the door, following the sounds of sheer chaos coming from KK's bedroom. By the time she found her friend, the ex-anchor was standing in an defensive stance and wielding a curling iron like a shortsword.

"What the bejeezus happened?" CC asked, taking in the room's state of moderate disarray.

"It was *huge*!" KK sobbed. "I left the window open just a crack when we left so it wouldn't be so stuffy in here, and then I guess a badger or raccoon or muscled its way in! It *hissed* at me! And it had these craggy teeth ..."

CC's eyes scanned the room. "Where is it now?"

"It ran back out the window!"

"You said it hissed? Do badgers hiss?"

"How should I know, CC? I live in Bridgeport! I don't even know if there *are* badgers in Bridgeport! I only saw it for a second. It might have even been a huge rat. In New York, they have 'em big as beavers! What difference does it make?" KK's composure crumbled entirely as she plopped onto the side of the bed and sobs wracked her tall frame. "Why is everything going to shit? I worked my tail off for 18 years to be a good journalist, respected in my field, and one stupid ladder-climbing bitch destroys it. Then I try to surprise my best friend, the only person who's ever stood by me, and the entire Universe is conspiring to ruin that, too!"

CC sat on the bed beside KK, leaning against her as comfort until the crying gave way to sniffles and hiccups. She wanted to hug her friend, but carrying the groceries had already aggravated her sore body. "Listen, sugar, nothing's going to ruin this vacation. We're together, and everything else is gravy. You've had a hell of a week. And I'm sorry. It's going to get better, I promise."

A few minutes later, the women were curled up on the overstuffed living room furniture with cups of tea. CC took a cautious sip of her oolong and sighed as the smooth and steaming beverage calmed her nerves. "Did you say something earlier about going on a hike tomorrow?"

"There's a trail not far from the cabin I thought we might check out. When was the last time you went on a hike?"

"When I was working in Houston, I found a women's hiking club I used to go out with."

"In Houston?"

"You'd be surprised how many lovely trails they have down there, if you don't mind the heat."

"Well I do mind the heat, and you know it."

"Then you must be absolutely ecstatic with how cool it is here," CC chuckled. "I know I am."

KK laughed too. "I don't think I've been hiking since we graduated," she said with a wistful sigh. "I really miss it. I've missed you, too."

CC wished she had something more potent than Tylenol. Her whole body ached and all she could think about was crawling into bed for a good night's sleep. The night had gone cool and the smell of impending rain was heavy in the air. A nearly full moon shone through the trees, its halo creating a prism effect that was both mysterious and calming. Tonight would be the first night CC had slept in months without worrying about what Rube might do. If he had a bad day, she had a bad night. Well, not anymore. This would be the first of many nights without having to worry about what he might take out on her.

"Maybe we should just call it a night," CC suggested. "Maybe we can do s'mores tomorrow."

KK didn't argue, but she studied her friend's ginger movements. "Did you see the bathtub in the master bedroom?"

"No," CC said. "Is it nice?"

"If you want a long hot soak, there are some perfumed epsom salts in the cabinet."

"I wouldn't say no," CC grinned.

"Don't think I haven't noticed," KK said kindly. "I probably have a couple of hydrocodone in my purse left over from my root canal."

CC looked down. "What? "

"You move like a woman in pain." KK took her hand. "You didn't fall off your horse, again, did you?"

"No," CC muttered, embarrassed. "It's nothing."

She snatched up her suitcase and disappeared upstairs. "I'll draw you a bath," Karen called after her. "You like it hot, right?"

CC stopped at the top step and looked down over the railing. "Yes, please." KK gave her a smile and nodded.

CC was stretched out beneath the foaming waters that steamed up the entire room. KK tapped on the door and stepped in, handing her a refilled cup of tea. "I figured with the hydrocodone, a glass of wine would be ill-advised."

CC accepted the cup as KK stepped out, returning a moment later with her own. She closed the toilet seat and put the clean towel on it for a cushion. "You wanna tell me what happened?"

CC closed her eyes and inhaled the scent of her tea. "Not really," she said. "But I know you won't let up til I do."

"No," KK stood. "If you don't want to ..."

"Rube ..." CC interrupted her. "He ... he's changed."

"They always do," KK muttered, sitting back down.

"He started coming home later and later. If dinner wasn't hot and ready on the table, he'd get angry. If the house wasn't spotless, he'd pitch a fit. When I had to go on a work trip he'd call every evening to make sure I didn't stay out late, and to ask when I was coming home. Then he'd grill me for hours about what I'd done and who I'd traveled with."

"How long did it take for him to hit you?"

CC winced and set her cup aside, sinking into the tub. "At first, it was just insults, then shoving me or raising his hand without ever striking me, but … it didn't take long. A few months." Tears ran down her face. KK slid down off the stool and caught Caryn's hand. "It caught me off guard the first time …"

"How long has this been going on?"

"Six months …" she sniffed.

"How much does he weigh?" Karen's question caught her friend off guard.

CC looked up at her with red eyes, looking baffled. "Huh?"

"How much does this asshole weigh, CC?"

CC shrugged. "I don't know, maybe 195? 200? Why do you ask?"

"Just calculating how much lye I need to decompose his sorry-ass body when I bury him."

"Huh?"

"Fifty pounds of lye per one hundred pounds of body weight."

CC looked stunned. She sniffed but then smiled conspiratorially. "There's a hog farm not far outside of town. I just haven't figured out how I'm going to get him out there."

Now it was Karen's turn to look stunned. A wide grin spread over both of their faces. CC started laughing first, but Karen didn't hesitate to get in on the moment. They laughed until they cried and CC wrapped her arms around her friend's neck, getting her soaked.

"Okay, okay," KK cajoled, as she escaped her embrace. "Finish your bath. I'm going to put my pajamas on and get ready for bed. We need some sleep if we're going to hike tomorrow. Are you up to it?"

CC nodded and reached for the drain, letting the water out. KK glanced back as she climbed out of the tub, wincing at the bruises that marred her friend's lean body as she pulled the towel around herself.

The rough pine steps squeaked as bare feet padded down the stairs from the loft above the master bedroom. A moment later, the handle jiggled, and the door groaned as it opened. Karen rolled over, pulling the covers over her head when the bathroom light came on and the bathroom door closed. "It's not even daylight," she groaned.

"No," Caryn said. "It's just past 3:30, but ... a storm blew in and ... all the water running in the creek behind the house and the rain on the roof ... I had to pee."

Karen sat up, throwing back the blankets. Her hair was disheveled and her make up smeared. "What moron builds a house with only one bathroom and puts it in the master suite?"

"Clearly not someone who intended to stay here," Caryn said. "Sorry if I disturbed you."

Karen lay back down. "It wasn't you. It was those creaky stairs."

"I'll tread softly in the future."

"Well, if it's still raining when we get up, that might delay our hike."

"Maybe," Caryn said, coming out of the bathroom. "Good night."

"Night."

Caryn did her best to keep from lumbering up the stairs. The planks in the loft, she couldn't help. She made her way to the bed, careful not to bump her head on the low rafters as she climbed into the antique bed. The springs made a high pitched noise as she settled. The room was bitterly cold, but she wasn't one to complain. She liked to sleep with a bit of chill in the air, and there was a lovely quilt and comforter to keep her warm.

Lightning flashed and thunder rumbled. The rain pounded against the metal roof over her head. Caryn sighed and lay in boneless rapture in the cradle of the tempurpedic mattress. The pain pill had helped more than she expected, and she drifted back into a healing and restful sleep.

The trilling of a mockingbird outside her bedroom window jostled KK into wakefulness, and she rolled luxuriously in the starched sheets. It was much nicer than waking up to an alarm on her phone, she decided, and made a note that when she re-invented her public persona, she'd make sure there was nothing in her life that had to happen before 8 a.m.

She looked at her fitness tracker. 8:15. *Glorious. Just glorious.*

Karen felt better than she had in years. As she replayed the previous day's events in her mind, she blushed at how rude s he'd been to the cabin's owners. She didn't blame them for not bothering to respond. She plucked her phone off the night table and fired off a text of apology through the booking app, stressing how horrified she was at her own conduct. The tension of the day had been no excuse. She hoped they'd accept her apology, and promised a top rating on the app at the end of their stay.

That task done, she pulled on a fuzzy pair of socks and padded into the kitchen, where CC had already put the coffee machine to work with the Kona blend they'd bought at the store. She poured herself a cup and splashed in some of the vanilla bean creamer they'd also bought. *Folgers and powdered creamer? The last guests must've been savages.*

"Morning, Sunshine," CC's voice cooed from the overstuffed chair next to the fireplace. She was buried under at least three inches of afghans.

"Hey, there." KK plopped herself down on the sofa, it's mocha leather as soft as butter. "How come you didn't start the fire? It's chilly in here this morning!"

"I tried to, but I couldn't figure it out. There's no wood anywhere, or matches. I wiggled all those switches, but nothing happened." She wagged her jaw at a series of silver levers along the left side of the stone hearth.

Karen thought about messaging the hosts for instructions, but thought she'd better wait until she was sure they'd received her apology. "Ah, well, we'll try it again later. How about we have some of those chocolate croissants we bought and head for the trail?"

"Sounds good to me. A bit of vigorous walking will warm us up."

"Not too vigorous for you, madam." KK pointed out. "A gentle hike is all you're getting."

"I'm actually feeling a lot better after a good night's sleep," CC protested.

"We'll start out easy and see how you feel," KK insisted. "And if your ribs start hurting, we either rest or head back. We've got all week. Okay?"

"Okay. I promise."

They filled their bellies with carbs and coffee, packed a few snacks and water bottles for their hike, and headed for the hills, literally.

The night's rain had abated, but the grass was damp with dew and the morning sun glistened on the forest around them. The carpark at the trailhead wasn't abandoned, but a work truck for the park service was the only vehicle parked there. "Looks like we have the trail to ourselves," KK said, shouldering the backpack. She'd insisted on carrying the pack that contained basic emergency supplies. Today's hike was a warm-up to get them acclimated to the elevation more than anything. If KK had known about Caryn's injuries, she might have taken them to a spa instead. Maybe they'd get a pedicure before they headed back to the airport.

CC tucked her cell phone into the pocket in her jacket, along with a pack of tissues. "Ready?" she asked her friend.

KK nodded. "Good to go."

"The backpack's not too heavy, is it?"

"Not for me," KK said, flexing. "I've been working out."

The trail was covered in gravel for the first quarter mile. Pine and sycamore trees shaded the path, drilling rain on their heads as the branches waved in a morning breeze. Birds chirped and squirrels scattered in the leaf-litter on the forest floor. "I know it rained, but did it storm?" KK asked, noticing fallen trees ahead of them.

"The thunder and lightning got pretty intense around 4:00," CC said. "Wind howled all night."

"Aw ... did it keep you up?"

"No, not really. I mean, I was aware of it, but the rain made the loft so cozy, and the bed was so comfy. Once I got comfortable, I slept pretty well."

"Good," KK hooked her arm in CC's. "I didn't realize you needed a get-away worse than I did."

"You saved me," CC leaned her head on her friend's shoulder. "And what a gorgeous place you picked."

"I needed a change," Karen said. "I didn't expect it to be this beautiful, but I couldn't be more excited to really get out here and explore."

"Me, too."

A half-hour into their journey, the path turned, and they found themselves at the edge of a creek, where downed trees blocked their way. There, a man in a park service uniform struggled with a chainsaw that was bound up in one of the large trees. He turned as they approached, and eyed them warily, sniffing as he reached into his pocket for a handkerchief.

"Whatchu lookin at?" he demanded.

"Uh, just trying to figure out the easiest way around this treefall," CC said. "Did the storms last night do this?"

"Partly," he said. "Had severe weather a few days ago, too. What that storm didn't get down, last night's weather finished."

"Oh," KK took a step back, picking her path over the tree that lay before her. She struggled over the tree before turning back to help CC.

"You girls goin' out to the waterfall?" The worker asked, picking up his ax, studying the blade.

"Warming up for a longer hike tomorrow," CC said with a genuine smile.

"Be careful out there ... wouldn't wanna run into the Booger."

"Excuse me?" KK asked. "The Booger?"

"You know," the man sniffed. "Bigfoot."

"Yeah, okay," KK laughed. She expected the ranger to laugh, too, but he didn't. Instead, he just shrugged and started using the ax to chip free the trapped chainsaw. KK and CC exchanged glances, and continued their walk along the trail, leaving the curmudgeonly ranger behind. An ominous creaking came from the left, where an embankment rose to a copse of trees, some of which leaned on each other at perilous angles. "What was that?"

"That was the trees settling, probably," CC answered, pulling her phone out of her pocket and glancing at it for maybe the fourth time since they'd left the ranger behind.

KK stopped in her tracks and leveled a look at her friend. "Rube?"

"Yeah," CC sighed. "He's called twice and left messages, and now he's texting me."

"What did he say?"

"I don't know. I haven't opened them. I don't want him to see that I've read them. I only saw the first word or two in my notifications."

KK nodded. "Smart. Plausible deniability."

The trail opened out into a wide meadow with a thin red clay line winding through the tall grasses and wildflowers, and the sweet fragrance of spring tickled their noses. Along either side, the dense woods stretched out as far as they could see, rising to gentle foothills in the distance. Both women gasped in delight.

"It's *beautiful*!" CC snapped a panoramic shot on her cell, then wandered around to take close-up shots of the yellow and purple and pink blooms all around them. A glint of metal caught her eye, and she gestured to KK that she was going to investigate.

"Looks like some old framing for a building or something," Karen theorized, examining the rusted poles and beams which made up the shapeless heap. "I wonder if it's stuff that was used to build that." She pointed to a tower poking out of the treetops in the distance, probably used for fire-spotting. But her fascination with the structure didn't last long. "Look! A stream!"

A small wooden structure no larger than two pallets nailed together crossed the span of a stream that, even swollen from the night's rain, couldn't have measured more than four feet across. "This is nice," CC smiled, taken in by the natural beauty. "How about if we sit here for a little while and have a snack. Then maybe we can head back." The sun was high in the sky, and she definitely wanted to get back in time for another luxurious bath before dinner.

They sat on the little bridge, which groaned ever-so-slightly under their combined weight, and pulled out the water and protein bars. CC had slipped off her hiking boots and was dangling her toes in the icy water. KK leaned back to take a long sip from her bottle when a loud *whoooop whoooop!* split the mid-day air.

"What in the world was *that*?" she choked.

"I don't know," CC replied around a mouthful of granola. "Maybe an owl?"

"Can't be. It's just past noon. What else makes a sound like that?"

"Maybe it's the Booger," CC snickered, earning her a sideways glance before KK broke into a grin as well.

"Well, if it is, it sounds like he's celebrating something."

"Maybe he found Mrs. Booger."

The two of them broke into a fit of giggles at the thought, and in the magic of the moment, cell phones, grumpy rangers, and rotten boyfriends were forgotten.

Rejuvenated and rested, they decided to press on. They hoped to reach the overlook at Snake Falls, but after walking for nearly an hour, the convivial spirit of the day quickly turned perilous. The first rumbles of thunder preceded the torrential downpour by only minutes. Before the girls knew it, the sky had turned as black as obsidian, and the trail into a sticky quagmire. They stood with their backs to an outcropping of rock, miserable and soaked to the bone. After waiting a few minutes for the storm's intensity to slow to a drizzle with attitude, they began to carefully pick their way back to the car.

They had to stop several times and try to find cover when a wave of heavy rain would wash over the area, and the trail itself was slow going. By the time they made it back to the RAV-4, they were chilled and covered in mud. They tossed their boots into the back of the small SUV and jumped into the front seats, cranking up the heater to fight their shivering. KK backed out of the parking spot just as the skies opened up again. As she approached the log fence marking the entrance to the trailhead, she spotted the ranger's truck sitting just outside the entrance, with the surly man himself stationed in the front seat. As she passed, KK gave him a friendly wave which he did not return.

"Why do you suppose he's just sitting there?" CC asked, craning her neck to see the ranger's headlights spring to life as they pulled away.

"He was probably debating whether or not he needed to have us rescued," KK pointed out.

"Yeah, good point. That explains why he looked so angry."

"Speaking of angry, you're going to have to tell Rube something eventually," KK grumbled. "I'd advise that *something* is '*goodbye and good riddance.*'"

"Yeah, you're right. I guess I should read those messages. I haven't even looked at my phone since we stopped at that bridge." She pulled her folding smartphone out and glanced at the front screen which would give her a hint of her text messages without having to actually open them.

Karen carefully maneuvered the vehicle down the slope of the steep and slick road. "Well, why don't you wait until we get to the cabin so we can be showered and cozy first. Then we can talk about what you want to say." The thought of the warm, dry, snuggly blankets which had been scattered all over the rental home was like envisioning heaven. It was fortunate that the trail had been so close by. In another couple of minutes, they'd be turning up the drive and ...

CC's hand flung out and gripped KK's wrist, almost causing her to swerve dangerously on the precarious road.

"CC, what the actual hell?"

"He knows, KK. *He knows!*" Her voice trembled in terror.

"What? What are you talking about?"

"Rube's latest text," she breathed, her voice barely above a whisper. "It says, 'I know where you are.' KK, what if he thinks I'm here with another man? I left him a note that I had an emergency work trip and ..." CC couldn't find the words to finish her sentence, and her shaking now wasn't from the cold.

"How would he know where you are, CC?"

"He must've tracked my phone ..." Without another word, CC rolled down her window, dousing the interior of the vehicle in chilly rain, and flung her phone out into a massive field where a lone white horse stood, munching the soggy grass, unbothered by the weather.

"You're being irrational, CC." KK reached over and took her hand, not taking her eyes off the narrow bridge. The river beneath was rising—fed by the onslaught of rain—and the waters churned violently beneath the narrow wooden structure. "He's just trying to scare you."

A bolt of lightning crashed to their left, striking a tree. The ground around it lifted then spewed out as the bark on the tree flew through the air. A limb struck the side of the car and KK shrieked almost as loud as CC did. The miasma of rain, ozone, moldering earth, and charred oak permeated the car as KK pulled over. An old homestead once stood along the road, but all that was left was a chimney and a scorched foundation.

"Well, it's working." CC covered her face with her hands. "You don't know what he's like, KK."

"Uuh," KK's tone made Caryn look up at her friend. "What does this guy look like?"

"About six-foot-three and a Neanderthal brow to match his personality. A real knuckle-dragger."

"And you dated that guy?"

"Love is blind," CC shrugged.

"Really? No redeeming qualities?"

"Can we talk about something else? Anything else?"

KK sat and considered her a moment, then put the car in drive and turned up the winding road towards the cabin. "What sounds good for dinner? I vote for soup and a nice salad."

"Stop!" CC barked, slapping her hand over her mouth as KK slammed on the brakes.

"What in the love of Pearl—" KK said, turning. She stopped mid-protest when she saw CC's face.

The color had washed from her skin and her eyes locked on a form that moved like a lumbering shadow through the windows of the cabin. CC's finger lifted. "It's him!" She ducked in the seat and pulled her hood over her head. "Oh my God. What are we going to do? We have to get out of here. Back up. Back up!"

Karen put the car in reverse, just getting a glimpse of the man CC had so accurately described. He was big, like ... *Dallas Cowboys linebacker* ... big. She had caught a glimpse of dirty blond hair that grew into a mullet from under his John Deere trucker hat. "Stay down," KK instructed as she watched in the rearview mirror to see if they'd been spotted. He wouldn't know Karen from Taylor Swift, and she was driving a rental, so as long as he didn't see Caryn they should be okay. But he was *inside* the cabin. It was pouring down rain, and all their gear for the long trek they'd planned to make was still in there with him. "I don't think he saw us." She pulled away from the cabin and back toward the main road.

"What are we going to do, KK?"

"We'll go to town. We'll tell the local authorities you have VPO against him and send them back up here to arrest him."

"But I don't have a Victim Protective Order," CC sniffed.

"Then we'll get ..." her voice cut off as she slammed on the brakes, skidding and nearly fishtailing on the slick road.

CC looked up, then sat back in her seat. "Where's the bridge?" A massive downed tree lay across their path, and it looked to have taken the edges of the two-lane bridge with it.

Karen glanced back over her shoulder, then made an illegal U-turn in the narrow road, nearly backing into the pasture where the white horse—*was that the same one?*—now stood at the fence, watching them intently. KK got the car back on the road and drove back up the winding road, passing the entrance to the drive that led to their cabin.

"Where are we going?"

"Maybe this road goes over the hill and back to the highway. If not, maybe the ranger is still at the trailhead."

"He's got a chainsaw," CC said.

KK glanced at her, with real concern washing through her. "We might need a chainsaw."

While it might be technically accurate to say that there was a road down the other side of the mountain, it was not the kind of road that filled one with confidence. It narrowed to a path that would have been two lanes if everyone drove Fiats, but even the small SUV would be hard-pressed to keep from pitching down the steep slope if another car came by in the other direction.

Praying that no other car would come up behind them, KK backed up very slowly, returning to where the road was wide enough for a three-point turn.

"Looks like we're going to have to take our chances with *Ranger Bob*," KK quipped, trying to lighten the mood and failing miserably. "The trail head is just a couple of minutes away, and let's just hope he's still sitting in his truck."

CC closed her eyes, and KK wasn't sure if it was in panic or prayer.

As it happened, the ranger's truck was still there, but the grouchy old coot wasn't in it.

"Where would he have gone in this rain?" CC whined, then took a deep breath. "Come on, Caryn," she whispered to herself. "You are a strong, independent woman. This is no time to fall apart! *Think, dammit!*"

KK rubbed her friend's shoulder and pulled out her own cell phone, which showed a miserable lack of signal. She tried dialing 911, hoping that somehow the Universe would pick up the call and put it through. No dice. "Shit. We're on the wrong side of this mountain for me to get a decent signal." She tossed her phone angrily into the cup holder. "We're going to have to find the ranger. He wouldn't be working in this weather. Were there any side paths that might lead to a ranger station? A bivouac? Maybe he took cover when the rain hit."

The women racked their brains, accompanied only by the sound of the rain pelting the roof. Suddenly, CC sat up straight, her eyes sparkling with hope. "The fire lookout tower! I bet he's there watching for lightning strikes or something!"

"That was over a thirty-minute hike in good weather, and this is NOT good weather. Should we sit here and wait for him?"

CC's eyes grew haunted. "If Rube was watching my location, then he knows where we were this morning, and it'll only be a matter of time before he finds my phone in the field unless that horse eats it. He *will* find his way up here, KK. He will. If he flew out here from Texas to find me, he isn't going to give up."

Karen shivered involuntarily. CC was probably right. "Okay, we head for the tower." She crawled into the back seat and reached over into the cargo area to reclaim their muddy boots. Then she maneuvered back into the driver's seat and slipped the shoes on with a squelching sound and matching sensation that made her want to cry.

"Slow and steady," CC advised. "The trail will be slick, and we can't afford for either of us to roll an ankle."

After a deep breath, they said goodbye to the warm and dry RAV-4 and stomped dejectedly toward the trail they'd followed only a few hours earlier.

The females had returned, probably searching for high ground, though it was unclear why they had abandoned their shelter. They were not suited to navigate the terrain in this place, and he had tried to warn them earlier that it was not safe. They did not have warm coats like the other beasts of the mountain, and they did not seem as hearty as those of their kind who usually passed through here. One of them smelled heavily of injuries. Beasts with injuries did not survive long here.

"I'm beginning to think that this was a stupid idea," CC yelled above the steady rain. The gravel of granite chips which had, no doubt, been laid down by the ranger service as a favor to novice hikers, had ended a quarter mile into their trek. The red clay that took its place had been hard-packed and dry when they'd been here the first time, and when they'd made their way back in the light rain, it had been muddy but still solid. Their only goal then had been to make it back to the car, not to judge travel conditions.

The continuous rain had loosened the top layer of earth, and the mud now was deeper and sucked at their boots as they walked. As if that weren't enough, the wet boots were chafing against the even wetter socks, and that would mean blisters sooner rather than later.

"What's the alternative?" KK called back over her shoulder. "You said Rube would find us. He beat the shit out of you before, and I think it's pretty certain he'd do it again. Somehow I don't think my Zumba classes particularly prepared me to fight back against a pissed off caveman. Finding a ranger, calling for help, that was the safest bet."

"Maybe we should have just hidden in the woods or something until he went away, or until the rain stopped, or ..."

KK stopped and looked at her rain-soaked friend. "Do you want to go back and wait in the car? Maybe try to hide somewhere? We're only about a mile out. But if we're going to turn back, we should do it now."

CC tried to think logically, strategically, but she was tired, wet, cold, sore, and scared. She took a deep breath and KK grabbed her hands, holding them tight. "No, you're right. Let's not second-guess it. The meadow can't be that much farther, and then we'll be able to see the tower. Worst case scenario, there will be shelter there where we can wait out the storm."

KK nodded in agreement. "We'll be okay because we're together," she smiled as rain streamed down her face.

"We'd better keep moving, though. It's getting colder, and we need to keep our bodies warm."

A half a mile later, they spotted the edge of the meadow with the tower's tiny silhouette poking above the trees in the distance. They whooped and cheered at the sight, heedless of the racket of their voices rising above the storm.

"We're going to make it!" KK exclaimed. "It looks like it's not even that far into the treeline." She felt a surge of adrenaline and excitement at the thought of having a roof over her head. "Last one there's a rotten egg!" She set off at a jog across the field, only vaguely noting CC's tone of warning before her foot found uneven ground, sinking into a foot-deep puddle of water and turning her ankle painfully.

She felt herself falling in slow motion, her arms windmilling and trying to decide whether she should fight for balance or reach out to break her fall. The resulting contortion accomplished neither, and she landed hard on her left wrist. Sharp pain simultaneously spiked through her arm and her leg, and sparks of pain erupted in her brain. Karen fell with a squeal and landed with a grunt. CC was at her side instantly.

"Oh, God, KK ... how bad is it?"

KK lay in the wet grass, her body racked with sobs of pain and frustration. She rolled onto her stomach and screamed into the ground, banging it with the non-injured fist.

"Come on, honey, how bad are you hurt?" CC asked, gently feeling the twisted ankle for torn skin or worse. Finding none, she heaved a sigh of relief. "Can you walk? We're almost there. Come on, I'll help you."

"Leave me here," KK finally said, insistence and despair heavy in her voice.

"Now you just knock off the crazy talk," CC ordered. "I'll carry you before I'd leave you here. Now, come on. Get up. I'll help you."

Karen realized she was serious, but she wasn't sure it would work. CC was already hurt enough as it was. Still, CC was determined and she managed to haul KK up. Both of them winced as CC put Karen's arm over her shoulder and they started with a tentative step. *One step at a time*, KK told herself. *Once we get to a safe place, we'll build a fire, find something to eat and I'll rummage through the supplies for Advil.*

The ranger station that looked so close was actually much farther than it seemed. A tenuous trail winding up the mountainside separated them from sanctuary and security. "No," KK protested, looking at the steep incline. "I can't make it and you can barely breathe, trying to support me with your hurt ribs. We need to stop."

CC was in no position to argue. She led her friend over to a large stand of trees and lowered her gingerly to the ground before collapsing beside her, rolling onto her back, trying to take a deep breath. It was impossible to tell if the sun had set. "Give me ... a minute ... to catch ... my breath ... and ... I'll find ... shelter ... for the night. We can ... try ... for the station ... tomorrow."

The rain turned to hail and the *chink* of a heavy ball of ice made a noise that caught CC's attention, even as she moved to shelter her friend with her own body. "Was that metal?" KK asked.

"Too close ... to be the roof ... up there." She nodded toward the ranger station. "It was ... nearby." The hail seemed to abate almost as quickly as it started but a flash of lightning, followed by a rumble of thunder, got CC to her feet. "Stay ... here."

KK shrugged as rivulets of water coursed down her face. "Like I could go anywhere."

CC followed the sound away from the trail and down a slight slope until she found a metal shack that looked like it'd seen better days. Rust marred the corrugated walls and one of the windows had been busted out. A piece of plywood suggested that someone had tried to patch it back up, but the plank had come down and lay on the mossy ground. CC went around to the door and found it had been lifted from its hinges. Inside, she discovered that it appeared to be a well house. It had pipes and valves that appeared to be in working order. Tools lined one shelf, each neatly hung on pegboards, outlined in yellow paint. Nothing appeared to be missing. It appeared dry except for where the rain had dripped into the window, and it looked like there was just enough room for two haggard travelers to hide from danger. CC wasn't the most handy, but she could manage a screwdriver, so she went to work replacing the wooden plank over the window, then put the tool back where she found it and set to work putting the door back on its hinges. There was no re-attaching it, but she managed to lean it across part of the entryway to block the worst of the rain.

She went back for KK and found her curled up in a ball, looking miserable. "Come on, girlfriend," CC said, grunting as she hoisted KK to her feet. "I found someplace dry to take cover. We'll feel better after a good night's sleep."

"I can't go another step," KK groaned.

"It's not that far," CC said, ignoring Karen's protestations as she pressed forward, leaving her friend with no choice. "Don't make me drag you."

The metal building might not have been the best option in a lightning storm, but the girls had no other choice. It was dry (mostly), and it kept them out of the wind and the rain. "Now if we only had a first aid kit and a battery charger," CC said, once she got Karen settled.

"A battery charger? Who do you think you're going to call?" KK reached into the backpack and rummaged around for her phone.

"Well, if I could get a signal, my first call would be to UberEats. I could really go for a Quarter Pounder right now."

"A Quarter Pounder, hell! If we could get out, we'd get something a lot better than McDonald's."

"Like what?"

"I don't know." The trembling had left Karen's voice and CC noticed she was starting to relax a little. "Cheesecake Factory? Wait, what was the name of that place that claimed they had the best Cheeseburgers in Georgia? That would work for me, especially if they have fried pickles."

CC had to laugh at that. She'd never had a fried pickle in her whole life until KK introduced them to her in college. Now, it was the measure of a good restaurant in their book.

"At this point ..." CC started, but froze when she heard a rustling above the din of the rain on the metal roof. She locked eyes with Karen as she listened. The noise didn't return. "At this point, I'm tempted to go hunt down a squirrel or a rabbit or something."

"With what?" KK smirked. "You got a slingshot in your hip pocket or something?"

"No," CC sighed. "Besides, there's no way we could build a fire in this rain, and I am ***not*** eating anything raw."

"Not even sushi?"

"No," CC said, shivering with disgust.

"Oysters?" KK asked. CC nearly gagged. "Never mind."

"Let's talk about something else."

"Tell me about this jerk, Rube. How did you meet him?"

CC didn't want to talk about him either, but considering they were in this mess because of him, she owed Karen that much. "One of the guys I worked with got tickets to a pub crawl. They were giving me a hard time about never going out with them, and I guess they finally wore me down and I gave in. He didn't tell me who was going, and it kind of surprised me when I found out it was his girlfriend and her brother, and that they were actually setting me up on a blind date. Rube could be charming ... when he wanted to."

"Most sociopaths are," Karen said, fighting back a yawn.

"We had a good time, and drank way too much."

"You didn't end up at his place, did you?"

"I woke up on his sofa," she said. "Unmolested, it appeared."

"Uh huh," KK said it in such a way to suggest she was suspicious.

"I didn't see him again for almost two weeks. When he did call, it was awkward, but I figured he was just as shy as I was. We talked a few times before he got the nerve to ask me out. Once we were together he was polite, chatty, and we had a lot of fun."

"Did you do any kind of a background check on him?"

CC was taken aback by the question. "Do I look like the FBI?"

"You don't have to work for the FBI to look someone up. I'm a reporter. I have connections. I know things."

"Well, it's too late for all that now," CC said. "The sooner we get to the ranger station, the better. Might as well try and get some sleep. I'll head up as soon as the sun comes up. Maybe the rain will let up."

"Maybe," KK said. "And I really hope the station has a radio." The despondent tone in KK's voice raised alarm bells, and CC felt her blood pressure rising.

"What's wrong, KK?'

"My phone. It's not in the bag. I ... left it in the cupholder of the car."

The females had taken shelter from the mountain night. That was good. But one of them had fallen, and now both of them smelled injured. They would need meat to regain their strength, but their claws were small and ineffective. They had no weapons. They would not be able to hunt, which would further weaken them.

A scent tickled the Guardian's nose, and he sniffed the air. Then he listened to the night noises while the females talked. The rain made it difficult to discern, but he could tell that he was not the only large beast aware of them. Had it been another of his kind, he would have picked up the familiar scent even in the wetness of the night. He was glad that he would not have to fight another for dominance of the territory tonight.

Still, it was unlikely that a prey animal would prowl so close to the den the females had chosen. There were other predators in the darkness, to be sure. He must attend to the hunt quickly so that he could keep watch.

The Guardian crept around the back side of the den, but found no trace of the beast he'd sensed earlier. He did, however, find one of the tools he'd seen the mountain's visitors use ... a stick with sharp metal attached. This was good. He would leave it for them, and the females would have a weapon to defend themselves if a predator got too close. He took the weapon and went in search of a night creature that would provide sustenance for the females.

The hunting was poor, and the only source of meat he could find was one of the bald-tailed scavengers that came out after dark. The creature hissed and bared its teeth, but he grabbed it by the tail and swung it toward a nearby tree. There was a cracking sound, and the creature fell limp.

He stood for a moment outside the den, wondering how the females could eat the meat. Their teeth were not pointed like a predator's ... they would not be able to rip fur and muscle. He looked again at the weapon in his hand and chuffed proudly as an idea hit him. There was a fallen log near the opening to the den, and he tossed the scavenger's carcass across it, listening carefully to see if the females had been alerted to his presence.

Their continuous noises told him they had not been, and he wondered how any of their kind survived if they spent their time announcing themselves to predators rather than listening for danger. Satisfied that he would not be noticed, he chopped at the carcass a few times until it was sufficiently mutilated that any creature would be able to get at the meat.

Then he crept a little closer and tossed the meal and the weapon through the den's narrow opening and stepped back, keeping an eye out for any beast of tooth and claw that might think this was an invitation to easy prey.

Blood oozed out of the opossum's carcass, saturating the entrance. A second later, a bloody hatchet sailed through the doorway and landed beside the mutilated animal.

The gruesome sight took a second to register, but then both women's screams ripped through the pattering of the rain, the echoes lost in the woods around them.

"Oh my God! Oh my God!" CC hollered, but then her voice dropped to a terrified whisper. "He's found us already. He was right behind us all the time!" She edged away from the gory mess until her back touched one of the pipes in the farthest corner. Her eyes were haunted with the memory of her cracked ribs.

The look in her best friend's eyes filled Karen with righteous rage. No one had the right to bruise CC's spirit. "Well, he has both of us to contend with. And Hell hath no fury like two pissed off women." She edged her way over to a wooden crate that was strewn against the wall with the intention of using it as a brace to stand up, despite her sprained ankle and wrist. But the box was more rotten than she guessed, and it collapsed nearly as soon as she put weight on it, sending her tumbling to the ground again. She cursed and raised her hand to check for splinters, half-expecting the annoying prickling pain that accompanied them. Finding none, she sighed in relief and brushed the remains of wood out of her way.

"What. The hell. Is that?" CC gasped.

KK turned her head to orient her gaze to match her friend's. At first, the sight didn't register. *No, it can't be ...* The box had been hiding a sealed mason jar. In itself, that was out of place enough, but the longer they looked, the more the grisly truth came into focus.

It was like looking at a jar from an old science museum exhibit. The fluid within appeared ochre in the dim light, but the hue may have been tinted by the pulpy contents within, varying shades of peach and brown. It was the glints of metal that first translated the mash into distinct shapes.

A bent silver wire pierced one of the solid bits, and dangling from the wire was a charm of a smiling silver sun. An earring. CC had stepped closer, forgetting her fear of Rube.

"Is that ... a hoop?"

It was. Another earring. Which meant that the globules suspended within the jar were ...

KK dropped the jar and spun away just fast enough to be sick in the opposite direction. Her mouth filled with the taste of bile and granola, she raised her watery eyes to Caryn. "What is happening?"

"Well, now, that's just unfortunate," came a gravelly voice that grated dissonantly against the sounds of the *clink-clink-clink* of pea-sized hail on the metal roof. The door slid aside a few inches, revealing a shadowed figure in a wide-brimmed hat. The ranger stepped inside and shook water off his rain gear.

CC almost wept in relief. "Oh, thank God! We were out here looking for you!"

"Were ya now?" His tone was flat, his eyes clearly fixed on the mason jar.

"We were!" KK felt almost giddy at the sight of his uniform. *They were saved!* "We're in danger, and ..."

"I should say ya are. Whatcha got there?" He waggled his chin toward their grim discovery.

"What? Oh, that's not ours!" CC protested. "We just ..." But something in his eyes told her that he knew very well that the jar and its contents didn't belong to them.

"You was just holdin' it for a friend. That it?" He almost sounded amused.

KK reached over and grabbed KK's hand tightly, a gesture of warning. There was no way that the ranger could have discerned the contents of the jar from the doorway ... unless he already knew what it held. "My friend's boyfriend is looking for us," she said pointedly. "He followed us up here, and, well, he's not a very nice guy. So when the road washed out, we came looking for you, hoping you knew a way to get us off the mountain. He's liable to catch up with us any minute." Her voice wavered in a nauseating combination of pain and fear.

"Is that so? Not a nice guy. But you thought I was?" The ranger arched an eyebrow and took a step deeper into the shed. "So you just thought you'd poke around in here waiting for me, eh?"

"We ... we weren't poking. My friend ... sprained her ... her ankle in t-t-the m-meadow, and we needed to take shelter from the hail, and ..."

"Oh? And ya just thought you'd chop up some wildlife while you were at it?" He toed the carcass. "You know what I think? I think there's no boyfriend, and y'all weren't expectin' to find me up here right now, and you thought you could snoop around. I bet you dames fancy yourselves brave and clever. I bet you watch those true crime shows and now you think you know what's what. But you don't know nothin' and you ain't so smart. Thought you were gonna catch me and get yourselves on the TV, huh? Yeah, I know who you are, Ms. Karen Hardaway of WYNK News. I did a little research when you showed up this morning. You stood out like a sore thumb with that dye job of yours. You ain't no outdoorsy girl. That nice lady at the rental car company sure hopes I'm able to find you and get your keys back to you." His voice dropped in pitch. "It's a real shame I won't be able to find you or your friend."

The ranger looked down at the old hatchet, and seemed satisfied that it was out of the women's reach. Then he took another step forward. "Looks like I'm going to get some pretty new dangles for my jar."

CC shrieked as he moved towards her. A deep grumble seemed to make the metal shake and then something hit the building so hard, even the tools on the pegboards rattled.

The ranger stopped and turned, scowling at the girls before he took a step out. He scanned the area around the shed, but when he found nothing, he turned back. "Damned cougars," he muttered. "Now, where were we? Oh yeah, ears." He pulled a jagged knife from the sheath on his hip. CC scuttled back into KK and covered the scream that attempted to escape her throat, making it come out as more of a squeak. The ranger brought the blade down and CC closed her eyes, wincing as she heard it penetrate something solid. When she opened her eyes, the knife was buried in the wooden work table like Excalibur plunged into the stone.

"I wasn't plannin' on addin' two sets to my collection today, but sometimes the Lord just provides." His smile was greasy and slid across his face as he drew a pistol from a holster on his belt. "Mighty considerate of y'all to deliver yourselves to my work space."

KK's mind spun, trying to figure out how to avoid bullets. This sick bastard didn't seem inclined to reason, and since they'd found his little treasure trove, she was pretty sure he had no intention of letting them live. It was then that the smell hit: a noxious mix of rot and kitty litter, sour and thick.

Despite their terror, Karen and Caryn grunted in unison at the stench.

Without thinking, CC blurted, "What, you keep the bodies like right out back?"

The ranger wrinkled his nose. "Naw, I ain't stupid. That's ... somethin' else." A dark look passed across his face for an instant, but then it was gone and replaced by the cold glint of hunger. "Not that it's gonna matter to you two in about a minute."

CC moaned as the ranger leaned over her, a sound saturated with rain water, despair, and horror. Her vision narrowed until all she could see was the round *o* at the end of the shiny black barrel of a snub-nose revolver.

Rube had been tracking them for some time, and he wasn't surprised at all when the signs told him one of the girls wasn't walking quite right. *Injured*. That would be Caryn. *Such a clutz*. The treads of the hiking shoes painted a picture of their desperate flight, which told him they were onto him. But they were slow and sloppy. It was like they weren't even trying to hide their trail. *So stupid.* He didn't know who the other woman was, but it was clearly a woman by the smaller tracks and the belongings he found at the cabin.

As he came up the hill, he could see a shed hidden in a clearing surrounded by a stand of trees. A commotion came from inside the metal building and echoed down the hill. The trail led to the shed and he realized he'd caught up with him. He broke out into a dash at the sounds of moaning and the shuffling of bodies on the dirt floor. *He knew it! She was cheating on him!* Not only that, she was having some freaky threesome in the woods!

"Blast it, woman!" he snarled as he came up to the door of the shed and reached for the figure in the doorway. The man in the uniform turned, startled, with a pistol leveled at Rube's chest. A ball of fire erupted from the barrel and hot pain like lightning shot through his chest. Rube staggered backward.

Caryn screamed. She hated that woman-beating bastard, but she didn't want him dead. Not like this. Her rage filled her with adrenaline, and she vaulted herself from the floor, leaping onto the ranger's back, wrapping her arms around his neck and clawing at his face.

She could see Rube's startled expression as he stumbled back a few more steps, his eyes lowering to the blood that soaked his hand—the hole in his shirt. Caryn snarled as the ranger flailed about, trying to throw her off. He staggered forward, then spun around, back into the shed wall as Karen scrambled to her injured foot and wrapped her hand around Excalibur, finding the blade unyielding, despite the age of the crumbling wooden table.

"CC!" Karen tried to edge past her friend who held on for dear life, even as the ranger slapped her hands away from his face, and tried to swing the gun around to hit her. Her hand found the jar of ears and she raised it high over her head. Reading her friend, CC let go of the ranger and landed in a crouch, turning toward Rube, who stumbled backwards out of the shed and dropped to his knees in the wet loam.

"Rube ..." she gasped, starting for him.

He lifted a hand, as if to push her away. "I'm ... sorry." His eyes rolled back and he collapsed, just as Karen brought the jar down over the ranger's head and the glass shattered, raining the vile contents onto their attacker. CC turned to help her friend just as a dark furry paw reached through the window, grasping the gore-covered fern green uniform shirt by the collar. One minute the ranger was there, the next, he'd been lifted off his feet, his boots disappearing out the broken window. The girls couldn't see the ensuing chaos, but they could hear the melee punctuated by the sharp *crack* of breaking bones and wet *squelch* of tearing flesh. Bestial growls and very human screams echoed in the treetops as the women clung to one another, falling into the corner and shielding their eyes.

The ranger's agonized screams fell silent, and all the women could hear was the labored sounds of their own sobs. CC hazarded to open her eyes just a slit, but squeezed them shut again as another cry ripped through the night.

WHOOOOP! WHOOOOOOP!

The sound that had been so distant earlier in the day was now all around them, shaking the shed with its horrible power.

The male had no respect for the mountain or the way among beasts. He preyed on the weak, as many predators did, but he did not use them for meat or even leave them out to feed the scavengers. He was one of those rare beasts that hunted purely for pleasure.

That was not the way of the mountain, but until now, the Guardian had largely ignored him. He had taken the females under his protection, though, and this male had no right to defy him. No other predator would have dared to challenge his dominance once he had provided food for the females. Yet this male had. The Guardian tolerated many things, but he would not tolerate this type of encroachment onto his territory and authority.

This was **his** *mountain. The insolent male had to serve as a reminder to any beast that might think the Guardian had become weak. He let loose his great cry, reminding all the creatures of the mountain who was the alpha here.*

He did not want the females to think that he'd abandoned them. The Guardian's duty was sacred. He had protected them, as was his right, and they did not need to fear. Their kind did not understand the law of the mountain. So he remained quiet, hoping they would know they were safe.

The girls huddled against each other, but realized the battle was over. The mountains had gone silent once again. Even the rain had become no more than a whisper. CC rose, offering KK a hand. KK was the first to muster the courage to peer out the window.

"What is it?" CC whispered

KK seemed to struggle for the words. The best she could do was lift a finger and point. CC cocked her head around to see, her jaw falling slack. "Is that ... a ..."

"Bigfoot," Karen said, in answer to the question CC couldn't quite finish.

They both ducked down, but the creature didn't stir. Instead, it sat in a meditative pose like a yogi. KK finally moved to the door and hesitated as she limped out, peeking around the corner. CC moved in behind her. The beast opened his eyes and matched their gazes, nodding beatifically. It then rose slowly and seemed to give them a knowing bow before it turned and disappeared into the trees.

KK stood, breathless, as CC moved to take in the bloodbath that stained the meadow dark in the diffuse moonlight. Hunks of the meat that had once been the homicidal ranger lay scattered across the wet grass, and a torn arm lay near the entrance to the shed. Rube lay where he had fallen ... face down, unmoving ... and CC knew it was too late. Still, she rushed over and knelt beside him, rolling him over. She felt for a pulse, but as she suspected, there wasn't one.

Choking back a sob, she rose and returned to Karen, who leaned against the ragged doorway with her hands on her hips. The women hugged each other tightly, trembling as the terrifying reality of the past few minutes seeped in.

Squeezing her friend gently so as not to aggravate CC's sore ribs, KK whispered, "One thing I can tell you for sure: I will not be giving this park a decent rating on Tripadvisor."

www.ingramcontent.com/pod-product-compliance
Lightning Source LLC
LaVergne TN
LVHW090551110826
845146LV00001B/103

* 9 7 9 8 9 9 9 0 7 9 9 8 5 *